The WEDDING ALBUM

The WEDDING ALBUM

MARIAN WELLS

BETHANYHOUSE
MINNEAPOLIS, MINNESOTA

982 2834

Published by Bethany House Publishers
A Ministry of Bethany Fellowship International
11400 Hampshire Avenue South
Bloomington, Minnesota 55438
www.bethanyhouse.com

Printed in the United States of America

Library of Congress Cataloging-in-Publication Data
Wells, Marian, 1931-
   [Wedding dress]
   The wedding album : two novels / by Marian Wells.
     p. cm.
   ISBN 0-7642-2592-8
   1. Mormon women—Fiction. 2. Historical fiction, American. 3. Christian fiction, American. 4. Love stories, American. I. Wells, Marian, 1931- With this ring. II. Title.
   PS3573.E4927 W4   2002
   813'.54—dc21
                                       2001006149

The Wedding Dress

Preface

History could be compared to a handful of multicolored beads. At first glance they appear to have been strung together at random, without design. Bit by bit as time passes, through the process of stringing, a pattern emerges. It helps occasionally to take a backward step; this changes the perspective, reveals the pattern.

The history of the Latter-day Saints Church began with its founder, Joseph Smith, Jr. Mormon historians tell us that at fourteen years of age, in the year 1820, Joseph had his first vision. In September 1827 he received the promised Golden Plates and began his translation of them, which resulted in the Book of Mormon. This was only the beginning of his writings—all claimed to be given by the inspiration of God. The church was formally organized on April 6, 1830, in Fayette, New York.

From the beginning, the church was marked by persecution, unrest, and upheaval. This new gospel presented some beliefs so divergent from the Christianity revealed in the Bible and practiced down through the ages that fierce opposition was inevitable. To survive, it was necessary for the church to move away.

From New York to Ohio they migrated as a body; missionaries were being sent even farther. As early as July 1831 these early emissaries were in Missouri. When Joseph Smith received the revelation that named Missouri as the new Zion, Independence in Jackson County, Missouri, was chosen to be the site of the temple.

Back in Kirtland, Ohio, in June of 1833, preparations were begun to build a temple there. This was still the church headquarters. Joseph Smith and a large group of his followers were living in the area.

Life wasn't easy in Missouri; the heat of opposition was growing, no doubt fueled by the church members' declaration that Independence was to be their Zion, and with God's help they would "possess the land." At this time, Independence was a frontier town, peopled with typical frontiersmen—crude, rough, and protective of their solitude.

Until after the dedication of the Kirtland, Ohio, temple in 1836, there was constant moving back and forth between Ohio and Missouri, as Joseph Smith and church members were called upon to support the harassed Saints in Missouri.

In 1838, Joseph Smith moved from Kirtland, Ohio. Financial problems helped make the move advisable and the new church headquarters was established in Far West, Missouri. In addition, the church itself was in a turmoil at this time as members struggled with the communal pattern of living handed down from the Lord to Joseph Smith, as he believed.

By August 1838, the hostilities, which would finally lead to their exodus from Missouri, had broken out between the Missourians and the Mormons. During their time in Missouri, the group had been forced to move from Jackson County, to Clay County, and then in 1836, to Caldwell County.

Their treatment was unjust and brutal. Often driven from their homes, they were left destitute and shivering in the cold without food or shelter. It was during this time that the Haun's Mill tragedy took place.

Eventually the Mormons migrated back to the eastern shore of the Mississippi River. Here, in 1839, Joseph Smith bought two large farms and the Mormons began to move in. The small town of Commerce was renamed Nauvoo, and the straggle of huts became the largest city in the state of Illinois before the Mormons moved on west. *The Wedding Dress* begins in the years just before Joseph Smith's death and the migration to the Great Basin in Utah led by his successor, Brigham Young.

———————

Notes and an annotated bibliography for *The Wedding Dress* follow *With This Ring*.

1

·····················

*R*ebecca Wolstone pushed the small trunk toward the open window of the loft and dropped to her knees in front of it. While her heavy taffy-colored braids coiled across the surface and her fingers stroked the dusty leather, she looked out the window. She had to peer through the branches of the apple tree to see down the hill. In the distance there was the shining strip that was the Mississippi River. Trees and buildings hid the curving bank. "Nau—voo." Rebecca practiced saying the name as Cynthia would, but her voice lacked the contempt Cynthia's carried. Her eyes were searching out the white spot on the hill.

In the dark clamor of the town the building rose silent and pure, capturing her imagination, forcing the words: "I'd fancy me a spot, more quiet and holy than any place on earth." She blinked and tried to focus her sunstruck eyes on the little trunk. "Do you suppose, Ma and Pa, that if you'd a-lived long enough to see that place, it would have changed everything?"

Now tears swelled her eyelids and constricted her throat. She was thirteen. Today was her birthday, this April 15, 1844. Three birthdays ago there had been the three of them—her mother, father and Rebecca. Now there was only Rebecca and the little old trunk.

And the Smyths. She reminded herself as she heard the commotion in the yard below. For just a moment she wanted to hug her loneliness closer, but there was that shrill, demanding whistle. She leaned out the window. Joshua and Jamie Smyth were waving. "Becka, happy birthday!" A flower-laden branch sailed through the window.

Joshua, seventeen, was grinning up at her. "I'd throw you an apple, but since it's only apple blossom time, have a posy instead."

His eyes were intently studying her face, and she wondered if the tears showed. Joshua was prone to discover her tears before anyone else, and they made him uncomfortable.

Another face danced into view. It was Prudence Smyth. "Looking at your ma's wedding dress, huh? We remembered it's your birthday, and Pa has a penny for you. That's so you won't be sad because your ma and pa are dead."

"Rebecca!" The voice seemed to float up the ladder that joined the loft with the kitchen below. "Hurry and do your looking; it's near suppertime."

"Yes 'um," Rebecca settled back on the floor, surprised to discover that her mood of sadness had disappeared. It was the first time in the three years since her parents had died that she was able to lift the lid of the trunk without tears ruining it all. She braced against the window frame and peered inside.

The trunk held only two items, the dress and a little black book. She rubbed her dusty fingers against her faded calico before she peeled back the cocoon of cotton that shielded the silk dress. She touched the lace and the pink velvet rosebuds centered with seed pearls; then she bent to sniff greedily of the musty fragrance.

She tried again to pull the memories of those people back into her life. Each year it was becoming harder to recall their faces, and each year it seemed more important to hold them close. Not that she wasn't grateful for the Smyths' taking her in, treating her like kin; it was just this need to draw the reins up tight, to pull all of her past about her.

One thing she did know. The wedding dress worn by her mother was hers. It would be her wedding dress too. Even today her mother's final words burned through her. Her lips had been blue with the life seeping out of her when she whispered, "Rebecca, take care, guard the trunk. There's in it your only hope."

"Becky!" Rebecca slammed the lid of the trunk and flung her long yellow braids over her shoulders as she ran to the edge of the loft.

Swinging down the ladder, she took the water bucket from the bench and slipped outside. As she approached the well, she saw Mr. Smyth and Lank Olson leaning on the fence.

It was Tyler Smyth's granddaddy who had settled this land. Now the apple trees were gnarled and the barn sagging, but the view below was as fresh as a new penny. The river gleamed; the houses on the bank rose sturdy and dark among the fringe of young trees. The shacks and clutter of the old town of Commerce (now called

Nauvoo) were being eaten by the rows of neat brick and new log houses, but the houses were also eating farmland, the forest, and even beginning on the hill on which the Smyths' house stood.

Turning to the men, she saw the bitter set of their faces as they talked. She couldn't help noting the rusting plow, the tumble of firewood, and the broken gate to the corral. The chickens were loose again. It was a dismal picture.

She raised the dripping bucket and rested it on the logs encircling the well. Her eyes found the shiny white building rising on a hill in the center of Nauvoo.

"They say they have a temple in Ohio." Tyler was speaking; "Why don't they go back there? They're worse'n grasshoppers takin' over the whole place."

"They say," replied Lank, shifting the straw in his mouth, "that round part's going to be covered with gold. Let's not run them out until they get that on."

Tyler chuckled. "Depends on whether we're still eatin' when they're done."

"They say—" Lank glanced at Becky and lowered his voice.

Mr. Smyth turned to Becky. "Better hurry the water in."

Becky crossed the porch and entered the kitchen. Before she could close the door, ten-year-old Matthew charged into the house. His tousled brown hair was on end and his eyes blazed with excitement. "Pa's coming. Let's eat; we're going to Nauvoo!"

Mr. Smyth entered the house, "Don't go gettin' them excited; this is just for the menfolk." Before Prue could protest, the door swung open again. Seven-year-old Jamie slipped through and Joshua followed. Ten years' difference separated Joshua and Jamie, but their sameness was apparent. Their hair resembled halos of corn silk and their eyes were blue. More than once Rebecca had seen Jamie throw back his shoulders and pattern his gait to match Joshua's.

Now Joshua's eyes were troubled. He accepted the bowl of rabbit stew and sat across the table from his father. "Couldn't pull a fish out of the crick. Even Tike couldn't, and he's apt to find fish in a mud puddle."

"Till 'thirty-nine they'd jump into your lap," grumbled Mr. Smyth. He glanced at Rebecca, and she ducked her head.

"It's the Mormons, isn't it?" Prue peered over Joshua's arm as he reached for the cornbread. Everyone knew she was repeating a well-worn phrase when she said, "Before they came there was enough for everybody."

Matthew lifted his head. "I heard tell that there's almost twenty thousand of them now. Today I watched a paddle-wheeler dump them out like grain."

"Matt, what were you doing on the docks today?" His mother's dark eyes pinned him while he squirmed. "You were sent to town for nails, no one told you—"

"Pa was waiting for those nails," Prue's accusing glare wilted him.

"I ran the whole way," he muttered around his spoon.

"Bluff Street is a long way from the docks," his father commented.

"Where are you going tonight?" Cynthia Smyth asked. Matthew was relieved that the attention was no longer on him.

Tyler glanced up. "Me 'n Lank are going to mosey down Mulholland Street."

"You can't get enough of each other? Before 'thirty-nine you stayed away from any neighbor."

"We set a lot of store by our land, and they're about to overrun it." They looked at Rebecca. Mr. Smyth reached into his pocket. "Here, birthday girl."

She accepted the penny and tucked it into her pocket.

"Thank you, Mr. Smyth."

"Going to spend it?" Matthew asked eagerly. She shook her head.

"At least someone's got a nest egg." Tyler grinned and tugged at her braid.

"What's going on down Mulholland?" Joshua pushed aside his bowl.

"Holy Joe's fixing to be President of the United States," Matthew said.

"Boy, are you all ears?" Cynthia asked. "Besides, you can't depend on gossip."

"Holy Joe," Prue snickered and glanced at Rebecca.

Rebecca dropped her spoon and straightened. Her voice was low. "Prue, it makes no difference to me what you call him. I'm not one of the Saints."

Cynthia was shaking her head. "You young'uns know nothing about it."

Four pairs of eyes turned to Mrs. Smyth, hanging on her words. Tyler cut in, "Now you've got them ticklin' with curiosity. Better tell the story."

Mrs. Smyth waved the serving spoon toward Rebecca. "True, the Wolstones were fancied about Joe Smith and his book. But they never did become a part of it."

"They came to Illinois when the rest did." Joshua was watching Rebecca.

"The others came from Independence. After they wore out their welcome elsewhere and had to move, Commerce was their choice. I have no call to discriminate against 'em, but it makes me mad that they had to be so uppity to change the name to Nau—voo."

"They made a pretty spot out of a bunch of old shacks," Joshua said thoughtfully.

Mr. Smyth snorted, "Anybody could've done the same with that size crowd pullin' on their team."

2
· · · · · · · · · · · · · · · · · · ·

*O*n the day Mrs. Smyth walked into the garden to dig tender dandelion shoots, she said, "Time to air bedding and wash hair."

Rebecca sat on the chopping block under the apple tree and loosened her braids while she listened to Joshua. His voice was pleading as he tagged along after his mother, carrying the feather comforter and lifting her buckets of water. For the past two springs Joshua had tagged after his parents with the same arguments.

"Oregon—you want to go off to Oregon when your pa needs every bit of help he can get." Cynthia put him off, "Wait until Matt's big enough for the plow."

Joshua's pleading resumed. For a moment Rebecca's spirit forsook the familiar and reached restlessly beyond security. She closed her eyes and saw wagons with their billowing canvas and creaking wheels pulled by plodding oxen.

Cynthia's voice cut through the picture, and Rebecca opened her eyes. Mrs. Smyth was standing beside Joshua, but she was looking toward Nauvoo. Was she seeing the tide of houses moving up the hill toward their land? Rebecca followed her gaze. Beyond that shimmering line of river there was a dark spot. Another paddlewheeler was puffing its way into dock. Cynthia was saying, "Maybe it won't hurt for you to talk to your pa. The way this place is growing, it'd be best for some one of us to be scouring the face of the earth for a bit of land."

Rebecca saw the hope on Joshua's face. A light breeze touched the apple tree and ruffled Rebecca's hair. A lonesome chill touched her heart.

Matthew stood beside her. "You look like an angel with your hair floatin'."

"You caught a fish!"

He lifted his prize. There were two large catfish. "Ah, no mush tonight." His eyes were still on her hair, and she wondered at the thoughtful expression that suddenly gave way to a spark of amusement. She thought about it for a moment, but Matthew scampered off before she could question him.

Later Rebecca would rationalize that it wouldn't have happened if Joshua hadn't left for Oregon that next week.

But Joshua was leaving. All that last week Rebecca pretended life would be the same after he left. Surely Joshua's constant kindness and understanding wasn't as necessary as cool water.

With his father's approval, Joshua soon found a wagon train heading for Oregon. The spring plowing was finished within a week. Too soon the day arrived and there was Joshua mounted on the pale horse, wearing new buckskin breeches and a fringed leather shirt. The sun touched fire from the metal of his rifle while the mare pawed her impatience. Matthew's face was full of awe. "You look like a real scout."

Joshua leaned down and tweaked Rebecca's braid. "Take care, you hear? You grow up, but only enough to fit that pretty wedding dress."

Forgetting the tear that wet her cheek, Rebecca stared up at him. Under the brim of his new hat his eyes were serious. Behind her Mrs. Smyth chided, "Joshua, don't you go planting notions."

When he was gone, Mrs. Smyth moved reluctantly. She touched the bowed shoulder of the graying man beside her. "You don't suppose you'll regret selling that parcel? Seems a high price for gear for a young man."

"I guess I'm gettin' to be a gambler." He was looking down the hill.

Rebecca hacked at the weeds. Perspiration ran down the sides of her face, plastering her hair to her head. The weeds, like the tender corn, were shooting up faster than she could walk the rows, at least it seemed that way.

"Psst!" She blinked perspiration out of her eyes. Matthew waited in the shade.

"Matt, how come you're resting so close to suppertime? You haven't finished that row, and you'll stand to get skinned for it."

"Water," he groaned. "Have some." He was watching as she

drank. "Ebner has a penny for you if you'll give us a hand after the corn's finished."

She lowered the cup. "A penny? Where's Ebner getting money?" He shrugged, avoiding her eyes. "I can't imagine what Ebner's cooked up now that's worth a penny."

"He's just of a mind to play a little trick."

"And who's going to get hurt?"

"Nobody."

"That's hard to swallow. Seems like last time I was hauled in on your scheme, I ended up taking the blame for everything."

"Who'd a-guessed Mrs. Burton wouldn't spook but her chickens would."

Rebecca shook her head, "Uh-uh. You're thinking I'll play on your terms. I've learned my lesson. That last time I'd never have done it if I'd known it was to help you steal melons. And me pulling up the lid on a box 'cause you told me to. I thought that was a possum in there, not a skunk."

"Ah, Becka, don't hold a grudge. It wasn't my fault. Besides, that old skunk was so feeble he couldn't run, and I don't think he could have heisted his tail if he'd met a bear."

"Maybe so, but Mrs. Burton's chickens didn't know that."

"I helped you look for them."

There was a shout from the house. "That's Pa. Guess it's supper-time." Matthew hung the cup on the tree. "I'll tell you about it later."

During supper Matthew said, "How about me 'n Becka going fishing first thing in the morning? We could be back early enough to finish the weeding by noon."

Mrs. Smyth wrinkled her forehead and looked from Rebecca to Matthew. Rebecca poked at her greens while Matthew said, "Well, with Joshua gone, someone needs to come with me. What if I drown?"

Prue snorted, "What about me or Jamie? Becky needs to hoe."

Tyler frowned, "Young lady, maybe it's time you learned to swing a hoe."

"I gotta do house chores," she whined.

"Maybe Jamie," Rebecca said. A toe caught her in the shin.

Cynthia nodded. "Mrs. Olson said they've gotten good bass from the springs."

———

When the last of the dishes had been dried, Matthew stuck his head through the door. "Goin' ta finish that row?" Rebecca hastily followed him out the door.

Matthew's hoe dipped and cut with unusual vigor. Soon he drew even with Rebecca. "You know that old barn down on Hulfords' section?"

"Yes." Remembering the tumbledown shack, she added, "Your ma said stay out of that place; it's dangerous."

"Naw, she said that 'cause the Hulfords' kids were smoking corn silk in there. Ebner wants us to meet him there before sunup tomorrow."

"Why?"

"Bishop Ellis and some others go in there to pray. Ebner thought . . ." His voice trailed away as she vigorously shook her head. "I figured you wouldn't. Told Ebner you was too much Mormon yourself."

"That's not so!" she exclaimed hotly. "I just don't trust his shenanigans."

"Ah, you and your ma and pa lived too close to them down there in the gulch. It rubbed off." She shook her head and he pressed, "Then prove it."

"What else does he have in mind?" Her voice was cautious.

"Well, he says the bishop's been praying for a miracle or a visit from an angel like Joseph Smith had. Ebner figured you'd be just the one to give it to him."

"What do you mean?" She stopped hoeing and turned.

"If you unwind your hair and wear something white, those old men won't be able to tell the difference between you and an angel."

"That's terrible!" Rebecca exclaimed, suddenly remembering Matt's impish grin when he had seen her with her hair down the week before.

"You'd have to climb up on the rafters and stand there so's the sun would hit you just right. I told Ebner you's too chicken to stand that high."

"What else am I supposed to do?"

"Just say something pretty, so they'd think you're an angel."

"It'll make them mad and besides, I don't have anything white."

"Ebner says he'll take care of that."

"A penny?" Rebecca was thinking of the meager store of coins she had.

"You'll have to decide now. Ebner's waiting in the willows."

By the time they reached the end of the row, Rebecca was

caught up in thinking of the men awed by the vision of her. "What'll I say?" she asked Ebner.

His brow puckered. "It's gotta be a revelation or it won't count . . . Pa's worried about their taking our land. Say something so's they'll go."

───────

Dawn was only a gray promise when Matthew touched her shoulder. While Rebecca pulled on her shoes, Prue groaned and rolled over. "I'd rather hoe all day than go fishing in the middle of the night."

Matthew stashed the fishing poles at the stream. Quickly he and Rebecca cut across the plowed field toward the barn. Ebner was a dark shadow in the trees. When they reached him, he handed Rebecca a white cloth, muttering, "Hurry up, now."

Rebecca held up the white cloth. "What is it? Where did you get this?"

"Just put them on over your dress and quit fussin'."

"Well, I should say. What are these funny little holes? It's big enough to fit the bishop—say, where did you get this outfit?"

Ebner's voice was indistinct. "Never mind. Undo your braids and come on."

In the pale light the old barn seemed to droop with fatigue. Loose boards complained as they stumbled across them.

At the rear of the building, Ebner pulled them close. "Me and Matt'll wait out back. Becky, you get up that ladder and hide in the loft. Wait until they really get fired up, and then when the sun strikes that beam over there, just stand up and spread your arms out. You can say 'peace,' or something to get their attention. Don't say more'n you have to. I don't think angels do too much talking."

A dog barked. Ebner shoved. "Get up there, I think they're comin'."

The fellows disappeared, and Rebecca grasped the crossbars and swung herself into the loft. Settling herself in the musty hay she heard the retreating rustle of the loft's occupants. She clamped her chattering jaws tight.

A twig snapped. There were muffled voices. From the creak and vibration of the building, she guessed the men had entered.

She chewed her fingernails and waited. The rumble of voices broke and then one lifted, smiting the rafters in petition. "O Lord, we know we are your people; we have followed your prophet back and forth across this land. Show us, like you did him, show us that you are with us."

The sun broke through the trees and streamed into the skeleton of the barn. It touched the back of Rebecca's head and banded the rafters with light. That was the signal. She coaxed her feet under her.

"O Lord," it was another voice, "show yourself to your people. If you did it for the prophet, won't you do it for the bishop?"

Rebecca stood and took a step to the edge of the loft. She raised trembling arms, and the long white sleeves flapped. The voices ceased. There was a whisper. "Peace." Now louder, she cried, "Peace, my good men."

"An angel," the breathy sigh floated up to her, and she was courageous.

She took a step nearer the edge. "Do you have a message?" the voice wavered.

"My brethren. Within a year you'll be in the promised land—"

"Boom!" There was an explosion of dust, and the building vibrated. The men shouted, "An earthquake! Let's get out of here before the place goes."

Rebecca stepped backward and felt a board break beneath her feet. There was a swish, and the contents of the loft poured through the opening. She was still gasping for breath as the thunder of feet faded.

Frantic burrowing hands found her and yanked her to air. While one pair of hands brushed away the straw, the other hands tugged at her costume.

"Let's get out of here; they may come back."

Matthew and Rebecca ran for the trees, while Ebner with Rebecca's costume was a white streak disappearing down the road.

———————

While Matthew tied worms to the fishing lines, Rebecca picked straw out of her hair. "Lucky I had that thing on, or I'd be straw all the way through."

"Eb's going to have a hard time explaining the straw in that outfit."

"What did you two do?"

"We rolled a boulder down the slope behind the barn. Worked better'n we expected. The whole place shook. We got to thinking they might figure you looked more like Rebecca Wolstone than an angel."

"Well, if I didn't look like an angel, then I suppose we'll hear about it right soon." Rebecca sighed heavily and tried to imagine the consequences.

3

· · · · · · · · · · · · · · · · · · ·

*W*e're going to town. Pa says so!" Prudence flew out of the house and down to the chopping block where Rebecca was sitting. She seized Rebecca's pan of beans and pulled her to her feet. "Ma says forget the beans for now and get ready. They're going after supplies, and we all get to go."

As Rebecca crossed the porch she heard Mr. Smyth say, "Smith's announced he's going to be runnin' for president of the United States. Nauvoo's in an uproar."

Mrs. Smyth was tying her bonnet. "There's going to be shortages. Everything affects the markets. We could use another length of piece goods. Rebecca's growing out of everything. We need a sack of flour too."

In this June of 1844, Nauvoo was a bustling city—the largest city in the state. Its wide streets and rows of neat red brick homes spelled comfort. There was an air of permanence, a settling-in-at-home feeling that marked not only the neat homes but also the markets, blacksmith shop, the two newspaper buildings, and the church offices. The limestone building being built on the hilltop lent an air of opulence and sanctity to the town. It seemed these Mormons were prospering.

As the Smyths drove slowly through Nauvoo, Rebecca looked eagerly around. "Becky," Cynthia murmured, "you've no call to crane your neck. It's rude."

"There's so much to see. Wonder whose pretty house that is?"

"Joseph Smith's. Looks like they're adding a few new touches."

Matthew studied the group of workmen and the neat row of flowers and shrubs. "Pa, if you were a prophet, Ma could have flowers and someone to fix the roof."

"And have six wives like Bishop Ellis does," Prue added, glancing at her mother. "Then you could sit in the rocking chair all day while the younger wives fixed your dinner and ironed your clothes."

"That's enough of that, Prudence!" Mrs. Smyth snapped. "You're repeating gossip."

Prue continued, "I heard tell that the bishop had a vision. He told the Prophet that God's going to send them to the promised land."

"And what did the Prophet say?" Matthew asked, leaning close to Prue.

"He told him that only the Prophet gets visions, and he just had a pipe dream."

The penny was warm in Rebecca's pocket. "I'm going to spend a penny," she announced. Would squandering that bit of money on candy ease her conscience?

As Mr. Smyth turned the oxen down Knight Street, they heard a crash of breaking glass. Tyler hauled back on the reins. "Sounds like a gunshot." Again there was a crash and then the shouts of angry men. Smoke puffed above the trees.

A horse galloped toward them. The rider shouted, "If you're Gentiles, better not go down there. Joe's gang is on the rampage."

A woman hurrying down the street called, "Don't you go blackballing the Prophet!" She waved the newspaper she carried. "Like as not Brother Smith had nothing to do with it, but those apostates deserve everything they get."

"What's happening?" Cynthia asked as the woman reached the wagon.

"You don't know? Well, here. I've had enough of these lies. I wash my hands of the mess and you're welcome to it." She thrust the newspaper at Cynthia. "That *Nauvoo Expositor* lies; 'tis set up to make the Prophet look bad. Now, how can the poor man say anything other than what the Lord told him to say?"

"Are you saying that the Saints are tearing up the newspaper office?" Tyler asked.

The woman's bonnet bobbed. Her lips were a grim line. "They scattered type from one end of Nauvoo to the other." She added with satisfaction, "One edition was enough. There'll never be another." She turned down the street.

Mr. Smyth was studying the paper in his hands. His lips moved as he carefully spelled out the words. "Those rascals said a mouthful." He folded the paper and handed it to Mrs. Smyth. "They're accusing the Mormons of straying from the true doctrine of Jesus

Christ. You tuck that paper in your valise. I wanna show it to Lank."

"I reckon Lank's in no mood for more trouble," Cynthia said slowly. "They say his missus is in a bad way, probably won't make it this time."

"I heard." He flipped the reins along the backs of the oxen. "Since we're here, might as well see if we can get a sack of flour." He turned the team.

Wistfully, Matthew said, "I'd sure like to see what's going on. Bet it's good!"

Rebecca eyed the corner of the newspaper sticking out of Mrs. Smyth's valise. Finally she took a deep breath and whispered, "Could I read it, please?"

Cynthia studied her face. "I know you never get enough to read, but you're only a child and this is grown-up material." Cynthia's eyes were compassionate but she was shaking her head, saying, "This is the beginnings of bad times. The less we get caught up in it, the better for all of us."

Soberly, Tyler said, "They don't want us around any more than we want them. Almost since they've come, there's been one heap of trouble after another."

"Seems they ought to be left alone," Cynthia sighed. "A body can't be so bad that they can't be helped, but they sure can't be helped if others are running them out. Now take that Haun's Mill thing in Missouri. I say it's bad blood that makes a man kill his brothers with no call."

Rebecca strained forward. "What happened?"

"A bunch of men just rode into that peaceful settlement, shooting it up. They say about thirty or so of the Mormons hid in a blacksmith shop, and the renegades got in and shot them. Even the little children. Said one little fellow begged for his life, and they shot him through the head. Wasn't no older than Matt."

They rode down the hill to the gristmill. Within minutes after Tyler entered the mill, a dusty man with a heavy sack slung across his shoulders appeared. He thumped the sack into the wagon while Cynthia's forehead puckered into a frown. "That's an awfully big sack," she said as Tyler paid the man.

The miller turned, "There's enough rumbling down there to start a fight right now. If'n the Saints ain't tearin' up the place, the others for sure are."

"What's the problem?" Cynthia asked.

"Politics, and don't you think nothing else. After Joe got his Gold Plates and wrote up the Book of Mormon, then got himself a bunch of followers, things started happenin'. Every place they's been, they start pushin' and people push back. When things back in Kirkland, Ohio, were going good, they built themselves a temple. Things hotted up there and they pushed on to Independence, Missouri, and set up to do more temple building. Said this time that it was to be Zion. But people don't tolerate their pushin' and their strange beliefs. People don't take kindly to bein' put down as Gentiles and livin' with the rumors that they'll be Latter-day Saints yet. Seems most folks are set on makin' Joe's revelations come untrue. I'm guessin' they won't be too happy here in Illinois either." He rubbed his dusty hands together.

"Smith's determined he's going to grease the political machine with Mormons, and the rest of us are supposed to be too dumb to know what's goin' on. Don't like havin' my religion served up and don't like seein' a church stick a long arm and a sharp nose into politics and try to call it democracy. Joe's doin' a good job of leadin' these people around by the nose. I sure don't want to see him doin' that with the whole country." He paused and then added, "If'n a guy sets himself up as a prophet and people agree with him, then they are obliged to toe the lines set down and don't do no complainin'. Prophets don't make no mistakes."

4

· · · · · · · · · · · · · · · · · · ·

Prophets don't make no mistakes—the words were still buzzing around in Rebecca's head that day only a fortnight later. All day the air had been heavy with a brooding storm. In the afternoon as the air chilled and a stillness gripped the land, the clouds dropped low over the hill. Rebecca and Prudence quickly gathered their corn and greens and ran for home.

They were on the porch when Jamie came flying across the road with the first raindrops pounding at his heels. "It's a bad sign," he said as he huddled by the fire.

"Superstitious, you are," Cynthia proclaimed, anxious and out of patience. "Did you think to look for your pa when you were up the way?"

"No, I came from Olsons'. They laid Mrs. Olson out today, and the poor little babe too. They said not to come, Ma. The house is bursting."

The door banged against the wall. Mrs. Smyth's relief burst in irritation. "Oh, there you are, banging like a banshee and wet as a hog in the holler."

Tyler dumped his burden on the floor and said, "Joe Smith's dead and Hyrum too."

"Dead." The words echoed around the room. Shock moved from face to face as they turned to him. Wonderingly, Rebecca watched. They had expected Lank's wife to die and had accepted it. But this fact was rending like tearing a dress, newly made. Even patched, it would be ugly forever.

"Didn't know things were workin' up so bad." Tyler's voice was a low rumble as he stepped out to the bench to wash for supper. The Smyths clustered behind him.

"Cooper brought me up on it while I had the plow welded. Said things been gettin' hotter by the minute, since they put the *Expositor* out of business. Seems there's talk of war. The Illinois militia's been moving in pretty close. Governor Ford ordered Joe to disband the Nauvoo Legion and surrender their arms.

Ford was supposed to have his troops protecting them, but they say Gentiles made a fuss. Ford asked Joe and Hyrum to come over to Carthage for a little gab. Give folks time to simmer down. They had a night in the hotel, but Ford moved them to jail. Gentiles rattled the bars and finally a bunch got up their nerve and broke in. There was no stopping them. Shot Hyrum and a Mr. Taylor, then Joe Smith jumped out the window, and they pumped him full of lead. They say Taylor's alive."

Cynthia set the kettle of greens on the table. "So Joseph Smith is dead. What'll this do to them? Maybe he *was* a prophet, maybe—"

"Because he died? Because he was killed by a mob? That doesn't prove it."

"What would it take to prove he's a prophet?" Rebecca asked slowly.

"I don't know," Tyler said thoughtfully as he sat down on the bench. "I don't know, and I expect nobody will know just what he is until we're on the other side."

"But if he is and we're wrong . . ." Cynthia's voice trailed away, and the hand on the spoon was trembling as she served the greens.

———

For the remainder of the summer, the residents on the hilltop farms kept to themselves and listened to the reports carried up the hill. Through July and August, 1844, Nauvoo was a seething caldron, but out of the heat and unrest a few facts trickled. In August, a man by the name of Brigham Young won the support of the church and assumed the role of leader. Soon the city rang with the sound of saw and hammer. Informers carried the news up the hill. "They're leaving. Brigham Young has half of them building that temple as fast as they can go and the other half's building wagons."

By spring and Rebecca's fourteenth birthday, it was rumored the Saints were moving west; California, Oregon, and the Great Basin were mentioned.

While the new gold dome on the Mormon temple rivaled the glory of the spring sunsets, the streets of Nauvoo began to wear the air of a rejected lover. A fleet of wagons with huge wheels and bare ribs waited for the decency of canvas.

On weekends pinch-faced women watched their furniture and flower-sprigged china depart in the arms of their new Gentile owners. But as earnestly as ever the fields were planted.

In August, Tyler sold the oxen. Two skittish mares, more suited to the saddle than the plow, took their places. Now there was calico for dresses and a slab of bacon. Tyler and Matthew sported new boots, but Jamie mourned the oxen. "How'll we get to Oregon when Josh comes back for us?" he asked.

"Seems silly," Tyler said, "to be considering Oregon when there'll be land to grab."

"By this time next year," Cynthia added, "the West'll be more crowded than here." She spread the calico across the table. "Becky, you'll need to be fitted this year; you're a yard longer now."

"I think we have a young filly about to jump the fence," Tyler said, looking at Rebecca thoughtfully.

Rebecca shook her head. "All I want is to go to school when it commences."

"You know more'n the teacher," Cynthia commented. "Your ma saw you had more learning than most see in a lifetime."

"But they have books. I've almost forgotten how to read."

"You'll be getting married, and then you won't need that kind of learning."

"Becka, Pa's got two sacks of apples here. I'm going to Nauvoo to sell them. Wanna come along?"

Rebecca raised her head and sighed. She was sitting on the edge of the porch, squinting at the tangled mass of black yarn and the steel needles. "I'm knitting stockings for this winter. I don't 'spect your ma'll be too happy to have me go."

"Winter stockings on a day like this?" As Matthew raised his arms to wave at the cloudless sky, a bright yellow leaf detached itself and drifted to his feet. He kicked at it. "Well, there's no frost on the punkins yet. You can knit later."

"Ask."

"Ma, we've apples to sell; can Becky come?"

"Don't know who'd buy an apple; there's lots of trees in the bottoms."

"Maybe we'll trade."

"Go, then."

As the mare meandered her way down the road, the sun was warm on Rebecca's back. She sighed contentedly and settled back against her bag of apples to enjoy the day. Matt grinned at her from his mount.

Already reds and browns of fall had touched the foliage. Wild plums hung heavy with fruit. Beside the creek the willows were yellowing.

She slipped her fingers into the top of the sack and pulled out an apple. "Here, Matt." She reached for the second. While Matthew disposed of his in huge bites, Rebecca held hers to her nose and breathed deeply. With eyes narrowed against the sun, the landscape mellowed into a blur of color.

"I'd like to trade apples for a cookstove, so's Ma could make apple pies," Matthew announced.

"You know they're not going to let a cookstove go for a bag of apples."

Matthew slipped off his horse and knelt beside the creek. "Wish I'd brought my pole." He splashed water to his mouth.

Rebecca went to kneel beside him where the water rushed/over the stones and gurgled on its way. She drank and settled back on her heels. "Matt, what do you want most of all?"

"A doughnut with sugar on it."

"No, I mean out of life. Do you always want to stay here, or do you, like Joshua, want to go places and see things?"

"I don't rightly know," he said slowly.

"Me either. Josh was always talking about going. He seems to itch to see all there is to see." She was quiet a moment and then admitted, "Your pa's and Lank's talk makes me uneasy. Like all that's safe and sure just isn't anymore." She raised her face. "They say this going west is a fever."

"Sometimes," Matthew returned, "I forget that you don't belong."

Rebecca chewed her lips; she was thinking of Lank. Since his wife died, he had come to visit all too often. That in itself was no cause for alarm, but the clean shirts and slicked up hair was telling her something. Seems Mrs. Olson's mother would have enough to do with those six little ones without ironing shirts for Lank in the middle of the week.

Sighing, Rebecca stood up. "If we're going to trade apples, we'd better go."

They wandered down Knight Street, so caught up with window gawking and returning the stares of the passersby that they forgot their mission. On Main Street their horses slowly carried them past the unfinished hotel and the match and powder factory. When they reached the newpaper office, Matthew poked her. "That's the

Mormon newspaper. That one didn't get torn apart; guess they're living right. Hey, I hear a boat! How about going to the docks?"

"To sell apples?"

"Well, we could try."

"Matt, we'd better well try or not go down there. You know what'll happen."

They reached the docks just after the boat's gangplank had been lowered. "Out of the way!" A sailor with a bag slung over his shoulder elbowed them aside. "If you're looking for mail from the West go to that building."

He set off with his burden and Rebecca called, "From the West, mister?" His head bobbed. "Matt, I'm going to see if there's a letter from Joshua."

He nodded. He was studying the knot of people at the railing of the ship.

Rebecca hurried after the man and entered the building almost at his heels. Already a group of people were pressing forward as the sailor surrendered the bag.

Eager hands tore at the bag. A foghorn voice boomed out the names on the letters. The bag was nearly empty when he pulled out the rumpled letter and held it up. "Smyth, Tyler Smyth."

Outside Matthew was holding the horses minus the bags of apples. He flashed a shiny bit of silver and then saw the letter she held up.

"From Josh?" She nodded and he whistled, "This is our lucky day."

"Who bought the apples?"

Matthew waved at the boat behind him. "They bought the whole lot."

"Let's cut up the hill to the temple before we head for home."

"Seems you're sure curious about that temple bunch," Matthew retorted.

"It's a pretty place, but there's a nagging to know more about them."

They turned their horses up the hill behind the general store. The path led through tall grass and wild plum trees. When they reached the street bordering the temple grounds, Matthew moved ahead while Rebecca allowed her horse to graze her way up the street. As they moved from one grass clump to another, she studied the building.

The afternoon sun's slanted rays had turned the gold dome into a blazing halo of light. Behind the dome fluffy clouds passed with majestic slowness that seemed to put the dome in motion. Rebecca swayed, blinded by the brightness. Suddenly from behind her came the solid thunk of a horse's hooves striking the packed dirt of the road. Rebecca's mare raised her head and wheeled. "Oh!" She scrambled for the reins just as the mare sidestepped again. With flying calico and petticoats, Rebecca ballooned over the horse's side. With a startled neigh, the mare dashed after Matthew.

Rebecca gasped for air and shoved herself away from the swinging earth. Strong arms were lifting her and a blackness moved close. It took a second for her to realize the blackness was a coat covering a tall muscular man.

Those arms were still supporting her. "Are you all right, sister?" She looked up into dark blue eyes topped with a worried frown and dark curly hair. His beard tickled her nose, and she almost sneezed and tried to back away from the arms.

From the corners of her eyes she was liking what she could see. Freeing herself, she brushed her rumpled dusty calico back into place. When he was satisfied that she was all right, the stern line of his mouth crumpled, and a chuckle made the broadcloth heave. Head back, he now laughed.

With eyes sparkling with fun, demanding that she share his amusement, he took a breath and gasped, "That poor horse. I'm sure she thought she'd been attacked by a schooner in full sail when you flew over her head."

He sobered. "Actually, it is a good thing she was frightened, otherwise she would have stepped in the middle of you. Do you always dismount like that?"

She moved as if sorting reality from dream. "My horse? Where is she?"

"That's a problem. Let's look." His big hands clasped her waist and lifted her to the back of his horse. Now he was in front of her, and she grabbed his coat.

Within a block they caught up with Matthew and the horses. "That's a quick lad." The stranger wheeled close to the mare. Matthew looked at Rebecca and then the stranger. His eyes widened. Quickly Rebecca slid off the horse.

The stranger followed. "That was an awful jolt; are you certain—" She nodded and fumbled with her filly's reins. "I'm Andrew Jacobson," he offered.

She scuffed her shoes in the dust. "Rebecca Wolstone," she whispered. He studied her face, and his expression softened. Behind his head the clouds moved as they had behind the blazing dome. The dizziness threatened her again.

"Rebecca Wolstone," he said slowly. "I have a feeling that one of these days we shall get to know each other." Again his hands clasped her waist, and she was lifted to the back of her own horse. "Good-bye for now." His blue eyes met hers again.

She was watching the black coat disappear into the trees when Matthew moved his horse close to Rebecca. "Sure is big. Must be one of those Mormons."

"Are all Mormons big?" She was still feeling that detached, drifting dizziness.

"Do you still have the letter?"

She patted the front of her dress. "Yes." Her fingers touched the crisp paper as her eyes followed the dark, distant figure.

5

....

Cynthia baked a johnnycake for supper. Matthew placed the silver coins and the letter in the middle of the table.

Tyler fingered the coins and grinned at the letter. "You got twenty-five cents for the apples, and Joshua hasn't forgotten us."

After they had eaten, he handed the letter to his wife. "Do us the favor."

Mrs. Smyth took the pages and pulled the candle close. "Dear Ones," she read slowly, "I take my pen in hand. Don't suppose you will receive this for some time. It is October now. We made good time to Oregon, but we really pushed to get here before cold weather. We'll stay here with the trappers until spring. The country is fair, lots of trees and water. The beaver and fox are so thick they beg to be trapped." Cynthia's voice labored over the pages and in the droning, Rebecca's mind slipped away from the fireside scene; her thoughts were filled with drifting clouds, the shining dome and the dark-coated stranger.

She caught the final words. "I won't be home this next year after all."

Rebecca visualized the prairie of golden grass, the buffalo, and towering mountains. Looking around the room at the quiet faces, seeing the resignation creeping across Cynthia's face, she felt her restlessness build.

Tyler spoke, "I hear tell this place will be deserted once all the Mormons go. Seems a body would think twice before leaving. The West will be covered with them." Cynthia nodded, but Rebecca felt her spirit had been plucked free by Joshua's letter. She closed her eyes and felt the sway of a prairie schooner.

During the winter, the state continued to rumble with the unrest in Nauvoo. Hardly a day passed without a new tale of woe. One day Tyler returned with an old newspaper. He spread the pages on the table and they hung over it.

It was the *Alton Telegraph* dated October 11, 1845. "Well," Tyler said, "things are gettin' pretty serious. I don't reconcile their carryin'-ons with religion, but this here says the good people of Illinois have determined to see them out of the state by spring or there's going to be trouble."

Rebecca frowned. "They'll force people to go because they don't agree?"

"There's law. When there's a bunch who want to make their own laws and don't abide by what's on the books, well, guess they'd better go."

"But what are they doing?"

He turned to Rebecca, "They're settin' up their own charter, like they're a separate state within a state. Brigham Young's printin' his own money. The state's buzzin' 'counterfeit.' That's not settin' easy."

The snows came early that year, and they were heavy. It was nearly Christmas when Tyler stomped into the house with a new tale. "They say a bunch raided three families on the outskirts of Nauvoo."

"Mormon families?"

He nodded. "Drove them out, and they had to spend the night in the schoolhouse while they watched their houses and barns burn. Lost everything."

Cynthia sighed and said, "Well, at least no one we know would act like that."

Tyler said slowly, "Might as well know; there's rumor Lank's been in on it."

They looked at Rebecca, and she knew what they were thinking. As she turned away from their eyes, she studied the shabby room, thinking about Matthew's wistful wish for a cookstove for his mother. She thought of Lank's slicked-down hair and hungry eyes. Overlapping her thoughts was the memory of the laughing, dark-haired stranger. Rebecca wiped moist hands across her apron. She was conscious of her new slender waistline and the tightness of her dress across her bosom. Try as she might, she couldn't recapture last summer's desire to stay a child just one more year.

In January, Tyler drove home in a smart new buggy. It was as light and trim as a sugar scoop. He had acquired it for the price of a bag of wheat. While they rejoiced over their good fortune, Rebecca was thinking of those women who would be riding in awkward wagons behind plodding oxen. In some ways she was wanting to weep for them, but her curiosity was beginning to feel like envy.

In February of 1846 the grip of winter loosened its fingers long enough for winter-wearied folk to take one deep, sweet breath of spring; and then in paralyzing force winter clamped down once again.

Tyler came home, stomping, steaming, and worried. "They're moving out. The silly fools are moving out in this cold."

Matthew pried Rebecca away from the fire. Swathed to the ends of their noses, they rode the horses to the bluff overlooking the river.

Like a long snake writhing its way across the frozen river, the wagons moved in majestic slowness, winding the life out of Nauvoo. "The fools," Matthew echoed his father with awe in his voice. "It's near twenty below zero, and they're moving out. No one could possibly hate them that much to send them out now."

During the spring, like echoes rebounding from barren cliffs, the news trickled back. On the first night across the Mississippi, in the poor shelter of canvas at minus-twenty degrees, there had been nine babies born.

The Saints were learning to live with hunger, miserable cold, and then the clutching hands of spring-thawed mud. Slowly but surely they were inching their way out of a miserable past into a unknown future. Rebecca found herself being pulled into a sympathy that lifted her beyond the Mississippi and the farm on the hill. More and more her thoughts wandered away, wondering, imagining, straining toward those prairies, those towering mountains Joshua talked about.

And then there was another letter from Joshua. In April 1846, amid blossoms and baby chicks and lambing time, with Rebecca's fifteenth birthday, the letter came.

That day Rebecca had again crept away to the loft to lean against the old leather trunk, to part the layers of cotton and touch the creamy silk and pink velvet.

It had been so long. Now the faces of her mother and father were dim, the sound of their laughter forgotten. Even this reminder of their love failed to stir the memories. She smelled the mustiness of the trunk and wondered about those words her mother had spoken. Why did the trunk hold her only hope of true happiness? Rebecca touched the wedding dress and wished she could cross that barrier to touch her parents once again.

She replaced the cotton slowly, tucked the bundle back into place. Underneath was a hard object. It was her mother's Bible. Pulling the Book from beneath the dress she turned the pages carefully. In the middle was the record of her parents' marriage and on the next page, the record of her own birth: Rebecca Ann Wolstone, April 15, 1831. The page for recording deaths was blank, and she moved her fingers over the sheet, wondering when she could bring herself to write in those facts.

There was also a page for children's marriages. She imagined herself clad in the silk dress with the pink velvet rosebuds spilling down the front. She would toss back those deep lace ruffles and, taking a pen, would write on that page. Beside her would be her bridegroom. Even her vivid imagination wouldn't supply a name.

Rebecca sighed and turned more pages. Strange, as much as she loved to read and had yearned for books, she had never tried to read this Book. She closed the cover and gently ran her hands across the scuffed and faded leather. It was too precious to be read.

Just then Prue called. "Becky, Pa's back from town, and there's a letter."

Rebecca spilled down the ladder and took her place at the table. "Almost a year!" she exclaimed, watching Tyler carefully open the soiled sheets. "And it's come on your birthday," Prue added. "Is that better'n a penny?"

"Today," Cynthia said briskly, "there'll be cake. Not many more birthdays will that young lady be having in this house, and we'd best make the most of it."

Their attention was on the letter now. Tyler cleared his throat. "Dear Pa and Ma, Matthew, Becky, Prue, and Jamie," he read slowly. Jamie pressed against his father's arm and studied the pages. "I take my pen in hand. It will be harvesttime at home. You will probably receive this letter about the time you expect me home. I must delay coming another season. I am trying to make this camp tight for next winter. I don't want to put in such a time as I did last year. The cold is worse than at home, although in the valley it is mild. I didn't expect to see fruit like this but at home. There is a doctor and his wife here making a mission among the Indians. They have planted the familiar fruit trees—apples, pears, and peaches. To bite into one of their apples is almost enough to fool me into thinking I am home. I hanker for a fried apple pie." Tyler stopped to clear his throat and

Rebecca felt her own throat tighten over the stilted, lonely words.

The letter described the territory and his neighbors. Now he returned to the doctor missionary. "Dr. Whitman is a true Christian gentleman. It seems a shame to waste a good doctor out here on the savages, but it is humbling to see he doesn't consider it a waste at all. He keeps saying something that nags at me. He says it is God's secret what He will do with our lives. I can't take my eyes off those people, but at the same time it makes me want something more than I have."

Joshua's words bounded through Rebecca's mind, pounding in a disappointing flatness. "Won't be home for another season," she murmured. "Will he keep saying it?"

All spring and summer the prairie schooners continued to trail out of the state. Each one left behind another empty space in the forlorn city.

As the unwanted ones moved on, Rebecca was drawn down to Nauvoo. Leading her mare down those empty streets, she listened to the silence, experiencing the loneliness,

On the day that Rebecca passed the building and found the door ajar, she murmured, "Even the temple's forgotten and sad." The door was creaking in the wind, and instantly a resolve was born in her heart. She tied her mare to the branch of a tree and walked around the building. Staring up at the pilasters, the high windows, the gleaming dome, stories she had heard rebounded into her mind. These people believed in baptism for the dead. She shivered and listened to her footsteps echoing as she crossed to the portico. Could it be true that God was not pleased to dwell with His people unless they built such a temple as this? Would He not reveal himself without these rituals? There were no answers, but she discovered a deeper questioning was born.

With heart hammering, she slipped through the doors. Like a bird lured, she darted through the rooms. Disappointed at the barren, stripped emptiness, she dashed up and down the stairs. Now, in the subterranean reaches, in the dim shadows, there was something.

Twelve oxen, cut skillfully from wood, supported an oval basin. It was the font for baptism. She touched the satin-smooth oxen, marveling at the beauty of wood turned nearly lifelike. This labor was a testimony. These people believed in the importance of all they did. These people believed enough to follow a man who was leading them away from home and all that was dear to them.

Now she admitted the reasons for her enthrallment. There was this vision of sacrificing, suffering humanity and it was demanding answers. Like stones buried in a smooth-surfaced pool, she must stumble over these questions or forever cast them from the pool of her mind.

The summer passed, and it was harvesttime. While picking apples with Jamie, Rebecca was reminded of the previous autumn. This year there would be no surplus to sell. She glanced down the hill toward the nearly deserted town. Indeed, there would be no market for apples.

She stood looking at the scene before her. The trees were a complex pattern of greens and golds and browns, a carpet in harmony with the blue of the sky and water. In the distance the gleaming dome caught the sun. The day was an echo of that day last year. She thought of the broad-shouldered man. Silly Rebecca. She threw a spoiled apple at the chickens.

"Becka." She looked into Jamie's wistful eyes. He seemed so little and frail for his nine years. She reached to ruffle his hair. "Becka, you can read, can't you?" She nodded. Looking down at him she thought he was much too old for kissing but she ached to squeeze him close. Now he said, "Ma won't let me go to school, but I sure wish I could read."

Gently Rebecca said, "It costs money and they don't have it." Once again that pang, that guilty reminder that Rebecca was keeping the Smyths just one step poorer than they would be without her.

She glanced up the hill to the Olsons' house and tried to imagine caring for those children in the same way she loved Jamie and even the prickly Prue. She was also remembering the birthday cake and that one precious gift.

Cynthia had explained the cake by saying there wouldn't be many other birthdays for Rebecca under that roof. While Rebecca's heart had been heavy with that thought, Cynthia had given her the shiny jewel of a gift: abruptly she had turned to Rebecca and, with a glimmer of moisture in her eyes, had said, "I hope you don't move far away. Seems like I couldn't face never seeing you again." Rebecca had hugged that unusually warm response from Cynthia like a warm blanket around her heart.

Again Rebecca looked at Lank's house and moved her shoulders uneasily.

She shrugged and turned back to Jamie on the limb beneath

her. "Jamie," she said, "I promise you, if you really want to read, I'll teach you."

"We don't have no books."

"I have a book. It's my mother's Bible. It won't be as nice as the primers they have down at the school, but it'll do."

6

....

The snow was piling against the windowpanes, draping its white velvet higher and higher. Jamie crouched before the fireplace. In front of him were a plank and a chunk of charcoal from the fire. Painstakingly he lettered his name. With tongue clenched between his teeth, he wrote, "December 15, 1846."

His mother had been watching each stroke. Her knitting was forgotten, but her fingers moved as if in anticipation of each stroke of the charcoal. "You're going to be our scholar yet." Her voice was filled with pride, and Rebecca was glad to see the worry lines around her mouth soften, but then they tightened again as Jamie coughed. The spasm seemed to tear at his slender frame.

Quickly Rebecca reached for the black Book. "I'll read to you tonight, Jamie."

After Jamie had gone to bed, Tyler came in, stomping and blowing on his hands. "We'll have a good hard freeze tonight. Guess we might as well have winter and get it over with." He grinned down at Cynthia and glanced about the room. "The young'un in bed?" Rebecca picked up her knitting, and Cynthia moved uneasily.

"I'm of a mind to send Rebecca to the doctor tomorrow if he's not better."

Tyler nodded. "Good idea. He may have a tonic for the lad."

"I hope Matthew is keeping warm and dry," Rebecca said to break the tide of thought. For the past two weeks Matthew had been staying in the valley with the Perkins', since Mr. Perkins had broken his leg.

By morning Jamie's fever had climbed, and he was content to stay in bed.

At midmorning the sun burst through the clouds and turned the countryside into a fairyland of crystals and rainbows. The worried frown hadn't left Cynthia's face, and now she said, "The snow's deep. I wish Matthew were here to go."

"I'll love getting out in it," Rebecca insisted, winding herself into shawls.

The mare was glad to be out and she galloped down the road, throwing crystal confetti into the air. By the time Rebecca reached the city, her nose was a fragile thing. She hurried the horse toward the doctor's house.

Dr. Mason was leading his horse out of the barn when Rebecca stopped at his gate. "Jamie again?" he asked. "Cough," he guessed, leading the way into the house.

Mrs. Mason was already tipping the kettle of hot water. "Have some tea," she offered.

"Jamie's cough about tears him apart," Becky explained as her numb fingers curled around her cup, "and there's fever."

The doctor was lifting a dark bottle. "Maybe I'll just go have a look at him."

Rebecca caught her breath and lowered her eyes. "I doubt Tyler can pay."

"There's a bad lung fever going around," he said slowly. "First, I need to stop down the street; guess you can go with me, young lady."

She finished her tea and followed the doctor into the crisp air. When they stopped at a log hut, Rebecca said, "I thought these people left last summer."

"The Campbells did. These are new folks, came in this fall. Wright's the name."

The door opened and a girl Rebecca's age greeted them. She nodded to Rebecca and took the doctor's wraps. "She's in there," she said in a low voice. Dr. Mason entered the other room while Rebecca unwound her shawl.

"Would you care for tea?" the girl asked. "I'm afraid it's just herbs, but—"

Rebecca shook her head. "I've just had some. I'm Rebecca Wolstone. You folks haven't been here long." She wanted to ask, "Mormon or Gentile?" but didn't dare. "Is your mother quite ill?"

The girl looked surprised, but she continued, "I'm Cora Wright. She's very ill." She hesitated and then asked, "Where do you live?"

"Up the hill. My parents are dead, and I live with the Smyths."

"We'll be here only until spring, and then we plan to head west."

Rebecca was guessing her question had been answered. Slowly

she said, "There's been a lot of folks head out this past summer."

She nodded, "I know, and there'll be more—lots." There was a lilt to her voice, and briefly a happy smile touched her narrow face. "It'll be heaven."

Dr. Mason came back into the room and closed the door. "The fever has broken. She'll mend. Try to keep her down or the fever will come back."

"Rebecca Wolstone," the girl said slowly. "I hope you'll come visit me again."

Today was Rebecca's sixteenth birthday. In the late afternoon, Cynthia took the hoe from her and said, "You've talked about visiting that little Mormon girl all winter. Your birthday is as good a day as any. After shunning the Mormon tykes all these years, why you should take up with them now is beyond me, but go."

Rebecca turned her horse down the street that bordered the temple. It was here she and the stranger had galloped after her mare nearly two years ago.

Today the temple door was tightly closed, and there was a quiet dignity about the place. Her excursion into its halls seemed like a distant dream.

The route she was taking past the temple was the long way to the Wrights' cabin, but there was the nagging desire to see the place again.

Old Nell's feet were dragging as she passed clump after clump of tender new grass. In front of the white fence bordering the temple grounds, she gave up all pretense and nuzzled the succulent weeds. Rebecca tilted her head to gaze at the dome.

"Hello." She turned.

"Cora Wright! I was on my way to see you. What a surprise!"

As Rebecca slid off the horse, Cora said, "I thought you'd forgotten me."

"No, but there's not been much time for visiting."

Cora looked at the temple. "Why are you here? I'd guessed you to be a Gentile."

Rebecca nodded and said, "Just curious. It's, well, such a beautiful place."

Pulling her shawl around her shoulders, Cora said, " 'Tis a holy place and it draws." Curiously Rebecca studied the towering limestone building. Holy. Was that the answer? "I like to come here," Cora continued. "It's all quietness."

Rebecca followed her to the steps. "Two years ago this place was like a hornet's nest. Seems quiet and peaceful now."

"Tell me about it."

"Well, I don't rightly know all the details, mostly hearsay."

"Were you here when the Prophet was killed?"

She nodded. "The whole town was in a turmoil. You know he made them mad, tearing up the newspaper office."

"There's no call to print such stuff. Apostates, that's what they were."

"The people who didn't believe like he did? Seems to me a person's got the right to believe like he wants, right or wrong."

She set her lips firmly, "Not if you believe Mormonism has the only true, restored gospel. See, we are really convinced and we're obliged to help others see the error of their ways."

"Seems to me like it's mighty risky being so sure everybody else is wrong," was Becky's spritely comment in spite of her inborn courtesy.

"Come," Cora patted the steps. "I'll tell you about it." Rebecca sat down and folded her shawl closer. "When Joseph Smith, the Prophet, was just a little lad, he wanted to know more than anything which church to join. He read in his Bible that God says we're to ask for wisdom and He'll give it to us, so he asked."

"But that doesn't mean just anybody," Rebecca said. "Seems to me there ought to be some strings tied to it. I doubt I could get wise just asking."

"That's your problem. You must believe or there's no way you'll receive."

"I guess I don't stand a chance."

"Ah, don't say that. By the time I get through telling you about it, you'll find it just as easy to believe as I did. And I sure didn't think I could. Well, anyway, the Prophet asked, and God told him that none of the churches were right. See, one of the miracles of it all is that God chose a mere boy to reveal the fullness of the gospel to. When He came to Joseph Smith there was no doubt that it was a miracle and that he was the chosen vessel."

"What do you mean?"

"He was praying in the woods. Then he saw two people. One of them spoke to him and called him by name; then he said something like this: 'This is my beloved Son, listen to Him.' So you know who that was.

"Well, anyway, then he asked which church he was to join, and they told him not to join any of them. He was persecuted something awful when he told people about his vision. The most wonderful part of it all was that this was the first time that the Father and the Son appeared before mankind."

She stopped for breath before continuing. "Well, not too many people were able to believe. Mostly just his own family. So he had to keep it to himself. Later he was praying in his room, and an angel appeared—said he had a message. Then he told him God had a task for him to do. Next he explained that God had a book hidden away, all written on gold plates. It was about the people who used to live here in America."

Rebecca had been watching Cora's face as she talked and the excitement that sparkled through her eyes. "You really believe this, don't you?" she asked.

Cora nodded. "Yes, I do with all my heart." She clasped her hands. "It's the most thrilling thing that's ever happened to me."

For a few minutes the girls sat together in silence. Below them they could see people moving about the docks. Dimly they heard the shouts of working men, but up here they were surrounded only by the sound of wind and the call of a bird. When Rebecca sighed and moved, Cora took up her story again. "Anyway, the next day the angel Moroni came again. Joseph went to the place where the book was hidden and saw it. But the angel wouldn't let him have it. It took four years before Joseph was allowed to have the plates of gold."

"I've never seen a Book of Mormon," Rebecca said. "What does it say?"

Cora shrugged, "I don't read too well, but I've heard it talked about at meeting. It tells you that you've got to be righteous to go to heaven."

"Like the Bible?"

"Yes, only God told Joseph Smith that the Bible hasn't been translated right. But we know the Book of Mormon has. Word by word it's been given through the power of God. Joseph Smith himself said it is the most correct book on earth."

Rebecca said, "Then it doesn't matter too much what it says, if it's correct."

"That's right. There's just been too many miracles connected with the whole thing to make me ever doubt it. I know it's the restored gospel, the true one."

With a sigh, Rebecca stood up. "It's getting late. I must go." She turned to look up at the towering limestone. "It's beautiful. I've never belonged to anything like this. Is it hard to join?"

"No, it's easy, Becky, and you're mighty welcome." Cora followed Rebecca down the walk. Pulling the mare close to the fence, Rebecca stepped on the top rung, and threw herself across the bare back of the horse.

"Bye, Becky. I hope you come see me again." The happiness faded as Becky said good-bye, and her face became wistful. As Rebecca turned the horse, she wondered about Cora's expression.

7

. . . .

*W*ith all the churches there are, why must another church be started? It seems to be causing an awful lot of trouble," Rebecca said as she frowned at the book she held. Again she and Cora Wright were sitting on the steps of the temple.

In the months since her meeting with Cora, Rebecca had thought often about the girl. Cynthia was right; Becky was completely caught up with the friendship.

This morning Cynthia had turned to Rebecca. With a gentle push, she said, "You're chattering about that girl. Take Nell and go. 'Tis your last chance before that bunch moves out."

As she rode into town, Rebecca raised her head and took a deep breath of the warm air. The familiar farmyard smells were overlaid with the river tang. Mud, fish, water—it all stirred her senses. In her mind it was coupled with a promise of freedom. The throaty toot of the riverboats seemed to beckon her on.

Today she had gone directly to the little log cabin. Cora greeted her, drawing her into the cabin. The dark, scowling woman in the rocker had been ill the first time Rebecca had visited the cabin. Now Cora introduced her, "This is Mrs. Wright," she said stiffly, "and my friend Rebecca Wolstone."

With a whirlwind change of mood, Cora touched Rebecca's hand saying, "Come, let's walk up the hill to the temple. It's too nice to stay inside."

Tugging Rebecca toward the door, she told the woman, "We'll be back shortly."

As they climbed the hill, a tiny question tugged at Rebecca's thoughts. "Is she your stepmother?" Cora threw her a startled glance and then shook her head as she paused to pull a stalk of marigold growing through the fence.

When they had settled themselves on the steps, Cora dropped her shawl and held up the book. "You asked about the Book of Mormon. I brought ours."

As Rebecca thumbed randomly through the book, she realized Cora seemed interested in nothing except her religion. Disappointment dampened Rebecca's enthusiasm, but she gave her attention to Cora, listening as she told of her conversion and the move west.

"It's hard, really hard to make the change." She touched a finger to the tear in the corner of her eye. "Everyone treats you like you've developed two heads. I don't know why there's so much prejudice. Seems people would be more eager to accept the new teachings. After all, Joseph Smith *is* a prophet."

"Look"—Rebecca closed the book and turned to Cora—"I'll confess. All this is like a rope around me, drawing me on. The Mormons have suffered terribly over the death of that man. The more I hear, the sorrier I feel." She pressed her hands to her face. "I just ache over what's happened. I've watched these sad people for so long I feel a part of them. But every time I get close to you all, I end up whirling around inside like Cynthia's old butter churn. Why? Why am I fearing?"

Cora's eyes were wide as she searched Rebecca's face. "Maybe God's calling you to be a part of us. You're fearing because you don't want to suffer like us. Becky, don't be afraid. I'll help you understand and be brave too."

"You won't be here." Even then Rebecca was afraid to admit that next step.

Cora whispered the words, "You can come with us. You can travel in our wagon."

Rebecca closed her eyes, and Lank's face flashed in front of her. Quickly she opened them and said, "I'll have to think hard about it all."

"Don't take too long; we'll be leaving before the month is out."

When Rebecca turned Nell up the hill to the Smyth farm, she was still filled with the churning emotions of the afternoon. "Me thinks I should have stayed home," she murmured into the mare's ear.

Matthew was back from his winter job with the Perkinses; and when the riverboats tooted he was prone to look down the hill with a wistful expression in his eyes. Rebecca said, "You're feeling it too, aren't you?"

"What do you mean?" He turned back to his hoeing.

"You've got that same expression Josh had before he left for Oregon."

"Won't do me no good," he said bitterly. "Pa'll never get along without me."

"Never you mind. I have a hunch Josh'll be back to take you all to Oregon."

"What you going to do? Won't you come too?"

———

In the week that followed, Rebecca found herself echoing Matthew's question. At the back of her mind, Cora's invitation was pressing. By turns it seemed enticing, compelling, and then totally impossible.

Through it all, she discovered a sore spot that needed understanding. It was Joshua. Like a fading photograph, he was becoming dim to her; even his parting words were losing their promise.

In the limbo of that final week, when indecision settled into a nagging worry, the problem of Lank took on a new dimension.

At the end of a hot day in the garden, she carried her hoe to the barn and found Lank waiting. With his hair slicked down and the hungry look in his eyes, he followed her.

"Lank, what are you doing here at milking time?"

"Miss Becky, could I talk to you?" He followed as she hung the hoe behind the door. He cleared his throat. "It's been a long time since Mrs. Olson passed on." He took the plunge, "Could I come courtin'?"

"No," she said simply. Walking past him, she carried her bucket to the well. As she poured cold water over the greens she viewed herself with astonishment. The crisis had been met and answered. Really, there was no crisis at all.

She watched Lank head back across the fields to his own house and wondered why she didn't feel sorry for him.

The following day Cora came to visit. Rebecca and Cynthia were washing clothes under the apple tree when she heard Nell's welcoming nicker.

Reaching her hands to Cora, she said, "Cynthia, this is Cora Wright." Cynthia's glance was cool, but then she had been frosty since last night when Rebecca had confessed her refusal of Lank's offer. Prue's reproachful "I think Mr. Lank is very nice" hadn't helped matters either.

"There's a jug of fresh buttermilk cooling in the well," Cynthia said.

Cora flushed, "That would be nice." Her voice was low, and Cynthia melted.

"Becky, fetch it. We don't have many visitors. Seems the trip up the hill is a mite too far." She retreated into the house.

After the buttermilk, Cora said wistfully, "This is a pretty place; you can see the whole valley and the river. It has a home feeling. Sometimes I wonder if we'll ever know that feeling again."

She caught her breath and said, "We're leaving next week." The words dangled until she said, "There's a dozen wagons taking the ferry Thursday. Mr. Wright said if you want to go, you'll have to travel light. Just your clothes and grub."

"I'll have to think more," Rebecca said, but under the thread of conversation her mind was busy sorting and packing.

———————

On Thursday the Smyths drove Rebecca down to the wharf. Although it was early, wagons had formed a line down to the ferry. In the drifting mists they seemed to issue from that white limestone with the gleaming dome.

Tyler found the Wrights' small wagon. It was crammed with bundles and barrels. The canvas top barely covered the load bulging out the sides. A small brown and white cow was fastened to the rear of the wagon.

"Oh, Becky," Cynthia said, looking at the cow, "do you really want this?"

There was a lump in Rebecca's throat, but she nodded as she watched Mr. Wright shaking hands with Tyler. Her heart sank. She tried to corral her leaping thoughts; but how could this spindly, middle-aged man calm those fearful, lonesome thoughts that were already running around in her head?

Tyler returned to the buggy and lifted down the bundle of bedding and the bag containing Rebecca's clothes. Mr. Wright took the sack of flour and one of cornmeal. When Tyler reached for the black leather trunk, he shook his head.

"But it's the wedding dress!" Rebecca exclaimed. "It belonged to my mother."

He continued to shake his head. "There's no room." Rebecca watched him lift the piece of bacon and the sack of dried apples. "You'll have to leave it behind."

Prudence spoke, "If Josh comes, he can bring it to you."

Cynthia was shaking her head. "She could be going to the ends of the earth."

"Josh." Rebecca was hanging on to the thread. She knew she had to hang on to that hope or she must stay. "Will you tell Joshua to write to me? I'll let you know where I am."

"There's some talk of Brigham heading for Oregon."

Rebecca turned to Cynthia, "I may see Joshua," she said eagerly.

"Are you taking the Bible?" Jamie asked. "You could carry that."

Mr. Wright nodded, and Rebecca knelt beside the trunk and pulled the Book out from under the wrapped dress, For a moment her fingers caressed the cotton, feeling the crispness of the heavy silk through the wrappings. The pain of leaving the dress was trying to reach through the shell she had built around herself. It would be impossible to tear herself away from these people if she allowed one lonely thought.

She closed the trunk, and holding the Book tightly in her arms she turned. "I'll not even *think* that I'll never see you again."

Shouts were moving down the line, and the wagons began to pull out. Cynthia snatched her close and then gave her a gentle push. Rebecca stumbled after Cora and crawled into the wagon. She was knowing only the ache inside.

The first night, when the stars had brightened and the fires dimmed, Cora lifted her chin and said, "I'm going to sleep under the wagon with Rebecca. 'Tis too nice to be inside."

There was a moment of silence, and Mr. Wright said, "If you wish." He moved off in the darkness. Without comment, Mrs. Wright climbed into the wagon.

During the star-filled nights, Rebecca and Cora talked. With sweet grass under their cheeks and the gentle cropping of the night-grazing animals nearby, Rebecca was beginning to feel the pull of this new life.

8

• • • • • • • • • • • • • • • • • • • •

𝒥t was nearly three weeks before the little wagon train reached the first permanent camp. On the evening the wagons rolled into the settlement of Garden Grove, the setting sun painted the sky with scarlet plumes. The color was a banner of triumph over rows of waist-high corn and bright grain.

Rebecca watched people spill out of the houses. The welcoming arms were for all. She felt the peace of the place reach out to her.

There was fresh-baked bread and milk still warm from the cows. A handful of wild strawberries was shared, and the meal became a feast. After supper, weary travelers were spread around the neighborhood.

Even before bedtime the plan was revealed. The welcoming settlers would leave for the next camp, and the newcomers would take their place, resting and bringing the crops to harvest while they waited for the next wagon train to arrive. The few weeks of respite from travel were busy from sunup to sundown with planting, hoeing, and harvesting.

July heat was upon them before they moved on. There were more wagons to join them on this leg of the trip. "New York will tilt to the sky, and California will sink beneath this mass," Rebecca said, looking out the back of the wagon.

In the hurried pace of the past weeks, Cora and Rebecca had seen little of each other. Now Rebecca was looking forward to renewing their friendship. This leg of the journey would be brief, and at Mount Pisgah, twenty-seven miles west of Garden Grove, there would be more harvesting and replanting.

On the first morning that Cora lost her breakfast, Rebecca had been sympathetic. In the days that they traveled to Mount Pisgah,

Cora's indisposition didn't improve, and Rebecca began to worry. Cora was wan and listless, but it was Mrs. Wright's indifference that plagued Rebecca. She was grateful when the journey was completed.

They settled into life at Mount Pisgah, caught up with the busy harvesttime. One day Cora arrived at the community garden patch while Rebecca was hoeing. She carried a basket, and her sunbonnet was pulled low over her face. "Lucky you," Rebecca called to her. "You'll be picking beans while I have the hot work."

Cora shoved her bonnet back. "One advantage of being in the family way." Her smile was strained.

Rebecca caught her breath as she studied Cora's face. "I don't know what to say . . ." She paused. "You don't seem upset."

"Well, it's bound to happen sooner or later. I was hoping that you'd just accept it without making me do all this explaining. I'm Mr. Wright's wife."

Rebecca sucked in her breath. She was trying desperately not to let it make a difference.

"Becky, I just couldn't bring myself to put it all in words when I saw that you didn't catch it at once. You're . . . well, you're so young."

"How can I be young when I'm sixteen, the same as you are?"

She turned away. "Becky, you have a lot to learn. When I'm feeling better, I'll have a lot of teaching to do. Someone's got to do it."

"Bessie seems—"

"Mrs. Wright isn't taking it well. After all, they've been married fifteen years, and there's no young'uns." She shrugged, "I'd not like it either. But, then, it's his only chance to make it in the next world. Hers too. And me . . ." Her voice trailed to silence, and with a sigh she headed for the bean patch.

———

When it was time for the wagon train to move out, Cora's cheeks were again round and red with health. As her waistband tightened, her spirit expanded with joy. More often now she rode in the wagon while Rebecca walked alongside, watching Cora use the needle on the pile of white cloth.

One morning Mr. Wright announced, "There's a touch of frost in the air. Talk's for pressing hard to Winter Quarters. Old timers are saying it's to be a hard winter."

"What's Winter Quarters?"

He turned to look at Rebecca. "The camp Brigham set up on the

Missouri last year. It's pretty close to Council Bluffs and the last likely spot for a settlement before heading west." He paused, "You might say it's the jumping-off place."

"Does that mean we'll be spending the winter there?"

"I expect so. It'll be like these other camps. A place to fortify ourselves and help those who'll be coming after us."

Later Rebecca learned that the Winter Quarters had been settled in June of the previous year by the Saints who had left Nauvoo in February 1846. Crippled by the binding mud and inclement weather, that first weary train had been ordered by Brigham Young to settle and plant crops there. Before the first month was out, before Brigham could send out a scouting party west, the United States government had requested a battalion of five hundred men from the group to serve in the war with Mexico. With such a number of their most vigorous young men gone, moving west that summer was impossible. During that summer and fall, a gristmill and a council house had been built. Each family raised their food and constructed shelter for the winter.

When Rebecca and the Wrights were ferried across the Missouri, they could see the town and appreciate the struggles that had brought it into existence. After being welcomed, the newcomers found cabins and, with the help of the settlers, they were moved into their new homes.

The Wrights had only a tiny cabin over against the bluffs, and Rebecca was taken into the home of the Samuels. Mr. Samuels was the overseer of the camp and his home was comfortable and large, in contrast to the poor huts that surrounded them.

Rebecca was caught up in the routine of daily living as the Saints settled in for the winter. There were vegetables to harvest and wild fruit to dry. There was laundry to be washed and a packed-earth floor to sweep smooth.

With her hands submerged in suds, she carefully handled Mrs. Samuels' dishes and marveled at the contentment she was feeling. Almost she could forget the Smyths' fireside and cease wondering whether Jamie had found someone to teach him to read.

One evening while Rebecca bent over the fire, stirring the kettle of stew suspended above the flame, the youngest Samuels boy dashed into the cabin. "Come on, everybody!" he shouted. "They're coming. I saw them!"

"Who's coming?" Mrs. Samuels continued to cut thick slices of bread.

"Brigham Young and some of the twelve. We were on the bluff

and saw them coming." He yanked at Rebecca. "Come on."

"You go with him, Rebecca. I'll follow along later."

Rebecca threw her shawl about her shoulders and followed. "You've never even seen him." Timmy was dragging her by the hand.

By the time the wagons wound their way into town, the streets were lined.

"Brigham, Brigham, Brother Brigham!" The children took up the chant, and it spread to the adults. There were eager, reaching hands as the wagon approached. Someone grabbed the lead horse, and the wagon stopped. Rebecca watched the man get to his feet. He moved as if extremely tired, but his smile flashed across the faces turned to him. She saw a chunky man of medium height, undistinguished except for his bright blue eyes.

He raised his hand; the shouting stopped. "It's been a weary five months," he said, "and if I start answering questions now, it'll be a weary six months. Let me go home to my family, and I'll tell you all the details on the Sabbath."

Brother Brigham kept his promise. In two days the Saints gathered in the shelter of the stockade walls to listen to Brigham Young tell them about their new home.

"It's the Great Basin. We've named your Zion the Great Salt Lake City of the Great Basin of North America." A joyous cry went up. He continued, "As soon as I saw it I knew that this is the land to which we are called." He went on, "It won't be an easy life. We'll labor diligently.

"I must warn you about the Indians. These people are savages; they will murder and steal. We must be on guard against them, but don't you once forget that these are the people we must reclaim for the Lord. They are the lost tribes of Israel; they are our brothers in the Lord. Joseph Smith has given us the sacred message from our Lord that we are to convert these people. You will be called upon to suffer at their hands, but God will deliver us."

He paused, and when he spoke again, his voice had deepened. "We are a people oppressed and hounded. We've been driven from our homes and for no other reason than because we are living the true, restored gospel of Jesus Christ. We are a thorn in the side of the government. Washington would like to see us wiped from the face of the earth, but we will prevail. We shall win our new territory and set up the kingdom of our Lord on this earth. It won't be easy. If Washington has fought us in the past, they will do so again. You must be strong."

The people around Rebecca were shifting. It was as if they must be off and running to reach that place. The feeling was contagious, and spirits were high. Soon the winter would be over and they would be on their way.

The next week Brigham Young announced that Winter Quarters would be vacated. All the Saints would be moving to the east bank of the Missouri where a permanent settlement would be built.

The new community was named Kanesville in honor of Colonel Thomas L. Kane, who had proven himself a true friend to the Saints in their effort to obtain land.

————————

The new year had dawned before Rebecca wrote her promised letter to the Smyths. "Dear Ones," her letter read, "it is the first day of 1848 and I must celebrate by writing to you. There is a good feeling in the camp of the Mormons. Brigham Young has returned to us from his Zion. This next spring all the Saints here will be moving west to the promised land. The worst of the struggle is over. The hunger and fear is behind, and we will have a home.

"Although the houses were poor at Winter Quarters, the crops were very good. There is hay for the cattle and grain for bread. We have moved back across the Missouri River to settle a new community. It is called Kanesville, and it will be a permanent post, a link between the Great Salt Lake City and the emigrants.

"There is much talk of Saints from all over the world moving to this new land; indeed, Brother Brigham is urging them to do so. I am feeling that I am truly a part of a whole new era. The most sacred commandments of our Lord have been revealed, and these people will hasten to bring peace and harmony to the world. They cannot fail; they possess the glorious fulfilled gospel of Jesus Christ.

"I am lonesome for all of you. Jamie, are you continuing with your reading? Even the newspaper is better than nothing. Have you heard from Joshua? I will write next when I am settled in the Great Salt Lake City. I will look forward to hearing from you. If you go to Oregon, we will see each other." She signed her name slowly, still caught by thoughts of those she had left behind.

9

· · · · · · · · · · · · · · · · · · ·

*T*here had been a slackening of outside tasks as autumn crumpled into winter. When the snows began, Rebecca discovered a whole new community. It was the sisterhood of the women. If the Latter-day Saints as a group were isolated, there was within the isolation a nucleus of life, and it was the women.

The men could build houses and erect communities. They could guard their homes and run their church. But in the end it was the women who held together the rough fabric of daily life.

And rough it was. Rebecca wryly surveyed her cracked fingers and watched her tougher sisters. They were struggling with the task of preparing wagon covers and tents for the springtime move. Like busy birds, they had been flying from spot to spot. As they hovered in one cabin after another, clustered about the canvas, their tongues flew as fast as their needles.

One day, as the din of the children competed with the woman talk, Ann Samuels lifted her head. With a sigh, she said, "What we need is a school." Eyes fastened on Rebecca. Hadn't she admitted to teaching Jamie to read?

No reply was needed. Slates and pencils were produced. A Bible and a Book of Mormon were donated. A battered primer appeared. A fireside was selected, and then Grannie Holstow made her contribution—a stout switch. Only the twinkle in her eyes kept the children from bolting. After her initial terror, Rebecca gladly surrendered her needle and marched her pupils to Ann's house.

Soon the lively students made Rebecca realize her own shortcomings. "If only we had a dictionary," she mourned, "and interesting books."

Brother Samuels tried to help with arithmetic. As they struggled together, Mrs. Samuels said, "Rebecca, you like teaching these young'uns. I'm going to speak to the bishop. We need more schools around here. I have the feeling he should be helping others learn to teach."

The idea caught on, and Bishop Taylor was given the task of educating the teachers. On the first evening, Rebecca looked around the room and her heart sank. Tired housewives harbored little enthusiasm for learning. But there was David Fullmister.

Immediately Rebecca was drawn to David. When she heard the deep cough, she guessed why he wasn't in the woods helping the men cut and haul wood. His gentle eyes made her think of Jamie.

On the evening of their first meeting, Brother Taylor rapped smartly on the table. "We've our school cut out for us. Brother Brigham says we're to teach religion, and if they by chance learn any reading, writing, and arithmetic from the Scriptures, so much the better. Becky, commence reading."

"Sir, I was hoping that we'd learn a little arithmetic and history."

"We'll start with the feeding of the five thousand and divide them into groups. How's that? Then we'll study the history of the American Indians."

"American Indians?"

He gave her a puzzled frown, "Surely you're familiar with the Book of Mormon."

———

Ann Samuels picked up the dishtowel and began drying the dishes Rebecca had washed. "I hear things are kinda dragging for the teachers at the school."

Rebecca nodded, "It's hard to keep interested when there are no books."

"But you have the Bible and the Book of Mormon."

"Brother Taylor's scratching the bottom of the barrel," Rebecca admitted; "he set us to memorizing the Bible."

"I hear that David Fullmister's a little soft on you."

She laughed, "He's just looking for someone to snip at him. I've never seen a person who could cause an argument over so little. Now he's decided he's going to memorize more Scripture than I can."

As winter wound down through January, the morale of the Saints was beginning to spiral down too. There was much sickness. The inadequate houses were drafty, and spirits sagged with the effort to keep ahead of the demands of living.

One day Rebecca pried herself away from a cozy fire and crossed the settlement to Cora's house. Under her shawl she was carrying a tiny knitted cap. As she walked, Rebecca's skirt dragged through the heavy wet snow, gathering a crust on its hem. She paused to shake it before she hopped the ice-bound creek.

"Rebecca!" John, one of her pupils, ran toward her. "I hear tell that you and David Fullmister are going to be treatin' us at the Valentine's party."

"What party? I didn't know—what are we to do?"

"Oh, they're trying to get up a little funnin'. The bishop said since you and David were good at scrappin' with each other, you'll do your Bible memorization."

"A contest," she wailed, "I'll not—"

"Everybody's betting on you to put that uppity David down." He ran off laughing, and after a moment, Rebecca shrugged and continued on her way to Cora's.

———

As Valentine's Day approached, the late winter air was astir with excitement. The talk began by centering around valentines and ice cream; now the excitement of ice cream took second place. Talk focused on David and Rebecca.

Bishop Taylor warned her. "It looks like the whole settlement is going to be at this party. Are you prepared to give them a good show?"

"Of quoting the Bible?"

"You can't let them down."

"I didn't expect our little funning to come to this."

"Neither did David. Plan on living up to their expectations."

With dismay she said, "I don't feel right using the good Book this way."

"At this time of the year," he said dryly, "anything, even a dog fight, would draw a crowd."

At dinner that evening, Mr. Samuels asked, "Well, how's the Scripture memorization coming? I hear that you've even taken up talking in your sleep."

"She mutters between bites of supper," Andy said.

"I know three hundred, I think."

The Samuels' eldest howled, "We have to listen to you say three hundred?"

"Not hardly," Rebecca said ruefully. "I'll probably make a mistake on the first one, then it'll all be over, and you'll have your ice cream."

"Oh, mercy!" Ann exclaimed. "You'd better not do that! We aren't starting the ice cream until seven o'clock. You'll finish before we're done churning."

————

The night of the fourteenth arrived with a touch of spring softness in the air. As Rebecca watched the steady stream of people moving toward the council house, she moaned, "Oh, the whole town's coming. It'll be a disaster, I know it will."

"It'll be a disaster if the whole thing takes until midnight and I go to sleep before I have my ice cream," Andy muttered.

When Rebecca entered the council house, she felt the excitement. David was waiting on the platform, and a whisper reached Rebecca. "They make a sweet couple."

"Oh, oh, that's it, Valentine's Day," she muttered. "David, we're being put up to this."

While Bishop Taylor addressed the crowd, David whispered, "It'll learn you to argue with my greater intelligence." She wrinkled her nose at him.

"Now, Rebecca and David." Bishop Taylor turned to smile at them. Holding his big pocket watch high, he said, "The Scripture must be quoted correctly with the reference given. A two-second pause will be allowed. There will be three matches of ten minutes or one error. Miss Becky, you will begin."

Rebecca jumped to her feet. " 'Jesus wept,' John 11:35." The audience groaned.

" 'He must increase, but I must decrease,' John 3:30," David said. More groans. With Jack-in-the-box movements, they continued to call their verses. The audience stirred.

"Come on, Rebecca."

"David, don't let a girl show you up!"

David got to his feet, and with a dramatic whisper he recited, " 'Come unto me, all ye that labor and are heavy laden, and I will give you rest. . . .' "

Now Rebecca was catching the spirit of her role, and as he finished she bounded to her feet and raised a compelling arm. Excitement was moving through the room again, and David was catching it too. The words bounced back and forth. Cheers rose first from the fellows and then from the girls.

"Do it, do it, Rebecca—show him!"

The bishop was right, Rebecca was thinking as she finished a verse and sat down. Even a cockfight would have served the purpose.

She was hearing the words David was saying. He was talking about faith and God and love while the crowd cheered, not because of his words, but because his voice rang with challenge and authority.

Now one match was completed, then two. Bishop Taylor raised his watch. "Time—it's a tie."

"No, it isn't, she won!" cried a female voice from the rear of the room.

"She didn't!" Confusion broke, but there were smiles and laughter.

Rebecca sighed. "I guess we did what we were supposed to do—entertain."

On February 15 Cora's baby was born. Mr. Wright stopped by the Samuels' cabin. Looking at his beaming face, Rebecca heard him say, "It's the most wonderful thing that's happened to me. It's like being given another chance."

Rebecca was still wondering about his strange words that afternoon as she readied herself to visit Cora. Ann handed her a jug of milk. "I hear things aren't going too well over there." She chewed at the corner of her lip. "I hate to poke in where I'm not wanted, but take this. It isn't much, but then I don't suppose Cora feels like much. You see she drinks some of it while you are there, hear?"

Now the settlement's most-traveled paths were bare of snow, and in the soggy mat of old grass there was a touch of green.

Rebecca tossed her head back and breathed deeply of the freshness in the air. Woolly lamb clouds scooted across the blue sky. Back home things must be greening. Soon the buds on the apple tree would begin to swell. Back home. She caught herself. That place was no longer home. Strange how dear that shabby old cabin seemed.

In less than two months she would be having another birthday. She was thinking of the wedding dress. She could almost feel the heavy silk and the soft, pink velvet flowers. Would Joshua think it important to bring the dress to her?

She recalled the things he had said before leaving. It wasn't like Joshua to be so wordy. Even his joking hadn't wiped out the seriousness in his eyes. For a moment her throat ached with loneliness.

She caught sight of the Wrights' cabin and began to run down the path.

Cora was in the tumbled bed. Now there was a tiny scrap of crying humanity beside her. Her pale face brightened with joy and pride when she saw Rebecca. "Oh, come and see our little Joseph," she whispered.

Bessie, who had opened the door for Rebecca, was inspecting the contents of the jug. "Milk—our cow's about dry. I haven't had a good drink of milk for ages."

She reached toward the cups on the mantel, and Rebecca said quickly, "Mrs. Samuels sent the milk for Cora." Bessie seemed about to speak; then, shrugging, she went to her chair beside the fire.

Cora was fumbling at the wrappings around the fussing baby. "I don't have any milk yet, and I think he's getting pretty hungry." Rebecca accepted the tiny bundle, noting the distressed groping and the thin hands.

"Takes milk to make milk. Have you had any?" Cora shook her head, and her eyes reflected her worry. Rebecca returned the baby and went to the row of cups. "Mrs. Samuels said I was to make sure you drank some while I'm here."

There was an uneasy expression of Cora's face as she looked past Rebecca, but she accepted the milk and drank it eagerly. Later Cora tried again to nurse the child. Rebecca could see the infant was either being satisfied or exhausted. He soon went to sleep. "Mr. Wright's sure proud of the little one," Rebecca said.

As Rebecca plodded home through the mud, she recalled Cora's reference to Bessie's childless state, but what were the words she had used? Hadn't Cora referred to their marriage as Mr. Wright's chance to make it in the next world?

She shoved aside her questions as she wiped her feet and entered the Samuels' cabin. "I made her drink two mugs full," Rebecca explained, returning the jug. "I don't think they have much to eat. You know, I think Bessie would have drunk it if I hadn't told her what you said."

"Oh, dear," Mrs. Samuels murmured, "I think you'd better carry a little milk over there every day or so until Cora's back on her feet."

"Mr. Wright doesn't seem to notice that anything's wrong."

"Well, Bessie's first wife. Sometimes men are blind to facts, don't forget that."

Rebecca was watching Ann's face. "Well, I know one thing; I'll never get mixed up in a plural marriage like Cora did. I don't think she realized—"

Ann was shaking her head. "Don't say that. If it's what the Lord has ordered, we'll all do it sooner or later. Make up your mind to it."

Rebecca shook her head. "Never. I don't even want to get married. Brother Taylor's promised me a teaching position when we get to the Great Basin."

"But you don't understand the principle—" The door opened and Mrs. Samuels said no more.

10

••••••••••••••••••

$\mathscr{K}$anesville vibrated with the news. Brigham Young had set the departure date for the 15th of March. On the Sabbath the congregation listened as the bishop detailed the plans. Even now there was much to be done to prepare for the last leg of their journey to the Great Basin.

A week later, while Rebecca and Ann Samuels were stretching canvas across the ribs of the wagon which would be home during the coming months, Ann said briskly, "Rebecca, I've talked to Mr. Samuels, and he's of a mind to have you travel with us rather than the Wrights."

Rebecca's hands dropped to her lap, and she sat back on her heels. She knew her relief was showing on her face as she grinned up at Ann. "Oh, Mrs. Samuels, I would like it so much. You don't know how I've been thinking and wondering."

"You'll be able to spend lots of time with Cora later," Ann said gently, "more than now. She really needs your friendship. The young wives suffer most."

Rebecca glanced up at her, but Ann's sunbonnet hid her expression. Quickly she said, "Let's get this finished. There's lots of baking to be done before we go."

"Will Brother Brigham be traveling with the train?"

"No. He'll be moving most of his family out later this spring."

"Does he have a big family?" Her voice was timid, "Wives and children?"

Ann's face was still hidden and her answer a short, "Yes."

———

On the day the big wagons began moving out, spring put on her best show. With the dawn had come wind and a fierce sprinkling of rain, just as quick and impatient as a housewife sloshing water around her dooryard to settle the dust.

In the early sun the tender green things gleamed with the moisture. Blooming meadow grasses, dandelions and nestling crocus all seemed to snatch at wagon wheels and plodding oxen as they passed that one last time.

At the Samuels' cabin the rooms had been stripped of all except the makeshift furniture, and the children's voices echoed from the chinked-log walls and bare rafters. It was a lonesome sound, catching at Rebecca, winding the good-bye feeling around her. As they left the cabin, she realized the lonesome feeling was wrapped around the unknown future, not the secure past.

The wagon train quickly settled into a daily routine. In the pattern set by Brigham Young on the first trip across the plains, the train was organized into companies with captains set over a group of wagons. Each morning the bugle was heard at five. At seven, after morning prayers and breakfast, the call came to move out. In the evening the sound of the bugle came at eight-thirty, signaling the Saints to retire to their wagons for prayer and then bed at nine.

At the end of the week there was the Sabbath rest. This, Rebecca discovered, was also an ordered part of their routine. The entire train accepted the pattern. First came worship and then there was the heartening aroma of freshly-baked bread and stewed apples to flavor the air, enhancing even the smell of the ever-present rabbit stew.

As March was waning, the cold was leaving their bones. Chilblained hands and reddened noses disappeared, and little Dee's nose began to show sunburn.

Brother Samuels watched them discard shawls for sunbonnets. "Summer's coming early. We'll reach Great Salt Lake City in time to plant a good crop of corn."

Ellen's pinched face brightened, "Oh, roasting ears. I can hardly wait."

"I'd just like to see some Indians first," grumbled Andy.

"Hey, hey," his father teased, "the trip isn't over yet. We've just begun, and it's a three-month stretch between here and the Great Basin."

"Then we'll see Indians?"

Rebecca shuddered, and Tim teased, "They'll take a real hankering to you, thinking that stuff hanging over your shoulders is real gold."

"Maybe it would be a good idea to wear your hair tucked up," Ann worried.

"Ah, we'll solve the whole problem by marrying her off to the Indians. She wouldn't even have to go through the temple for that."

"That's enough of that, young man," Tim's father said sternly. "Remember, we're to be converting the Lamanites back to their origins, not picking fun."

"Lamanites." Rebecca straightened up. "What's that?"

"The Indians. Rebecca, you really should read the Book of Mormon."

"It tells about the Lamanites?"

Brother Samuel nodded. He turned to Tim, "Now, Brother Brigham has already instructed us that one of our tasks is to bring the gospel to these Indians in the Great Basin. They are your brothers and sisters in God, and nothing will be spared to bring them to the church. Quit thinking of them as enemies, and start calling them your friends."

At the next Sabbath stop, Bishop Taylor approached Rebecca after worship. "A word with you, sister," he hailed her as she hurried after Ann. "Brother Samuels tells me you haven't been baptized. Are you ready?"

"I was thinking it would be nice to wait and be baptized in the temple. The one in Nauvoo kinda took my fancy."

"It'll be years before we have another temple. You don't understand. Becoming a part of the Latter-day Saints Church is not something you can put off without endangering your soul's welfare." When she didn't reply, he said, "I think you should plan for it when we camp on the Platte."

"I'll be thinking about it," she answered in a low voice.

Rebecca was baptized on a warm May day in the muddy North Platte River. Beaming Saints lined the bank, and she tried to pick up their excitement. She was still pondering it all when her golden braids came up limp and wet, and the elders circled her and conferred on her the gift of the Holy Ghost by laying their hands upon her head.

When the Platte River separated into two forks and the wagon train turned to follow the North Fork, spring's freshness disappeared. By the time the wagon train reached Fort Laramie, the heat lay heavy on the prairie.

The word moved back down the train. "We're going to hole up at Fort Laramie for a few days, long enough to set up a forge and repair wagons."

They camped close to the junction of the North Platte and the Laramie rivers, snugged in a grove of cottonwoods, knee deep in meadow grass and close enough to hear the river's talk. Rebecca wished they could stay forever.

During their days of rest and freedom, the women used their time to do laundry and bake innumerable loaves of bread. While older children romped and played in the river, the men repaired and strengthened the wagons.

As if the Saints couldn't tolerate idleness, the evenings were given to dancing and singing. Old Elmer Nils wore out the horsehair on his bow and broke one string on his fiddle. But the frenzy of activity continued, building always to a greater peak.

But peaks are topped, flattened. Before the week was finished, David Fullmister was dead.

It had started as innocent fun and the need to repair Elmer's bow, but the mare was young and nervous, barely broken to the saddle, and hardly apt to stand still when her tail was pulled. Later they told Rebecca that David had tried to stop the mare as she ran toward the wagons. He had seized her neck and was nearly astride when she stepped in the prairie dog hole.

When Mr. Samuels came after her, he warned, "Unless there is a miracle, he will die. A man can't have a horse that size fall on him and survive."

In the dimness of the wagon, David's face was a white square. Rebecca knelt beside him and tried to talk. "It doesn't hurt," he assured her in a whisper, "I'm all numb. They say that's good, but I know it's bad."

"Oh, David!" She bent her head, and he touched the braid that swung forward.

"It was fun, wasn't it?"

"What?"

"Last winter, the studying and all. I was hoping that we would teach school together when we got to Great Salt Lake City, but I guess that's not to be."

"David, don't say—" She remembered Mr. Samuels' words and couldn't continue.

He was shaking his head. "Let's not pretend. There isn't that much time. It's all okay, except . . ." for a moment he was silent, and then in even a softer voice he said, "I'm glad you were baptized." After more silence he said, "You know the teachings of our church. Rebecca, I'm only nineteen." In the shadowy wagon he turned his face toward her, and for a fleeting second his face twisted. The agony in his eyes forced her to drop her head against the hand that clung to hers.

"It doesn't seem quite fair." His voice rose in despair. "I didn't get a chance to marry and have a family. There's nothing in the revelation to take care of a problem like that. You might say I've been left out in the cold."

"Oh, David!" Her tears were on his hands now. "I'll do anything on this earth that I can to help you." His face brightened, but before she had time to say more, the dreadful spasm shook him, and when it had passed his eyes remained closed.

David died during the night without regaining consciousness. The next day he was buried on the hillside in full view of the rivers and trees while the prairie glimmered beyond. There were words and promises, but Rebecca was conscious only of the damp earth and the clunk of steel against wood.

On the following day the wagon train moved on, trailing the north fork of the Platte. Rebecca kept her eyes on the lead oxen and refused even a backward look.

11

....

*R*ebecca Wolstone, letter, Rebecca, Rebecca!" Her name bounced around the fort like pebbles in a pail. Quickly Rebecca wiped her hands and ran out the door. The heat struck her and she gasped and slowed to a walk. The excitement of their arrival at the Great Salt Basin had been overshadowed by the midsummer heat. She was prone to forget that the adobe walls of the fort trapped the heat and stilled the air. At least the huts lining the inside of the fort were cooler, thanks to their thick adobe.

She walked through the powdery dust to the well at the center of the fort. "Here I am." She lifted her hands, and the letter was passed to her. Her eyes widened. It was from Joshua. She pried at the envelope as she walked to the cabin.

In the six weeks since they had arrived in the valley of the Great Salt Lake, Mr. Samuels had begun to build his cabin. But until that cabin was completed, the Samuelses and Rebecca were sharing a hut not much larger than the wagon.

Rebecca stopped on the threshold. The Samuels family lined the table. "You didn't eat much," Ann chided.

"I've a letter from a friend. I'll go sit in the shade and read it." She explained, "I'm just not hungry."

"Oh, ho, what kind of a friend?" Mr. Samuels called.

"A boyfriend," Ellen cried. "Her ears are red."

On the shady side of the fort, Rebecca found a patch of grass and sat down. She opened the letter, and the sheets of paper waved and crackled in the breeze. Holding them against her knees, she read: "Dear Rebecca, It sure was a shock to come home and find you gone. Wouldn't surprise me if we didn't nearly bump into each other. I arrived home the first of June, and the family thought you'd be getting to the Great Basin this summer. They are all fine and wish you well." She paused to let the memories of those faces flood her thoughts. She swallowed the lump in her throat and went back to the letter.

"I wanted so badly to see you. There's much to tell. Oregon is a fair land, and I am eager to get back. The matter most pressing now is money. There's land for the taking, but I must have money for stock and all the other necessary gear."

He went on to describe the country and his daily routine, and then a tentative note appeared in his writing. "I mentioned the Whitmans and told you a little about them. Well, they've been murdered by the Indians. It was heartbreaking after all the sacrifice they made to help these people. It's made me do a lot of thinking—about them and about life and God. I'm beginning to see that the living out of a person's life, if it is to have meaning, must be a glory. I could see their love for each other and for those savages was a glory. I aim to find out more about that."

Now the tenor of the letter changed. "Little Becky, I'm hungry-lonesome for you. I was ready to drop everything and head for the Great Basin until Pa talked some sense into me. He's made me see that unless I want the same kind of existence he and Ma had all these years, then I'd better do something about it now.

"There's talk of gold in California, and the idea of trying my luck there is picking at my thoughts. Pa says I can do enough digging to make my dreams come true in one season." Rebecca raised her head and stared at the flaking adobe wall of the fort. Disappointment was spreading through her, and she hugged the letter.

Words, like weeds in the wind, flailed her. Hungry-lonesome. Pa talked some sense into me. Glory. She rested her head against her knees with the letter sandwiched between. Finally with a sigh, she sat up and spread the crumpled pages.

"I'm going to dig my gold," she read, "and then I'm coming to Great Salt Lake City looking for you." She studied Joshua's signature, and her mind was full of the last time she had seen him. Tall and slim, bright in his buckskin on that fair horse with his hair reflecting the sun. He had said, "I'll see you next year." Cynthia had told him not to plant notions.

Rebecca was talking down to the letter, "Cynthia doesn't want me getting too close to you, Joshua. I think she's planned something different for you."

She closed her eyes, and a vision of the wedding dress floated before her. "I wonder if it still fits," she mused, looking down the slim length of her.

With a sigh she got to her feet and went back into the fort. How long would it take Joshua to dig enough gold to satisfy him?

———————

As the summer of 1848 had been hot and early, winter was hard and long. Snow piled around the Samuels' cabin and swirled through the cracks. Survival became the all-consuming thought. Food supplies dwindled, and illness moved from cabin to cabin. The war with Mexico was over and the Great Basin now belonged to the United States. Even as rumblings concerning this new situation were drawing together, Brigham Young and the twelve, plus the members of the Nauvoo Legion who had departed from Winter Quarters in the summer of 1846 to fight in the war, were trickling into the Great Salt Lake Valley.

With the returning soldiers came interesting facts. The first bit of knowledge produced the Mexican-style adobe, which provided the early shelters in the valley. They also returned with reports of the lush valleys and fair harbors in California. Later groups trickled back the news of gold, and Brigham Young promptly dealt with all the ungodly yearnings.

It was that winter, while Rebecca huddled beside the fire trying to remember to smile, that she recognized the change that had taken place within her. She was one of the Saints.

Until the letter from Joshua, she had not felt really at home. All last winter on the banks of the Missouri, even after her baptism, she had been but a spectator. "It's like putting on a slipper, but never wiggling your toes down into the very end. Comfort isn't there until you wiggle your toes and know it fits."

Ann had been poking a needle in and out of a stocking. "What doesn't fit?"

"Life. At the Smyths I thought I fit. But I didn't. I didn't realize it until they made me uncomfortable by pushing at me about Lank."

"That's the widower they wanted you to marry?"

She nodded. "I never could admit, no matter how much Josh and I liked each other, that I just didn't belong. Cynthia, well, she doesn't want me to have Joshua. But until this letter, I couldn't admit it. See, without realizing it, I'd been letting my life here just fill the time until he could come and get me. Now I know that down deep I've quit expecting it. He'll find his gold, but chances are, he'll never make it back to Oregon. His glory is going to be gold, not me."

"Those are dismal thoughts for a snowy day," Ann said.

"I'm just putting words to all I've been feeling since the letter. Now I'm wiggling my toes like I belong." Ann raised her eyebrows, and hastily Rebecca added, "Oh, not to you, but to this place and this time. I'll make my own glory, and I think I can. The first step's going to be to move from this fire and start. If there's a primer and a slate in this valley, I can begin to teach school."

"Better'n letting the young'uns run wild all winter."

Rebecca made good her promise, and before the Christmas excitement was in the air, she had been given a spot in the fort, a handful of primers and a group of squirming students.

By the spring of 1849 significant changes had taken place in the Great Salt Lake Valley. In February the first political convention was held in the old fort.

At this time the Deseret territory was designated as an area bounded by the Rocky Mountains, the Republic of Mexico, the Sierra Nevada Mountains, and the newly established Territory of Oregon. In March another convention was held, and Congress was petitioned first for statehood and, when that failed, for recognition as the Territory of Deseret. Even as this was going on, a constitution had been adopted and a government set up. Brigham Young was governor, and the laws of the church became the laws of the land.

The steps toward self-government gave the settlers a feeling of permanence and self-confidence. Now roads were built; irrigation ditches, gristmills and even a water-powered threshing machine came into being. A twelve-mile stone wall surrounded the community farmland. Newly planted trees had taken hold, and there was a promise of swelling buds.

Although many of the settlers had moved into their own cabins last fall, Cora and her family were still living in the fort this spring. It was March, and as Rebecca walked toward the fort the air was soft and light. The snow was melting, and doors stood open to the breeze.

"It's a gladsome time," Rebecca reflected, thinking that she sounded like Grandma Taylor. "Makes you happy we didn't just give up in January. Things do get better. Life is good!"

As she hopped her way through the soggy grasses, Rebecca felt icy water oozing into her shoes. On higher ground she surveyed the damage. The split along the side of her shoe gaped enough to reveal her heavy stocking. She remembered Brother Kimball's prophecy and smiled ruefully.

"If Brother Kimball's right—saying that before the year's up, we'll be getting all the goods we need—well, it'll make a true believer even out of me."

"Rebecca!" Cora stuck her head out the door of her cabin. "I thought I heard you. Talking to yourself? What brings you out today?"

"You. I've gone most of the winter without seeing you." Cora's dress strained over her stomach. "Expecting, huh?" She nodded, and Rebecca shook her head. "Only a year since Joseph, and you miscarrying last summer. You shouldn't so soon."

Cora's face reddened. "It's my duty. Children are a blessing."

"I hope you live to raise them."

Rebecca knew her voice was cutting across raw emotions when Cora snapped, "And if you were living your religion, you'd be married and in the family way."

She shook her head. "You've forgotten there're other things in life. I'm in no hurry. There's school to be taught."

"Then you aren't thinking about your soul's welfare."

"What do you mean?" Rebecca asked impatiently.

"The only way you'll ever achieve salvation is through your husband."

"I don't believe it."

"The principle. You know about it. The Prophet said you'll only achieve a higher glory by being married and having children. Do you want to end up just an angel? That's all right. I'll have you fetching and totin' for me for eternity."

"Oh, Cora," Rebecca burst out laughing. "This is funny. We haven't seen each other for ages, and here we are arguing. You live your religion, and I'll live mine."

"Trouble is, you aren't living it. I heard you say you would believe if Brother Kimball's prophecy came true. You're not to be trying the Father. The Prophet said we're to believe on someone else's faith if we don't have enough to believe on our own."

Ignoring Cora's words, Rebecca said, "Seems, for being the true followers of God, for having the restored gospel, we're not seeing too much evidence of His mercy. Looks like we ought to be experiencing some of the Lord's blessings. Last winter was more'n enough to try our religion. It nearly took our souls and bodies. I heard a woman on the other side of town went clear crazy and took off in the snow."

Cora nodded, "I heard too. Her husband spent half the night trying to haul her back. It wasn't the weather and the lack of victuals. She was just plain rebelling."

"The principle again?" Rebecca asked dryly.

Cora studied Rebecca's face. "You're still not quite in agreement, are you? Yes, her husband's second wife just got to her, and she flew apart. Poor thing. There's nothing to do but accept it. Remember, she's not rebelling against him; she's rebelling against God, and there's no way to handle it but to bring herself under control. They prophesied the way would be hard, but the harder it gets and the better we handle it, the greater will be our reward. Jewels in our crowns." She bent to pick up her baby from the floor, and Rebecca sighed impatiently.

"Where's Mrs. Wright?"

Cora brushed dirt from her baby's hands and wiped his mouth. "Outside settin' in the sun. That's what she does come summer, and it's the fire in the winter."

She got to her feet. "Come look what the Mister's done." She moved to the fireplace and pointed to the bed of embers heaped in the center of the fireplace. "Got a piece of sheet iron and made me an oven." Returning to the table she uncovered a pan of rising bread. "I'll show you how it works."

With a stick she shoved aside a stone and eased the pan into the cavity formed by the metal and rocks. Pushing the stone into place, she scooped the glowing embers close and tumbled a share of them onto the earth-covered metal. "Bread's not bad."

With a sigh of satisfaction she moved back to the table and sat down beside Rebecca. "There's some talk of us trying to start an ironworks down south."

"Down south?" Rebecca echoed. "You'd move away from here?"

She nodded. "About three hundred miles from here. Brother Brigham's had men down there looking the place over. There's iron ore to be had. You know how he's always preaching we must be self-sufficient. Well, right away he started looking for someplace he could set up a foundry."

"It's so far away."

"He's going to have Saints spread all over this country. From here to California. Rebecca, think of it. This is all going to be the Kingdom of God, and we're starting it. This is the place where Jesus Christ is coming to set up His kingdom. Isn't that reason enough to stick through all the trouble?"

"I don't find my thinking inclined that way right now."

"Then you aren't living by faith. You aren't really believing that Brigham is God's prophet and that God is directing him through all this. Rebecca, you can't wait until Jesus comes back before you're believing this is all true."

Rebecca got to her feet laughing, "Then I'll believe because you say so."

————

During that summer and fall of 1849, Rebecca saw Heber C. Kimball's prophecy come true.

While dust devils stirred the corn hanging limp in the July heat and the wagon trains continued to trickle into the Great Salt Lake Valley with their poor offering of tired and hungry Saints, a new force entered the valley. The sounds were different. The echo of their curses and the angry crack of whips was heard from dawn to dusk as heavily loaded wagons moved into the valley.

The commotion brought the Saints to the streets. They were mindful of the poor adobe of their homes and the graying calico and split boots as they watched Brother Kimball's prophecy arrive behind tired horses. Sweating men cursed the burden they had hauled across the plains, fearful of the tales they had heard of the dangers yet to come.

Ann and Rebecca had been watching the dust cloud when Ann's youngest rode in from the fields. His tousled hair was a banner of excitement even before he reined his panting horse. "Your pa'll whip you for winding that horse," his mother scolded.

With eyes dancing with joy he ignored the warning. "They's gold miners, heading for California with loads of stuff. Rough ones, they is."

"Are," Rebecca reminded automatically. Her thoughts were racing before her. Gold—what if Joshua were there? "Where are they from?"

He shook his head, "Don't know. They're powerful discouraged by the tales of the mountains and all. There's talk of their getting rid of their load. Pa's coming to get the oxen and see if he can dicker."

"Oxen!" Ann exclaimed. "Not Sue and Dixie. We can't get along without them." But her son was off, and she hesitated only a moment. Grasping Rebecca's arm, she said, "Come, we'll see for ourselves just what's going on. Let's walk down there."

"Wait up!" Cora was hurrying to reach them. She stopped for breath and shifted Joseph to her other hip. When she could speak, she said, "There's talk of them selling their goods that they're totin' to California. Now they're in too big a rush to get there."

During the following week, as the wagons continued to break

through the mountains, the teamsters held daily auctions in the streets. They were as desperately eager to dump their load and be on their way to California as the Saints were eager to acquire the merchandise and hurry the uncouth miners along. Fresh oxen and repaired wagons were traded for tired horses and collapsing wagons—at a profit to the Saints.

For the most part, the women clustered on the edges of the crowd and watched their menfolk dicker for merchandise. Clothing was sold for a fraction of the price it would bring back east. There was tinware, shoes, dress goods, and every sorely needed item imaginable from needles to nails.

Occasionally some of the braver of the women swooped close to the bulging wagons to peer and dart back with the news. "I declare, that wagon has a stove."

"Those barrels are packed with shoes. I saw them. I suppose they're just for men." The speaker studied her calloused feet. "I don't reckon these feet would fit shoes, for all their lumps."

As Rebecca watched the wealth change hands for only a token of their value, destiny stepped close to her and wrapped its arms around her. Brother Kimball's prophecy had indeed come true. She must be a believer now. The facts were there, touchable and ready to be possessed.

12

· · · · · · · · · · · · · · · · · · · ·

$\mathscr{I}$t was barely light when Rebecca heard the bird. It scratched and pecked at the crude shingles above her head. As if just recognizing the dawn, it gave a trilling call. Rebecca smiled and snuggled against the comforter under her cheek. A gentle breeze stirred the sheet dividing the loft into two rooms.

From the far end she could hear Timothy's snores. Beside her Ellen moved. Today was the Sabbath, and with a contented sigh she began anticipating the day. There would be no work except for feeding the stock. After breakfast there would be worship, but until then this precious jewel of empty time was hers.

She slipped from the bed and quickly dressed. As she reached for her bonnet, she noticed the black-bound Book of Mormon which Bishop Taylor had given her. It bulged with Joshua's last letter and some clean sheets of paper. She tucked it and the stub of a pencil into her pocket and crept down the stairs.

The sun was still behind the mountains, and those dark rugged lines shadowed the valley. Rebecca walked slowly to the street. Before her, to the east, stretched the city. Here and there among the adobe and log buildings, she could see the fresh green banners of trees newly transplanted from the mountains. To her left and behind her, the cultivated land was already a sea of green moving in gentle waves with each touch of the morning breeze.

Unlike Winter Quarters and Kanesville, there was a neatness and a sense of order here. The squatty houses huddled companionably close to each other. Gardens, chickens, cows and the outbuildings with their plows and harnesses created a homey picture. It spelled comfort and security—progress.

But there was a goad. She looked beyond the city and saw the gray-green of the desert. It seemed to push at them with a quiet pressure that reminded them of how little they had gained and how quickly it could be lost.

When she reached the creek, she settled herself in the shelter of the trees and tried to recapture the good glow of freedom with which she had greeted the day.

She fingered the pages of the book in her lap. Where was that holy feeling which had marked the Sabbath in the past? "I need to learn about God. I want to know the whys of all this." She looked about her, at the book, at the letter.

She smoothed the letter. It had been read so many times that the pencil marks were smudged and the creases worn thin. Still, she puzzled over it, feeling her heart respond and lift each time she read it. These Whitmans. What did he mean when he talked about a kind of glory?

She tried to fasten that word to all that surrounded her and even to her everyday life. There was drudgery, pain, the constant battle for life. Faces floated before her. Last winter's agony had etched them in a forever way. Ann's features had become lined with a kind of fatal gentleness. That kind of living didn't spell glory. Those people living in Oregon must have had times as hard and fearful as the Saints. What kind of glory could possess their days?

She shrugged off the questions and returned to the tender part of the letter, the part she couldn't quite grasp. It was unlike Joshua to be reaching out to her like that. What did it mean? At home he had been rough and silent. No, not rough. That wasn't the word. A youth can whip a team of horses where they don't want to go. He can push through stubborn soil and split a cord of wood faster than anyone on the hill, but rough? Not when he gentles his voice to speak and polishes an apple shiny bright before he gives it away.

Rebecca's heart strained with the effort to recapture the memories, and she hungered to relive those shadowy days. Why must Joshua have gold? She didn't want gold. She remembered the poor little house on the side of the hill and the helpless look on Tyler Smyth's face when little Jamie was ill.

There are things that can strip the soul from a man; sometimes it was as little as not having enough to give. Her heart stilled. She couldn't ask that of Joshua.

She opened the paper and spread it across her knees and picked up the pencil.

"Dear Joshua," she wrote. "You'll probably never receive this letter, but then that may make it easier to write. I have no idea where to send it, but I'll be thinking it off to you. I am still remembering the way you looked sitting on the back of that horse. You were all light. Joshua, why did you say that life must be a glory? How can it be a glory when there is no more to it than grubbing and fighting to keep alive? I don't have the roots of glory in me.

"Joshua and gold. I suppose it's fitting, the golden man digging gold out of the ground. Don't you get those pretty yellow buckskins all dirty.

"Gold. Is that really what you want, a something you can put in your hands and call glory? I am still looking for my glory. But I am so caught up in the fight to keep alive that most days I forget.

"You see, I am only one of a mass. We are people, we Saints, but thick as ants, mindless as geese, fruitful as cows to be ridden like horses. And in the middle of it all, I wish I knew a moment of standing alone, of knowing what I really am down underneath. Is it possible to be a part of a group, really belonging without first being a single whole person? I think I am meaning I feel like an ingredient in a johnnycake, and I need to know me as a pinch of salt first."

She dropped the pencil into her lap and stared down at the filled sheets. "Why did I say those things? I didn't even know I thought them."

The sun was high over the mountains now. Its heat pushed away the night coolness and, as it moved across the streets and adobe houses, life stirred.

Rebecca caught a glimpse of a black-coated man, and she remembered it was the Sabbath. She jumped to her feet and hurried back to the Samuels' house.

Cutting across the yard, she hugged the black book to her. Maybe this would be the day she would learn, really hear those things they said.

———————

When it was nearly autumn, Rebecca realized her town was becoming a city of strangers. No longer did she move down the streets, calling greetings to everyone she met. Some of these strangers didn't speak English. But bright, friendly eyes caught, there were smiles and nods. The smiles were saying, "I recognize you, I don't know your name, but you are one of us. You have suffered and overcome. We are kin."

One day Ann brought her worries home from Relief Society meeting. "There's talk," she said. "This last bunch of Saints that came in have a schoolteacher with them. They say she's real uppity.

She's been to some kind of a finishing school back east and knows all there is about teaching. Rebecca, could be you'll be out of a job this winter."

Rebecca's hands dropped into the kettle of beans she had been washing. "What'll I do?" she whispered. "I do love teaching, but I have no education except what Brother Taylor taught me at Kanesville."

"We'll just go see Brother Brigham himself."

"He'll never have time for such as us."

"I expect that we can just pester him until he listens. Besides, I've heard he has a weak spot for women, especially if it looks like they might shed a tear."

Ann made good her declaration, and before Rebecca could draw a deep breath, an appointment was set up for the two of them to see President Young.

The building that housed Brigham Young's office was one of the first buildings in the city that was neither adobe nor crude stone. Its white clapboard set with shiny windowpanes even boasted a smooth wooden floor covered with soft carpets. Rebecca could hardly remember the reason for their visit as she stared about.

Brother Brigham came out of his office to greet them, and Rebecca was tongue-tied with awe as she stood close to the man for the first time. A ribbon of thought spun through her mind. This short, powerfully built man with the twinkling blue eyes was the leader of the Latter-day Saints. He was revered as prophet, seer, and revelator. Her hands were damp, and Ann filled the silence, repeating the story she had heard at Relief Society meeting.

"Well, my dear," he soothed, "with Zion on the increase, I doubt you'll ever be without a job. Why, there's a perfect horde of young ones that have come into the valley this summer. We could use a dozen more like you right now."

His eyes became steely. "Only I want it understood. You are to be teaching things profitable to their souls. Reading and writing is important only as it enables them to understand the first principle of their religion and relate it to every day of their lives. You will dwell on the Book of Mormon, the writings of the Prophet and the Bible. Let's not have any frivolity and ungodly books."

"Oh, yes sir!" she gasped. "Besides, we don't have much except a few primers. We could use some dictionaries and a history or two."

"I suppose you need slates and pencils too?" he chuckled.

Not catching the irony in his voice, she eagerly replied, "Oh, yes, and paper and ink. It would be nice to have a blackboard. I heard tell of—"

He cut in, "And this year, I think we'll be doing good just to keep the victual box full. Maybe next year. Meanwhile—" he bowed. The interview was over.

He started for the door and stopped. "Young lady, are you married?" Rebecca shook her head. "Why aren't you? You're plenty old enough. There's many a man around here who needs a wife. I'll see what I can do."

"Please, sir!" she cried desperately, "I don't want to be married. There's—"

"Oh," he nodded wisely, "is he a Saint?"

She shook her head, and he snapped, "Then forget about him unless he wants to become one of us. We can't have anyone pulling you away from the church."

Rebecca was walking down Main Street. The sun was a pleasant warmth on her shoulders. Her stride lengthened, slowed. The basket she carried began to swing in a contented arc. She beamed and nodded at her world, acknowledging the changes.

The aroma of raw lumber still lifted above the scent of horses and dust. Hammers still banged and saws screeched as the city expanded. This spreading girth reminded Rebecca of a contented lady claiming her rightful share of the earth. Indians no longer roamed the streets, poking their inquisitive heads through every door. Now cattle didn't disappear as frequently, and in the evening it wasn't uncommon to see young people strolling casually down the city streets.

It was September 1850. The city of Great Salt Lake had existed for three years. During those years the poor adobe and crude log huts began giving way to more substantial buildings. Three sawmills poured milled lumber into the valley.

Streets, arrow-straight and wide, cut through the city. Bridges crossed creeks, and fences divided property. Beyond the city, the stone wall that had circled cultivated fields with a twelve-mile girth was now a line in fields that overflowed, pouring greenness beyond as far as the eye could see.

As quickly as people poured into the valley, Brigham pointed them on to create new communites. There was talk of a vast horde waiting to come from across the ocean—Saints eager for Zion. They would build this place for their home and then they would wait for the coming of the Lord of Zion. She shrugged away the thoughts that didn't seem quite real.

"Rebecca, Rebecca Wolstone!" She turned and watched the round little lady making her way through the crowd.

"Why, Mrs. Tucker, it's been such a long time since I've seen you." The two continued down the street together, stepping carefully on the slabs of flagstone that paved the street in front of the stores. "Where are you going? I'm headed for the dry goods store. I must have some paper, if there's some to be had."

"You'll be teaching again this year?"

"Oh, certainly." She looked quizzically at the woman.

"I just wondered. There's talk Bishop Willis is sparking you, and since he's moving to Fort Utah, I wondered."

"Sparking! He's old and married!" Rebecca said indignantly.

The woman turned to study Rebecca. "You aren't taking the principle seriously. Girl, you've got to live your religion."

"That's it, I'm just a girl," Rebecca said hastily to cut the tide of talk she was hearing more frequently. "I'm still young, and I'm happy with my teaching."

They traversed another six squares of flagstone in silence, and then Mrs. Tucker said, "I hope you do continue with your teaching. My Aaron is full of wanting to learn. It would be nice to have more books, something different."

They parted in front of the store, and Rebecca entered. "Good-day, Sister Wolstone. Come to smell the soap again?"

She laughed at the rotund little man whose cheeks looked as freshly scrubbed as his stiff-collared white shirt. "Indeed I have. It's a wonder there's any. I'd guess Mrs. Cassidy used it all to keep your shirts that sparkling white."

"Not this perfumed stuff. Besides, she says nothing whitens like lye soap. Now if you want some lye—"

"No, no," she shook her head. "I've come for paper and ink."

"Lots of paper, not too good a quality, but I expect you'll be inventing your own ink this year."

"There wouldn't be one book in that shipment?" She looked around the store. Every inch of the rough log walls supported an item. Curing hams were wedged between hoes and harnesses. Shelves held bolts of gingham and calico. There was even a single bolt of carefully wrapped silk. She knew, because, like most of the other women in the city, she had been permitted a glimpse before it went on the shelf to wait for a more affluent customer. Ann and Rebecca were holding a wager on which one of Brigham Young's wives would be wearing that length of silk.

Out on the street again Rebecca clutched the precious packet of paper and the one pencil she was able to buy. "Becky Wolstone," Granny Hicks was hailing her. She nodded at Rebecca's paper. "Nearly school time. The haze's on the mountains."

Rebecca lifted her eyes to the towering mountains. They were veiled in their smoky autumn haze. "I love this time of year," Granny continued, "but it sure makes me homesick to sink my teeth into a nice crisp apple."

"Yes." Rebecca's mind was flooded with the sight and scent of apples. Clearly she saw herself throwing an apple at the squawking chickens. "I regret every apple those silly chickens got." She stopped to listen to Granny's chatter. With the memory of home sharp in her thoughts, she glanced down the street.

At the end of the block there was a horse and rider moving swiftly away from her. The rider's broad shoulders were clad in black broadcloth, and memory tumbled her back into the arms of the dark stranger on that long-ago day. Andrew Jacobson. The tattle-tale pulse at the base of her throat pounded, and she quickly covered it with her hand. Silly, she didn't know for a fact that he was one of them.

As they walked down the street together, Granny Hick's chatter slid past her. She was musing over the changes that had taken place in the territory. Without the iron-fisted leadership of Brigham Young, it would never have happened.

Iron fist? Yes, but more than that. There was a mystical quality about the man that commanded love and respect—adoration. Without him they would have failed, with him they dared not.

Just this very month the territory had become a recognized part of the United States. Utah. Rebecca pondered the name. Deseret, the name the Saints had chosen for the territory, was a Book of Mormon name meaning honeybee. But the government had chosen to deny them this name, just as it had chosen to withhold statehood from them.

Already there were rumblings from the office of President Young. It was reported that he had sworn he would be governor. There was not a Saint in the new territory who doubted his word, and many already pitied those who would dare challenge him. And challenge him they would. It was rumored that by next summer there would be federally appointed officers here. Rebecca shook her head. Gentiles trying to govern the Saints while Brigham was around to wave the laws of the church at them?

"Why you shaking your head?" Granny Hicks peered at her.

"I'm thinking of the Gentiles charging in here where angels fear to tread. If this is the Kingdom of God, it's beyond the talents of Washington to handle it."

"Brother Brigham? I'll say the angels will be wary of him. Washington, huh? They'll be asking for a fight sooner than can be when they start moving their men in here."

"Well, no matter; next summer will tell it all. I'll imagine a dose of Brother Brigham's pepper will get us statehood in a hurry." They reached Granny's gate, and Rebecca went on her way, busy with her thoughts.

Thinking again of Brigham Young, Rebecca's lips twisted in a wry grin. She must admit that any people would have been this successful if their leader had promised them—as had Brigham Young—that they would obey or be damned.

But things were looking up. She sighed with pleasure, remembering the one piece of legislation that had particularly pleased her. It had been the move the provisional government had made to establish district schools. Already plans for the whole territory included a school in each ward.

13

....

In October of 1850 the first blizzard of the season whitened the prairie and swept through the streets of Great Salt Lake City. Horses huddled at hitching posts, their patient misery a warning that all of nature must bow before the battle of weather. On his last bit of strength, the wind led a lone straggler from California into the valley. He was distinguished by the packet of mail and the news he carried from there.

When Brother Samuels carried home a letter from Joshua, he also carried the tales of California.

"There really is gold and just for the taking. Men are making millions and nearly dying for lack of bread and a new shirt. There's a frenzy. Men are pouring into California to hunt gold, and another horde of men are pouring in to get rich off the miners. That's why we got the goods last year."

He paused in his story long enough to remind his family of the goods that had come into the valley just as Heber C. Kimball had prophesied.

"Not all's good in riches; there's greed and waste. Brother Young is wiser than we know. We've got to listen to him and not run after riches. I heard tell the wildest things. In San Francisco they say doctors walked out on their patients, judges out of the courtrooms, and schools closed for want of teachers. The city looks like the plague hit it. Three-fourths of the men left to look for gold, while crops rotted and the cattle were neglected. Even the ships that sailed into San Francisco lost their crews. Then the rains turned the streets of San Francisco into lakes of mud. They threw in bushes and even trees, but the mules stumbled in the streets and drowned in the mud. Then they threw in a whole cargo of cookstoves, right into the mud and used them for stepping-stones."

"Stepping-stones!" Ann's longing glance was on the makeshift stone oven.

After the Samuels had gone to bed, Rebecca knelt by the fire to read Joshua's letter. Fingering the stained paper and recalling Brother Samuels' words, she tried to imagine Joshua in that pack of cursing, pushing miners, fighting for gold nuggets. Joshua's steady blue eyes surveyed her from distant memory. She could feel his final handclasp, suddenly tender. What could possess a man like that to go after gold?

She spread the paper. "Dear Rebecca, how I want to say that to you. It has been so long, and the future is still black and empty. How much longer it will be, I don't know. One thing I do know, gold is a ghost here. It haunts our dreams and flits away when we reach for it. I wish she were lady luck and would smile on me.

"We've been dredging up the American River. Winter could come early and catch us; then we will hole up and hope for the best. Now we work from dawn until dark, dredging in icy water. My partner has been coughing for weeks now. He needs the sun and hot sand to cure his cough, but we dare not leave. Claim jumpers are hiding in the bushes. When you figure a lucky day can fill your bucket and keep you for a year, we dare not leave.

"At night I think about you and wonder. I hope things are going well with you and that you are able to teach school this year. They got a book for Jamie. I bought a Bible for myself. Just felt like I needed to be good to myself. Besides, I've ended up feeling it was the most important thing to have. I can't get away from the notion that there's a different kind of glory waiting out there.

"After thinking about the Whitmans I get to feeling that the most important thing a person can do with his life is to decide about God. The people I most admire in this world have got this all straightened out in their minds. I'm still working on it, and when I do, I'm coming. Becky, wait for me. Just let me see you again. That's all I ask for now. But then, you're young. The folks are still talking about moving to Oregon. Prue's big. Ma says there's lots of fellows sparking her. Matthew's working out. I am your humble servant, Joshua."

She sat looking at the blurred signature, pondering the stiff closing, conscious of the ache around her heart. That night Joshua walked through her dreams, and the golden radiance that he had become was trouble in her heart. She must creep away from thinking about him. In the press of this winter, she couldn't stand up to the pain of both this place and Joshua.

As if in a rage, the winds and snow whipped down across the land. Again the Saints were faced with dwindling food supplies, and illness moved through the city.

One day in late November, Rebecca packed a loaf of fresh bread in a basket and told Ann, "I'm going to see Cora. I've not visited her since before the snow started, and Tim says he thinks they're moving. I can't imagine that in wintertime."

She pulled her shawl over her head and closed the door behind her. The icy blast made her shiver. Last fall Brother Samuels had added on to the cabin. From two small rooms with a loft, the structure was expanded with two additional rooms in the back. Now there was a kitchen and a room for the girls.

The previous year a floor had dignified the cabin, and Mr. Samuels was talking about a cookstove for Ann. As she shivered, Rebecca was thinking the luxuries made stepping out into the cold that much more difficult. It also made it hard to visit the Wrights' cabin in the old fort.

There was another little boy at the Wrights' home. This one also resembled his father. Bessie still rocked, cocooned in her isolation.

Rebecca accepted the cup of sage tea and pulled little Joseph onto her lap. Cora cuddled the baby close to her breast and beamed at Rebecca. "You don't know how good it is to see you."

Glancing at the silent figure beside the fireplace, Rebecca explained, "I've been busy. School. There's been a pack of students this year. Two are just starting out and the rest of them are fighting for attention."

Cora sipped tea. "Did you get books?"

"No, and my arithmetic isn't any better. I try to keep them busy memorizing the Bible and making up dramas. Seems like everybody enjoys that come Fridays."

"What a boring life."

"Boring! It's better than being stuck by your own fireside all winter. Cora, why don't you come out for Relief Society? There's quilting this winter and with new stuff, too. Ann's gathered up every scrap in the valley."

"I'd like to get some wool. The little one could use some stockings." She dabbed at Joseph's drippy nose.

"Tim tells me you're thinking of moving."

She looked astonished. "My, the news flies fast! It was only last week that Brother Young called Mr. Wright in. I told you about the big plans to start an ironworks down south. Iron's aplenty down there and coal too. Some of the men will be going down pretty soon to look the place over. They say it's a pretty spot. Lots of red rock and cedar-covered hills. I suppose there'll be women moving out in the spring. If it weren't for the Indians—" She looked from Bessie to the youngsters and sighed. "A body doesn't worry as much when there's more of you than Indians."

She removed the towel from the bread and cut a piece for Joseph. "Oh, this visit is nice. What's happening with you? Still just wanting to be the schoolmarm?"

Rebecca nodded and cuddled Joseph close. "More than anything else in my life. By this time next year, we'll all have our own schoolhouse."

"I hear some's disgruntled because you're using the Bible so much."

She shrugged. "What else am I to use?"

"There's the Book of Mormon. The Saints set more store by it than the Bible. They say the Bible's not translated right."

"Cora, I've honestly tried to give the book a fair trial, but it's so hard to understand. I end up just telling the story; that's not teaching."

"Except the Book of Mormon is what we believe. You know Brother Brigham's been saying all along that's the most important."

"Sometimes I feel so uneasy about the whole thing."

"They're preaching it every Sunday. Aren't you going to meeting?"

"You know as well as I do that they don't spend too much time preaching. It's mostly about how we're to be treating the neighbors and the Indians."

Unexpectedly, Bessie spoke from her chair by the fire. "If'n you were really wantin' to learn, you'd be going to the fast and testimony meeting. It's the first Thursday night each month. That's comin' up day after tomorrow."

Astonished at her break with silence, Rebecca asked, "Do you go?"

"I've no call." She retreated into her silence once again.

When Rebecca rose to leave, Cora touched her arm. "I've been hungering for our talks; come back. I'll need them more than ever if we move come spring."

"I think it's terrible for Brother Brigham to send you so far away."

"It could be worse. Our family will be together. Some of the men are called to leave their families and go on a mission. How their families manage, I can't imagine."

Rebecca squeezed Cora. "I'm glad it isn't happening to you. It seems unfair."

Bessie's admonition about the fast and testimony meeting was forgotten until two weeks later when Ann met Rebecca at the door as she came from school. Her expression informed Rebecca that something was amiss.

"I've hardly known that Bessie Wright to venture away from her fireside," she began as she drew Rebecca away from the chattering children. "But it seems she's found a reason to leave it now. She's telling the world you've complained about the Book of Mormon and won't teach it. She's pretty well called your religion into disrepute. Knowing the neighborhood, you'd better draw the lines up tight."

"Oh, dear," Rebecca murmured, "what'll I do?"

"I'd start by getting just as religious as I could," Ann continued. "Brother Brigham really took that snippy little teacher from the academy to task when she didn't teach like he wanted her to. He said there was no call for any teacher to show off all she knew about newfangled ideas. He said he was satisfied the Lord gave it to us straight and that she'd better teach it that way or apostatize in a hurry."

Rebecca shuddered. "I'd be terrified to death if he thundered at me like that, especially right in the meetinghouse."

The next month, on the first Thursday night, Ann, with Rebecca in tow, attended the fast and testimony meeting. As they faced the biting wind and trudged through snow, Rebecca said, "This wouldn't be nearly so hard to take if we'd filled ourselves with that good rabbit stew before we left."

"Just you hush; you can have some after meeting. This is good for your soul."

"Oh, Ann, I hope you're right. I'd expect your chiding me in that motherly voice would do me more good. At least there's rabbit stew this winter, but I don't know whether it's any easier to go without when there is than when there *isn't*."

"The good Lord willing, we won't go through another winter like that."

The building held a handful of people, and Rebecca's rumbling stomach advised her that it was a miracle there were that many. Two coal oil lamps brightened the room beyond the glow of the fire. As Rebecca and Ann entered, a woman hurried to them.

"You're new, welcome. We'll be singing and after Brother Ellis leads us in prayer, we'll be bearing our testimony. The Lord bless you." She disappeared.

"Who is she?" Rebecca whispered.

"Leitha Ellis. That's her husband over by the door."

The man turned, and his booming voice greeted the people walking in the door. "Well, Brother Eppson, I haven't seen much of you since we left Nauvoo."

Rebecca eased herself lower on the bench. That ever-present fear had surfaced. Since the day of Matthew and Ebner's planned visitation from the angel, she had dreaded this day. Recalling that childish prank, she admitted her worst dreams were of Bishop Ellis recognizing her.

"Rebecca, pull that shawl away from your head or you'll be in a sweat before we get outside. That means lung fever most certainly."

Now Brother Ellis turned his back and bent his knees before addressing the Almighty. In the dimness Rebecca saw the round bald spot on his head, and she settled down with a sigh of relief.

After prayer the woman beside Ann jumped to her feet. Waving a black-bound book, she proclaimed her faith. "I believe this is God's Word, I believe Brother Joseph Smith was ordained of God, called to bring, by the gift and power of God, this wonderful work to us. I'd rather be here in this Great Salt Lake City than anywhere else on earth." She sat down. A bearded gentleman in the rear stood.

"Brothers and sisters, dear Saints and suffering emigrants," he entoned. Rebecca lost his words in contemplation of his rapt expression and the rhythmic motion of the snowy beard cascading down the front of his dark coat. When he took his place, Rebecca was aware of sobs coming from the woman beside her.

Slowly the woman got to her feet. "I've sinned. I'm ashamed of my harsh tongue and complaining spirit. Brother Williams convicts me so. I've no right to complain under the yoke of the principle. I intend to live my religion."

"Sister, it's a blessing. Don't look on the hard parts," the high clear voice rose. "It's God's way of providing salvation for you. Without that good husband and the little ones you have, you'd never progress to being anything other than a servant of us all in the eternity. Brother Brigham says so. Rejoice!"

Rebecca snorted, and Ann's sharp elbow found her ribs. Just then a high sweet sound filled the room. Rebecca strained to hear the words. They eluded understanding; could this be the gift of tongues she had heard about?

In awe she strained to hear, to see more clearly the face lifted and the hands stretched heavenward. Those hands described an arc of enchantment and the face glowed in the lamplight. Now the woman shook her head, and her snowy hair shed its pins and cascaded down her back. The sounds encircled Rebecca, enveloped her. When they finally faded, she was alone, more alone than ever before.

Ann and Rebecca stepped out into the snowy night. The crisp clean air rushed across their faces shocking them to life. In silence they walked homeward.

————

During the following week, Rebecca found herself recalling the meeting and pondering the significance of it. Try as she might, she couldn't understand, and she yearned to talk over her feelings with someone.

One afternoon Rebecca walked to the fort. When Cora greeted her at the door, she said, "It's warm as spring. Let's bundle the tykes and walk down the street."

"Rebecca, that street's a mudhole. Joseph would be in to his armpits."

"I'll carry him."

When they closed the door behind them, Cora gasped, "Oh, Rebecca, I'm so glad you've come. Another day and I would have gone as stark crazy as Sister Walker."

In dismay, Rebecca listened to Cora pour forth her woes. Her impatient waiting for a turn to talk was arrested, trampled. It was dawning on her how desperate Cora was. They turned down the street toward the Samuels' cabin.

"Cora, I just don't know what to say," Rebecca admitted. "Let's talk to Ann. I can't take care of my own problems, and I certainly can't advise you."

Ann had just put bread into her rock-walled oven. She was heaping coals around the stones as they entered the house. Releasing Joseph and unwinding his shawl, Rebecca said, "Ann, Cora really needs help. That woman is driving her mad."

Slowly Ann turned. Her placid features crumpled into lines of concern. In a low, miserable voice, Cora said, "It's the principle. Don't let your man go into it."

"I can't stop him once Brother Brigham puts his finger on him," Ann said sadly. "But, Cora, much as you women scare me to death talking about the problems, I don't think God meant it to be so. The good Book tells us He'll help us overcome. It's the enemy making this so hard, and it's because it's earning us such glory."

Tears were sliding down Cora's cheeks, and her hands trembled as she dabbed at them. "I'd forego the glory for a little peace on earth. That woman harps constant when no one's around. I wait on her like I was a slave, but nothing suits her. She keeps the Mister wore out with her whining, and he's changing. It's getting so he's believing the complaints. I can see it in his eyes."

"There's nothing I can do except pray the Lord will make you stronger."

The troubled look was still on Ann's face when Cora and Rebecca left to walk back to the fort. Rebecca mused over that expression. Why hadn't Brother Samuels taken another wife? They were saying it was the only way to reach the highest glory.

As they entered Cora's cabin, Rebecca asked, "Do you believe that everyone who isn't in the principle will be just a servant in the hereafter?"

"I wish I didn't have to believe it. But if they say it, it's true."

Cora eased her sleeping baby into his cradle and turned to Rebecca. Now it was her turn to study Rebecca's face. "You look like you've got something on your mind."

Rebecca glanced at the impassive figure beside the fire and lowered her voice. "I do. I've been doing lots of thinking, and I wanted to hear how you'd take to my thoughts, but I sure don't want Bessie passing them all around the city."

"She will, and they'll come out worse than they started," Cora warned. "Looking at you, I'd guess you're as down as I am. There's no call for that. You're free to go out and have a good time. There's no man and young'uns to pull you back. Rebecca, have a good time. Go to the parties and everything else you can. Let the fellows spark all they want, but put off getting married."

"That doesn't sound like the last sermon you preached to me. You told me to live my religion."

"I've changed my mind. There's plenty of time to get married and start working toward earning your glory."

"There is?" Rebecca questioned. "I can't help thinking about David Fullmister. He didn't have time. He's been cheated out of a chance to earn any glory, if the only way's through living the principle."

That night Rebecca started another letter to Joshua. At first her words were stilted phrases detailing the events of her life, at the same time her thoughts were busy. Joshua bought a Bible. Why did he talk about the Whitmans and a glory?

She wrote, "You talk about a glory, and I know it has something to do with the Whitmans. I'm guessing it's a spirit thing you've got a hankering for. We get lots of that kind of feeling around here. Mostly it confuses me. I don't doubt there's a God, but I find myself wondering if He's like they say He is. They say He's kind and loving. That He's trying to help us live right. But there's much that's fearful. We hear sermons from the twelve apostles and the first presidency where they're passing out curses on everyone who opposes the Saints. At first I was kind of glad, but then it started drawing such fearful pictures of God. I've begun to wonder if all those curses were deserved. Right now I'm relieved to see that not many of them have been carried out.

"But I must confess, I'm convinced more and more that the Latter-day Saints are really God's people, and that only through believing like they do and accepting the restored gospel given through Joseph Smith will anyone ever make it to glory. You see, there's just too much happening to show that God's with them. I am constantly hearing stories about how Joseph Smith had visions and how he could heal people. Others, from the apostles on down to the bishops, are able to heal too.

"Just this last month I've been to a fasting and testimony meeting, and one woman there spoke in a strange manner. I couldn't understand her, but Ann had told me about the gift of the Spirit that's called speaking in tongues. It gave me gooseflesh to listen to her, but it was beautiful, all high and almost like a song. I guess with all these things happening, I must conclude that these people really do have God with them and that I'll have to admit Joseph Smith is right—he's proven it by his visions and prophecies. There's just no other way. Mormonism is right. They have the witness."

When Rebecca finished the letter and folded it, she found herself straining to check that inner pulse of her being. The declaration she had made didn't seem to satisfy some deep resistance within. She was almost relieved that she had no way to get the letter to Joshua.

14

•••••••••••••••••••

The summer of 1851 saw the beginning of a regular mail route established between Utah Territory and California. As news of success and failure trickled in from the gold mines, Rebecca had another letter from Joshua.

She studied the familiar writing, seeing Joshua's bright hair and his intense blue eyes. At the beginning of his letter Joshua said, "I'm going to write Ma to send that wedding dress to you so's the first chance I get I can come marry you before one of those Mormon guys gets you."

In a more serious vein, his letter went on to describe the poor living conditions and the profiteering that was taking place on the gold fields. "Me thinks," the letter said, "the only ones getting rich are the ladies doing the laundry for the miners, and the cattlemen and farmers who are feeding us. Potatoes and beef could be gold for the price they bring. The gold fields are a poor place for a man and family. I'll not stay much longer. Becky, it's me and you for the green forests of Oregon. I respect Pa's advice about having a nest egg before I think of taking on family responsibilities, but I think I had better snatch you before someone else does."

"That Joshua," Rebecca said ruefully as she carefully folded the letter. "It's impossible to know whether he's teasing or serious. My common sense tells me to take his fine words with a grain of salt."

Autumn was fast approaching. With new excitement Rebecca prepared for school. This year her district had a new schoolhouse, but then this was so for nearly every ward in the city.

As Rebecca worked in the small, frame building, setting her classroom in order for the opening day, her lips were twisting with wry amusement. She sighed and shook her head. "Oh, your hasty tongue!" Last spring, looking at the discontented faces of her pupils, she had said, "I prophesy that within another year, we'll have lots of school books and fun books to read."

The effect had been electrifying. "Rah, rah, for Miss Becky's prophecy." The room had vibrated with the shouting as faces brightened with anticipation.

Now Rebecca was looking at the poor line of books: the primer, the Bible, and the Book of Mormon. She was also remembering that one of Brigham Young's wives had a new grand piano, pulled across the plains by a team and wagon which could just as well have been bringing books.

She scoured a spot on the floor and muttered, "I'll be eating my prophecy when I'm trying to explain the piano."

She tidied her desk and sighed over the little stack of paper. Easily, she would forfeit a parlor stove for school books, paper and one of those newfangled blackboards which were decorating the walls of eastern schools.

Barely had Rebecca begun to tame the spirits of her summer-wild students when rumors began to fly thick and fast. At first Rebecca believed none of them. But it was true. Through a grant, Congress had appropriated the Territory five thousand dollars to establish the Utah Library. Close on the heels of the Utah Library appropriation came more good news. Two tons of school books were being shipped into the valley.

When Rebecca made the announcement to her pupils, their joy brought tears to her eyes. She couldn't forget the wistful eyes of little Jamie Smyth.

Great Salt Lake City was still rocking with the events of summer and autumn. At midsummer, the three federally appointed officials had arrived in the valley to take up their responsibilities of governing the new territory. Thinking back on the events, Rebecca winced as she recalled the mood of the city.

Like a sore tooth that had been probed and then ignored until it became a throbbing pain, the Saints had tolerated the status of territory with the demeaning threat of federally appointed government. But until those three Gentiles had erupted full voice into the midst of a people already ruffled by years of oppression, the pain had been ignored.

True, Brother Brigham's tart words at the Founder's Day celebration had set the stage for the equally tart words of government-appointed Judge Brocchus when, in his address to the general church conference, he had exhorted the women of Utah to give up living their sinful life and return to a life of virtue. During the coming weeks the city had continued to rock with outrage. The territorial officers quickly and quietly packed their bags and their records and rapidly headed back to Washington.

The dust behind their heels hadn't settled before every Saint in the valley realized the implications. Without a doubt, Brigham Young and his people would be fought every step of their way toward statehood.

Later, Washington reverberated with the Brocchus report. Words conceived in Utah trickled back to them: lawlessness, sedition, absolute control by the church, coining and issuing money, sanctioning polygamy as part of their religion.

But life must go on, and it was moving forward with confidence in the Great Salt Lake Valley. Trim carriages and sleek horses became commonplace on the streets. The little shops with empty shelves turned its bulging stores with enough variety to entice every housewife. While looms and spinning wheels were still evident in most homes, more and more often silk dresses and plumed hats were making their appearance at the Sabbath services and the many parties and balls.

With the advent of a library, Brigham Young instigated a new level of education. A school, called the Parent School, was established to train teachers. Rumor reached Rebecca that her visits to the new library had been noted, and she began to hope that she would be appointed to teach in the new school.

One afternoon she dared mention her hopes to Ann. Her stern glance was enough to settle her inches closer to the ground. You'd stand a better chance of getting your wishes if you'd go back to living your religion."

"Why, Ann, what do you mean?"

"You've been flitting around here like a princess ever since they opened that library and gave you a stack of books for your school. The last straw was that wall they painted black for you." She snorted, and pounded the bread she was kneading.

"Ann, I didn't dream I was becoming uppity. I'm just glad for all we have." She studied the woman's face, noticing the lines and the puffiness under her eyes. "You don't feel well." Ann moved abruptly, and the wooden bowl she held slipped to the floor.

"I'm fine!" she snapped.

"But you aren't, and I've been inconsiderate. Here, let me finish the bread." She reached for the bowl, and Ann snatched it away.

"You tend to your school teaching. Trying to take even this away from me?" Rebecca stepped backward and looked at Ann. The woman's mouth was compressed in a tight line of anger, and her eyes flashed. "You hear? Tend to the teaching, and let me have the kitchen."

Slowly Rebecca said, "It's Dee, isn't it? She's been following me around like a puppy. Ann, I'm not trying to take your daughter away from you. But you have been a little short with her lately. Be patient; she'll be your own dear daughter again. It could be she's having troubles of her own. She and Lisa are scrapping."

Ann was watching her closely. The tight lines on her face gave way to astonishment, and then she smiled, "Oh, Becky, forgive me. Why must I always be suspicious? You're as dear as my own daughter." Abruptly she turned away.

In November of 1851, the ground was broken for the construction of a new meetinghouse. Brigham Young was already calling it a tabernacle. The old bowery constructed during 1849 and 1850 now seemed inadequate and poor in comparison to the new buildings being erected about the city.

With the twenty thousand dollars appropriated by Congress, construction of a State House on Union Square was begun on the first day of September 1851. But now all eyes and attention were focused on the tabernacle.

In January of 1852, work began in earnest while every person in the valley took his turn inspecting the edifice. Brigham Young proclaimed completion would be in time to celebrate the twenty-second anniversary of the founding of the Church of Jesus Christ of the Latter-day Saints.

While the city seethed with this new excitement, Rebecca received the letter from Cora.

"Dear Rebecca," she read. "I am so very lonesome for you. I think even Bessie misses you. I am expecting again, which does nothing to make matters happier around here. I do believe Mrs. Wright would take the first opportunity to return to Great Salt Lake City. The dear Lord knows she wouldn't be missed by me.

"Our homes are poor log cabins. None of the men have time to work on a meetinghouse. When one of the brethren is through here, we crowd into someone's cabin and feast on messages from home.

"Here in Pinto we are in the mountains. We scarce dare leave the house, thanks to the Indians. They seem to only want food, and they're thieving our cows.

"We have had many a jawing to gird up our loins and be content with what we have in order to build up Zion. Most of us would be content with enough to fill our stomachs. There wasn't time for planting last summer, so we must buy everything from the wagons. The main effort of the men has been toward the iron industry. The coke oven has been erected and roads hacked through to the coal mines. The iron ore is good quality and, the dear Lord willing, less than a year will see the first load into the furnace.

"How I miss you, but I wouldn't wish this place on you. Cedar City is a little better with more people and a proper fort. I long for the civilization of Great Salt Lake City. Just the trees and sidewalks, the gardens and new little orchards. I'd visit a store just to smell the bacon and soap. I'm thinking of those good feasts in Union Square on Founder's Day. I'd love to have some of Granny Hicks' ginger cake heaped with cream. I'd never complain again if I were allowed to spend the day, shoulder to shoulder with you, hoeing beans and chopping weeds."

Rebecca finished the letter and fingered the smudges on it as she reflected on its unhappy tone. "No wonder Brother Brigham has to fuss so much to get the people to move south. It sounds terrible. It's as bad as starting over again." She shuddered. "None of us would be willing to do that again unless we had to."

———

"Miss Becky, what does 'covenant' mean?" Rebecca raised her head and lowered the Book of Mormon she had been reading. She studied the serious eyes focused on her.

"I don't know, but we can find out." She crossed the room to the line of books on the shelf beside the blackboard. Plucking a dictionary from the shelf she went to sit on a low bench among her students.

"Covenant." Her finger moved down the words. "It says"—she paused to read and then raised her head—"it says an agreement between people. Ruth, were you thinking of the covenant mentioned in the Book of Mormon?"

Bewildered, the child nodded. " 'Course, what else is there?"

"Why it could be any agreement, but let's see what applies." Again she searched. "Oh, there. An agreement of God with man, 'as set forth in the Old and New Testaments,' " she quoted.

"That sounds like two covenants," Isaac said. "Are there more?"

"What was on the hunks of stone?" asked Ruth.

"I don't really know," Rebecca said slowly. "I've only heard it called the law or the commandments. But an *agreement*. I just don't know."

"Well, why don't you go ask Brother Brigham? Ma says he wants people to bring their problems to him."

"Oh, dear," Rebecca murmured. "He may not think much of a teacher who can't discover this on her own."

Redheaded, freckle-faced Alice jumped to her feet and, with a mischievous grin, thumped on the desk in front of her. "Here's tomorrow's assignment. Teacher, you are to come prepared to tell us all about covenants."

"Yes, ma'am," Rebecca said meekly. "Although I believe you're asking more of me than I can possibly do."

"Oh, ho!" Isaac hooted. "Anybody who can prophesy can find a little old thing like that. Last year you predicted we would have books before the next year was up. Look at all the books." He waved toward the bookshelf.

"Oh!" The awe was in unison, and wide eyes looked from her to the evidence.

"Children," she protested, "that was only coincidence."

"Pa doesn't think so," Isaac continued. "Just like Brother Kimball's, it came true. Pa says it shows you have the Spirit."

That evening, long after the others had gone to bed, Rebecca huddled before the fireplace, straining her eyes over the fine print in the two black books.

Ann came into the room. "Rebecca, are you ill?"

"No, my students want a full and complete report on covenants tomorrow. If only there were a dictionary to tell you where to find the answers in the Bible."

"Well, I suspect if I were looking, I'd commence at the place where it tells about covenants."

"Where would that be?"

"Doesn't covenant have something to do with Moses getting the stone plates?"

"Maybe the things that happened before the plates," Rebecca said thoughtfully. A verse she'd memorized popped into her mind. Pressing fingers against her forehead, she concentrated on dragging up the words. "Put them in their hearts."

"You are ill."

"No, I'm trying to remember—there it's Hebrews 8:11." She thumbed through her mother's Bible. She read, " 'For if that first covenant had been faultless, then should no place have been sought for the second.' " She sighed, "Well, that answers one question, there're two covenants." With a yawn Ann returned to bed.

The following day Rebecca stood before her students and confessed, "I'm only partly prepared. There's so much to tell you, and it will take days. First, I think there are two covenants. But the interesting part is the story in the Old Testament. If you think California has gold, wait until you hear about this!" The children clustered around her, and she began to tell them all that she had read.

Their eyes widened with amazement and they pressed closer. Rebecca found herself dramatizing the story. "God warned Moses and the children of Israel that every little detail must be perfect. See, part of the covenant was the building of a house or a tent which would be a dwelling place for God. That's the part I want to tell you about first. And God told Moses it must all be done according to the plan He gave Moses on the mountain."

"Perfect. He sure is particular," Timothy said slowly.

"Listen, Moses had all the people bring offerings of gold and silver. He used those gifts to cover the table inside the tabernacle and the ark which was to hold the stones marked with the covenant. It says here that over twenty-nine talents of gold were used in constructing the tabernacle. And that over one hundred talents of silver and seventy talents of bronze were used."

"How much is a talent?"

Rebecca threw up her hands. "I don't know."

"Why don't you go ask Brother Brigham?"

After two days of discussing the building of the tabernacle and the use of it for worship and sacrifice, May Taylor spoke up. "Miss Becky, we have to give a program for the big folks before spring. Why don't we do the tabernacle?"

"Ya, Brother Brigham might make ours more pretty—it's just adobe."

"Well, how could we 'do' the tabernacle?" Rebecca asked.

"We could make curtains out of blue and purple, red and linen. I don't suppose we could find any gold to use, but we could make an ark."

Now the students were bouncing with excitement. "We could write the commandments on pieces of wood."

"What do we do for manna?"

February moved into March. Rebecca's students were consumed

by their interest in the covenant and building the tabernacle. Many trips were made to Rebecca's Bible to verify details.

Rebecca's apprehension about the project disappeared as she saw Timothy's reading improve and the others develop new skills. Plans were sketched on Rebecca's precious supply of paper. Isaac must know how to spell pomegranate before he could complete his sketch. Old shawls and quilts were being modified for hangings and robes. The children learned about talents and could spell shekel, sardius, topaz, and carbuncle.

Scraps of lumber were hauled into the schoolhouse, and one mother arrived with plaster of paris. A reasonable facsimile of cherubim was produced—reasonable, Rebecca decided, since no one knew exactly what cherubim looked like.

During this time Rebecca received another letter from Joshua. It was short. "I'm coming," he had written. "Just as soon as I sell my claim, I'm coming for you. Ma said that she would send the wedding dress to you."

Rebecca's hands crumpled the letter in her lap. This couldn't be reality. The schoolroom was reality, as well as the mud and snow of Main Street.

"A letter from Joshua?" Ann asked. "Does the winter find him well?"

"Winter," Rebecca looked for a date. "He doesn't say. In fact, he doesn't say much of anything except that he's coming after me and that his mother is sending my wedding dress."

A strange expression crept over Ann's face. Rebecca studied her, wondering if the expression was relief or sorrow. "Do you intend to convert him to the way?"

"I think he intends to rescue me from the way," Rebecca chuckled. "He still can't understand that the principle is something practiced by just a few silly old men—beg pardon, Brother Brigham!"

"I guess you'd better beg his pardon," Ann muttered, "and you'd best watch your tongue."

"Well, I fully expect the whole business to die down and fade out of sight in another year or so, 'specially since Washington is so opposed."

Ann turned abruptly and walked into her bedroom.

15

$\bullet$

$\mathcal{O}$ne day, soon after the class had begun to work on the tablets bearing the covenant, Arnold Pickens said, "Miss Becky, you still haven't found more covenants. You said you *thought*. When are you going to talk to Brother Brigham?" There were fifteen pairs of unwavering eyes.

With a sigh of resignation, Rebecca lifted her hands. "I promise, I'll go soon."

Spring was definitely moving into the valley. First came the softening and sweetening of the air. Now the snow was retreating, revealing tufts of green.

On the day that Rebecca went to see Brigham Young, her mind was so full of a new problem that she scarcely noticed her world. The problem was Brother Samuels.

Ann and Brother Samuels had children not much younger than she. Despite her twenty-one years, come next month, she felt terribly young and awkward. Still, Brother Samuels was sending out signals.

Since coming to Utah Territory, Rebecca and all the other unmarried women had become adept at signal watching. It was better than a gossip column for keeping account of who was interested in whom.

At first Rebecca couldn't believe the signal. But Ann was knowing it too. While Rebecca had tried to ignore the pointed conversations, the gentle pats, she couldn't ignore Ann's tightly compressed lips and unusual quietness.

In the months since the onset of the signals, Rebecca had been desperately seeking ways to divert them and to reaffirm her standing as Ann's friend. But she was not being successful.

Today's walk toward Brother Brigham's office was taking her past the old fort. She knew that Cora's cabin was vacant, and that had given Rebecca an idea. It had also served to remind her that this evening was the monthly fast and testimony meeting for their ward. She was still busy with her thoughts when she reached the office.

Despite the constant assurances of Brother Brigham's willingness to counsel, she felt first cousin to a field mouse after an encounter with him. Remembering the Parent School, she smoothed her hair and squared her shoulders.

He took the initiative. He had heard about the play and his piercing blue eyes never left her face as she explained why the project had been chosen.

When she finished, he chuckled and said, "It seems to me that you've picked quite a task. It's always good for our people to know as much about their heritage as possible. I'm going to have your pupils present their program to the other wards."

It took Rebecca a numbing minute to recover. "Oh, that's wonderful!" Was dismay showing in her voice? "But that isn't the reason I've come."

"Let's set it up for the tenth of April," he continued. "Now what?"

"We've discovered that there seem to be two covenants. I haven't read the whole Bible, but Mrs. Samuels reminded me of the Ten Commandments and the covenant. Now my students want to know if there is another covenant."

He nodded. Leaning forward he rested his arms on his desk and studied her. "That's the whole purpose behind this dispensation. Because of the wickedness of the people and the broken covenants— the Prophet Joseph Smith referred to it as the people's dead works— there needed to be another covenant. A new and everlasting covenant. There are more revelations to this, and this year we'll bring them to the people. You just be a good student yourself, and you will hear about them. Now the tabernacle is nearly complete, we will be able to bring all the teachings of the Prophet to the people.

"Go back and tell these little children that they must be baptized and enter into living the laws and ordinances given through the Prophet."

"Well, that doesn't lend itself to dramatizing," she said, following President Young as he got to his feet.

"Let's hope it lends itself to being worked out in the daily lives of the Saints," he said dryly, bowing her out of the office.

When Rebecca reached the house, Ann gave her a curt nod and continued to stir the stew. "Ann," she said, determined to carry out her resolve, "I haven't been living my religion lately. Would you like to go to the fast and testimony meeting tonight?"

Rebecca could see the refusal forming on Ann's face. The door behind Rebecca slammed and Brother Samuels called, "Stew? That smells good enough to eat."

Ann glanced toward him, and then looked at Rebecca. "Yes," she answered, "I think it would be a good idea for both of us."

Rebecca was very conscious of her empty stomach and tormented heart as they walked the six blocks to the ward meetinghouse. During the walk she tried to think of a way to break the silence and clear the air.

Bishop Ellis was presiding over this meeting. His presence no longer worried Rebecca. She was confident that he had forgotten the silly incident in the barn.

After singing hymns, they knelt to pray. Rebecca stifled a yawn and knew she dared not close her eyes. The prayers seemed to drone on forever. When the high sweet sound began, the shock of it ran through the room. Rebecca was lifted and carried on the crest of feeling. Even after the voice became silent, the group continued to kneel beside the rough benches.

Now Brother Ellis' heavy voice boomed through the room. The thunder of it reminded Rebecca of that barn prayer meeting. As he prayed, she felt as if she were being jolted back to earth, out of the heavenlies back to harsh reality.

When they had taken their seats once again, Sister Ellis stood. "You know, Brother Brigham has said that he would just about rather hear of our personal experiences than anything else. It does encourage, and I want to tell you a story. Sister Turner tells me about a friend who had one of the Nephites visit her. She was positive it was. They lived out in the country, so's there's no possibility it was anything else. Fact is, she fed him and he ate, but when she went to clear the table, there was the whole meal, not even touched."

When they started home, Ann linked her arm through Rebecca's. "It was a good meeting. I'm glad we came. Lifted my spirits, and I think I'll find it easier to live my religion now."

"Ann, I've been thinking. I've enough salary to live on my own now. I'm of a mind to see if I will be allowed to live in Cora's old place."

Ann's arm trembled. When she finally spoke her voice was low. "Rebecca, don't think I'm opposing. I just suppose I'm being jealous and female."

"Don't!" Rebecca's voice was sharp, but she could say no more.

They were nearly home when Ann asked, "What did you think

of what Sister Ellis had to say?" Rebecca shrugged. Ann's voice was wistful. "It would be wonderful to have an experience like that. I've prayed for it. It would sustain me too."

"I'm afraid I'd just be scared to death, having a fellow with a long white beard come in like that. Guess you can't discount the food being left, no matter."

In April, 1852, the new Tabernacle was dedicated. Two thousand two hundred Saints were seated at the first meeting, while others strained at the doors. On the heels of the dedication came the semi-annual conference of the church.

On the morning of the first meeting, Rebecca left the Samuels' early. President Brigham Young was to address them and she wanted a good seat. The new Tabernacle was filling rapidly, and Rebecca tried to make herself as small as possible as she pressed through the crowd. Behind the pulpit the band was beginning its warm-up. The first presidency, Brigham Young and his two counselors, Heber C. Kimball and Williard Richards, entered the building. She watched Brigham Young cross the platform with a confident stride and an air of authority.

With hymns behind them, the audience settled down, and Brother Brigham stood. Immediately he launched into his sermon, saying, "It is time for us, my dear brothers and sisters, to get down to the hard doctrine task of understanding all that the Prophet Joseph Smith learned at the hands of the Almighty and to transfer that into our lives."

In his sermon he began to explain how Adam came to the Garden of Eden with Eve, one of his wives. At that time, he said, Adam possessed a celestial body. Rebecca was wondering what a celestial body was when Brigham Young said that Adam helped make and organize the world and that he is Michael, the archangel, the Ancient of Days. "Adam is our Father, our God—the only God we are to be concerned with. It was the forbidden fruit that Adam and Eve ate that caused their immortal bodies to become mortal."

Rebecca was still trying to grasp the significance of the message when the President's words penetrated her thinking again. She heard him say, "It was God the Father who, with the Virgin Mary, conceived the child Jesus, making Him in reality a Son in the likeness of His Father." Emphatically, President Young stressed that it was not by the Holy Ghost that the child Jesus was conceived, but by the Father himself in the manner of men.

Later Rebecca followed the crowd out the door into the bright April day. As she hurried down the street, she murmured, "He said that spirits were born first, then the body is born. And that God is really our Father—just like our earthly father, only of our spirits. He has wives in heaven to produce these spirits. Adam was really God."

She was nearly home when Mary Jane Holman caught up with her. "Oh, Becky, wasn't that something! I nearly died when he said what he did right there at the last."

"What was that?" Rebecca asked, wrinkling her brow.

"Oh, it was when he said that Jesus wasn't conceived by the Holy Ghost, otherwise the elders would have to be very careful about confirming the Holy Ghost on females because He might start them in the family way, and then the elders would get blamed for all the extra children!"

"Do you believe all those things he said?"

"Yes, I've heard them before. Do you mean about Jesus? That's true. It's in the writings of the Prophet; that means it's a revelation from God himself, and it will never change. It's found in the book of Moses, and it plain out says that Adam, the man of holiness, is the father of Jesus Christ."

———————

On the evening of April 10, Rebecca and her little cluster of students filed into the dark, empty social hall. Isaac was saying, "Okay, you young'uns, this is it. We're giving the play tonight. No more funny business."

Timothy, who was to be Moses, mourned, "I wish I had a beard. I can't imagine Moses without a beard."

"Never you mind," Amy said. "We gotta pretend about a lot of stuff. That yellow paint isn't real gold either."

Rebecca's oldest student, Isaac Gilpin, had been chosen as narrator. As she helped him into his robe and adjusted the turban, he confided, "I'm glad the building is dark, otherwise they'll see me shaking. Do ya guess there'll be lots here?"

"Likely. It sounds like a good program and Brother Brigham has been talking about it. You know people like these things. Don't worry, you'll do fine."

She turned to the foot of the stage and surveyed the line of coal oil lamps which would serve as footlights. "Only ten? That won't be much light. I thought I saw more coming in." Timothy squirmed, and she comforted, "Never mind. Their eyes will adjust and they'll be able to see just fine. Did you bring the tablets of stone?" Timothy nodded. There was a thumping behind the curtains and John scooted across the stage carrying a bundle.

Amy poked her head through the curtains. "It's getting late," she warned. "We better get in the corner so's they can't see us when they start coming."

"I hope John remembers his father's trumpet." The door creaked and Rebecca whispered, "Timothy, light the lamps."

When the door creaked for the last time and the chatters quieted, dim shapes moved about the stage. John lifted his trumpet, and the brass caught the gleam of lamplight. One strong clarion call and Isaac strode into the light and lifted his scroll.

" 'Thus shalt thou say to the house of Jacob, and tell the children of Israel.' " Rebecca caught her breath as Isaac's voice rose majestically: " 'Ye have seen what I did unto the Egyptians, and how I bare you on eagles' wings and brought you unto myself. Now therefore, if ye will obey my voice indeed, and keep my covenant, then ye shall be a peculiar treasure unto me above all people: for all the earth is mine.' "

Now Moses appeared in the light and lifted his hand to speak. The children surged forward and in unison said, " 'All that the Lord hath spoken, we will do.' "

They disappeared from sight, and Isaac stepped forward. He told the audience how God spoke to Moses on the mountain, and how God gave Moses the commandments written on stone. The listeners could almost hear the tablets crash as Isaac described Moses' fierce anger when he saw the golden idol the people had made in his absence.

Isaac paused dramatically and then continued, "But God in His love and patience forgave the people because of Moses' prayer. Again Moses came with new tablets, and again God gave him the commandments. This time, Moses was ready to tell the people God's instructions for building a house to honor God. Now hear the commandments." Isaac stepped back, and Moses moved into the light and lifted the tablets of stone.

" 'I am the Lord thy God, which have brought thee out of the land of Egypt, out of the house of bondage. . . .' " The now-familiar words slipped away from Rebecca. The children were handling their parts well, and she sighed with relief. From the corner of her eye she could see the social hall was well filled, and the audience seemed to be hanging on every word.

Timothy lowered the tablets and said, "Who will help me build a house for the Lord?" The children shouted and surged forward with their offerings.

Andy brought boards for the tabernacle; Alice brought curtains. Little Carey backed onto the stage dragging a cowhide. The crowd tittered as he said, "You have instructed us to make a roof of leather skins."

Ralph, carrying blue garments, appeared, saying, "I have made the priestly robes, and I will help the priest prepare to offer the sacrifices to God."

"Now, O Moses," Deborah cried, stepping forward, "we are ready to place those items in the Most Holy Place, to be forever sealed off from the eyes of all except His chosen one. Have you prepared the ark?"

"I have." There was a murmur of appreciation as the yellow box with its cherubim was slowly carried on stage. Moses continued, "Inside I will place the tablets of the covenant, Aaron's rod which budded to show his power, and also the jar of manna which God has provided to feed His people."

Moses supervised the completion of the tabernacle. Then he paused and raised his voice, "The tabernacle is built. We are ready to consecrate the priests, and they will be able to offer sacrifices to our God."

In majestic silence the priest slowly walked toward them. "Bring the bull to the front of the Tent of Meeting. Aaron and his sons shall rest their hands on its head. It is to be slaughtered in the Lord's presence, and every sacrifice must be done strictly according to God's Word."

Suddenly there was a thump and a blast from the trumpet, followed by a scream. Above the gasp of the audience, the narrator explained, "God gave specific directions for preparing the sacrifice. But Aaron's sons were not careful to obey God's directions, and fire from the Lord came down and killed them."

While silence still gripped the audience, the narrator continued, "God gave detailed instructions to the people through Moses. He told them just how to worship Him with sacrifices and on what days the sacrifices were to be made. Each year the people were to assemble before the tabernacle to honor the day of atonement. Remember, it is the blood that makes atonement. The law requires cleansing by the blood; without the shedding of blood there is no forgiveness."

Behind the tabernacle there was a movement and a glow of light. From her front seat, Rebecca realized that the children had lighted more lamps. Knowing the narrator's final speech, she smiled with appreciation for their foresight.

Isaac was saying, "The Lord reminded the people that in His covenant with them, He said He would do wonderful things for the people and that those around them would see awesome things if only they would obey the Lord in all that He asked of them.

"He instructed them that in all of their travels they were to look to the tabernacle for His guidance. There was to be a cloud settling over the tabernacle by day, and at night they would see fire in the cloud. Only when the cloud lifted were the children of Israel to move."

Rebecca caught a shadow of movement and looked with astonishment at the rafters over the stage. A billowing cloud of white was floating down. It settled over the tabernacle and the audience gasped their appreciation.

Just as Rebecca raised her hands to clap, the white cloud burst into a ball of flames. Screams were filling the air as she rushed toward the quilts. In seconds the flames were out, and quilts were gingerly lifted away from the still-smoking lamps.

"What was that? What happened?" Both Isaac and John stood with heads bowed.

Isaac spoke, "We didn't think about the stuff catching fire."

"What was it?" she asked again.

"Milkweed down. Isaac's ma had a whole barrel full of the stuff. We knew because we helped pick it last fall. We got to thinking it would make a pretty cloud floating down over the tabernacle."

"Well, it did," Rebecca said slowly. "I was all set to start clapping." She shuddered. "It was all a little too real."

"Well, thank the dear Lord that He is watching out for you." It was Bishop Martin speaking, and he patted Isaac's shoulder as he turned to leave.

16

•••••••••••••••••••

It was July before Rebecca had time to consider moving into the fort. On the day she went to see Cora's cabin, she met Mary Jane's mother. "I'm heading for the fort," she found herself explaining. "Want to see Cora's place. At the Samuels', with the tykes growing up, we're about to split out at the seams."

"I'd be expecting him to be adding on." She studied Rebecca.

Hastily Rebecca said, "There's the prettiest piece of watered silk down at the Mercantile Company. Have you seen it? It's blue."

"I don't like blue." She was persisting. "Everyone's talking. It's about time you-all start living your religion."

The next day, Rebecca decided the Samuels were talking too. Ellen and Deborah Samuels cornered her as she weeded the vegetables. "Are you going to be Father's second wife?" Ellen's eyes were wide. Shocked, Rebecca shook her head.

"I wish you would," Dee said wistfully. "It would be nice to call you Aunt Becky like they do at Jessica's house. It would sure be fun to have little ones around again." Rebecca guessed that she was quoting someone.

"Well, just don't trouble your ducky little heads." Her grin was forced. "I don't intend to be anybody's plural wife."

Over dinner Brother Samuels watched her with troubled eyes, and Rebecca decided the sooner she moved, the better for all.

It was a hot, muggy day in July. The corn was ready, and everything else seemed to be moving rapidly toward harvest. Rebecca and Ann worked from dawn until dark caring for the garden. That evening as they cleaned vegetables together, Ann asked, "Rebecca, what's troubling you?"

"The girls are talking." Taking a deep breath, she dropped her knife and faced Ann. "They were wondering if I'm to be Brother Samuels' plural wife."

"Well?"

"You know how I feel about it. I have nothing against either you or Brother Samuels, but there's no way on this earth I could go into a plural marriage." For a moment relief flared in Ann's eyes, and then she turned back to her task.

"Sometimes we are all asked to do things that we don't like to do. But when your eternity's at stake, you don't rebel."

"I'll never believe that."

"You'd better be doing some deep thinking about it. You know, it could be worse—there's always Joe Dickson."

"Oh, Ann!" Rebecca leaned against the table laughing helplessly. Joe was the city's most active polygamist. With unquenchable relish, Joe aimed at proposing to every woman in town, married or single, young or old. Judging from the number of Mrs. Joe Dicksons, he couldn't be considered unsuccessful.

———

August 29, 1852, was a clear, sunny Sabbath. Rebecca was imagining a touch of autumn in the air as she and Ann walked toward the Tabernacle. Mr. Samuels had left early to attend a priesthood meeting, and the children had long since run off to be with their friends.

"Law! those peaches should be ready in another week or so," Ann exclaimed. "I'd like to get a few of them. It's been a long time since I've tasted a juicy, ripe peach."

"Oh, Ann, don't mention food. This is apt to be a long session this morning, and there's more to come this afternoon."

"Don't those clouds look like a bridal veil trailing out behind a pretty little bride?" Ann asked comfortably. "Her dress is a mite long, but it'll do." She turned to Rebecca. "Your Joshua was supposed to have your dress sent. Hope it isn't lost."

"I do too," Rebecca said slowly. "I've thought of it several times this year. Wish I'd told him never mind. Those mail runs aren't dependable."

"Too bad you couldn't bring it."

"My mother set a lot of store on that dress. Before she died she told me to take good care of the trunk. I'm not too certain what she meant, but she told me the trunk held my only hope. I guess she was meaning the dress, saying it's important to make a good marriage."

The band was playing by the time they took their places. More than one foot tapped time, and Rebecca was feeling the promise of an exciting day. President Young was the first speaker, and the morning passed in a froth of jokes and laughter.

When Rebecca and Ann took their seats for the afternoon session, Ann said, "I'll settle me down for a good sermon or a good nap. I can't sit down in the afternoon with no call to stay awake."

"Brother Pratt is a good speaker," Rebecca said. She was watching the people around her. Directly in front were two women chatting. Their precise British accents intrigued Rebecca.

Suddenly one woman poked the other. "There, Brother Pratt is saying it. He's bringing it all out in the open now. He's saying that it's God's will for us to practice plural marriage. Law, what will Washington do now?" Someone hissed, and the women were silent.

Orson Pratt was saying, "I want you to understand these are not my ideas I'll be presenting to you. They are revelations given to the Prophet Joseph Smith by Jesus Christ. In the inspired translation of Genesis we find the preexistence of man explained. We know God has fathered all spirits. These spirits are waiting for us to provide tabernacles for them. This is our task on earth."

As the sermon continued, Rebecca found some of the statements were hitting her, colliding with her thoughts. She heard: "God has provided plural marriage as necessary to our exaltation in the future world." So it wasn't just a silly old man's ideas. "We are the most righteous society on this earth." Righteous? Rebecca cringed. It was impossible to consider herself righteous.

" . . . one thousand million spirits every century, and they must have tabernacles provided for them." Did all the still-born babies and the poor little children who died soon after birth count?

"There will be an endless increase of worlds." The stars? We are to multiply without end? "The promises made to Abraham, Isaac and Jacob—your seed shall be as endless as the sand." Well, most certainly one wife couldn't do it all, even in eternity. "To fail to do the works of Abraham will deprive a man of his blessings. Denying the provisions of the church to make marriage eternal will end forever a man's chance of marriage and children in the hereafter."

Brother Pratt raised his voice and lifted his arm. "And what's to become of those who have the principle revealed to them and who reject it?" A voice echoed through the Tabernacle, "They will be damned." Rebecca caught her breath. For one moment her heart nearly failed her, and then she heard the apostle explain that being damned wasn't always forever. The erring individual would lose only the privilege of exaltation in the coming eternity.

When Rebecca and Ann were finally free of the noise and press of the crowd, Ann breathed a sigh of relief, settled her collar and smoothed her hair. "I declare!" she exclaimed, "that was an excited crowd. But that's to be expected. That's the first time the apostles have come right out in meeting and preached these things."

"I thought they'd been living it for a long time."

"They have, least some of them 'way back to Joseph's time. Pressure's kept them from talking too free. I heard there was to be no announcement until we were a state, but I guess they're all pretty confident that Washington won't give us problems because of the freedom of religion part in the Constitution."

"Well, I still don't like the idea of it all, and I'm glad Brother Brigham hasn't seen fit to put the pressure on. I'd just plain turn a deaf ear."

"Rebecca, you've no call to be selfish. It's your duty just as much as the rest of us, to provide tabernacles."

"Ann, you're not providing more. Looks to me like the Lord could use the instruments before His hand without troubling those of us who don't want the job."

"I don't quite understand that either," Ann said slowly. "I'm willing, but there's just no more little ones. But that doesn't relieve you of responsibility."

She touched Rebecca's arm. "There's Brother Samuels hailing me. I'll join him now." She was off, and Rebecca watched her retreating back. Responsibility? That sermon changed everything. She was suddenly filled with the need to run.

When Rebecca reached the cabin, she stood in the doorway and looked around. This place had been home for two years. Could it be she was rejecting it? The empty rocking chair and half-knitted sock, the chipped bowl on the table, the rumpled quilt at the foot of her bed were parts of a picture that no longer existed. Rolling up her sleeves, Rebecca bundled her possessions together.

Cora's place had been empty for months, and she found it easy to keep herself busy. She heated water to scrub the furniture and shelves above the table and bench.

She was finishing her dinner of bread and a mug of Brigham tea when she heard steps. Ann called, "Mercy, child, I didn't know you intended to move on the Sabbath. For shame, I'll tell Brother Brigham on you," she teased, as she entered the cabin and placed a basket on the table. "I'm glad you took the bread, but that's not enough to keep your body and soul together. Here's some stew, and

I brought you cornmeal for your breakfast. There's fatback, some dried beans and a melon from the garden."

Ann took a deep breath and sat down on one end of the bench circling the room. "It was hard for you to get the whole load dumped on you at once, but it's not like we haven't known about it. Mostly we've guessed that sooner or later it'd be put to us to live the principle."

She waited a moment before adding, "Becky, I don't like it any better than you, but that's the last time I'll say it. Brother Brigham has been after Brother Samuels for nigh onto a year to get with it. He was full of the rebels with the idea, but after today he's placed in the position of rejecting the covenant if he doesn't do as he's told."

"It's horribly unfair. We're not allowed to live our lives as we wish."

"You've got to obey every ordinance of the gospel if you want to make it in the hereafter."

"I was thinking, fussing around here and trying to get settled, just like a nesting mouse. One of these days I'll wake up and realize I can fit in with it all. After all, it's become home."

"You're not talking about this place, are you? Becky, you know how we feel. Since it's to be, I'd be pleased to have you as second wife."

"Oh, Ann, this is too much. Give me time to get settled into the idea. Maybe next year we can talk about it again. Now I just want to teach school."

Ann was shaking her head, disappointment clouding her eyes. "I have a feeling that he's not going to wait," she said slowly.

———————

Since the winter of 1851, Rebecca had wanted her own home, surrounded by her possessions and answerable to no one. Wouldn't that help her become the complete person who haunted her dreams?

In the short time before school began she did experience the beginnings. With confidence she moved around her domain, secure in her privacy and happy with freedom.

She slept late in the morning and ate dinner as the moon rode slowly across the sky. She had squaw corn for breakfast and pancakes swimming in molasses for dinner. She shoved her table in front of the fireplace and squandered three candles at once as she read until midnight.

One evening just after school had begun, there was a knock on Rebecca's door. She opened it and discovered Brother Samuels. He was carrying his hat and wearing a humble expression that poorly fit his commanding figure. Dismayed, but feeling cornered, she let him in.

Embarrassed but determined, he explained that it was the principle that brought him. "Brother Samuels," she paused and discovered that the mentally rehearsed speech was there and ready. This was not like the monosyllable she had said to Lank. She liked and respected this hard-working farmer who was trying to live up to his religion and follow Brother Brigham. But there was Ann. As the words flowed, Rebecca realized that if it weren't for Ann—if Brother Samuels were a widower—she could be tempted. There was a family feeling that she was missing.

The words tumbled out, and they added up to a simple no. "You can live with the principle," she told him, "but I can't. From one end of me to the other I am as full of rebellion as Brother Martin's old mules. That's a terrible way to enter marriage and an unthinkable way to inflict myself on others. Besides, I want to teach. I want to read books and find out about everything, and then I want to teach your children, not have them."

"But you can't go on like this." His voice was low. "You know I'm not thinking just about me. There's you and Ann. Brother Brigham makes it pretty clear that if you women are to be saved, it will be through accepting the principle and living your religion. No woman can reach the highest order of heaven unless her husband takes her. Don't you want us to make it together? Don't you want to be part of that kingdom of gods, a queen instead of an angel serving others?"

Rebecca was still shaking her head when he got to his feet and picked up his hat. "Remember, this is a revelation given by Joseph Smith. This is the new and everlasting covenant. It will never pass away. Until the second coming of Jesus Christ, it will endure. There is no other covenant to be had."

Rebecca watched the door close softly, and then threw herself across the bed. While she sobbed and trembled, she determined to visit Brother Brigham.

17

· · · · · · · · · · · · · · · · · ·

The frost was on the pumpkins before Rebecca made her way through the city to the church offices. Probably she would not have gone even then if it hadn't been for goading questions that had arisen the past Sabbath.

During the passing of the sacrament, while she had grasped the fruit jar and lifted the water to her lips, she heard the bishop's words. "Take this and drink; it is a symbol of the covenant." She had fallen to musing about the covenant and wondering how the water played a part in this symbolic offering.

When Brother Heber C. Kimball stood to speak, she abandoned her thoughts as she listened to him talk about the new Iron County settlement. She shivered at the stark picture he drew. As Rebecca thought of Cora and her babies, she heard him say, "You know who holds the keys offering life and salvation to all of us. Brother Brigham is prophet, priest, seer. If he wants you to settle Iron County and leave your comfortable homes here, then you'd better do it. He has the power to curse or bless you. He's got it by the authority of the Prophet Joseph Smith, and I can show you in his revelations where it says it."

But today Rebecca was finding that the nearer she drew to the office of the President, the more reluctant she was becoming. Her steps slowed, and her mind raced. Did she dare demand that he satisfy her need to know? She shivered. But also she knew there was something rising up within that demanded satisfaction, and the rebel that was Rebecca would have her way.

She reviewed facts and rehearsed her speech. She walked twice around the block before she dared approach the building.

He had the first word before she could open her mouth.

"Brother Samuels tells me"—he fastened her with those keen blue eyes; she was a bug on a pin—"that"—he paused—"you'll have nothing to do with his proposal. Young lady, you make my job very difficult. I'm trying hard to live up to my religion and to help you people live up to yours. That includes encouraging the reluctant to quit delaying and go along with the principle. Now I'm finding it a burden too, but if I feel I must live up to my religion, pray tell me, why shouldn't you?"

"Brother Brigham," she began.

"Do you have some other gentleman in mind?"

"No, sir."

"Then why do you delay?"

Her back stiffened. "Sir, I do not believe that the kind Father in heaven would cut anybody out of His kingdom for being unmarried."

"But can you prove to me that He wouldn't cut out everybody for disobeying His commands?" There was no answer. More gently he said, "We're all called upon to make sacrifices and forget our own wishes in order to be holy people. I have explained that the promise of the priesthood is only to men. If a woman wants to make it to the highest of the heavenlies, she's going to have to do it through the good graces of her husband. In other words, as the Prophet was fond of saying—if he doesn't see fit to take you to heaven, well, you won't make it."

The words were out before she could stop them. "But the Bible says that in Christ we are neither male nor female; we are all one. I want to be a priest; then I won't have to be married."

"Young lady, are you toying with apostate ideas?" She wilted. Quietly and firmly he said, "You know what that means. It's hell and damnation without a doubt if you carry on in that manner. Now, let's get these problems out in the open and turn your mind around so that you can follow like a good little girl."

She sucked in her breath, but the words exploded in a torrent. "There's so much that contradicts. Why do we drink water in the sacrament?"

There was a second of stunned silence, and then Brother Brigham cleared his throat. "We do it to honor the sacrificial death of Jesus Christ. Read it for yourself in the Bible; since you've determined to do all that study do some that will instruct your mind properly."

"But Jesus called it the cup of the new testament in His blood. That means covenant, doesn't it? The church leaders said, and they were reading the Prophet's revelations, that all the old covenants had been abolished because they didn't work and that only the new and everlasting covenant was in effect. If that's so, then why do I have to go to church and drink water out of a chipped fruit jar and eat soggy bread to celebrate something that doesn't work?" Brother Brigham was getting to his feet. Rebecca turned and flung herself out of the room.

———

The morning sun was still making pink smears in the sky when Rebecca let herself into the schoolhouse. She started a fire and then went to her blackboard. As she swished down the aisle between the crude desks and benches, she couldn't help the tingle of excitement and pride of ownership. True, the blackboard was only black paint carefully layered into smoothness on planed lumber, but it helped make her feel like a real schoolmarm. Besides, she must admit, it was so much fun to fill the board with her careful penmanship.

She had nearly finished placing the morning's lesson on the board when the door behind her creaked. "Mercy," she murmured, "I didn't know I was that slow."

"You aren't, I'm early," trilled a voice behind her. Rebecca turned quickly. This wasn't a student. She was very obviously a schoolteacher, and Rebecca didn't recognize her. She set down her armful of books and removed her shawl.

"I'm the new teacher. I understand you are moving. I didn't expect to find you here today."

"Moving," Rebecca repeated stupidly. "No, you're mistaken."

"Brother Brigham gave me your post since you'll be going south."

"Brother Brigham," Rebecca repeated. Her hands were limp at her sides. "Then there's not much sense in fighting it," she whispered. "His word is law."

———

Cedar City was set in a broad, long valley. The fort with spindly new-planted trees stood alone in the flatness of sagebrush and sand. Beyond the fort the land bunched into rolling hills studded with the evergreens for which the town was named.

Even in October the air was warm and dry. Dust devils still sprouted across the barren flatlands.

"Whatever possessed Brother Brigham to settle a place like this is beyond me," complained Sister Morgan. She was tall and spare, as weathered as the country that surrounded her. Her mouth was a thin, grim line and her eyes spoke more often than her lips. Rebecca watched her move around the tiny cabin that was a part of the fort.

"Wasn't it because of the iron?" Rebecca asked. She was still a stranger in this town and this home. She didn't know what to do with her hands or when to sit instead of helping out.

The woman snorted. "That's a losing proposition. They've been at it for a year now, and we're no closer to getting started than before. There's coal to dig and haul. That furnace is putting out, but I don't know what you'd call the stuff it's putting out. Oh, well, if we get a handful of nails, I suppose that's better'n nothing." She turned abruptly. "I suspect you'll produce more good."

Rebecca blinked, "What do you mean?"

"Getting the kids out of the house and giving them something to do."

Rebecca thought of the little log shanty just outside the fort. "I understand you've been having problems with the Indians."

She nodded. "You'll be safe in the daylight. Just keep that hair bundled up. They seem partial to towheads." She paused to knit a few stitches and said, "Miz Tomkin's little girl was bothered something fierce. Finally the Indians run off with her. Her pa caught up with them. Poor tyke, scared to death, hanging to that Indian pony. All they were interested in was her purty hair. Her pa cut off a braid and passed it to the Indians, and they were happy. That's how come she wears her hair cut off up to her ears. Aren't taking no more chances."

It was impossible to keep from sighing over the schoolhouse. Not even black paint graced the wall. A small stone fireplace provided warmth, and one window added light. The benches were crude and the floor packed earth. It was back to shingles and charcoal; even slates were not to be had. She was grateful for the small pile of books she had been allowed to bring from Great Salt Lake City.

At Christmas, Rebecca received a letter from Joshua. This Christmas was shared with the Morgans at the fort, and the luxury of plum pudding and new ribbons was substituted with sage hen roasted on a spit and cornmeal pudding with molasses. Rebecca was introduced to piñon nuts bartered from the Indians; and she decided, after the task of shelling them, they were hardly worth the effort.

It was after the children had received their handmade wooden toys that Brother Morgan gave the letter to Rebecca. It had been written in the early spring. Now she understood why it had been such a long time since she had heard from him. He had suffered a broken leg in an accident high in the mountains. The compound fracture had produced a fever that had kept him only semiconscious for weeks and totally useless for months.

His letter reflected a weakness and hopelessness that deeply touched Rebecca, and for moments, while she held the letter tight against her, she contemplated the journey she would make to find him. But it was winter. She watched the snow fall, knowing her dream was folly. She returned to the letter and read, "Before the autumn is over I hope to find you in Great Salt Lake City." She stared out at the snow and slowly crumpled the letter.

The spring of 1853, Rebecca dismissed school early. Every hand was needed in the fields, and even the smallest child could carry rock. During the winter, progress had been made at the foundry, and more buildings had been erected around the fort.

In March only snow shadows remained under the sage when more Saints began to move into the valley. Some of the new members of the community were Welsh, and their expertise at the foundry lifted the hearts of the discouraged workers.

In the week before Rebecca's twenty-second birthday, Mrs. Morgan announced her intention of going to Pinto. "Pinto!" exclaimed Rebecca. "That's where the Wrights are."

Mrs. Morgan nodded, "There's about fifteen families there now. My sister's there and I want to go visit before the Indians move back into the hills."

"I'd love to see Cora again."

"No reason you can't. We'll take horses and be there before supper."

It was well into the morning when Rebecca and Mrs. Morgan set out for Pinto, but Rebecca was still uneasy. "Don't the Indians scare you?" she asked.

She shrugged. "Brother Brigham ordered the lot of us to get out of here a year ago. People only stayed away a few months. We need land for farming; there's sure none around the foundry. It's in the mountains."

They reached the end of the valley and began to climb into the foothills. Rebecca discovered the soil of the cedar-studded hills was red. Sister Morgan pointed, saying, "That's suppose to mean there's iron. At first I expected it to produce red turnips."

It was past noon when Sister Morgan slowed her horse and waved across the little mountain valley. "That's Iron Town." She pointed out the beehive-shaped coke oven and the quarried stone buildings surrounding it. "Doesn't look like much's going on today. On good days the smoke fills the valley."

The town of Pinto was a cluster of log and adobe huts sprinkled in the hollow between the hills. When they stopped for directions at the first house, their ways parted. Rebecca turned down the valley, and Sister Morgan continued on.

As she rode, Rebecca could see the sparse sunbonneted figure moving along the slash of raw soil with hoe in hand. For a second there was a lump in her throat, and then she could call, "Cora, Cora Wright!"

They hugged like long-parted sisters before stepping back to study faces and then hug again. Cora was very thin, but the lines of strain on her face had eased. She gave the reason as she led the way to the house. "Mrs. Wright died this winter." She dismissed the matter with a shrug. "Didn't guess you were around here."

"I sent word with Brother Allen. Said he'd tell your husband. Probably forgot."

The house was snug and dark and tiny. Three pairs of eyes stared up at Rebecca from the middle of a quilt-covered bed. "This is Mattie." Cora lifted her.

"And Joseph is four now." Rebecca touched the thin child with the serious face. "I may get to teach your youngsters yet."

Cora lowered the child to the bed and asked, "You still teaching? I was expecting you to tell me you'd followed a man out here. After that announcement last summer, I don't know how Brother Brigham has missed seeing you married off."

"You mean the principle sermon? There was a regular marriage mill, mostly older men picking up on the young girls. They say some of the apostles have lines of young ladies forming outside their offices, just waiting to add their names to the apostles'."

"From the way you're sounding," Cora said as she went to stir up the fire and pull a pot into the heat, "I'd just guess you aren't about to get in line."

"I like teaching." Reluctant to pull at the bones of contention, she paused before saying, "Still seems there's got to be some way for people to get to the highest glory without marriage. I can't forget David Fullmister."

Rebecca spent three days with Cora and her family. Cora

admitted, even while she still gloried in being free of the strain of Bessie, that Mr. Wright was looking around for a way to build up his family again.

Back in Cedar, Rebecca found herself living much the way she had lived that first year in Great Salt Lake City. From dawn until night, she and every available hand worked in the fields and gardens. Getting water to the crops was the prime concern. This year more ditches were dug and fences erected. For the women, each moment free from the fields meant busying themselves at the loom, weaving the wool of their sheep into the fabric from which every item of clothing must be made.

The isolation of these southern communities was apparent when news and goods did arrive from the north. In April, the people of Cedar were told that the cornerstone of the temple had been laid in February of that year. Rebecca was lost in homesickness as she listened to news from the valley and visualized those tree-lined streets, those ample shops, and the sound of music and laughter.

They also learned that when Franklin Pierce became President of the United States, it was rumored that Brigham Young would be replaced as acting governor of Utah Territory. They were informed Brigham's roar had reached Washington: "Until the Lord Almighty says otherwise, Brigham Young will be governor over these people."

Later they heard President Pierce appointed Lieutenant Colonel Steptoe to serve as civil governor and military head. With friendly diplomacy, Steptoe stationed himself at a discreet distance from Great Salt Lake City. For all practical purposes, Brigham Young continued to act as governor.

Since spring, mail from the north had been coming through on a regular basis. In vain Rebecca waited for a letter from Joshua. She had finally sent a letter to California but it remained unanswered; she had nearly abandoned hope of reaching him. Still, there was that promise, and in this barren land, the promise shone more brightly.

July passed. Founder's Day in Cedar was a celebration of progress. There was a picnic on the grounds of the new ward. The spindly saplings didn't provide shade, but there was food and company aplenty. True, the food leaned hard to corn prepared a hundred different ways, and the company was largely Indian; but there was a spirit of celebration.

In August a new copy of the *Deseret News* arrived in Cedar. It carried part of Brigham Young's sermon about the Indian problems. The newspaper was passed from hand to hand, and its contents became the most important subject of conversation.

Rebecca was delivered the sermon in bite-sized servings every mealtime, and Mrs. Morgan served her own particular seasoning. "Brother Brigham has no real understanding of this," she fumed. "It's well to fuss about us living together in harmony in the fort, but he doesn't know about things being so crowded that at night you all arrange to turn over at the same time to keep from knocking knees. He says we need to be baptized into the church again, and then get the Spirit of God. Then he goes fussing about the cattle again, wanting us to send every cow to Great Salt Lake. Maybe we weren't going to put them through the tithing office, but they're better off here. At least we'll have something to eat this winter."

"If the Indians don't get them," her husband replied, stabbing his pancakes with vengeance.

Sister Morgan watched him and replied, "Well, Brother Brigham has the right idea."

"What's that?"

She referred to the tattered newspaper. "Says every man, woman and child get himself a butcher knife and be good for one Indian."

"Oh, I don't believe he said that." Rebecca reached for the newspaper. She read silently and then said, "Well, I don't know, but it seems hard when you remember they're part of the lost tribes of Israel." She looked at the paper again.

"Read it aloud," Brother Morgan instructed.

"It's saying we're to meet them with death and send them to hell if they come at us." She shivered. "I hope I don't have to make that choice."

"Does seem a little stout, considering he's just started the mission to them."

"Goes back to the Prophet's new translation," Brother Morgan said. He pushed away from the table and wiped his mouth. "In Matthew and Mark both it says something like this, that if our hand offends us, we're to cut it off because it's better to go into life maimed than to go to hell. Now this new translation tells us that the hand or foot talked about in this passage really refers to our brother and that God intends for you to do him in rather than to put up with his sinning. Then it says it's better for us to be saved alone than to be pulled down to hell with him."

"That's pretty hard," Rebecca said slowly.

"Yes, siree, but it's no mistake. It's in the other revelations, too."

"You mean the blood atonement," Sister Morgan said. "I hear tell"—Cyrilla Morgan's eyes were wide with curiosity as she stared up at her mother, and Sister Morgan got to her feet, brushing the child aside.

———————

Summer slipped into fall. The harvest hadn't been good, the crops had been first drenched and then scorched. Now the Saints faced a hungry winter.

Coal was being delivered to the foundry on a regular basis, but the toil involved with producing a wagonload of coal was costly, and the route down the mountain was steep and dangerous. Each measure of crude nails seemed precious beyond price.

18

•••••••••••••••••••

The spring of 1854 found discouraged and disheartened Saints, winter-whipped and hungry. Isolated from the man who in the past had chided, cajoled, and encouraged them into stiffening their backs and throwing their shoulders to the wheel, they moved at a halfhearted pace through the spring ritual of plowing.

As Rebecca watched her neighbors, a new uneasiness was born in her heart. It wasn't the fear of Indians or starving; instead, it was the hopelessness she was seeing in their eyes.

She watched helplessly, guessing her neighbors were beyond being lifted by a cheerful word. She, too, was becoming aware of her own inadequacy. She saw herself swept and battered by life, moving swiftly toward a poverty of spirit which offered no resource for herself and certainly no reservoir of sustaining grace to share.

In the midst of her anguish, there were those up-tilted faces of her students. Those questioning eyes, with fear pooled in their depths, were her salvation. She must be lifted beyond herself and, miraculously, she was. In forcing her eyes away from the elusive horizon of hope, she found sustenance in the activities that brought smiles and laughter to her pupils.

On this bright day, the last day of school, Mary Morgan watched Rebecca pack the picnic basket. "You're spoiling those young'uns with all the funning. Seems with the stories of Indian troubles still comin' in, you'd be more concerned with saving their hides."

"Seems to me," Rebecca answered tartly, "if their spirits aren't rescued pretty soon, there'll be no call to save their hides." For the third time, she reminded, "We're only walking to the clump of trees behind the school. We'll only be gone for an hour. After all, it's May Day, and we must celebrate."

Momentarily, an expression close to envy slipped across the woman's face, but she watched in silence as Rebecca finished the basket and swung out the door to the group waiting for her. "There's Miss Becky!" They added their bundles to her basket. She was guessing the picnic basket would yield a few raisins and dried apples, probably some cold cornbread. Her offering was a griddle cake drizzled with honey. No matter, the poor fare would seem special eaten out-of-doors and shared with the others.

Ruth Haight skipped ahead of the others. "Miss Becky, say the poem about larks."

"I can't remember it all." She knew they were referring to the poem by Wordsworth, and she tried the phrases she remembered: " 'I have walked through wildernesses dreary, / And today my heart is weary; / Had I now the wings of a faery / Up to thee would I fly.' There's more about having joy and being a happy liver."

"I wish we were happy livers," Anthony said wistfully.

"I think we might be with practice," Rebecca said gently.

"Let's practice. Let's make Miss Becky into a fairy princess."

Catherine darted ahead, and the others followed her into the trees. When Rebecca caught up with the children, they had collected tiny button bouquets of wild flowers and a long trailing vine. "There, sit on the rock," Anthony instructed. "We must make you a fairy princess. Here's your wand. Turn us all into happy toads."

"I want to be a happy lark," Cyrilla protested as she pushed Rebecca to her rock and plunged her hands into Rebecca's hair.

As it tumbled down, Rebecca cried, "What are you doing?"

"Princesses have their hair down. Oh, that's pretty. You should wear it down always. Now, here are your flowers, and we must make a ring and dance and sing until we turn into larks."

There was a shout, and a horse crashed through the underbrush. "Why are you children here?" The angry voice reached them as the rider plunged through the bushes.

Spilling flowers and vines, Rebecca jumped to her feet and straightened her shoulders. "I'm their teacher, and we're taking a nature walk."

The man slid from his horse and pulled off his hat. Those blue eyes. Her hands fluttered to her tumbled hair. His dusty beard and rough clothing were a contrast to the spotless black broadcloth she remembered, but she knew him.

"We're being larks."

He turned, and his voice gentled. "Weren't you counseled to stay in the fort?"

"But our school isn't even in the fort," Anthony protested. "Miss Becky takes good care of us."

He walked to her, and his eyes began to question, "Haven't I—"

"Yes," she said breathlessly, "in Nauvoo."

"Ah, yes." His grin lightened his sun-darkened face. "The lady in full sail."

The group was ushered back to the fort. Mr. Jacobson walked beside Rebecca telling of the Indian troubles up the valley. "We found a house burned to the ground. No sign of anyone, but the Indian trail was fresh and they were leading cattle. These are the kinds of things that get Brother Brigham's ire up. Now, you stay in the fort," he ordered swinging back into the saddle.

Throughout the summer, Indian attacks on the Saints' cattle kept the women and children close to the fort. The men worked in the fields in groups. In the evening the conversation was low and tense as everyone listened.

Brother Jacobson was a frequent visitor, and Rebecca learned he had been recently appointed by President Young to enforce his orders in the small towns.

It was during one of the unexpected times Andrew Jacobson appeared at the fort that Rebecca began to realize how much his visits were meaning to her.

Her tentative questions about him were met with a raised eyebrow and a shrug. They did say that he lived south of Cedar. He seemed to be a lonely man.

By mid-July the problems with the Indians abated, and the settlers began to relax. The wheat and corn crops were doing well. Just outside the fort the kitchen gardens were progressing nicely. Squash, beans, potatoes and yams promised a better winter.

Now the daylight hours found more Saints outside the adobe walls. There was talk of moving from the fort into more comfortable homes before winter.

One hot July evening, Rebecca went to the well for water. As she turned to leave she nearly bumped into the horse pressing eager lips toward her bucket. Andrew Jacobson's voice spoke out of the shadows, "Aren't Rebeccas known for giving drinks to weary servants?"

As she poured her water into the drinking trough, she replied, "Seems to me Rebecca was paid pretty well for her troubles."

"Silver and gold have I none, but such as I have . . ." His voice trailed away and Rebecca caught her breath. She noticed her foolish hands were trembling when she raised the bucket. They were inclined to do so around him.

"More Indians?" she asked.

"No, this is a pleasure trip. I was hoping to entice a certain young lady into taking a walk in the moonlight."

"We've been given strict orders not to leave the fort after dark," she teased.

"I've just rescinded the orders. In fact, there's a new order. Pretty ladies with golden hair are hereby ordered to entertain tired travelers by taking them for a walk in the moonlight."

Down by Coal Creek, the air was sharp with the scent of willows and damp earth. The water of the creek reflected restless silver in the moonlight, and its spray was a gentle benediction to the day. Rebecca lifted her face to the dampness while Andrew plucked at her sleeve and motioned toward the trees.

Following him, she realized the creek had all the conversation. "Noisy, huh?" She sat down on a stump, and he leaned against the trunk of the nearest tree. "You know you're nearly as mysterious as the priest Melchizedec, without beginning or end. No one seems to know anything about you."

"Ah." His grin was white in the darkness. "Then I have the advantage; even Brother Brigham knows you." Rebecca winced. "Don't look like that, it wasn't bad; he just said you were a filly who needs to be tamed."

"Where is your home?"

"I have a house in Harmony, but I don't spend much time there. Brother Brigham gave me the job of looking out for all these little towns between here and Great Salt Lake City."

"Why?"

"Because some men are sent as missionaries. I'm sent as Brigham's eyes."

"Don't you kind of yearn to settle down, or do you like living in the saddle?"

The silence lasted long enough for Rebecca to become aware of the crickets in the woodpile and the frogs by the creek.

"I suppose," he said softly, "I've given it a thought or I wouldn't be here tonight." Now he squatted beside her and lifted his face to the moonlight.

She watched him, liking the open honesty she was seeing. Now a subtle change moved across his features. The strength was changing to indecision. He dropped his head. She studied the bowed shoulders, feeling loneliness reaching to her.

"Rebecca. Often I've remembered meeting you in Nauvoo. But it

was an impossible dream to think I'd ever find you again. Now—"
He paused and his eyes searched her face. "Life is unrolling at a
pace that doesn't seem to leave much time for long courtships. You
know I'm serious about this, don't you?"

She could only nod. Her heart was pounding, and she pushed
her hand against the silly thing. He stood to his feet and reached for
her.

She remembered the strength of him and lifted eager lips.

Later when their shoes clinked against the stones outside the
Morgan cabin, she murmured, "I can't believe how far the moon
has traveled."

She saw his grin as he pulled her close again. "I'm leaving before sunup and I don't know when I'll see you again, but I'll be back
as soon as possible."

The summer had ended and school was in session before she
saw him again. And when he left, the pain of farewell was almost
sharper than the joy of seeing him. But this time there were words
that offered hope. "Brother Brigham won't be keeping me on the
road so much this winter. I'll be back soon."

Several of the families did leave the fort and move north for the
winter. Rebecca was bereft of some of her prize students. The handful of pupils who gathered each day were lonesome and unhappy
without their friends. Rebecca tried to find inspiration in the few
books she had, but she was guessing it would be a poor year.

Unexpectedly, Andrew was there again. He was feeling the strain
of separation as much as she. It was clear on his face. "Rebecca,"
he pleaded between kisses, "come away with me, and let's be married now."

She clung to him and replied, "The children. I've promised to
stay the year."

"You can stay right here and keep on teaching. But let's not wait
longer to be married." She leaned back to study his face. "I'm still
traveling most of the time, and I don't want to wait for you. Marry
me now, and put up with a part-time husband." Words weren't necessary. He left, promising to be back with a bishop.

"How do you plan a wedding in a week?" Rebecca cried, standing in the middle of the Morgans' cabin. But she did. She was
moved into a tiny cubicle next to the Morgans' cabin, and household furnishings came in from people whom she knew to be as
poor as she. Anthony's mother carried over a beautifully pieced
quilt.

She explained, "We've not been able to pay for school like we should, so maybe this'll help make up the lack."

The wife of Nathaniel Thackett lent Rebecca a dress. It was a flower-sprigged calico, as near bride-colored as anything in the community. Rebecca closed off her yearning for her mother's dress and accepted the calico.

Flour and eggs were garnered from the community, along with a precious hoard of white sugar. A troop of women produced Rebecca's wedding cake. On that November day, only winter-weary sumac and aspen decorated the schoolhouse as Rebecca and her groom exchanged their vows. But looking around the packed building, seeing the beaming faces and the heap of wedding gifts, Rebecca felt the warmth that circled them. Was it a good omen for their marriage?

After the wedding, the party moved to the clearing in the middle of the fort. There was square dancing to fiddler Charlie's music tucked between eating the roast pig and fried chicken, and the nipping bottle was passed with the wedding cake.

When the sun disappeared and the embers of the bonfire were scattered to the wind, babies were carried off to bed, and the party seemed to be over. Rebecca and Andrew slipped away to their cabin. In the tiny intimate enclosure, Rebecca wondered how the awkwardness would be bridged.

Andrew sailed his hat across the room, and she watched it rock precariously atop the new butter churn. His arms were reaching for her, blocking out the sight of the trembling churn. With a sigh she raised her lips to him. The night outside suddenly erupted into one giant clanging cymbal.

"Oh, every washtub in the fort and there's someone behind each one," Andrew groaned. With a shrug of resignation, he reached for the door just as it burst open.

The last of the cake disappeared and then the new-baked bread and the jar of wild current jelly. Every inch of the cabin was filled with people, but still more came. Charlie the fiddler came, bringing his instrument and a new jug.

When a bar of light appeared across the eastern horizon, the last guest left the cabin. "Teacher," called a voice from across the fort, "will there be school tomorrow—er, today?" Andrew banged the door shut, and the laughter faded.

In 1855, the Endowment House in Great Salt Lake City was completed, and the Saints whose marriages hadn't been previously solemnized at the Nauvoo Temple began to flock to Great Salt Lake City.

On the last day of school, Andrew appeared at the schoolhouse while Rebecca was tidying the room for the final time. He was wearing a happy grin and saying, "Pack your valise, Sister Jacobson, we're going to the city to say our vows right before God, for time and eternity."

"Oh, Andrew!" She clapped her hands and pushed away tears. Already her mind was running away with the thoughts of all those she would see. "I'm sure we can stay with the Samuels. They'll be so happy for us."

"And we'll find a pretty new dress for you, a wedding dress." For just a second her heart leaped.

"Yes, a dress." She tried to sound enthusiastic. But then, "It's just possible they've sent my mother's wedding dress. It was over a year ago that I wrote for it again. It would be so wonderful—somehow I would feel more married."

He grinned down at her, "Well, now, I'd think that even without the dress you'd manage to feel married."

She blushed, and he pinched her pink cheeks. "I'd like to have this over and have you moved south before we start having little ones." There was a question in his eyes, and she shook her head.

They traveled to Great Salt Lake City in a light buggy. It was a pleasant trip with balmy days and mild nights. Rebecca was discovering the many changes that had occurred since she had moved south. New communities had been established, each with its adobe or log fort and its circle of green fields. This year the crops were doing well. Andrew remarked, "They'll have corn soon."

"The thing I like most is the feeling," Rebecca said. "It's different. People are more relaxed and friendly. There's not the worry strain on their faces."

The Samuels weren't as happy to see Rebecca and her new husband as she had expected. Almost immediately Rebecca sensed the tension in the household, and she was grateful that the ceremony in the Endowment House required only a brief stay in the city.

The day before the ceremony, Ann and Rebecca went shopping for a suitable wedding dress. The only one Rebecca could find was black watered silk. Shaking out the heavy folds, she held it against herself and exclaimed, "This is not right at all, but Andrew will be disappointed if I don't manage to come up with something! At least it will do me for years as a Sabbath best."

After paying for the dress, Rebecca joined Ann at the front of the store. With a bright smile Ann said, "I expect I'll have to be getting a new dress."

"That sounds exciting. What's the event?"

"Brother Samuels will be taking another wife before the first snow. There's all the signs." Rebecca searched Ann's face, but the serene features revealed nothing.

After the ceremony at the Endowment House; Rebecca and Andrew stopped at the Samuels' before starting south. Ann had prepared dinner for them. There was even a small cake baked in her new cookstove.

Just before they climbed back into the buggy, Ann handed Rebecca a package and a note. "I'm ashamed of myself and I need to clear my conscience. Don't hold it against me."

Guessing that Ann was referring to her cool welcome and that it was because of Brother Samuels' rejected proposal, Rebecca hastily kissed Ann and said, "Of course I forgive you, always. And thank you again for this lovely dinner."

Rebecca snuggled against Andrew's arm and watched the changing countryside. It was the going-home time of evening and it always filled her with great contentment. The sun's deep red glow added warmth and serenity to the scene. Even the log cabins seemed cozy. She could hear the lowing of the cattle and the clink of milk pails. She sighed softly.

"What's that for?"

"It's the family feeling. I'm so content just being with you."

"Little Rebecca, I'll be so glad to get us settled in as a real family. This running around the country has about made an old man out of me." He wrapped his arm around her, and she lifted her face. His eyes were watchful, questioning. "What did you think of the ceremony?"

Rebecca rested her head against his arm and thought. It would be well to say everything that was on her heart, but there were so many untried areas of their relationship. How would he react to her forthrightness?

She began slowly, "I kept wondering if it were all necessary. I don't like these terrible garments. Is it true that we're to wear them always?"

"Yes. Not only do they protect you, but to fail to do so is to incur God's wrath. This is His ordinance. You know that they say the reason Joseph Smith was killed was because he failed to have on his holy garments." Rebecca sighed and waited. "What about the rest? Did the ceremony seem to have a deep significance to you?"

"The oaths," she said slowly; "was that necessary? Why must we swear to avenge the deaths of Joseph Smith and to teach our children to do the same? I don't want my children to murder. I would rather never have children. And to obey the priesthood in everything . . ." She shook her head slowly. "How do I know what they'll ask? And the penalty of not keeping the vows: bowels torn from us while we are alive and our throats slit and our heart and tongue to be cut out, plus damnation in the world to come." She shivered, pressing close to him.

"But why should that bother you? Surely you intend to keep those vows."

"It's just that I don't like being under such a terrible oath."

"Look at the other side of it," he insisted, lifting her chin to see her eyes. "Now you have eternal life promised to you. You will be my wife for all eternity. We will fill the heavens with our children, and you shall be my queen."

"And you will be a god, ruling over your own kingdom," she said slowly, knowing the words were hitting the bottom of her heart like stones. There was no circling spread of belief in her. Could she hide from him the doubt she was feeling? Could she ever believe her salvation was only through him? She looked up at him, and her heart melted. Accept that he was as god to her? This she could and did. Her eyes caressed his dark wavy hair. She moved her hand across his square shoulders, loving the hard muscle of him.

At Cedar, they gathered her belongings and took the road through the mountains. They passed the ironworks and Pinto before cutting south to Fort Harmony.

At Pinto there was a brief visit with Cora. Her children were growing and she was again pregnant. Back in the buggy, Rebecca became aware of Andrew's silence. Studying his profile in the fading light, she decided that already his thoughts were leaving the trip behind and pressing to life ahead.

In the midst of her musings, he hauled on the reins. "Whoa. Let's spend the night here." He waved toward the snug shelf of rock and clump of piñon.

"But you said it was only a few more miles." Rebecca was thinking of a soft bed.

"It's not much more than that, but I'd rather reach there in good daylight."

They dined on bread and milk with fresh berries and then settled to sleep. Andrew was still remote, and Rebecca went to sleep troubled by his separateness.

It was nearly midmorning when they broke through the trees into the little cup of a valley that held Fort Harmony. Andrew halted the team on the hilltop and pointed. "There's the ward. They hold school there, too." As she listened to him name the buildings clustered around the fort, Rebecca's impatience grew. "That's the general store." He grinned at her, "Our place is behind the fort, back in the trees."

He held her close as he studied the scene. "Looks like there's more building. Don't recognize those rigs. Probably the Clara bunch moving in. Well, no matter; there's room enough for all. Wasn't too good an idea to settle the Clara anyway. There's been nothing but trouble. First the floods and then the Indians. I expect Hamblin will have the Indians under control in a year or so. He's done a goodly share of baptizing already. At times we're hard put to remember these are our brothers." She tried to control her impatience. "Well, let's get down there."

When they pulled through the gate in front of the log house, the first thing Rebecca saw was the children. She stared, numbness flowing through her. "Pa!" Like swooping birds they came at him as he jumped down.

While Andrew was pulling the children close, the door of the house swung open and a tall, rawboned woman with a solemn face came out on the porch. She thrust her hands under her apron and watched as Andrew captured the last child and pushed him forward. "John, Margaret, Billy, Angie"—he touched them briefly and said—"this is your new Aunty Rebecca." His eyes were bright, challenging Rebecca. Now he extended his hand toward the woman on the porch. "My dear, come meet Rebecca."

The day grew dim, seeming to float past Rebecca like faded gray photographs. The first photograph was the house. Andrew was saying that it would be most practical for them all to live here together.

Like a wooden soldier, she toured her new home. The main floor was divided into two big rooms, both containing a fireplace and comfortable furniture. In each section there was a large bed shoved back in the corner. One room was obviously used as a kitchen. About its fireplace clustered a long table and benches. A cupboard hung from the wall beside the fireplace. Nearby, another table was loaded with a jumble of pans and sacks of dried corn and flour. The disorder jarred the numbness in Rebecca.

The next room contained, besides the second bed and bureau,

comfortable chairs and a desk, holding a china lamp. The only reality for Rebecca was seeing the tumbled bed and the puffs of dust
on the floor, even as she noticed the pink roses on the base of the
lamp and its smudged chimney.

19

· · · · · · · · · · · · · · · · · · · ·

*D*uring the days that followed, the gray haze which had settled over Rebecca seemed to lift gradually. Life began to pick a new pattern, but Rebecca found herself thinking only in terms of the before and after days.

Now she knew each moment as a deliberate, self-conscious one. No longer did she move with ease; she jerked, conscious of every muscle, every stray hair, every wasted movement. She was growing thin and silent. Andrew's worried face slowly assumed an angry frown. Seeing it, she made herself merry and productive. The house became filled with activity, and the stern features of that woman, Sarah, became pleased, relaxed. Andrew expanded into the genial, indulgent head of the household.

Through the numbness of those beginning days, Rebecca had groped her way to acceptance as a way of life. In the quiet of the nights he spent with Sarah, Rebecca had taken to lecturing herself. There would be no call to charge her with being the troublemaker. There were all those stories of plural marriages. Now that the lot was cast, she would settle in and make the best of it.

But in the lonesome nights and quiet times, the sense of destiny crept upon her. How silly of her to have thought all that time she could fight against the order of things.

She grew to accept the dividedness of Andrew, trying to deny her need for his nearness and caresses. Constantly she must remind herself that her honeymoon was over.

Slowly, Rebecca was beginning to know the town and become acquainted with people. In the beginning, while her mind was still wrapped in its gray blanket of shock, she had rejected the friendly people reaching out to her. Now in her loneliness, with approaching winter and Andrew's absence becoming more frequent, she began searching for friendship.

One day as Rebecca sat on the front porch, trying to card a tangle of wool, a woman stepped through the gate and approached. "You're not going about that right," she stated. "I'm Matilda Davis, and I'll be glad to help you with that."

"Not Grandma Davis," teased Rebecca, glancing at her graying hair.

She snorted, "Not everyone is grandma. I married Mr. Davis while he was on his deathbed, and I was old enough to know what I was doing. I married him just to have the endowments and earn my place in glory. I wouldn't have it any other way. He'd had a flock of young ones with his first two wives and didn't need more children, just that third marriage."

"Weren't you interested in having a family?"

She shook her head. "I just wanted to teach school. But they come along and preach that if a woman wants to get to the highest heaven, she's gotta let some man take her there by being married to him." She shrugged. "They say it, I'll go along."

"But you haven't had to live with another wife?" Rebecca asked in a low voice.

Matilda shook her head, "That's enough to send anyone to glory. You'd better believe the atonement is the only thing that makes a lot of these marriages work." The woman squinted up at her. "It pays to be a good gossip, but this isn't gossip, it's gospel. It's in the Doctrine and Covenants; that means it's a revelation given to Joseph Smith by the Lord Almighty himself, and it isn't ever going to change. For now and until eternity it's there. Where it tells about the new and everlasting covenant of marriage for eternity, it says all who have the law revealed to them must obey it or be damned. Any man in the priesthood who has a wife who doesn't believe and minister to him, well, he has a sacred obligation to kill her off just to keep her from being damned. Kill her body to save her soul. I tell you, there's some men who think any little old thing is enough to damn a woman, and they're ready to go great lengths to save her soul."

Rebecca stared at the woman. Not believing her, she skirted the topic by asking, "Is it commanded that men have plural wives?"

"Well, depends on who's talking about it. It says in the same place that we're to go do the works of Abraham, which means taking more than one wife. Sounds like a command. There's no other way to get to the highest heaven and be gods."

"Seems so unfair."

"Why you complaining? Seems an easy way to earn the highest order of heaven."

"I'm thinking of those who've never married."

"They've had the right."

"Sometimes they die before they've had the chance." She was thinking again of David.

"Well, there's plenty of unanswered questions. You could get so caught up in asking questions that you could just talk yourself right out of your faith. Brother Brigham comes down pretty hard on this. Calls them apostates."

"He doesn't have much patience with them, does he?"

"No. In a sermon I heard him say rather than allow apostates to flourish here, he'd unsheath his bowie knife and conquer or die. My, what a commotion that caused! People were hollering and shouting, 'Go it, go it!' He said we should call upon the Lord to assist in this and every good work."

———

A year had passed since her marriage, and as Rebecca prepared dinner, she tried to keep her thoughts from wandering back over that year. She stirred the braised quail in the iron kettle while she gave instructions to Margaret. "You can cut the bread, just watch your fingers. Angie, carry the knives and forks to the table." She watched Angie pull a chair to the cupboard and climb onto it.

The door flew open, and Andrew came in. With a happy grin, he made his rounds kissing each child and then his wives. His eyes caught and held Rebecca's for a moment before he turned. She felt her heart leap. He went to hang his coat on a peg.

"Aunt Becky!" Rebecca turned and caught Angie as the chair tipped.

"Aunt Becky, dinner's burning." She dashed to the fire.

Andrew was drying his hands. "Sarah, why don't you give Rebecca a hand?"

"I think I'm in the family way." Sarah stood slowly and moved to her place at the table. "I've been feeling poorly for a week or so."

A grin split Andrew's face. "That's wonderful!" He patted her shoulder and gave her a quick hug. Rebecca turned to hide her disappointment.

During the coming weeks, Rebecca discovered that Sarah's delicate condition changed her disposition even more—she retreated from all responsibility for her children. Rebecca was reminded of Bessie Wright as she watched Sarah continue to rock and knit.

On the first warm day of February, Rebecca moved the laundry outside and built a fire to boil the linens. Then she worked in the fresh air, scrubbing the clothing and stretching it to dry across clotheslines and bushes. The sun was as warm as a friendly hand on her back, and when she finished her task, she noted with glad surprise how her mood had lifted. She hummed a little tune as she sloshed soapy water across the porch and scrubbed at the mud with her broom.

Filled with gladness to be alive, she paused to look at the town. Sister Lucas was shaking rugs out her door. There was a cluster of tiny folk frolicking in the middle of the street. Smoke curled from chimneys in the lazy manner of spring.

As she eyed the dark house, a thought was born, and Rebecca voiced it. "It seems to me a body deserves a joy once in a while. Couldn't it make the rest of life a little easier?"

That distant line of hills had beckoned her for months. With Indian problems cooling, wouldn't it be a joy to walk there?

Quickly, before she became timid, she hurried into the house. Removing her apron and smoothing her hair, she said, "I'm going to walk for a bit."

"You'll be mud all over."

" 'Tisn't muddy. You should look for yourself; the fresh air would be good."

Nodding briskly at her neighbors, Rebecca headed for the line of trees. Once in the midst of the piney perfume, her pace slackened. A dreamy calm crept over her as she wandered, listening to the birds, pausing to chew a pine needle.

It was a glory, a kind of glory. Joshua had talked about a glory and about some people who lived that way, the Whitmans. They had been murdered by the Indians. What kind of glory could end in tragedy?

While she snuggled in her shawl and mused on the word glory, the sun dipped behind the trees, and the streets of Fort Harmony became shadowed.

Tonight was fast and testimony meeting. Sarah and Andrew would be going, and she would be expected to feed the children and then trail along behind when the meeting was nearly over.

She left the trees and quickened her steps on the slope. New resolutions were forming in her mind. They made her uneasy, but they also shone like a ray of bright sun in a dark day. "I think," she said slowly, "it wouldn't hurt to prove I'm still my own self. There must be enough room in Mormonism for me to think one different thought and walk one lonely mile."

She was breathless as she burst through the door. Andrew was already there and Sarah, wearing her bonnet, was dishing up the porridge for the children.

"I'll do it!" she exclaimed breathlessly. "You go ahead, I'll not be going."

Andrew frowned at her. "Where've you been?"

She smoothed her hair. "Walking in the trees. I've had a heart to do it since I first came. I'm not going tonight," she repeated.

Andrew's glance slid off her face, and he turned, "Come along, Sarah. She can take over now." Without looking at her, Sarah adjusted her shawl and followed him.

When the door closed, John spoke around his mouthful. "Pa's mad at you. Ma told him about all your gallivanting when there's work to be done."

"But I did the laundry and scrubbed the steps!" Rebecca exclaimed. "I—" Suddenly she realized she was trying to justify her actions. She smiled down at them. "I needed a joy, and I've supplied it for myself."

Angie raised her face, and the cornmeal dripped from her chin. "I wish I had a joy," she said wistfully. "With raisins in it and oatmeal instead of corn mush."

"You baby pumpkin." Rebecca circled the table and pushed a kiss down into the child's tangled curls. "I'll give you a joy. Shall I make you a pancake with molasses or shall we read a book together?"

"Book, book, read to us!"

Rebecca shoved aside the dishes, and Margaret ran to the shelf of books. She selected the red one and returned to the table. "Oh, good!" Rebecca exclaimed, "the stories and poems. This book was given to me by a dear lady just before I left Great Salt Lake City." She settled herself to read.

The fire burned low, and she interrupted herself to say, "John, please put on another log." She was still reading when Andrew and Sarah returned. With a start, Rebecca realized the laundry was still unfolded, and the dirty dishes waited.

She jumped to her feet and handed the book to Margaret. "Let's get at the dishes. Surely we've all had enough joy to last us for a time."

Later, when the children had climbed the stairs and Sarah's door had been closed, Andrew demanded, "Why?" She studied his face, and only then saw the trouble her willfulness had caused. His face was tight and his lips cold.

"Andrew." She tried to move close and found she dared not. "I'm not trying to cause trouble; it's just that—" she stopped. Her thoughts flew back to Cora and she remembered her saying, *They don't listen to anything against the first wife. You waste your time talking; they don't see it. I guess it's because there's a romance, a kind of love in the first marriage that isn't in the others. One word of complaint and they get the wrong idea. I hear him saying I'm trouble, so I keep it all to myself.*

She turned away from him. "It seems life runs better when there's a little joy. I've had mine because I snatched it. They needed theirs."

He moved impatiently, "I want you to be more careful of Sarah. She isn't as young as she was and this birthing could be hard on her. I'd say another two months and she'll be on the bed." He hesitated, and his face melted. She flew at him.

"Oh, Andrew, please," she begged, "let's not quarrel. I need you so badly."

"Rebecca"—he studied her face—"you've got to realize there's a difference in this kind of marriage. It can't be all honeymoon; there's too many feelings to be considered. I make a pet of you and there's no living with Sarah."

She closed her lips tightly to stop the torrent, but the words burst through. "Andrew, it wasn't that way in the beginning. We were as close as it was possible. I did think you were a lover in love. You acted the part. Now this. Why? Why didn't you tell me this was to be a plural marriage?"

"Because you would never have married me."

Quietly she said, "That is true. I had refused better positions than this. True, I didn't love the man, but I love his family and that, I do believe, is where the real marriage is anyway."

He stepped close and wrapped his arms around her, forcing her face upward. "But you are mine. That ceremony at the Endowment House sealed it for time and eternity. You are mine." He bent to kiss her. When he lifted her in his arms, Rebecca couldn't dwell on the love. She knew he was thinking of the child that must be.

————

Rebecca was part of the group around the quilt frame. It hadn't taken her long to discover the Relief Society meeting was the best place in Fort Harmony to get acquainted with the women of the community.

"Sister Jacobson, I do believe that you've not heard a word I've said to you. You're doing that section all wrong. See, there are the lines you're to be following. I declare, you must be in the family way to be so absentminded. Never you mind. After six or seven, it ceases to be a wonder and becomes a way of life."

Rebecca was shaking her head, and Sister Wilkes said, "That's the problem with these plural marriages; sometimes there isn't enough husband to go around." Over the titters she continued. "Never you mind, you'll get that way soon enough, and then there'll be no rest."

"But after a year and a half."

"Yes, even then. Don't give up."

"You could trade off favors," saucy little Cindy exclaimed. "There was a woman in Cedar who did that. It was whispered around that the first wife didn't care all that much for the nighttime activity, and so between the two of them they managed the mister just fine. The second wife had a passel of young'uns."

Rebecca's trembling fingers tried to manage the needle as she listened. "There's advantages to not living in the same house."

"I don't know about that," came a voice from the far end of the quilt. "I wear myself to the bone just trying to keep up with the first wife. Sometimes I wish we did live in the same house; then the difference wouldn't be so noticeable. She changes the sheets every time he steps in the house. I believe in making him feel like a king in his own home, but there's limits, especially when she's got only one half-grown son, and I've five little ones."

"Sadie, quit your worrying. Surely he knows how busy the little ones keep you. I'll bet she just scrubs to make up for not having children to keep her busy."

Cindy continued, "I hear tell that Miz Duncan's oldest gal ran her pa out to the barn the last time he came to visit. The little snip told her pa to go sleep in the barn because they had too many mouths to feed already, and every time he visited they got another."

Rebecca awakened during the night. The day's events moved through her mind, and she tossed restlessly. Beside her Andrew stirred. "Rebecca, are you having another bad dream?" His arms drew her close, and his beard tickled her face. "Seems you've been a restless sleeper lately; I'm guessing you have something on your mind. Is it about not being in the family way?"

Rebecca fastened her arms around him and relaxed against the warm hardness of his body. "No, my dear husband, I was not thinking about babies. Do you suppose God uses nighttime quiet to make us think?"

"About what?"

"About Him and living like He wants. Andrew, do you sometimes feel that no matter how hard you try you just aren't really getting better—progressing?"

"Well, I've noticed you've been a little hellion lately. Both Sarah and I know once you get your own little one it'll be different."

"But it hadn't ought to be," Rebecca murmured, still troubled with the guilty feelings that had awakened her. "You can both be patient with me, but that doesn't do anything about changing me inside."

"You've got to live your religion, lady." He bent over and tweaked her nose.

"I guess my problem is that I don't really want to live it except in the middle of the night when I see how terrible I've been, and I don't like the guilt. Why don't I want to change when I'm screaming at the children?"

His lips moved across her chin and found her lips. After a moment he murmured, "You're going about this all wrong. I know you need to love and get along with people; but, Rebecca, concentrate on producing your kingdom instead of perfecting it. You're not doing the big sins, so don't be such a fuss."

"It isn't the sins so much as the ugly way I am inside." He slid his arms around her, and she sighed heavily. Now was the time to start practicing her religion. She tried to shut out Sarah's face as Andrew bent over her.

Even though it was late March, it had begun to snow heavily while Rebecca was at Relief Society. As she walked home, she bowed her head to the storm and pulled her shawl close, but it was impossible to hurry her feet. She was thinking about the lesson Sister Lee had brought. It was about Hannah, the mother of Samuel.

Recalling Hannah's prayer, she muttered, "If I had a prayer to pray, it wouldn't be for a child, but I'd pray to be away from here and for these last six years to disappear." She thought of the turmoil that was home. Daily it was becoming more unbearable. She must acknowledge it was her fault. For a second she closed her eyes and saw herself warped into an ugly creature of darkness. The picture pressed upon her, and she knew that one of these days, her spirit would refuse to be lifted.

She shivered at the thought, feeling her powerlessness. There were the sleepless nights when the slightest whisper from Sarah's baby, or even Andrew's snoring drifting to her through that adjoining wall, would be enough to send the tears cascading down her cheeks. To say she despised the trembling mass of emotion she was becoming was to accept one more defeat.

Sister Lee had painted a word picture of Hannah as a beautiful, childless, plural wife with never a complaint. Rebecca rejected the picture, and anger burned through her rebellion. She stormed down the path, kicking puffs of snow.

At the door, her anger vanished. Andrew was home. She crushed her impulse to fly into his arms as she glanced quickly at Sarah.

Andrew's face was gray and lined with fatigue. He moved restlessly about the room while Sarah held her baby and rocked.

His nod was curt, and he went on with what he was saying. "It isn't good. There's a bad feeling brewing across the territory. I'm certain God is leading us, but nothing seems to be going right." He wheeled and paced to Sarah's chair. "It's like Zion is about to be snatched from our hands. The government won't grant statehood— they don't want us to be self-governing. These territorial officers will continue to be a thorn in our flesh."

Sarah sighed and shifted the sleeping baby to her lap. "I don't understand why they won't give us the right to practice our religion the way God tells us to."

"If this is God's will for us," Andrew said slowly, "then God will permit it."

"If—" Rebecca cried. "How can you question? Don't the revelations Joseph Smith received instruct us to live that way? If God isn't fickle, then we're stuck with it forever. I can't believe God would change His mind."

Andrew thoughtfully studied her face. He turned to Sarah. "I'm leaving now. I'll ride as far as Hyde's place and spend the night. He's going with me."

"You're leaving." Rebecca's voice was flat, and Andrew looked at her. For just a moment she caught a glimpse of the old tenderness, and her heart responded. "In the worst of weather you must go; doesn't that man have a heart?"

"There's work to be done and a kingdom to be kept in order. It's my job, and there's no sense in fussing." He moved past her, and on impulse she reached out.

"Andrew, you spend so much time on the road. It would make sense for you to have a home up the way. Least you'd spend more nights under your own roof."

He studied her closely. "You're right. No matter the reason, you're right." He took his bundle and pulled on the heavy coat. With a brief wave he was gone. Again Rebecca's heart sank to its slow dismal beat, and with a sigh she turned away.

Sarah lifted the baby and got to her feet. Her steps were heavy as she carried the child into the other room. As Rebecca watched her go, she was wondering if Sarah could be feeling as she felt, missing the closeness and love.

20

. . . .

$\mathscr{I}$t was well into the new year of 1856 when Rebecca had her urge to put her house in order. With Andrew gone so often the household seemed to lack purpose, and, at best, the house reflected indifference.

While straightening her bureau drawers, she found the little bundle of towels which Ann had given her. The memory of that day and the trip to Great Salt Lake City overwhelmed her, and she choked back tears as she remembered the happy, carefree people she and Andrew had been. She fingered the towels. There was Ann's coolness. The letter. She had tucked it away unread.

Rebecca began searching the contents of her drawer. At the bottom was her Bible. Of course! She had carried the Bible to the Endowment House and later placed the letter in it. She found the letter and pushed it into her pocket to read after the children were in bed.

Later Rebecca watched Sarah shoo her children upstairs and settle the baby on her shoulder. She nodded curtly to Rebecca and closed her door behind her. Rebecca had long since ceased to be disturbed by Sarah's silence. Always Andrew would stand between them. She understood. She fingered the letter and whispered, "No matter what, Rebecca, you're learning."

With a sigh of relief Rebecca took Sarah's rocking chair beside the fire. As she looked at the letter, she felt a strange reluctance to open it. Finally she slipped her finger under the flap.

"Dear Rebecca," she read, "I've been so ashamed of myself. I determined in the beginning to never tell you this, but now I must. My conscience won't give me rest. Last fall a young man, he said he was Joshua Smyth, came through the valley looking for you. Everyone was loath to give him any help with information, since we'd already concluded that he was a Gentile. I just let him know that you were gone out of the territory and didn't tell him that I knew your whereabouts. He said he was on his way to Illinois to pack up his family, and they were all moving to Oregon. Seemed very disappointed, but I hardened my heart. I had visions of you throwing off all you've worked for and apostatizing because of this young man. I told him for all I knew you'd headed for Oregon territory on your own.

"Rebecca, dear, I know that was a terrible lie, but I couldn't stand for him to be upsetting your life, and he seemed so determined. Please forgive me. Now that you're married, I thought I would tell you and we would have a good laugh over it. But when I saw how upset you were about the dress, I just couldn't tell you. I'll give you the dress when you come again."

"Dress!" Rebecca cried. "My wedding dress. Ann had my dress and didn't tell me!" Her hands trembled to her face. She was only vaguely conscious of the letter slipping from her lap.

When the fire was ash and she was trembling with cold, she realized the letter was gone. There remained only a tiny fragment of gauzy ash still supporting the shadow of Ann's writing.

As she prepared for bed, Rebecca wondered about the remainder of the letter. How did Ann get the dress? Oregon. How could she send a letter to the Smyths now?

In April, when Andrew returned, he told Rebecca there was a cabin in Pinto and he was moving her there. She nodded, still caught in the mesh of life that drew her mindlessly on.

They were packed into the wagon and well on their way before Rebecca began to comprehend all this move would mean. There would be no more living with Sarah. She took a deep breath and sighed with relief. Cora lived at Pinto. Andrew must have felt her excitement; he smiled down at her.

"It's Cora," she explained; "it's been so long, and now we'll be neighbors again. I really love Cora. I think we must be soul sisters."

"Well, of course you are," Andrew said. He was using his teaching voice. "We are all soul brothers and sisters. Our god is truly our father. He birthed our spirits thousands of years ago. There are still millions of spirits waiting to be born. That is why—" he paused, and Rebecca winced.

"You forget"—her voice was low—"I'm not childless because I wish it that way."

Awkwardly he patted her shoulder. "We'll have more time together, and that'll be remedied." For a moment he was silent, and she waited. "You know I'm going to have to take another wife." She bent her head, and the sunbonnet shielded her face. "It's the working out of the trinity in our lives. You know enough about the priesthood to know that. Besides, there's this need to provide more bodies."

There was that question Rebecca dared not ask. But later, as she looked around the cabin, she decided it was answered. The cabin was much too small for another wife. But the one tiny room would be home, their home.

They had carried Rebecca's bed and bureau with them. There was the bundle of household goods she had acquired before leaving Great Salt Lake City. As Andrew carried in the bundles, Rebecca scurried about placing her belongings in order.

Now Andrew came to the door. "Close your eyes," he commanded, "I've something in the barn." It was a rocking chair. He placed it beside the fireplace on a scrap of rug. While she clung to his neck and kissed him, he added, "There's a cradle too."

While he returned her kisses, he said, "I've put it in the loft for now. I understand that your friend Cora has four children. Go learn her secret."

Rebecca busied herself setting out the pots and pans on the shelf built into the wall. Andrew returned to the cabin with a bundle of his shirts. She watched him place the bundle on the table and carefully unroll it. Rebecca caught her breath. It was a china lamp like Sarah's. "Andrew, it's beautiful!"

He placed it in the middle of the table, and she said, "All we lack is the good Book. I'll bring out my mother's Bible."

"It looks home-like already. I hope you won't be lonesome when I'm gone."

"I'll have Cora to fill the lonesome times." She thumped the feather tick into shape and reached for the sheets.

Very soon Andrew was on his way again, and Rebecca was left to settle the cabin and care for the cow and chickens he had purchased. She struggled with building a fence and repairing the barn, but when she contemplated the soggy garden patch, she decided she could go visiting with an easy conscience.

Cora's cabin was across town. Rebecca walked slowly, thinking as she walked of the common thread running through the lives of these women. There were no strangers when the warp and woof of lives were the same. Through one direction ran the common cares, the poverty, work, and little children; in the other direction ran their religion, the principle, and Brother Brigham. The principle seemed to be a double thread that held more securely than any other tie. Tie, or was it a shackle? She was sensing that the answer would be in her ability to accept life as she found it now.

For the first time in months she found herself whispering, "Please, God, help me—" She groped for words. "I need to find glory in life."

And there was Cora. They held each other and then sobbed together. There was a bond. Rebecca recognized it in its completeness. It had cemented them together despite the years and miles that had passed between them.

When Cora finally released her and pulled Rebecca into the cabin, there was Jessie to meet. She seemed barely sixteen. Her face was petulant and her stomach swollen with child. While they were having a cup of Brigham tea, the children came in.

Rebecca was holding the baby, Carrie, who had been born the previous winter. Joseph, a lanky, serious boy of seven, with Todd, nearly six, and little Mattie, who was almost four, filled the little cabin. Rebecca caressed the down-headed baby and listened to Cora explain that she had lost two babies since coming south.

Looking around the poor, crowded cabin, Rebecca's forthrightness surfaced. "Cora, haven't you provided enough bodies for spirits? If this is God's will, why do so many live such a short time?" Cora winced, and Rebecca immediately regretted her hasty words. How worn the woman was. Rebecca rose to leave.

She embraced Cora, saying, "Please come. I need you so much."

Cora followed her to the road. "I'm sorry it's so dismal. Jessie isn't well, and she never ceases to remind us of it." Tears welled up in Cora's eyes.

"Is it as bad as it was with Bessie?"

She shook her head. "I'm being oversensitive. I still can't feel good about another wife. I was getting silly, letting my thoughts run away with the idea of being the only wife. I knew it wouldn't last." She sighed heavily. "I spend most of my time trying to kill love. Seems to be the only way to be content in marriage."

Walking back to the cabin, Rebecca mulled over Cora's words. She had wondered how the young, beautiful Cora had been so attracted to that scrawny, timid man she had married. Now Cora was admitting her deep love for him and at the same time trying to deny it life.

The corn was knee-deep when Andrew came. In the bliss of having him all to herself, Rebecca wondered if she were as vulnerable as Cora. She tried to tighten the reins of her emotions by reminding herself of Andrew's promise to take another wife.

When he prepared to leave he said, "I'll be making a trip to Great Salt Lake City about conference time in October. Would you like to go?"

She hesitated, and asked, "Will Sarah be going?"

"No, she's in the family way again."

"I'd enjoy going. I'll see Ann again; her children'll be grown." He nodded and kissed her again. She watched until he disappeared around the curve, and then walked slowly back to the house.

Filled with new loneliness, she hesitated in the doorway and finally settled on the steps. The robins were carrying worms to their nest. Did robins have only one mate or would that male robin soon be off to find worms for another family?

Rebecca reluctantly got up from the step and opened the door. She couldn't resist one last glance toward the nest.

21

....

$\mathcal{C}$ora came to visit. When she walked into Rebecca's house, she dumped the sleeping baby into Rebecca's arms. The shock of the sweet warm flesh nearly reduced Rebecca to tears. Cora was saying, "All the talking you did. I never expected to see you married. Now you're a plural wife to boot."

"How did you know Andrew was married before?"

"Everybody around here knows him, and Sarah too. They settled in Cedar that first year."

"The folks in Cedar have known him for a long time?"

"The ones who settled there with him. I couldn't call their names."

"They could have told me," Rebecca said slowly. She wondered at her blindness.

Cora asked, "Would it have made a difference? If you're in love, I'd suppose it wouldn't. Everybody's got to get married."

"Not everybody," Rebecca said slowly. Today Cora was the plural wife, not the emotion-torn woman.

"If you're going to live your religion, you'll marry."

"I'm still not convinced that God operates that way," Rebecca declared.

Cora looked shocked. "I thought you'd got all the old feelings out of you."

"Cora, I'll go crazy if I can't talk. You're the only one who'll let me say what I think."

She looked uneasy. "Maybe I'd better not listen anymore. I've troubles enough of my own without letting you feed me something to think about."

Rebecca touched her friend's hand. "Don't deny me that."

Cora admitted, "You say things I don't allow myself to say. You're bringing out the doubts and scary nighttime feelings. You always have. As long as I've known you, you've dug at the things they've told us were wrong to question. Becky, don't. That's apostasy. You've got to have faith. Start this, and you'll drag us both down."

Later Rebecca walked down the street with Cora, still carrying the baby and loath to surrender her at the end of the street.

When Cora reached for the child, Rebecca noticed the lines on her face, the unhappy shadows in her eyes. "Much as you pretend, Cora, you're no more content with life than I. Do you suppose it would harm us if we were to lay our questions out in the open and try to find answers?"

"I don't know. Becky, I'm scared to own up to my questions. That means weakness."

"Maybe it means we're searching for a stronger faith. Right now I feel a good wind would blow my faith all over town."

Cora turned away, and her voice was muffled, "I'd be willing to talk. Sometimes I think if I don't start having a good hard case for my faith, I'll blow away too."

Rebecca said, "It sticks in me to find out what 'holy' is."

"It can't be much to worry about. Adam is our God and look how he was taken to task just for eating a little fruit. We all end up getting death as a reward."

"And sweat and hard times."

"And terrible childbirth." Cora shrugged hopelessly. "We'll talk again."

Rebecca watched her go. Using pines as patterns, the sun was laying long thick shadows. The cows were lowing as they moved toward the barns. But the evening clatter of milk pails and shouting children failed to draw the familiar picture of contentment for Rebecca.

With a sigh she turned. How defenseless and lonely the cluster of little log houses seemed, how fragile the stick figures of men and women. "We could disappear tomorrow, and life would go on without a hitch. It is only by the grace of God that we even survive," she muttered. "Must we forever be beat down before we are fit to be called the children of God?"

As summer expanded, Cora and Rebecca wore paths to each other's homes. Through the sage, down the dry wash and up the hill the path went. If the early years had made a friendship, these months served to reveal a deeper bond.

It was to Rebecca that Joseph ran with the news that Jessica was about to birth, and her time was hard. While Joseph ran on for the midwife, Rebecca flew to Cora. But already the child had burst from Jessie and was dead.

As Rebecca entered the cabin, Cora turned with an anguished cry, "And the Saints and Prophet say this is God's way! This spirit didn't have a chance."

"Cora, save your energies for Jessie," Rebecca said sharply. Already the girl's face was blue. Rebecca bent over her, trying desperately to guess what must be done. But now Cora was herself, and she pushed Rebecca away.

Jessie did recover, but there was a scene etched on Rebecca's mind and with it the thoughts that would not leave her. When next Cora and Rebecca were together, she said them.

"Cora, I think sin is much worse than we've been led to believe, than we'd ever guess. I think it is something we can't recover from."

"That's the first childbirth you've seen?"

Cora settled her baby on the floor, and Rebecca took the black Bible from beside the china lamp and opened it to Genesis. Her fingers traced the words, "It says that God cursed the serpent, and told Eve that He would multiply her sorrow in bringing forth children. To Adam He said the ground was cursed because of sin."

"I wonder if we're to take that or if we should just go by Joseph Smith's translation," Cora said slowly. "It gives a different slant. In the first place God tells them not to eat the fruit, and then says that they can choose for themselves."

Rebecca frowned, "He's saying no, but do what you want? I wonder why?"

"Ah, the answers are found later!" Cora exclaimed. "It goes like this; Adam was filled with the Holy Ghost and prophesied, saying because of his transgression he got his eyes opened, and that meant in this life he would have joy. Then Eve said that if it weren't for eating the fruit, they would never have known good and evil and would never have children. She also said they wouldn't know about the joy of redemption and eternal life."

"Then that makes eating the fruit a good idea, not a sin of disobeying God." Rebecca thought about it all and then said, "I had such a horrible picture when I saw Jessie; now I don't know."

Cora gathered up her baby. "Well, I find the Prophet's words much easier to live with. How else do we progress except by working at it?"

"Cora, do you suppose we have this all wrong? Is it possible that the Garden of Eden was supposed to be our home, and that we weren't meant to struggle and sweat and hurt? Right now I don't see all this as better. I can't see progress in the lives around us. I think things are getting worse."

"Becky! We're surviving and creating homes. We're having big families and doing what is necessary to become gods in the next world. We're creating a beautiful place for Jesus Christ to return to." Cora got up. "All our talking and asking questions just makes us doubt and wonder."

"I think I'm going to read some in my Bible," Rebecca said. "You know, for a fact, I couldn't tell you what it really says."

After walking part way with Cora, Rebecca returned to her lonely cabin. As hot as it was, she was glad to build a fire to chase the shadows. She busied herself making a pancake for her supper, when she knew she could have been satisfied with a scrap of cold bread and a sip of milk.

When her supper things had been cleared away, Rebecca lighted the china lamp and settled down to read the Bible. She had finished the third chapter of Genesis when she heard the crunch of footsteps on her path. She was trembling against her chair wondering whether she had latched the door, when she heard her name called.

Before Andrew reached the steps, she was out of her chair. "Oh, Andrew, Andrew!" His beard bristled against her cheek, and she discovered how foreign his hard body seemed to her. "Oh, it's been so long. I've nearly forgotten the feel of you."

She drew him into the cabin and quickly prepared a meal for him. "That spring house is doing its job. You shall have cold buttermilk and fresh-churned butter. I'm glad I didn't eat this scrap of bread."

As she watched him, she was reminding herself, as she always did after days of denying her heart, that this tired, dusty man was hers and for these few days she needn't share him with anyone. Caressing his arm, she pushed the plate of bacon closer to him and began, "I've been thinking, hoping—"

He looked up quickly. "I've missed you too. If the water isn't as cold as this milk, I'd like a quick scrub in your washtub."

She asked, "Are you on your way to Great Salt Lake City?"

He nodded. "Brigham's wanting a report on the Indian affairs."

"There's troubles again?"

"No. Jacob Hamblin's doing a fine job. It's disappointing, though. There's not the quick change we've wanted. Joseph Smith prophesied their dark skins would begin to lighten after they were converted.

Right now a bunch of us would be happy if they'd quit stealing cows."

"There was a family murdered over by Beaver."

"Well, they're still savages. We've got to convert them and live with them, but it pays to be cautious. Hamblin's gone to great lengths to settle them down and make farmers out of them. Now he's talking about the Washington rumbles; says it's making the Indians edgy. One strong word and they'll be more'n glad to dispatch any white man who steps into their territory."

As Rebecca watched her husband bathe in the light of the china lamp, her mind was spinning off on its own. With a tingle of shock she realized how separated they were. For a moment she tried to imagine her conversation with Cora taking place between the two of them.

She handed him a towel. As he embraced her, a corner of her mind and emotions clamored for a touch that went beyond the physical.

Later, when they were moving toward sleep, the words slipped out and Andrew asked, "What did you say?"

"Spirit touches spirit."

"What have you been reading?"

"Not reading, just thinking. That's the way it is." Her voice was tired.

It was several days after Andrew left before Rebecca again thought of her Bible. When she lighted the lamp and lifted the Book, a sensation of foreboding slipped over her. "Why?" she whispered. "No possible harm can come from reading this Book." The quietness of the room held her.

On the doorstep the crickets chirped. From the creek came the chorus of frogs. She looked from the Book to the fire and thought about herself.

She smoothed her hair and rubbed at a dandelion stain on her hand. There was this feeling of approaching God. Hadn't something ought to be done to overcome the sense of unworthiness when she picked up the Book? What if He were to communicate with her as others claimed had happened? As she stared into the fire she forgot her uneasiness. A tingling sense of anticipation crept over her.

The last embers of the fire were winking out when she said, "God, I think I need to know about You. I think I'm ready, but I'm as naked as bare bones and afraid to have You see me."

Cora pushed open the door and stuck her head in. "The mister left?"

Rebecca turned, "Come in, Cora. Here's the middle of August; you know he hasn't been here for weeks." She caught the expression on Cora's face. "Why do you look like that?"

"Oh, nothing." She extended her cup. "I've come begging a pinch of soda. I've got to sweeten some milk before I can stir up a batch of biscuits." Her gaze slid quickly beyond Rebecca as she handed over the cup.

"Cora, you're as guilty as sin this morning. What's the trouble?"

"Oh, Rebecca. I'm sorry. I've never hidden anything from you for long. Your eyes haul out the deepest of secrets. I should have watched my tongue."

"You thought Andrew was here." Shame washed over Cora's face, and she dropped into the rocking chair.

"I was really thinking that you knew his intentions. Becky, I could cut my tongue out before hurting you. I know how it goes. You've never been as easy about it all as I have. I've seen it in your face when you look at him. Don't torture yourself, girl. The only way to live with it is to cut it out of your heart; otherwise it'll drag you down to your grave."

Rebecca was understanding. Through stiff lips she whispered, "You're talking about my selfish loving, aren't you? This clinging to Andrew. I can't help it. When I married him I was completely given to the idea of loving him. I never dreamed he didn't feel that way about me."

Cora's face was twisting. "Don't be that way. None of us can, or it'll cut us to pieces. Why should you have anything better than the rest of us? You've got to cut the feelings out of your heart. There's no place for feelings in the principle." Cora's eyes were reflecting the misery back to her. She muffled her voice against the baby's chest. "Get your chin up. Not a one of us will respect you for blubbering about it."

Rebecca was saying slowly, "She's about to die—his other wife. The thought is like expecting to be let out of prison. I was even thinking about how I could take those young'uns and raise them. I'd do it gladly, gladly."

Cora filled in the thought as if the same thoughts had crossed her mind hundreds of times. "If you could be the only wife." With a guilty glance at Rebecca, she suddenly stood and restlessly began pacing the room.

"Who is it?"

"Priscilla Yost." Rebecca's head jerked. She felt as if her face were turning to stone as Cora watched. "Yes, her. Every young fella in the country's been sparking her. Sixteen, pretty as a princess, and your husband's been sparking her like a young fool, taking her fancy hankies and settin' on her folks' porch."

"They're not married yet?"

"I understand she's going to Great Salt Lake City with you two."

"Oh no, she isn't!"

"Rebecca!"

"Cora, I'll hear no more about it. Marry her, he probably will, but I'll have my say first, and she's not going with us."

Cora was still shaking her head when she left. Rebecca flew about her house and garden. During the two weeks she waited for Andrew, she cared for the garden produce and cleaned her house. When time hung heavy, she mended the chicken house and corral—chores she had been saving for Andrew.

As she stretched wire and rope, pounded nails and stacked hay in her crude barn, her fury grew. Even the capricious cow calmed before her storm, and the chickens flew before her swishing skirts. Weeds were pulled and a new shutter fashioned. She was ready for Andrew.

Had he come conquering and arrogant, she would have cut him to ribbons, but this was her hungry, tired bridegroom. She felt his humble yearning in his first embrace.

For three days there was peace and contentment. Cora's face and words faded while Rebecca was Andrew's wife.

Andrew puttered around while Rebecca finished trying to sew the new quilt to take to the city with them. It would be a good warm cover for those cold autumn nights.

"Andrew, why are we leaving so long before the conference begins in October? We'll be there at least two weeks beforehand."

"Brigham has a bunch of us coming in for meetings with him and the twelve. We'll be standing in line for our turn." He touched her cheek. "Besides, you'll be seeing your friends and emptying every store in the city."

"I only wish," she said wistfully. "There's so much we need. Andrew—"

He laughed, "You'll have your fair share to spend."

"Share," she echoed, her mind busy with the implications.

"Rebecca." He took a deep breath, and suddenly Cora's words dropped on her.

"Yes, Andrew?" She lifted her chin. He turned restlessly, unable to meet her eyes. Was he remembering these nights just past? Could he possibly open his arms to welcome another into the intimacy that was hers? Even as she was thinking, feeling her body respond to the memory of his arms holding her close, the sharp picture of Sarah intruded. Must she again be reminded that Sarah suffered too?

"Rebecca, I'm planning on taking another wife. I have asked Priscilla Yost to marry me, and I'll take her along to Great Salt Lake City. You can be with us in the Endowment House while we take our vows."

Rebecca said sharply, "Andrew, don't forget, I haven't consented."

"I don't need your consent!" he snapped. "I've given you the privilege of going to Great Salt Lake with us. I could take only Priscilla."

"You're to get our consent, mine and Sarah's, before taking another bride; but if that's not easily won, you'll have your passion in Zion regardless." His quick hand caught her across the mouth, and she felt warm blood.

"Rebecca, my dear!" She swayed dizzily against him, seeing his horrified eyes. "I've heard tales, but I never dreamed I'd be driven. My darling wife!"

————

Rebecca's mouth was still sore and swollen, but she must speak again. She dropped the shirt she had been folding and closed the lid of the trunk. "Please, Andrew, may we have this trip alone?" She clasped her hands to keep them away from her swollen mouth. "You know I've counted on it. Please? I understand about your taking another wife, but can't this be our time alone?"

He was studying her face. "If only you would have a child."

"Andrew, I can't understand God. Why does He give us this principle and yet, even while we cooperate with Him fully, He won't allow us to have a child?"

Andrew was shaking his head slowly. "I keep thinking it's our fault. Maybe it's secret sin." His eyes were questioning.

She shook her head. "No, Andrew, you know there's been no sin." Suddenly guilt washed over her. There were those questions she held in her mind. Reading her Bible was starting to feel like a guilty quest for knowledge that was being withheld from her. She had been told to question was sin, lack of faith.

"What is it?" His voice was rough.

"Andrew," she whispered, "I must confess." She struggled with the lump of fear in her throat, seeing only the thundercloud expression turned down upon her. "Please, my love, I've been reading my Bible, and I—"

He threw back his head and laughed. "For a minute, I thought you were going to confess to sleeping with Brother Gardner!"

"Andrew, how horrible!" She clasped her hands to her face. "Never, why he's terrible! Besides—" She stopped, and he swept her close.

"Reading your Bible? Is that bad? You know we believe it's inspired too."

"Once I was told to read the Book of Mormon and stop asking questions."

"Well, you read the Bible all you want. If that's all it takes to make you happy, I give you my permission." He kissed the fingers cupped against his face.

22

· · · · · · · · · · · · · · · · · · ·

The road from Cedar City to Great Salt Lake City was narrow but clearly defined, even the stretch that cut through miles of sage and rabbit bush.

In the spring its length was marked by deep, muddy ruts. This autumn, powdery dust rose in a churning cloud to envelop the light wagon and its two occupants.

Andrew flicked the reins along the backs of his team, urging them up the slope away from the dry creek bed. "There's a pond ahead," he said. "We'll water the horses and rest." He headed toward a grove of willows.

Rebecca shook out her shawl. "Whew, dust!"

"From here on north things are pretty dry," Andrew said soberly. "The crops did so poorly that the most stouthearted Saint is worried this year. Brother Brigham is cautioning us not to waste a grain of wheat."

"I wish they could have had some of our water this year," Rebecca said, remembering the torrential rains of the summer.

"You'd have had more call to say that if you'd lived on the Santa Clara," Andrew replied as he maneuvered the team around a deep rut. "The rain washed out the crops and carried away the good soil."

"Seems the good Lord is bearing hard on the children of Israel. I'm hearing nothing but tales of suffering and hunger."

"Brother Brigham says our poor times show we aren't following the Lord as we should."

"How much more is expected? What new doctrine will he have us into next?"

"If you're wondering, I'll get some books for you to read. Not many women would be of a mind to dig it out for themselves."

"Oh, would you, Andrew? I've been hearing about the Book of Commandments and the Prophet's writings on doctrine, but I haven't heard enough to understand."

He smiled at her. "We'll be making a good Latter-day Saint out of you yet."

"You think I'm lacking?"

His smile disappeared. "Well, you do buck some of the teachings."

"Sometimes my heart shouts out it's wrong," she said slowly.

"Rebecca, my dear wife, you don't follow your heart; you listen to President Young. Might be you need those books more than most would."

"Because I'm rebellious? Andrew, I know we could be so happy if only—"

His jaw tightened. "Don't say it again."

"I will. I can think of nothing else. I can't believe that God intended for us women to live such lonely, destitute lives. There's nothing on this earth I want more than to keep you close and happy. Andrew, why isn't that enough for you?"

"Rebecca, I refuse to listen to your continual jawing. It's been this since we left Pinto. I wish I'd brought Priscilla; then you'd watch your tongue."

Rebecca caught her breath and drew away from Andrew. "I'll say no more."

"And you'll be cold and distant as you were in Harmony. Rebecca, I'll see to it that you'll learn to live your religion and like it."

"It would be a miracle to change how I feel inside." Her voice was so low Andrew could hardly hear her.

"Anyone can change how she acts and thinks and feels if the right elements are brought to bear upon her." Rebecca turned as the cold words hit her, but Andrew was unhitching the horses, and she couldn't see his face.

On the day they were to arrive in Great Salt Lake City, Rebecca spoke out of a long silence. "I've had a letter from Ann. She has my mother's wedding dress."

"Rather late for a wedding dress now, isn't it?" Andrew asked dryly.

"Yes, but there is this need to have it. Oh, Andrew, leaving it behind was agony."

"I can't believe only a dress would mean so much," he said curiously.

"It's more than that. Mother told me to guard the trunk carefully; it was my only hope."

"You think she meant the dress?" Andrew asked slowly.

"Of course. I wish now that we could have waited to go through the Endowment House after I received the dress." He was frowning, and she said no more.

Although it was two weeks before the October conferences of the church were to be held at the Tabernacle, the roads spiraling into Great Salt Lake Valley were marked with a dusty banner as the wagons moved into the city.

Every hotel and rooming house was full, and a city of tents was growing beside the creek. Rebecca and Andrew joined them and set up camp.

On the following morning, a quiet group split off from the tents and formed a somber line of shabby Sabbath best as they headed for the Bowery.

In its pungent pine shade, the crowd was packed knee to back and shoulder to shoulder. A heady sense of anticipation seemed to move among them.

"Good morning, Saints of God's own Zion!" The song leader raised his hand, and the chorus of greeting echoed back to him. "You know, this group of people is the prize of the Lord's earth. Don't let your problems keep you from remembering that you are the most holy people on this earth: the fire of affliction has purged you of your sins, the waters of baptism have lifted you sinless. Rejoice!"

There was a children's choir, and Rebecca's eyes burned with tears as she recognized some of her former pupils. There was Henry Fortner from Cedar—how tall and sober he had become. Except for the mass of brilliant red hair, she would never have identified Alice. The years were passing.

She blinked at the figure striding purposefully across the platform. It was Brigham Young, but his jovial smile was missing. His voice rang out across the building. "All you good people who honestly can say that you are desirous of salvation—no, I don't mean half-interested, I mean you who wholeheartedly want it. You, my good people, if you are now willing to admit an interest in salvation stand to your feet!"

The crowd surged to its feet, and in the pack of humanity, Rebecca stretched to study the faces of those around her. There were serious faces, worn and defeated faces. Brigham was speaking again, referring to the font that would soon be built. "I will take you again into the water of baptism," he said slowly, stressing the words, "when you repent of your sins."

Suddenly Rebecca seemed to be standing alone. She faced him like a defendant before the judge. The words thundered around her. "When you repent of your sins."

The spell broke. The people around her were taking their seats. Andrew tugged at her sleeve. She shivered and slid down beside him.

Heber C. Kimball was speaking now. He quoted from the Book of Helaman. She recognized the Book of Mormon illustration as Apostle Kimball thundered, "When God blessed the people they promptly forgot Him." She darted a glance at Andrew. So he was right. The apostle continued, "You people must repent and be baptized once more."

Her thoughts drifted back to the time of her baptism. How could she be in need of baptism again when the first time had been such a disappointing experience?

She watched J. M. Grant walk to the pulpit. The crowd stirred restlessly. Grant had a reputation as a forceful speaker. With his first words, sagging heads snapped upright. The words swirled around Rebecca. She mulled them over in her mind. Could she be hearing right? Was he telling these people sitting before him to go to President Young and ask that he appoint a committee and select a place where their sins could be atoned by the shedding of their own blood?

Their blood? The words hit her, and she gasped. Andrew glared at her. "Andrew, does he mean kill, die for what sinning they've done?" The line of backs on the bench pressing against her knees squirmed. "Does he mean there's things God won't forgive? And is he saying this is Bible doctrine?"

Apostle Grant's voice was rising again, and she leaned forward to hear. He was saying that water wouldn't do the cleansing for sins; their sins were too deep. Only the shedding of their own blood would suffice.

Now he was talking about the principle. She was hearing him say that there were women in the valley who were rebelling against the celestial law of God. She took a quick look at her husband and then saw other women giving the same glance to their own men. While the words swirled around her head, she looked about the room. The guilt on the women's faces made her realize how deeply the words were being felt.

Again the speaker was accusing the mothers in Israel of trying to break the ties of the church of God and to break it from their husbands. "Be baptized, cleanse yourselves!" His voice dropped to a deeper note. "Forsake your sins. Those of you who have committed sins which can't be forgiven through baptism, let your blood be shed as an atonement before God. I want the sinners in Zion to be afraid."

Rebecca watched Apostle Grant take his seat, and with a deep sigh of relief, she saw President Young go to the pulpit. She touched moisture on her neck and noticed others were fanning themselves. Conversation was a wind-soft whisper in the room, but the tide of emotion was a hurricane. Shamefaced women and somber men stared straight ahead. Andrew refused to meet her eyes, and Rebecca's hands trembled as she patted the perspiration on her cheeks.

President Young began to speak in a gentle voice. From her seat Rebecca guessed she saw a half smile on his face. But even in the beginning there was steel in his voice, and within a few minutes, Rebecca's heart sank. He would not let them off easy. He was following through on the theme that the Apostle Grant had started. His voice underlined the words. "There are sins for which there is no forgiveness." Taking a stance he leaned forward and said softly. "I've had men come to me asking to have their blood shed."

Rebecca shivered as his words hit her. "The only way forgiveness can be obtained in this world will be for the Saints to beg their brothers to shed their blood. 'Tis true that the Son of God shed His blood for sins, but there are sins that sacrifice won't touch. Shed their blood to save their souls."

————

In the warm, dust-laden night, Rebecca lay wide-eyed, staring at the ceiling of canvas over her head. An occasional leaf dropped from the willows and hit the tent with a plop and a swish as it slid to the ground. Moonlight projected patterns of branches and leaves against the canvas. Her weary eyes endlessly pursued the shapes, seeking substance upon which to hang her troubled thoughts. She was recalling the final part of President Young's sermon which had burst in upon her resolve to no longer listen.

He, too, had come down hard on the mothers of Israel who were bucking the principle. Rebecca winced at the memory of the scorn in his voice as he had denounced them for their unwillingness to live by the principle. When he had every woman ready to crawl to her husband and beg him to take another wife, Brother Brigham had let go his final shot. He had told the women that he would give them two weeks in which to make up their minds about the covenant of everlasting marriage. In two weeks, if they didn't agree to accept the principle without a whimper, they would be granted their freedom and allowed to leave.

Rebecca moved restlessly. Beside her Andrew's heavy breathing told of his untroubled sleep. Bitterness frothed up in her even while fairness demanded she not blame him for living up to his religion.

For a moment she toyed with the proposal of freedom. She had no children to brand her as a prostitute. While her heart soared with the thoughts of freedom, shame filled her. She thought of Cora and the others. They would live their religion, proving to themselves and their neighbors that they were cut of a more durable fabric than she. And there was Andrew. A tear dampened her cheeks and she discarded the faithless dream.

In the morning it was possible to address Andrew in a calm voice. Behind the screen of willows, she stirred her fire and boiled her water. The tent flaps were lifted and the bed straightened. He secured a rope and brought more firewood. The dailyness of their life together eased yesterday's memories, and they could talk.

There were the tentative questions, and finally he could meet them without anger, without crushing the mind that challenged his. He could even admit his own questioning, although he acknowledged it was faithlessness and apostasy to question. "Rebecca"—his hands grasped her arms, pulling her close—"these questions are wrong. The spirit tells me so, but I can't shut them from my own mind. How can I silence yours?"

"Andrew, is it wrong to need a sureness inside?"

His fingers traced the shape of her face, and in the shade of their tent he drew her even closer and kissed her. "Then tell me what I can do."

"You said books. What can I read that will tell me what I need to know?"

"You can't trust me to know for you?"

"Do you want an unsettled wife with only half a mind on what must be?"

When he returned with the books, he asked, "When are you going to see Ann? She's asked after you and reminded me that she has the dress."

"There's something fearful and jittery inside," she admitted, "I feel I must know more before I claim the dress."

"What does the dress have to do with you living your religion?"

She faced him squarely and said, "I keep feeling I'll never be married until I'm wearing that dress in front of the altar."

"Rebecca, we've married and we've had our endowments. Isn't that enough?"

She shook her head slowly, and the twist of bright hair on the top of her head tangled in the branch overhead. "Here, you're caught. Let me help you."

As he freed her hair, it tumbled down her back. "You're like a little girl with it hanging like that." His voice was husky as he caressed her throat. His hands slid around her and he held her close. "Tonight is the ball, and I'm glad I'll not have divided loyalties. I'll be proud to show you off at the ball. Get the dress; you can wear it tonight."

She pulled back. "A wedding dress to a common old ball? Andrew, it's wrong!"

"I think you're carrying this holy idea too far. I'm sure your mother never intended for you to place such store by the dress."

Rebecca moved away from his arms, shaking her head. "Andrew, I'll never forget her voice, the urgency—" she turned and walked away.

As late afternoon shadows spattered their campsite, Rebecca hurried back. "It's close to suppertime and I haven't a thing started."

"I'll get my supper!" he teased. "I gave up hope when you got the books."

She glanced toward the stack, "Somehow I'm almost afraid to start reading."

"Shall I fetch the dress?"

She faced him, "No, I've brought the black silk. I'll wear that." She knew he was displeased as he turned away. Why should the dress nag at him too?

The ballroom was packed with people, but almost immediately Rebecca saw Ann. In her eagerness to greet her friend, she didn't notice how quickly Andrew left her side.

The women fell into each other's arms. Old differences were forgotten and excited words tumbled from their lips. Ann's girls were grown tall. Both were married. Across the room were Brother Samuels' other wives. Ann pointed them out. Her graying husband was beside them.

Soon other women joined them. While the chatter was interrupted as a wife was claimed for her turn on the floor, Rebecca looked around. It was easy to spot the social groupings. She was standing with the older women, while across the room a younger group clustered. She guessed they were the second wives. Another group was visible, and clearly this was the most attractive group. It was also the group receiving the most attention.

"Just look at them," Letty March snapped, "absolutely shameless!"

Rebecca looked. "They don't look shameless. Most of them look terribly young."

"That's what I mean—no, no, not the girls. I mean the men. It's shameless to see a bunch of paunchy men old enough to be grandfathers out there strutting like young cocks. And those girls are lapping it up. I'll bet they're being treated to stories about the wonderful farm he has down south. She'll be flattered with a pretty trinket, and he'll march off with another wife on his arm."

"Well, Letty, what do you expect?" Bessy Lang's nose quivered. "It's the principle. No young girl'd marry a sapling when she can get an oak. If you have to take your chances nowadays, better make them good."

"What do you mean?" Rebecca asked.

"Might as well jump on the boat midstream. You could take your chances with a young one, but you might not like one of the wives who comes home with him later."

"Now take Brigham and Pratt and Kimball—"

The newcomer snorted, "Just try; they've about been taken for all they're worth. But I'd choose someone with a little money even if he has a hundred wives."

"Then you don't mind being a plural wife?" Rebecca asked.

"Of course I mind. But you heard Brigham. Like it or leave it. Where does a lone woman go with a flock of little kids? Think of the folks back home. Would they welcome her with open arms? Don't forget, these marriages aren't legal any place except Utah Territory. Far as they're concerned, we're living in sin. Far as the kids are concerned, they're bastards. What kind of a future is that?"

Now Rebecca realized the crowd around the talkative newcomer was thinning. From the sidelines Ann was beckoning, and Rebecca excused herself.

"Andrew has been glaring at you," Ann whispered. "I'd avoid that woman. Everyone knows she's a troublemaker. I have an idea that if she doesn't volunteer to apostatize pretty soon, she's going to have some help."

23

· · · · · · · · · · · · · · · · · · · ·

The next morning Rebecca carried the stack of books to the middle of the makeshift bed in their tent. Pushing the straw tick into a comfortable heap, she settled herself to read. As she thumbed through the books and stroked their covers, she was thinking of the one time she had determined to study the second covenant; yet, despite her hunger for reading, that resolve had never been carried out.

Andrew had included a Book of Mormon in the stack. "Now, he knows I have that," she muttered. Putting it aside, she picked up the next book. It was more of Joseph Smith's writings and, curiously, she turned the pages. There was the Book of Abraham and the Book of Moses. It was a full account of the Genesis story. The Book of Abraham, she knew, was a translation from papyrus given to Joseph Smith. She studied it and then went back to the Book of Moses. When she had finished reading it, she admitted, "It's like the Bible, but somehow everything's turned upside down and inside out." She did acknowledge that it clarified the sermons she had heard about the preexistence of souls and the beginnings of life on the earth, as the church taught it.

She picked up the next book. It was the Doctrine and Covenants. She knew parts of this book were originally called the Book of Commandments. "It is certain," she advised herself, "when I am finished with this book, I'll know what I must know. No longer will I have a need to question." She stared at the book, appalled by her statement. Would she really dare read it?

Words caught her attention. "This is saying," she whispered, "God revokes not judgment. He has woes, weeping and gnashing of teeth for those who are not keeping the commandments that He gave to Joseph Smith."

Throughout the day, Rebecca read—sometimes with keen interest, sometimes smothering a yawn, and sometimes trembling. When Rebecca realized it was getting late and again nearly time to prepare their evening meal, she turned to the end of the book. She must read that revelation, see with her own eyes just what the Prophet had heard from God. Rebecca glanced down at the book. A finger of light had found a tiny hole in the tent and there was a puddle of brightness on the page before her. Was it an omen? Was God telling her how important this revelation was?

Already she knew it was the culmination of the doctrine of the priesthood, the high and holy order revealed to the Prophet. Since it had been revealed to the world in 1852, Rebecca had heard countless sermons on its contents, but never before had she seen the revelation in print.

She found she was holding her breath as she began to read. The beginning words dropped into her mind: "Prepare your heart." "Rebecca," she whispered, "prepare your heart. It says here that all who have this law must obey it." She glanced down at the next words. She must believe them. They said that if she didn't abide by the covenant, she would be damned.

"Of course," she murmured, "this is the new covenant—this covenant makes the other two of no effect. Damnation is the result when it is rejected."

She was nagged by a feeling that something was escaping her attention. She went back to her reading, and the words lined up. Each word seemed to strike her with a greater impact. She argued with herself and then admitted, "If this is the final covenant, it's got to be strong medicine. Rebecca, listen to the words!"

There, "No one can reject—and be permitted to enter my glory."

She quickly skimmed the section that talked about the power of the anointed, the one who held the keys of the priesthood. She knew this referred to the president of the church—first the Prophet and now President Young.

The following paragraphs told Rebecca that Jesus had said that no man could come to the Father except by the word of Jesus which was His law. And nothing would exist in eternity unless it was ordained by Him. This was the heart of the covenant. Marriage, instituted by the word of the Lord, this new and everlasting covenant administered through the church, would last for all eternity.

Now she read that if a man or woman sinned against the new

and everlasting covenant, providing they didn't commit murder, they would still make it in the resurrection. Her heart chilled. She must read and go back to read again before the words became real. "This says that they will make it if they shall be destroyed in the flesh," she said slowly. "Why, that means they must be killed!"

Now she was reading that the Lord promised Joseph Smith that whoever the Prophet blessed, God would bless and that whoever the Prophet cursed, He would curse. Further on she read that any man endowed with the power of the priesthood could do anything in the name of Jesus, according to His law, by His word, and he wouldn't commit sin; Jesus would justify him.

The word *destroy* caught her attention, and she read that if a man in the priesthood had a wife who refused to believe in the new way, she was to be destroyed. She would be a transgressor. "So that's what we'll be if we follow through on Brother Brigham's offer," she murmured. "Transgressors, with no hope of heaven."

She heard Andrew's step. He was whistling a silly tune in the dusk. Sticking his head through the tent flap he asked, "Well, where's my supper?"

She looked at the grin on his face and saw the bemused expression in his eyes. The words of the covenant echoed through her, and silently she got to her feet.

The following morning Andrew pointed to the pile of books and asked, "Have you read all you want?" She nodded, not slowing her task of straightening the tent. After pausing, he asked, "Do you have any questions about what you've read?"

"I'm not certain," she answered as she folded a quilt. "Seems like I need to do some thinking on my own."

"Oh, come, it wasn't that hard to understand."

"It's in knowing how far to take it all." She faced him, and her eyes were searching his. His dreamy expression was gone. She was grateful she had been able to chase those dreams, but she knew he was determined to live his religion. There would be more marriages.

"Do you understand," Andrew asked, "that the new and everlasting covenant is saying women will be saved through their husbands, if indeed that husband is living up to the priesthood and is following all the rules and ordinances of the gospel?"

"Is that what you are wanting me to see?"

"Yes. According to the revelation, there is no way a man will make it to the highest order of heaven unless he has entered into the new and everlasting covenant."

"And it doesn't even mention women."

He reached for her. "Rebecca, I know life is hard and disappointing, but you mustn't focus on the present. Think of all that has been promised us for eternity."

Rebecca was thinking about errant wives, and the heaviness in her heart kept her from answering.

It was past noon when Rebecca finally pinpointed the burden lying like a brick on her chest. She was sitting on the ground, picking over beans for soaking, when the thoughts broke through the darkness of her mind. She straightened and dumped the last of the beans into the pot.

"Of course," she exclaimed, "that's it! I needn't fear or even try to understand it all. That's what they've been telling me all along. I need only to trust, have faith. Remember you've learned that faith is the important thing, the one that makes the difference." And then she thought of obedience. "Oh, it's true. I need only make up my mind that I'll follow through on my vows. I'll let my husband lead our family, and I'll be an obedient wife."

She recalled the episode over Priscilla. Would she really be able to share him and live her life without complaining? She hesitated only a moment before she said, "There's no other way. If I'm to follow the Lord and make my home in heaven, I'll have to trust my church and allow my husband to take me to heaven."

She stood up, "I do believe I'm ready to see Ann and claim the dress."

———

When Ann answered Rebecca's knock, she drew her hastily into the house. Rebecca watched her glance quickly around as she closed the door. Her greetings weren't hiding the anxiety in her eyes. As Rebecca pulled the shawl from her shoulders, she exclaimed, "Ann, what's troubling you? I'd swear you turned pale. Your peering around that lilac bush made my scalp tingle. Indians?"

"I'm sorry," she murmured, "I've just had, well, I'm afraid."

"Of what?"

Ann was frowning, her eyes were sharp as she studied Rebecca's face. "Girl, are you living your religion?"

Rebecca blinked in surprise. "Why, of course, Ann. What's got into you?"

"There's this foreboding spirit. Becky, answer me straight. I promise I'll never breathe a word of this. Have you been writing to that Gentile, that Joshua Smyth?"

The contempt in Ann's voice made Rebecca gasp. "Ann, of course not! I'm married."

"Well, he seemed awful agitated and way overly polite. Kept telling me he meant no harm, but he just must see you and make sure you're all right. He didn't know you were married. Said he's tried to find you down south but no one would give him any help. Seems likely. He looks Gentile."

A strange numbness built around Rebecca's heart. "After all this time, Joshua's come looking for me?"

"Yes, and don't you go looking like that. You're a married woman."

"He didn't say what he wanted?"

"No. You'd have thought he was on a holy mission, he was that persistent. I finally convinced him he'd best stay away if he didn't want a load of buckshot. I promised him I'd talk to you, ask if you wanted to see him."

"But, of course! Ann, he's practically family."

"You was sweet on him." She studied Rebecca's face again, slowly saying, "I had the strangest feelings while I was talking. It was like the Lord was telling me this was no regular call from kinfolks. Rebecca, my feelings tell me he's up to no good, that he's got the power to pull you straight down to hell."

"But there's no call to feel—" Rebecca's quick retort died, and the heaviness touched her again. She was remembering yesterday. Why had she suffered this strange compulsion to read, positive that until she was settled in her mind, it would be impossible to claim the wedding dress?

Now she whispered, "Oh, Ann, do you really think so? Yesterday I was fearfully torn until I settled it in my own mind I would cling to my religion and never allow myself to complain again. Is this some trick of the wicked one to lead me astray?"

Ann's eyes were wide. "I don't know. I only know it makes me fearful inside. Becky, if it were me, I wouldn't risk it, even if he's as dear as kinfolk."

"Then you'd better tell him—" Her voice broke; for a moment she closed her eyes. "Say it's inconvenient to see him now. Perhaps someday—" She turned and said brightly, "That's that. Now let's have our visit."

Later the trunk was carried out. Rebecca pressed her cheek against its dear, familiar lid. Just as she opened it, Ellen and Dee came in. There were more greetings, and then Rebecca must show the dress.

"Oh, Becky! How beautiful. To think you couldn't have it in time for your own wedding. How sad. I'd postpone my wedding forever if such a dress were mine."

Dee—still with shy eyes and silky hair said softly, "I'm afraid I'd never feel married if it were mine and I didn't get to wear it. Rebecca, try it on."

Rebecca rushed to wash her hands spotless and then before her reverent audience, she slowly removed the old cotton wrappings. "It's like a cocoon being burst open," Ellen whispered. "What will the beautiful butterfly become?"

Once the dress was unwound and lifted, Rebecca could only stare. She held the dress away from her to study every detail of the creamy lace and velvet rosebuds centered with pearls. "This is the first time I've had it completely unwrapped," she whispered. The heavy silk grew warm in her hands, the musty odor of age and faint perfume became the essence of her mother. The room dimmed while warmth and life seemed to step nearer. She clasped the dress against her. "Mother, oh, Mother," she mourned. She sobbed, knowing that her tears were wetting the dress, but more aware of the undeniable link stretching across the years. For precious moments the dress was healing the gap and shredding the curtain of eternity.

When the storm of her emotions had blown away and she was again only Rebecca alone, she was left with an aching sweetness.

Now she was shaking her head at their sober faces. "I can't—it's impossible. See, I've dampened it with my tears until it's all a soggy mess." She turned to Ann. "I'm sorry. I've spoiled your fun. But it was as if she were here." She took a quick breath and said, "Over the years I've dreamed of how she and Daddy must have been on that day she wore the dress. More than anything, I've wanted to wear it too. Somehow, just touching the dress—" She couldn't explain, and she turned, shaking her head. Eternity seemed more real.

The little trunk rode back to Pinto with Rebecca and Andrew. He carried it into Rebecca's house and tucked it in the corner under the bed. But he didn't ask to see the dress and, conscious as she was of that day at Ann's, Rebecca said no more about it.

24

....

The winter of 1856 came early and hard. Its heavy hand spread across the Territory with equal pressure. With the crippling cold, the loss of cattle increased. The drought's stingy yield of grain plus the heavy influx of emigrants made the position of the Saints precarious. Rebecca's harvest had seemed ample and comforting under the blaze of the autumn sun. In the dim light of a snowy November day it was a fearful little.

Barely had word trickled through the grapevine, informing her of Andrew and his new bride's housewarming, when the first snowstorm struck. Along with it came the plea to share the summer's harvest with the unfortunate of Zion. Later the frantic plea changed to frenzy, and the reformation was born. The word came from Great Salt Lake that the Saints were to pray, fast, be rebaptized. The Lord was pouring His wrath upon His sinful people. When God is pleased there would be food and freedom from the fearful attacks by the Indians.

Cora was heavy with child again, and Rebecca was filled with anxiety for her. While life had been slowly tightening its grip on Rebecca, paring her to a thin shadow, it was also moving rapidly on Cora. She, too, grew thin and pale, scarcely supplied with enough strength to care for her brood.

Fear for Cora lifted Rebecca from her own despair and loneliness. She hadn't seen Andrew since his trip to Great Salt Lake with Priscilla. Daily now, Rebecca was forcing herself out of the house, carrying extra food down the road to Cora.

One day, as Rebecca was preparing to go to Cora's, she noticed that her mother's Bible had slipped from its shelf. As she picked it up, she recalled her resolve to read the New Testament account of the second covenant. It was the resolve she had made while she and Andrew were in Great Salt Lake City.

She sighed as she looked at the snow drifted against her window. What a wonderful time that trip had been. Then the autumn had promised to last forever. She still remembered the return trip home. The oaks had been a blazing canopy of red, a cathedral of color, while aspen had shaken its gold dollars from the top of white colonnades. Had her determination to live her religion fostered the picture of cathedrals and colonnades?

Rebecca moved away from the window, thinking. For years the Bible had lain beside the wedding dress in the trunk. Hadn't it ought to be there now? On hands and knees, she pulled the trunk from under the bed and opened it. As she was tucking the Book beneath the cotton swathed dress, her hands stilled and her mother's words resounded through her. *Guard the trunk, in it is your only hope.*

Until Rebecca had left Illinois, the trunk had contained two items, the wedding dress and the Bible. Now Rebecca slowly withdrew the Bible and looked at it.

Was it possible that her mother had referred to the Bible instead of the dress?

She settled back on her heels and tried to recall her mother's voice. The urgency in her voice had been real. Was there something escaping her attention?

With closed eyes, Rebecca leaned against the bed, trying to bring back the memory of her parents and the life they had lived together. There had been good times as well as bad. Now the good times were only a memory of love. She recalled that restless time before they had settled in the little cabin next to the Smyths.

There were shadow memories of wagon-living on the banks of the Mississippi. It hadn't been good living, she recalled, and it wasn't only the flies and mosquitoes; there had been questionings and arguments. And it was her parents doing the asking. She recalled her father's protective arm around her white-faced mother. After that time, they moved up the hill away from the river, to be neighbors to the people who had befriended Rebecca that next year when the sickness claimed the Wolstones' lives.

Rebecca clenched her fists. "Why, oh, why didn't I ask Mrs. Smyth? She could have answered my questions."

But would she? Vividly she recalled the troubled expression on Cynthia's face when she had been questioned about the community on the river.

It was cold on the floor, and Rebecca was conscious of a

numbness creeping through her body. She closed the lid of the trunk and started to shove it under the bed. Now she hesitated, lost in a strange urgency to bring her mother close. Would it, by chance, be possible to bring that sweet presence close if she were to read the Bible? She hesitated and then plucked the Book back out of the trunk.

That evening, when she returned from Cora's, the Book caught her attention. She built up the fire and waited for the kettle to boil while she thought about it.

That evening Rebecca ate her porridge flavored with a touch of salt. Just a speck of bacon fat remained, and the flour was getting low. If only Andrew would come. She ate slowly, trying to make the meal last as long as possible.

Her thoughts kept returning to Cora's miserable cabin. Their dinner would be no better than hers. Recalling their shrinking bag of flour, Rebecca murmured, "Cora could be using the services of that young Jessie now, but I do believe they're lucky she apostatized and left the country."

After she washed her bowl and spoon and scraped the iron kettle to prevent rusting, she pulled her rocker close to the fire and bundled into a quilt.

The flickering light of the fire played across the Book, and Rebecca ran her fingers over the cover, recalling each time she had ventured into it.

The scripture she had memorized at Kanesville still surfaced occasionally, but most vividly etched on her mind were the passages she had studied for her pupils' presentation of the first covenant. Now was the time to read the second covenant; could it provide as much enjoyment as the first?

She found the New Testament and then thumbed the pages, wondering where the story of the second covenant began. Random verses claimed her attention. She read, skipped, and read again until finally she rubbed her weary eyes. She rose, piled on a backlog and went to her lonely, cold bed.

The next day a blizzard whited out all except Rebecca's front step. She settled by her hearth, thanking the foresight that had led her to winter her cow with Cora's. While the storm continued to rage, she found it in her heart to be grateful that she had eaten her last hen before the blizzard had come to claim it.

"Well, cornmeal and sweet potatoes with a bit of biscuit isn't much of a promise for Christmas," she acknowledged, trying to shut out the lonesome thoughts of that holiday, "but at least I'll be warm and dry until the storm is over."

The wind was forcing snow through the crumbling clay between the logs of her cabin. She moved the bed close to the fire and, as the cold grew more intense, she stretched a canopy of canvas salvaged from an abandoned wagon. Extending from the rafters over the fireplace to the posts of the bed, the canvas pocketed heat and light. Rebecca settled with her Book and her fire.

While anxiety gnawed at her as surely as the mouse gnawed in the corner, Rebecca turned pages and listened to the wind howl. But the world outside her canopy faded as her reading carried her to the sun-drenched land where she followed the story of Jesus. Occasionally she stirred uneasily to the howl of the wind and tried harder to concentrate on the words before her.

In the snowbound days that followed, every moment not claimed by the task of daily life was given to reading. There was a new something grasping for her thoughts, and she must deal with it.

She added the Book of Mormon to the table beside the Bible. Now twin fingers traced twin pathways down parallel passages and her wonder grew as she admitted the puzzle was becoming more complex.

She was seeing the Book of Mormon in a new light. In the past she had stood intimidated before it, not understanding it, nor even able to pick out the importance of it all. Now she read with a restlessness growing inside. She found she couldn't help comparing the two books. Finally she shoved aside the Book of Mormon and exclaimed, "Oh, why don't they just say something! I catch promises of something, and then it disappears like a cloud in the sky."

She returned the book to its shelf, announcing, "I'll not touch it again until I first understand what the Bible is saying to me. One thing is certain, and I'll cling to the thought, I'm on the right path. I heard Brother Grant has said himself that the Book of Mormon and the Bible agree with each other, and that both contain a true account of the gospel. I can rely on that and I need not fear that I will be led astray in my thinking."

———————

It was late December when Andrew came. Rebecca welcomed him with open arms, and then she carefully closed the door on all except the two of them. January thawed and Andrew joined the other men in bringing in wood from the mountains. Later, Rebecca and Andrew took the wagon to Cedar City to purchase flour from the gristmill there.

Returning home with the meager sack of flour, Rebecca knew their idyllic time had passed. The somber mood of the town they had just left opened the door to the harsh facts. Grain was in very short supply. The snowbound Indian villages seethed with hunger and unrest. In addition to the shortage of food, disease crept through both the Mormon towns and Indian villages. Rebecca moved uneasily on the wagon seat and looked at Andrew. His face was a reflection of the trouble she felt.

"I didn't visit a one that had a happy story to tell," she sighed. "I've never heard of so many people dying in one spot in a winter. The Thompsons' oldest boy tried to get from the house to the barn in the blizzard and froze to death. They didn't find his body for a week. The Martins lost two little girls from consumption. Seems the Lord's not dealing kindly with us."

He moved impatiently, and she was reminded that he didn't like to hear that kind of talk. She studied his face, remembering the time in Great Salt Lake and the resolutions that she had made. She tightened her lips, determined to say no more. But she was guessing about Priscilla. From the looks of his tired, careworn face, Rebecca guessed that the new marriage wasn't without problems.

At home she washed and mended his clothes. Carefully she sealed her lips against the questions she might have asked and tried to keep from thinking of the future.

Now that he was gone, Rebecca's life settled back into its empty days. She fought to regain a measure of tranquillity and purpose.

With her own cabin pin-neat and silent, she went to Cora's where she knew there would be noise, confusion, and work.

Cora's time was nearly upon her, and Rebecca's heart squeezed with fear as she looked from the woman's drawn face to the crowded, dirty cabin.

With chatter designed to hide her fear, with words poking at the woman like boosting hands, Rebecca set to work attacking the cabin with hot water and lye soap.

As she reached for a pile of tattered clothing, mice scurried for a new home. Giving a startled squeal, she exclaimed, "Oh, Cora! if cleanliness is next to godliness, you'd better start practicing your religion." Color flushed the thin cheeks, and Cora heaved herself from the bench. Already Rebecca was biting her tongue. Surprisingly, Cora responded with spunk.

"I know this is bad," she snapped, "but you've no call to

complain. I didn't send for you. It's easy to chide when you've no one to do for except yourself. I'd like to see you with four young'uns and a sloppy man." She stopped as Rebecca turned away. "Oh, Becky, I'm sorry. I know you'd settle for even one little one. It's thoughtless of me."

"It's all right, Cora," Rebecca replied, simply grateful for the ginger in her friend's words. When Cora tried to join her at the washtub, Rebecca said, "Now you go find yourself something else to do. I'll tend to the washing. Use that broom, and then we'll see what we can put together for supper. Is my cow still giving milk?"

"Barely a stream, but at least it's a swallow for the littlest one." Now Cora pressed her hand to her back. "Law, I don't much care about anything. I think I'll sit." Rebecca straightened and looked at Cora. The two bright spots on her cheeks didn't look right, and Rebecca was suddenly helplessly incompetent.

"Do you want me to run for Granny Haight?"

Cora's smile was almost amused. "No, my dear, just relax. I don't go to it for a while yet. By now I know. Just come and sit by me, and let's talk."

"I'll hang these clothes up to freeze, and then we'll talk."

When Rebecca returned to the cabin after stringing clothes on the bushes, Cora was comfortably tilting her bulk back and forth in the rocker. A dreamy expression had softened her face, and she nodded at the stool beside her.

"The little ones are asleep; now we can have our talk. Becky, I miss you something fierce when Andrew's here. Seems our talk's what keeps me going at times."

"Even when we're arguing?"

Her smile was wistful. "Seems a while since I had enough spunk to argue religion. Wanna set to?"

"Right now I can't think. Last fall I made up my mind to settle to it all and be content. Cora, the way Brother Brigham scorched our ears, I suppose there's not a woman in Utah Territory this winter who'd dare complain a snitch."

She chuckled, "I believe it, after hearing you deliver his sermon nearly word for word." She looked at Rebecca. "Does it answer the questions?"

"Well, right now I'm wondering what's really important to believe."

"What do you mean?"

"During the blizzard I read part of the New Testament and some of the Book of Mormon. Apostle Grant and Brother Brigham said there was enough in the Bible to help us live right."

"Remember, the Bible wasn't translated by anointed men. Rebecca, you know that Brother Brigham tells us that if we're living by the revelations we have, then there's nothing to worry about."

"Then nothing's important but what we've been taught. Cora, we don't hear much about Jesus, and there's so much in the Bible about Him. Is this important?"

"You know the principle is the most important."

"More important than understanding about Jesus?"

Cora looked puzzled. "Rebecca, I can't understand why you're agitated."

She took a deep breath, and the words came in a rush. "Oh, Cora, you are the only one on God's earth that I dare talk to. Please don't—" She couldn't say it.

Cora whispered, "Becky, I won't."

"There's all these questions I have. There's so much in me that's fighting against it. Even when I say I do believe, I wonder if I really mean it."

"You're saying you still question the principle?" She nodded, and Cora said, "Yet you're admitting that you understand from what you read in Great Salt Lake that the principle is more important than believing on Jesus. Becky, tighten up the reins. You've seen there's nothing more important; we've got to accept that. We've got to believe it's the final covenant."

––––––––

There was more snow and cold. The Saints were gaunt from short rations; but when the first green peeped through the snow, their elation turned to agony as their stomachs refused the new food.

Cora's baby came, lingered a day and was buried on the hillside that had been wounded with many graves that winter.

With the heavy burden of caring for the ailing Cora, Rebecca was unaware of the tide of life until her stomach refused to harbor her breakfast.

From the burrow of her quilts where she had fled in agony, she cried, "That's all for you, my fickle friend. If you can't tolerate the greens, you'll suffer worse." Suffer she did until it became a pattern. Then she flew to Cora.

"Tell me," she whispered her questions, and Cora's face answered her even as she hugged and kissed Becky.

The littlest one tugged at her mother's skirts questioning, "Ma?"

"It's all just fine." Cora patted the little head; "Aunt Becky is going to be a mama."

It was like walking into a new world. The trouble around Rebecca's heart dissolved. "God is good after all, isn't He?" she whispered. Knowing that her childlessness had ended unshackled a corner of her heart, freeing her from the fear of unknown sin.

She ached to tell Andrew, and her prayers flew upward, petitioning his return.

On the day she heard the horse at the gate, there was no doubt that her petition had been heard, and she flew to greet him.

The swathed figure was a woman. As she dismounted, Rebecca saw that she was young and very pregnant. "You're Rebecca?" she asked slowly. "Andrew said that if I needed anything I was to go to you."

"Andrew?"

"I'm Priscilla—Priscilla Jacobson. Andrew's gone south and it's been so long. I wanted to know you." She touched her swollen body. "He said you'd help."

"You're due very soon," Rebecca said dully, realizing this meant the child had been conceived before September. Surely Andrew wouldn't be guilty of adultery. The Saints dealt severely with that. There must have been a wedding, a secret one, earlier than the public November one.

She was nodding, looking past Rebecca to the neat cottage. "You've a lovely place here. I've been living with my folks, and there's no room for another. They've been tolerating us, waiting for Andrew to find us a cabin, Now . . ." her voice trailed away, and she looked at Rebecca, waiting.

Desperately Rebecca clung to the fence, thinking, *It's because I'm pregnant; she's got no call*. Then the torrent broke. Pressing her hands against her still flat body, trying to hold back the bitterness, her resolve crumbled.

"You've come looking for a home after you've taken my husband, denied me what is mine, to satisfy yourself. Now you want to give your bastard a home in my house!"

"It's not—" Priscilla started to cry, and the tears were streaming down her face. Through Rebecca's astonishment, she felt a thrill of power. Even as she acknowledged the words had been heaped up through the past two years, even as she was seeing Sarah's bitter face, Priscilla's words broke through. "It's not that. We're married."

She straightened and rushed on, "We are living lawfully under the new covenant. You should be grateful. You've denied your husband children, and now I'm chosen to help you in your posterity. Are you apostate that you can't welcome your husband's wife?"

In the end she left, and Rebecca crept to her bed like a mortally wounded animal.

It was Cora's turn now. It was she who came into the dark, chilled room, bringing light and food. It was she who washed Rebecca's face and helped her to the chair. It was her hard words that broke the spell. "You'll be losing that baby!" she snapped. "After all the praying and hoping I did for you, that's no thanks. Now you be setting yourself up to this table and having your supper. Not for yourself; you don't deserve a thing for that tongue, but take it for that dear little baby. Then you get down on your knees and ask the Father to forgive your rebellion against the principle. No better than any other quarreling second wife, you are, taking it out on those under her. Your husband will switch you good when he hears about this, and he will hear. It's all over Pinto. She crept like a whipped dog only 'til she was out of sight; now she's towering vengeance. I suppose they know about it down on the Santa Clara."

Rebecca was ashamed. Although her heart hurt like a well-pummeled prizefighter, life surged back. "Oh, Cora, do pregnant women always act so?"

"Don't excuse yourself!" she snapped, then her face softened. "Yes, I suppose we've all the instincts snarling mountain lions have. You're no different."

Rebecca was laughing and crying. Life broke in upon her fresh and new. But there was a desperate edge. After Cora left, as she prepared for bed, Rebecca dropped to her knees beside the bed. "O God, if You care even a little bit about this little baby inside, help me!" She stopped. She dared not plead for herself.

25

•••••••••••••••••••

*W*ith April came the breaking of ice, the bursting of spring in Utah. With spring came renewed reformation fires, and the Territory rocked with it. Although one of the primary advocates of reformation, the Apostle J. M. Grant, had died during the winter, his fervor lived on. Now the Saints were going again into the chilly waters, being rebaptized, renewed, recovenanted.

As spring melted the grip of winter, it melted Rebecca's heart. Her anxious fears yielded to the pressure of spring-cleaning and gardening. While sun warmed the soil under her hands, the pleasure of new growing things cheered her heart.

Spring also brought a letter from Joshua. She looked at his signature, read the closing line. With her lips forming the words in the silent cabin, she read, "I keep feeling that I must continue to offer you a chance to escape. The burden of these feelings grows stronger." Rebecca's smile faded. "Dear, sweet Joshua." For just a moment she allowed herself to wish she could see him. She went to the beginning of the letter. It was a miracle that there had been a letter at all. She had received it enclosed in a letter from Ann. That letter had informed Rebecca of Ann's reluctance to send it. She had said, "Rebecca, against my better judgment, I've finally told this man that I would send this letter. You know this is the first time he's asked. As I told you, I had such strange feelings when I found there was someone in the city asking about you. When I heard that he was walking the streets, mingling with the crowds looking for you, I nearly had the vapors. Thank God, he has no idea of your married name; otherwise he would have found you without a doubt. Anyway, I finally told him I would send the letter to you, and here it is. I regret it has taken this long to send it to you. Ellen's youngest has been took with the lung fever, and we've all run ourselves poor taking care of them all."

Joshua's strange letter began with a note of chiding mixed in with news of the family. So now all except Jamie were spread thither and yon. She read: "Mother and Father are settled with me in Oregon. The land is fair and kinder to us than we deserve. I would be content if I could see you and satisfy myself that all is well with you. I was taken aback when I heard you wouldn't see me. Rebecca, I come as a friend, almost a brother to you. Surely that is a tie to be honored. I bear your welfare heavily upon my heart. Will you be so good as to write? Settle our hearts with news of you."

Now came the final part. Again she must mull over the puzzling sentence that seemed to poke cold fingers at her. ". . . a chance to escape." Escape what? Slowly the frown on her face relaxed. She slid her hand across the tiny growing mound, and a smile tugged at the corners of her mouth. "Ah, Joshua, all is well." There was a noise at the door. Rebecca got to her feet as it opened. "Andrew!" She dropped the letter and ran to him. From the faintly horsey scent to the rough buffing of his beard, it was Andrew. She pulled him into the room and helped him out of his coat. As she chattered and fussed, his serious face lightened, and finally he smiled. "My girl," he gathered her close now, and only then did she realize the lack of warmth in his initial greeting. "It's good to be here."

Finally she dodged his kisses and held him off. "Andrew, I've something—"

"Yes, I know," he said quickly; "that's why I've come." The frown was back. He folded his arms and moved away from her. "No doubt you're ready to ask forgiveness. If I weren't confident of that—" He paused and paced the room. "Calling Priscilla's child a bastard is just about the most unforgivable thing a good Mormon wife can do. No doubt jealousy—"

"Jealousy! Oh, Andrew, I'm going to have our baby!" The emotion was fleeting as it touched his face and left. "Don't you see," she pleaded, "it was woman nerves. Here I was, wanting attention, and she was expecting me to wait on her."

The anger was disappearing, and an indulgent grin tugged at the corners of his mouth. "You women, you silly little children. No wonder the priesthood can't be trusted to womankind. You'd spend so much time scrapping with each other the kingdom business would be neglected." He scooped her up and went to the rocking chair. "Now," he instructed, "tell me all about it."

Much later he murmured against her hair, "I've got to be going."

Her head jerked, "Not staying? Oh, Andrew, it's been so long."

"I've been to Cedar and am headed south. There's no time to spare." His mouth tightened, and the shadowed expression was back. "There's turmoil across the territory, and it seems I'm kept busy flying from one end to the other."

"But why you?"

His smile was bitter. "When Brother Brigham says go, a smart man goes."

She followed him to the gate. "Things aren't going well, are they?"

He untied his horse, saying, "There's a strong feeling things will be worse."

"What is it? We haven't done anything wrong."

"There's a great deal that Washington thinks we haven't done right."

"Plural marriage? Is that why they won't grant statehood to us?"

"That's a big part. Brother Brigham isn't given to being the diplomat. Now there's his hot words flying across Washington. Already they're talking about a fight. That means we've got to be prepared."

"There's been rumblings ever since we came here."

"There were rumblings before," Andrew said bitterly. "The Saints have been oppressed from the beginnings."

She saw the dark shadows in his eyes and whispered, "It's the teachings. We know what's expected of us. We must be ready to avenge the deaths of the Prophet and his brother. We must conquer and bring all to accept this restored gospel."

"Or send them to hell. We know we'll be opposed. We'll fight for our doctrine, our territory, and our lives." He wheeled his horse and then said, "By the way, you didn't ask, but Priscilla has a little boy. She's named him Andrew."

Rebecca was pushing her needle in and out of the scrap of linen. It was a Relief Society meeting. She and her neighbors were clustered around the long table in front of Bishop Gardner's fireplace. The large room was pleasant with sunshine. The heap of quilt blocks on the table reflected every color to be found under the heavens, although most were only the better parts of used clothing. From the chatter, Rebecca decided it sounded as if these women had erupted full voice from firesides as lonely as hers.

But that was not the case. Some of the women were plural wives sharing the same house. Curiously, Rebecca watched Annabell and

Iris Cox trading thimbles and needles as cozily as sisters.

Rebecca's thoughts flew to Priscilla and Sarah. She knew, with a sharp stab of guilt, how far she was from living the principle. Andrew had done well to chide.

The door flew open and Lettie Harris came into the room, "Why, Lettie!" Rose Huntington exclaimed, "You're white as can be. Are you ailing?"

She snorted, "I'm sick to death of this whole thing. I suppose you've all taken it apart and put it back together. Well, that's what I get for being late."

"The quilt?" Ann exclaimed. "Why, we're still cutting."

"No, no, I'm meaning the Johnson affair—"

"The Johnsons," Mrs. Gardner muttered. "I hadn't said—"

Granny Haight nodded briskly, "Law, the things we get ourselves into just trying to do right." Her voice cracked, and the chatter ebbed away. Rebecca was thinking it must be the Johnsons over by Cedar. The story had been circulating all winter. Granny had the floor now. "That man was doing his best to live by the principle." She was still relishing her story. "I don't know I approve of a man marrying his wife's daughter; doesn't seem biblical."

"Tell me what's going on," Cora cried. "I've not heard a word."

Iris was the spokesperson. "Brother Johnson was wanting to take his wife's daughter for his second wife. They say both women were willing, but his bishop objected. He'd been casting his eyes that way too."

"She's pretty as a picture."

Another voice chimed in, "The council told him he couldn't have her; it wouldn't be fittin'. But law, we all know it's happening all over. What's good—"

"Well," Lettie said, her voice demanding attention, "if he'd just left well enough alone—"

She paused and Rose said, "Then tell us; you're dying to."

"He let it out to the bishop that they'd been keeping house already and after all the sermons—well, you can guess the rest."

Mrs. Gardner said slowly, "Adultery then—what I heard was right."

"What did you hear?"

"There was a bunch through here yesterday. They let it drop that they'd been dispatching a fellow over by Cedar. Made him dig his own grave, and then they just tumbled him into it after they cut his throat."

"Blood atonement."

In the silence that swept the room, Rebecca's thoughts were swirling. Mrs. Gardner said "a bunch through here yesterday." Yesterday Andrew had been home. Unwillingly the thought pushed into the center. Could it be possible that Andrew had been one of the group? Rebecca's hands were trembling against the quilt.

The sunshine had dimmed before Granny spoke, "Seems like a hard lot to live, but if the Lord says we're to do it—well . . ."

"Law," Rose said with a sigh, "seems like things are sure getting tight around the Territory. If it isn't the reformation fever, it's the Legion being stirred up. Heard tell the Indians are being riled up against the Americans. One of the bishops has been calling the Indians the battle-axe of the Lord."

While the conversation moved on to cozy woman chatter, Rebecca sat back and watched the faces around her. There was still a stony lump in her throat.

Cora got to her feet. "I've got to get home to my young'uns before dark."

"I'll go with you, Cora." Rebecca gathered her sewing.

Dusk was bringing out the sweet spring scents and the creek tumbled full from runoff. Rebecca breathed deeply of it all. "It's a right pretty day," Cora said slowly. "Kinda reminds you that at least there's something going on that's good."

"Cora, what's wrong? Seems like everything's out of control like a runaway team on a slope." Her shrug left Rebecca wondering until she saw the fear in her eyes. "You're thinking about that story, aren't you?" Cora nodded, and they walked in silence as Rebecca recalled the other tale that was being whispered about.

One of the missionaries had returned to find that his wife had been unfaithful to him. They were saying that rather than risk losing her place in heaven and her children for eternity, she had allowed her husband to slit her throat. Rebecca shivered, visualizing that young mother sitting on her husband's lap, kissing him while her blood was spilled over the two of them.

The wind was rising. Through the treetops its keening voice seemed like a dirge. For a moment she was sickened. "Blood atonement, how horribly unbelievable."

"I wish it were," Cora murmured, "but it's too real."

Inside her silent cabin, Rebecca moved quickly to stir up the fire, to light the lamp and chase the shadows.

There was one part of Rebecca's mind that wouldn't be still. That part was busy with the afternoon's conversation. That part continued to thrust before her the open grave. From out of the past, words surfaced in her thoughts. It was Jedediah Grant speaking at the Bowery in Great Salt Lake City last September. His words swirled around her, ". . . repent and let your blood be shed—rising up to God an atonement for your sins."

She shuddered. Escape. If only there was an escape from the horror. That word, it was the word Joshua had used in his letter. What had become of the letter? She searched, looking on the table beside her Bible, even shaking it. She poked under the bed and finally settled back in the rocking chair.

The loss of the letter meant only one thing. "Joshua asked me to write, and I've no longer got the information as to where to send it."

Perhaps Andrew. . . . Each remembered word of the letter dropped into her heart. Would Andrew see a pattern of conspiracy, of unfaithfulness in those innocent words? The Apostle Grant's words swirled around her. Repent, confess your sins, be rebaptized. The sins must be routed out of Zion. Joseph Smith's death must be avenged. Rebecca's hand crept to her throat. "I'm even doubting my own husband." She jumped to her feet and paced the room. "We're all being twisted into cruel, fearful people."

Rebecca snuggled her shawl close as she stepped into the road. The rain was falling, dismally drizzling its coldness and misery into everyone. Even the chickens and cows had pulled into themselves in misery.

At Cora's she unwound her soggy shawl in front of the fire. The house smelled of dampness, but the fire snapped and crackled, sending smoke and heat toward the chill.

"Here are the scraps of cloth," Rebecca explained. "I figured you'd want to get them cut before next week." Cora set her toddler aside and held out her hands.

"You'll need to stay awhile to dry out. The Mister's gone into Cedar and won't be back 'til late. Might as well visit until evening," Cora added. Rebecca was thinking of her own silent, cold cabin as she nodded.

The women smoothed the scraps against the tabletop and began cutting. "Cora," Rebecca straightened to ease the strain on her back "who was Jesus?" Cora sat down and looked at Rebecca, "Why law, girl, you know as well as I. He was the firstborn. He's God's Son and our elder brother."

"Then He's just one of us. Why was there all this fuss when He was born?"

"What've you been reading?"

"I started looking for the second covenant and didn't know

where it was, so I began reading the stories about Jesus. Seems there's something special about Him."

"Well, there's the dying. God told the spirits someone needed to go die for people so's they could be resurrected to eternal life. The way I understand it, the only ones who volunteered to die were Jesus and Satan so God chose Jesus. I'd guess that made Him special."

They cut and worked in silence until Cora said, "Also, He's the only one whose body was fathered by God. The rest of us have earthly fathers."

"Oh, yes," Rebecca murmured. "I've heard that sermon. Brother Brigham worked pretty hard to make us understand it wasn't the Holy Ghost who did it. That seems different than the Bible."

"I'd guess you'd better believe Brother Brigham, and quit fussing," Cora advised. "It's sure to keep you from having problems. Why spend your time hunting for trouble?"

"Cora," Rebecca touched her shoulder, "I'm not looking for trouble. I only feel obliged to read for myself. Seems there's this nagging in me since I was teaching the young'uns about the covenant. I keep wanting to sit down and read for myself and find out what the Bible really says about the second covenant."

"Rebecca, there's the evidence," Cora said earnestly. "I've heard Jedediah Grant say so himself that the gospel the apostles are preaching, as it is written in the Book of Mormon, agrees with the gospel written in the Bible; and he proves it."

"How?"

"He says himself that he's seen the sick healed and the deaf made to hear and so on—just like in the Bible. Isn't that proof enough?"

"Well, I guess so."

"It'd make you an apostate if you were to say you don't believe just because it's written up a little different in the Bible."

"But if there's disagreement, if we're accepting something different than the Bible, well—"

Slowly Cora said, "I'd rather believe like they're teaching us. It makes sense to think God'd give us another chance after the first two have failed."

"I don't know enough about the second one to say it's failed. We're taking Brother Brigham's word that it's failed."

"And the Prophet's word, and the apostles and all the others who've testified to its being right. Besides, how'd you prove otherwise?"

"I don't know. But it seems like if a person were meaning to prove it, and if God's willing, then He'd make it pretty plain."

"You're forgetting faith. You know the Prophet taught that to doubt means you don't have any faith. Don't throw away your faith, Rebecca."

Later, when Rebecca returned to her cabin, she looked at the Book lying on the table. "I have a feeling," she said slowly, "that I'm about to throw away my faith. But then, it really isn't much of a faith, is it?"

26

....

It was a glorious day, bright and warm. The high-blown winds touched only the tops of the tallest pines, wafting their perfume down the streets of Pinto.

Rebecca discarded her sunbonnet, rolled her sleeves high and loosened the button at the waist of her dress. "Dear little beets and turnips and carrots, I'll thin you for my supper this evening. Then I'll break up the ground so these tumbling clouds can pour water on you."

"And do you talk to the chickens and the cow too?"

"Andrew, I didn't hear you!" His arms were hard and eager.

"Oh, that's a nice little round stomach you're getting. I've ridden since sunup; come fix me some breakfast." He turned toward the chicken run and poked at the red hen under the bush. "Is there an egg yet?"

"Oh, leave her," Rebecca chuckled. "I've some in the house." She led the way, wondering and hoping. "You'll stay for a time?"

"A bit. After I eat, we'll talk." A heaviness settled on her. She tried to ignore her uneasiness as she cracked eggs into the sizzling skillet.

She sliced a thick cut from the bread and put it on his plate beside the smear of butter. "The brick oven is working fine," she reported. "When the berries ripen, I'll try my hand at a pie. Cora found a raspberry patch above the road to the foundry."

"How's the ironworks doing now?"

"Poorly," she said as she dished up the eggs. "Practically everything the Saints have set their hands to do is failing. Another couple of years of this and we'll all starve. The crops failed, they can't grow cotton or forge iron, the floods get us or else it's the drought. They can't manufacture sugar or produce decent paper."

Andrew finished his eggs and shoved his chair aside. She saw the frown on his face. "Andrew, I'm sorry. I didn't mean to be cantankerous. I mean to keep my 'whys' to myself. We see each other so seldom, and then I ruin it all."

"I intend to remedy that." He took a deep breath and faced her across the table. "I've been taking stock of my life. A man of my position and means is going to have to take some action to pull it all together." He paused, and Rebecca searched his face. "Brother Brigham has called some of us in for a conference."

"The Legion?" she asked, thinking of the unrest and the call to strengthen the military arm of the Saints. "Is it the fuss with Washington?"

"Yes," he answered shortly and added, "Also, I'm going to be married to Alma Whitehead. I'll be bringing her back here, and then I plan to move you both—as well as Priscilla—to Fort Harmony. I'm building a larger home."

Slowly Rebecca began to understand. Stone cold, she asked, "And you intend us all to live there together in one big house?"

"Yes. Several of the others are doing the same thing. It allows for spending more time at home and less on the road. I expect in the next year that Brother Brigham will completely relieve me of my duties and allow me to be a full-time farmer."

"And we four wives will keep your house and line up for a kiss or a good word from you. Well, I'll not go," she said abruptly.

"Yes, you will," he replied mildly as he picked up his hat. "You'll go if I have to hog-tie you and throw you into the wagon with the chickens and bed quilts." He lifted her chin, and his lips were hard against hers, demanding. "I'll prove my kingdom will work on this earth. Rebecca, think. If you can't live peacefully here, what'll your quarreling be for all eternity?"

For all eternity. She watched him go. Now the day was flat. She moved restlessly about, trying to recapture her enthusiasm for the garden.

For all eternity. The futility of it all crashed in upon her. Tears seeped from the corners of her eyes as she chopped listlessly at the weeds. "Why must it be that men don't have it in them to be satisfied? Oh, why must the principle be? Seems all those places in the Bible where it talks about being good to one's wife is really going against the grain of the Prophet's teaching."

In the days that followed, heading toward that day Andrew would return with his new wife, Rebecca's thoughts lined up with questions and ideas, which she rejected as quickly as they came.

There was no way to escape Andrew's plans.

Cora came. "Hear tell Andrew's moving you back to Fort Harmony." She nodded. Cora continued, "Hear tell he's bringing another wife. That got you down?"

"I suppose. More than anything, even more than being lonely, I'm dreading the move in with the other wives. Cora, how do I obey when every part's screaming about it?"

Cora's eyes were thoughtful as she studied Rebecca's face. Her voice was dull. "You just hang on and pray the dear Lord will give you strength. Life's not easy, but you can make it tolerable. The Prophet promised us that we have it within ourselves to live the holy life. Just make up your mind to it."

"Oh, Cora, I've made up my mind to it a thousand times, and every time I fall flat on my face. I don't know how other women handle it, but I know me. It's easier to hate than to love. No matter how much talking I do to myself, I'll never be convinced that it's within me to be different than I am right now."

Cora turned away, and Rebecca was surprised to see the thin shoulders sagging. "Becky, you're no different. I suppose the rest of us just don't have it in us to be so honest. But we try. There's got to be virtue in trying. Every night I pray the Lord will give me strength just to keep a smile on my face and my lip tight against all I want to say. To fail means to end up as crazy as Patty Smith or as mean as Edna or Margaret. The Mister tells me this disposition is the reason women are inferior to men so that they can't have the priesthood. We never get above the meanness of just living."

"And there's no hope."

"There's no hope on this earth except our striving toward being holy."

It was nearly sundown, and Rebecca was limp with fatigue. From the depths of her walk with despair, she had risen on the full wings of pride. As the day for Andrew's arrival drew nearer, she vowed, "I'll not be pitied."

She had looked around the untidy cabin with its pile of ashes and dirty clothing, and proclaimed, "I'll be a good Mormon wife. Andrew'll not be able to find fault and, least of all, that other one."

She had thrown herself into housecleaning—sweeping, shining, airing, scooping up the ash—and baking bread. Now as she pulled weeds beside the path to the gate, she discovered the cow was gone. She looked at the gently swinging gate while dismay filled her heart.

She flew out to the road. "Law, no, Miz Jacobson," old Hank

scratched his head. "No cow's come past here. I've been on this stump since noon." She was off down the street.

Noon? She must have grazed her way up the hill to the line of trees. Rebecca turned to look. Already the sun was gilding the tree-tops with gold dust. There was a touch of night chill in the air. Bunching her skirt in two hands, she started up the slope, striding as rapidly as her pregnancy would allow. She needn't be reminded that with night shadows and Indians, loose cows weren't in the habit of coming home.

At the top of the hill she could see the shadows were already filling the hollows. "Bossy!" she exclaimed as she spotted the cow across the ravine. "It's a good thing you're brown and white like a crazy quilt."

The cow was still eating her way up the far slope. It was nearly dark by the time Rebecca reached the placid cow, now contentedly chewing her cud as she waited under a pine. With relief, Rebecca slipped the rope over the cow's head and pressed her face against the bovine cheek. "Now hurry. Your condition can't slow you down more than mine can, and I'm running all the way home." Rebecca's soothing words were pure bravo; her heart pounded out her fear and her legs trembled with exhaustion.

She led the cow along the slope, peering through the shadows for an easier way to cross the ravine. It wasn't long until Rebecca realized the slope was becoming steeper and the shadows more threatening.

"You were right the first time, old dear. It's back we go. Hurry now. If you were fresh, I'd stop for a sup of milk." She was still whis-pering, all too conscious of her fatigue and the heavy, strange dark-ness surrounding her.

Was that a twig snapping? Rebecca froze, pressing against the cow, straining to hear. She dared not breathe as she waited for the next sound. The silence was unbroken, but when Rebecca moved again the darkness was complete. She fumbled for each step.

Continuing down the slope, she searched for footing as she tugged at the rope. Now the cow stopped and set her feet. Re-becca's frustration broke in a strangled sob as she pulled at the cow.

"Mormonee lost?"

Only at that moment did Rebecca recognize the scent of horse and Indian surrounding her. "Oh, please help me!" she cried. Her heart was sinking as her mind informed her: darkness, cow, Indian. They all added up to disaster.

"Mormonee lost." Now the two words were a statement, and she was beginning to guess she was hearing the extent of the Indian's vocabulary.

"Yes, yes!" she cried. "I'm from Pinto."

"Pinto." There was satisfaction in his voice. She heard a rustle in the darkness, and then strong hands were about her. She was swinging through the air, and the rope fell from her limp hands. No matter. It was all black space.

Through her fainting senses she grew aware of the warm horse beneath her. There was a mild protesting moo from Bossy. Now the Indian was in front of her on the horse, and they were moving through the dark night.

It had seemed forever—the darkness, the horse, and the silence—when through her numbness she heard a dog bark. Now she saw the shadows of buildings. They were entering Pinto from the far edge of town.

Quietly, the Indian pony walked the length of town with the reluctant cow plodding behind. Not a flicker of light shone. The houses were like roosting chickens, tucked in upon themselves, unknowing, uncaring as Rebecca passed through the streets on the back of an Indian pony.

Captured, rescued. Her world was upside down. Security was insecurity. Threat was safety, and Rebecca was defenseless. While her body was still numb, her mind was moving through strange corridors of thought. Looking at the houses, she thought: *They are unaware of this moment, this threat. He could steal our cows to feed his hungry people; instead, he is returning one cow and one frightened woman. I am totally defenseless before him, before the whole world. There's no hope. I'm in bondage through this poor weak body. How desperately I needed him.*

At her doorstep he lifted her down and led the cow to her pen. Still in the dream where surely all of life must be upside down, with chairs on the ceiling and the creek running uphill, she lighted the lamp and faced the bronze man across her table. He was looking at her hair, and she touched the mass that was tumbling down her back, remembering the stories. But his eyes stilled her racing heart. There was curiosity and a gentle peace in the dark depths.

She lifted the freshly baked bread and held it out. "How can I thank you?" she said, knowing he didn't understand. "Your kindness leaves me without defense. I would know how to fight, but to accept your kindness leaves me forever obligated."

Tiny lines crinkled around his eyes. Again he looked at her hair. Now he accepted the bread and gravely bowed his head. He left, carrying the bread as if it were a long-lost treasure.

She sat down before the cold fireplace and in stunned silence watched the sun lift above the hills.

It was while the sky was still pink with dawn and Rebecca was still in the rocking chair that Andrew came. He walked into her cabin leading a pretty girl with bouncy curls and big blue eyes.

Awkwardly Rebecca lifted herself from the chair, feeling every aching muscle and the clumsy swelling that was pushing at the seams of her coarse dress. She smoothed her tumbled hair, still aware of the scent of the Indian's horse.

Now there was Andrew and his new bride outlined against her night terrors. Her chin came up. She refused to see the timid hand extended and the thundercloud frown on Andrew's face. She saw only the patch of sky and cloud beyond.

"Andrew, I'm not prepared to entertain you and your bride right now." She knew her voice was high and singsong with tension. She suffered his startled glance without answering it. "You will take your bride and leave. Perhaps later, when you have built your handsome house, then I'll discuss moving. I've spent the night chasing the wandering cow you should have been seeking. I've ridden behind an Indian who delivered me from the wilds and has been my protector this night. I think he's turned my life upside down. You will excuse me." She crossed the room and, like a felled log, tumbled across the bed.

When Rebecca was able to venture from her house, she found herself drawn irresistibly to the mountain. In daylight, while the insects buzzed and the sun distilled pine perfume, she picked her way through the bushes and into the trees.

From up here she could see the little settlement of Pinto. Life seemed to move in miniature, and she said, "Is that all it is? God, do You see us this way? You are so far removed. Are our struggles, our pain and even the effort of living just little specks before Your eyes? Seems cruel to think You've given us such painful struggles. We're like pathetic bugs dropped in the creek. We struggle while You watch. Yes, You've given us all we need to progress, but must every breath we take be spent in a struggle that takes us one step before we slide back three? How I wish I could be reduced to the level of wanting nothing more than my daily bread and the chance to keep Sarah's kitchen clean. Why do I have this unending hunger to burst something that will allow me to be free of myself? God, how I hate me, how You must hate the little worm that is me."

She walked on. Part of her was terrified at her vulnerability, her empty humanness as she wandered through the forest where she had been rescued. But there was also a part of her alive with curiosity, seeking the unknown.

When she stood, panting, on the highest slope, she said, "The worst part of being human is in not being able to escape human thought. I am a prisoner to all I see and feel. I am a prisoner to a me that I don't like."

Almost she wished she could meet her Indian benefactor again. Was the calm that surrounded him a part of the forest? The sun seared her, and the pine needles pricked, and the peace she sought eluded her.

As often happened in her quiet times, snatches of the Bible verses she had memorized at Kanesville slipped back into her mind. Her lips moved with the words, ". . . my peace, not as the world gives . . ." She looked around. Was there a peace deeper than this peaceful spot, deeper than the tranquillity in the Indian's face?

Those were Jesus' words. John had called Him "the Lamb of God, which taketh away the sin of the world." Now she was remembering the school play at Great Salt Lake City. She was seeing the flames engulf the set, hearing the screams.

She rubbed damp palms together. "Why did I think of that?" she murmured. Lamb. The first covenant. She frowned again, wondering why Jesus was called "Lamb."

The wind keened through the tops of the trees, showering Rebecca with last year's pine cones. There were other words surfacing from that long-ago time and she quoted: "John 3:3, 'Jesus answered and said unto him, Verily, verily, I say unto thee, Except a man be born again, he cannot see the kingdom of God.'"

She traced her initials in the soil with a pine needle. She couldn't recall the bishop talking about being born again. There was another verse farther down the chapter; she quoted it slowly: "That which is born of the flesh is flesh; and that which is born of the Spirit is spirit." Born again, born of the Spirit.

"Why, that's talking about a spirit birth taking place after the flesh birth, but that's not what—" she stopped again. There was that funny upside-down feeling.

A cool breeze touched Rebecca, and she shivered. The afternoon was nearly gone. Getting to her feet, she hurried down the hill.

Cora was just leaving her gate as Rebecca approached. "Oh, there you are. I left a bit of new bread for you and some quilt scraps. You feeling poorly?"

"No, just a little tired. I've walked to the top of the hill."

Cora shook her head. "Come home and sup with us; the Mister will be along late. I declare, these meetings of the Legion are cutting into everything."

Rebecca was shaking her head and Cora asked, "Why not? You can't be doing anything important. I'd be glad of your company. You don't eat but a speck."

"I'm—" she swallowed; it would sound strange coming out. "I want to read."

"What do you have to read? There hasn't been a new *Deseret News*, has there?"

"No. Tonight I'm going to read in the New Testament. Cora, all that studying I did with David Fullmister must have gone right over my head. I'm remembering verses we learned, but I don't recollect really finding out what the Book says."

Cora's gaze was steady, questioning, and Rebecca looked at the ground. "Becky, all those things you were saying the last time you were over—don't you think you'd be better off just forgetting them? Seems to me a person can get too much book learning, and I feel you're right next door to being in that spot."

"Not when you're churning around inside like I am," she replied. "Cora, something tells me I'll never settle down to accepting life until I find the answers."

"About what? Who Jesus is?"

She stood silent, and Cora turned away. "Well, the tads will be disappointed. Don't stay away long."

"Even if I bring my questions?"

Cora paused, bent her head. Without facing Rebecca, she said, "Well, I guess I can handle them better'n anyone. Least, I know you so's it don't bother none."

Rebecca built up the fire and lighted the lamp. In its glow she studied her home. In the single room, the quilt on the bed was the one bright spot. The window was letting in the soft glow of moonlight, and she went to pull the scrap of cotton across it. Her pans gleamed from their hooks on the wall, and a row of dishes made pale circles above the table.

She saw there was plenty of room between the end of the bed and the wall for the cradle. Already kind friends were bringing diapers and bits of clothing.

She dreamed, filling the room with Andrew, the child and herself. He would be holding the little one, cuddling him close in the rocking chair, content to stay by their fireside. She sighed and rolled another log toward the fire.

Curiously she thumbed her way into the Bible, looking through the book of John to find the verses she had quoted that afternoon. There was John 3:16. Love—strange, she wasn't thinking of love in connection with God. Wrath, yes—that thought never left her. She stopped to read the last verse of the chapter, speaking the words into the silence of the room: "He that believeth on the Son hath everlasting life: and he that believeth not on the Son shall not see life; but the wrath of God abideth on him."

Slowly she continued to turn pages, "I wonder where it talks about the second covenant." Finally, she let the Book close as she watched the fire.

Her thoughts drifted, and she found she was recalling more verses. One after another proclaimed that Jesus was God, and she hugged the book to her as she thought of all the implications involved with the idea.

If He was God, then it was God loving those children, healing those people. She thought about the dying. "If He was God, He didn't have to die. Why did He say on the cross that it was finished? What was finished?" There seemed to be no answer to that.

As she prepared for bed and drew the quilt close, she remembered her afternoon on the mountain. "Then if He did come to earth, if that was God, then He's been through it all. He knows what it's like to be a man and be cold and hungry."

During the days that followed, Rebecca found herself caught up, unable to go on with life. She saw her house and garden and the tasks that waited for her, but she found herself unable to lose herself in them. The Bible became a compelling tryst. From it she snatched time to milk the cow and mix a loaf of bread.

Into the circle of quiet in her soul, the words she read fell clear as bells, tolling their measure of meaning into her heart. She puzzled no longer; instead, she stored up truth in her mind.

With childlike enthusiasm and curiosity, Rebecca discovered that the Bible said redemption is only through the blood of Christ, and that keeping the law would not make her acceptable to God. She needed to accept Christ's one-time atonement by faith, repent of her sins, and live by His power flowing through her life. It seemed too simple, somehow. . .

She found the book of Hebrews and read the eighth and ninth chapters. The words spread their richness around her. Jesus was the perfect sacrifice for sin and the ever-living High Priest. The first priests worshiped and sacrificed in a tabernacle which was only a copy of the original in the heavens; now Jesus was finished with His final, complete sacrifice. She paused, remembering the words, *it is finished.*

She placed her finger on the section and said aloud, "So the first covenant was only a pattern to point the people to the real one—to the one that God planned all along for His Son to fulfill." She was filled with awe as she said, "Salvation is in the blood of Jesus Christ."

Slowly she closed the Book. "How can it be possible that another covenant is necessary? This says that Jesus Christ died for all sins, for everyone—forever."

Now she became aware of what was going on in her mind. It was as clear as if she were seeing vividly a signpost pointing along the road she had been following while another sign pointed out a clearly divergent path. At the beginning the paths were together; now they must part. Just ahead she knew that they cut sharply away from each other.

It was a lonesome path down which she looked. Filled with all she had read, seeing the differences in the two paths, she knew she must choose; clearly, she couldn't stay on both paths. "Oh, Andrew," she whispered, "how I wish you were here to talk some sense into me."

27

· · · · · · · · · · · · · · · · · · ·

*I*t was June. The fires of reformation had dimmed; the months of deprivation and misery were past. The baptisms had been redone, and the fever of new marriages had subsided. Life returned to a more earthbound existence.

Fields greened with grain, and the kitchen gardens were filled with peas, carrots, and tiny new potatoes. Corn was knee-high, and the cows freshened, while new lambs, piglets, and downy chicks lent a promise of prosperity to the territory.

In the shuffling back to normalcy, there was a new element that spread more quickly than the *Deseret News*. The Washington problems were coming home to roost, and Brother Brigham was making no bones about his feelings.

"Mercy!" Sister Gardner exclaimed. The sisters were clustered outside the meetinghouse on this Sabbath, waiting while their husbands counciled inside. "I do wish Brother Brigham would just tolerate the situation a little longer. Seems like he was calming down nicely until this spring; now he's spouting words that won't set easy in Washington."

"Where did you hear about this?" Rebecca asked.

"There's been a bit in the newspaper, but mostly it's the men coming back from council with him. After that nice Colonel Steptoe fixed things with Washington so's he could be governor, I figured that would take care of the matter. But, law, Brother Brigham has things fixed so's the federal marshall can't do a thing without him and the twelve agreeing to it. Seems we ought to be working at being extra nice until we get to be a state; then Brother Brigham can have his way."

"I hear that Drummond is claiming we have a secret

organization to resist the laws of Washington. Fussing about the Legion and the blood atonement. I wish Washington would learn they can't interfere with religion."

"They're saying that when Judge Stiles ordered some matters brought into his court for jurisdiction, the Mormon lawyers declined to obey him. Then it turns out Drummond and Stiles hot-footed it to Washington with charges, saying secret organizations are resisting the laws of the country. President Buchanan's fussin' because federal officials left Utah. Now there's no federal officials in Utah except an Indian agent."

"We've got to make up our minds to live our religion or die."

While Rebecca walked home, her thoughts moved away from the conversation and became busy with the morning's sermon. "So Brother Brigham says we all must have the certificate of Joseph Smith before we can go into heaven. And Joseph Smith is holding the keys to the kingdom in the spirit world, and he's reigning there now. I recollect them saying the Prophet was foreordained to preside over this dispensation, just as much as Pharaoh was foreordained to be wicked and Jesus was foreordained to be the Savior because of the fact that He's the oldest son in the family." She stopped. "The Bible said Jesus Christ is God. There are verses in the Bible that say Jesus Christ has been set as head over all that's in this world and also the one to come."

As she continued to walk, she reminded herself, "If I were to believe that instead of what they're teaching, then no matter, there's no way that what Joseph Smith has said can touch me."

She prepared her meal and sat down to eat. While she lifted the spoon, the words rang through her mind. "All things under His feet." Jesus Christ had everything under His feet—all the black frightening things. In Jesus the wrath of God is escaped. Neither the principle nor the blood atonement would have power over her if she believed in Him.

———

The year was pressing past the halfway mark. In July there would be that tenth anniversary of the Saints' arrival in the Great Basin. The year was also pressing toward autumn, relentlessly dogging the steps of the Saints as they worked tirelessly to capture every morsel of nourishment for both man and beast.

Just as hard as the year pressed them, events were pressing too. War was becoming a common word. The *Deseret News*, the settlers' only link with the rest of the world, was carrying an installment story of the Nauvoo tragedy. With heightening suspense, the latest edition was met by eager hands. Each issue was passed around, to be read and reread. Tears crinkled the coarse paper as names were recognized and mourned. The Saints relived the story.

Now a traveling band of actors from Great Salt Lake City toured the towns and forts, presenting the play *The Missouri Persecutions*.

It was July when Andrew came. Rebecca had nearly given up hope of seeing him again. His face was stony. With a sense of detachment, she recognized that it had been increasingly so for a long time.

His face softened only slightly as he studied the contour of the growing child. "When will it be?" he asked.

"I won't count on it until the end of October."

"Past harvest. The house should be ready by then, and you can be confined in your own home surrounded by family."

She felt her spirit cringing. Quickly she asked, "How are . . . they all?"

His face tightened as he watched her. "I suppose they are all fine. I'll see Priscilla when I go to Cedar."

"She isn't with the others?" She tried to keep the surprise from her face.

"Thanks to you," he said bitterly. "She's declared she won't live in the same house with you, and if you can choose to live apart from the others, she has that right also. You rebellious wives make a man's life difficult. I'm fair beat down with handling the crops and building the house every spare minute."

From across the table, he fastened her with a steely glance, saying, "I expect my whole family to be in that house. You'll do your best to get Priscilla there."

"Then you won't be here long?" she asked.

"No, I'm headed for Great Salt Lake."

"Again? There's a bad feeling adrift, isn't there?"

"Yes. If we avoid a confrontation with Washington, it'll be because the Lord intervenes. There's rumbles about troops being moved this way."

"With the new highway, perhaps they'll just be moving through to California."

"Maybe." He reached for more bread. "You bake a better loaf than Alma."

"She's young," Rebecca said absently as her thoughts ran ahead. It was hopeless, this picture of Rebecca taking her place with the others.

Later he said, "You're quiet. Before when I've been here, you've run on like a young'un just let from school."

"Just tired, I suppose." She pressed her hands against the moving child.

"Do you need anything now?"

"No." She fell silent, picking at the bit of sewing she held.

"Do you still fit on laps?"

"Not very well," she said. "Being like this seems to move one beyond the need."

"You're going to be the usual mother," he said, his voice resigned. "It's the child first, then the father."

"But isn't that the reasoning behind the principle? It's the future progeny, the housing of souls, that's important."

Andrew lingered on, and Rebecca sensed in him a relaxing of tension. Lines softened on his face. Despite the sprinkling of gray over his temples, for a few short days he seemed youthful, carefree.

When the day came for him to leave, she followed him as he went to the corral and shook the spindly gate. "I'll plan on coming back before I head to Harmony," he said, giving Bossy a pat on her rump. "You need a bit of attention back here."

The following day at Relief Society meeting, Rebecca tugged her needle in and out of the quilt blocks as she listened to the patter of conversation. It was early in the hour and the thrusts of words were tentative, light, ready to be withdrawn at the earliest threat.

She was thinking of how these meetings had changed during the past months. From a cozy group of women who liked and trusted each other, the mood had warped, twisting into this wariness. It was the pressures, the fears that had been voiced in secret. But she knew the fears must be shared or soon they would become a divisive rope, capturing and pulling them away from each other.

Last winter's harsh sermons with the demand for unity and sacrifice now seemed a gamble that had worked. Rebecca knew it was because the call for action had come down from Brother Brigham. That had given sanction, eased the troubled minds, and allowed the hard doctrines to be accepted.

"Rebecca," Maude Cline shifted her bulk and addressed her. "If you intended to be this quiet, you might have saved yourself the trouble and stayed home."

" 'Twasn't my turn to talk," Rebecca answered smartly. "I've been standing in line for half an hour. See how much quilting I've done just listening."

"Well, it's your turn now. Hear tell that Brother Jacobson's been back and is on his way to Great Salt Lake. Been so long, 'spect you didn't think to see him again."

Maud had a way of getting a person's back up, and Rebecca deliberately thrust her needle twice before answering, "He's been pretty busy building a house."

"Reckon the Legion's more'n keeping him busy."

"Oh, Maude, what've you heard?" Sister Gardner was leaning forward. "My man don't do much talking, but he's looking grim after those meetings."

"I hear Washington's boiling mad over the Legion."

"Law, I don't know how the rumors build. Legion's no worse than the others."

"They're militia. Taken one by one they're pretty harmless, but together—"

There was silence, and for a time the needles moved rapidly.

"Rebecca, I hear your husband's heading up the Legion in this area."

"You don't approve?"

"Law, somebody's got to do it. My husband and every man's obliged to fight."

"It isn't the defending that's got me worried," Margaret said slowly. "It's the feeling that's boiling down underneath. Sometimes ideas catch on in a bunch of men, whereas on their own they wouldn't give them a thought."

When Rebecca and Cora walked home together, Cora asked, "Is it all right?"

"With Andrew? Of course!" she laughed. "Were you expecting him to do me in?"

"Don't joke about such things. A body can't be certain when things are cutting right down the middle of a man's beliefs."

They walked the length of the road in silence. Finally Rebecca said, "Cora, the thought of living out my life, raising my baby under the eyes of those other wives, just grabs me by the throat. I know I can't tolerate it. One thing about Andrew, when he comes he's different. It's not the same man who leaves my side later. If we could be together alone, it would be heaven."

"But heaven's going to be plural marriages. Forever and ever. It'll never change because it's written in the revelations. Becky, you'd better face up. You know as well as I that there's just no other way. Failure means—"

Rebecca's voice was breathless as she said the words she knew so well, "Means, being cut off forever. It means damnation—the wrath of God. It is only through the husband that the woman can be saved."

They stopped beside Rebecca's gate. Cora's eyes were dark, and the worry lines on her face had deepened. "Becky, you're my dearest friend. I wish I could gentle you down before something terrible happens. What if you'd die on the childbed before you reconcile yourself to accepting?"

Rebecca took a deep breath. "What if I were to believe the Bible in all the places it's different from what we're being taught?"

"What do you mean?" Cora asked slowly.

"I mean the places where it says that Jesus is God, and He saves from wrath."

"I don't understand. We believe just exactly the way the Bible teaches."

Rebecca was shaking her head. Inside she was feeling a rising excitement. "No, we don't, and I'm beginning to think the missing link is Jesus. See, if He's more than our elder brother, if He's really God, there's God power in what He did. It says that He died on the cross to be the Atonement Lamb, and if we just accept it—like a gift—then we'll have all our sins forgiven forever. We'll escape the wrath of God."

Cora was shaking her head. "It's too simple. At least with this, I'm living my religion. I feel like I'm doing something."

"You do?" Rebecca studied her friend's face and her shoulders sagged as she turned to fumble at the latch. "Me, well, knowing what's down inside of me, there's no way I can harness this rebellion. There's no way I'll ever be able to face God. Deep down inside I know I'll never be righteous. All I can think about is the wrath of God. If blood atonement is bad, think how much worse the wrath of God is."

She opened the gate. "Nights I wake up thinking. Seems the other way is the only way that offers a hope."

"The Saints'd never accept you." Cora was shaking her head. "I'm going to pray that the Heavenly Father will strip the blinders from your eyes and let you embrace the truth once and for all."

"Oh, Cora, please do that! Jesus said the truth would make us free."

Andrew returned hot and tired from his long trip to Great Salt Lake City. Immediately Rebecca recognized the restless, troubled spirit of him. She drew him into the dim, cool cabin and brought milk chilled by the mountain stream.

As she buttered bread, she asked, "It wasn't a good trip, was it?"

"The mood's bad. There's such a bunch of people ready to kick over the traces."

"Apostasy?"

"Yes, wanting to go to California and let Washington have the place. Doesn't help that practically everything we've set our hands to has failed or is on the edge of bankruptcy. California sounds a little like heaven compared to this place."

"Do you think it's all going to fail?" Her hands waved toward Pinto.

"No. Brother Brigham won't let it. He may be forced to excommunicate the lot."

"Excommunicate?"

"Send the whole lot to hell." There was silence while Andrew ate, and Rebecca pondered the contradictions. Brother Brigham claimed the power to do that, yet Joseph Smith's writings indicated that only the Sons of Perdition would suffer hell.

Before he left for Harmony, Andrew took Rebecca in his arms and kissed her. "My little Becky, please remember we are free. By the action of our parents, Adam and Eve, we have our eyes opened to live. We were redeemed from the fall by Jesus, and that frees us to choose good or evil. There's not one thing in life that makes it impossible to choose the right." He kissed her again and left.

Rebecca was remembering verses in Romans. The apostle Paul recognized the impossibility of doing right without God's help. After making up his mind to do right, he found himself doing the thing which he hated. He said sin dwelt in him.

———

Rebecca was standing by Cora's table. Her fingers rested lightly on the two books. One was the Book of Mormon and the other was her mother's Bible.

Excitement tingled through her body. "It's true," Becky insisted. Cora was still looking at her in disbelief. "I really searched it out. After Andrew left it was so hot, and I was feeling poorly. This time I started in the Book of Mormon. Now, because I've been reading so much in the New Testament, I could see the parallel."

"What's that?"

"Well, for one thing it says right in the Book of Mormon that Jesus is God." She thumbed quickly through the book. "I've read this before, but it never really made sense. Now here, in Second Nephi, it says there's a God and He is Christ. In Mosiah, it says that Christ was the God, the Father of all things. Later on it says He came to live on earth and take upon himself a human body. Later, in Alma, I read there's only one way mankind can be saved and that's through Christ. Oh, Cora, don't you see! It's just like the Bible—almost."

Cora looked up and her face was troubled, "But that's not what they're teaching. Rebecca, you've got to be willing to accept the new revelation."

"But that's a different way to God; that's not through Christ."

Cora was slowly shaking her head, "Rebecca, don't say more. I won't listen."

"Why are you afraid? Cora, this is the missing link. I've always felt there was something lacking. I knew there was no way I could overcome my sins. I've tried desperately to reach God; and now, all of a sudden, He's reaching me. I see such a clear picture of Jesus on the cross—it's like He's closing the gap between me and God."

"Rebecca, you scare me. You're getting mighty close to being an apostate."

"But how can you call me an apostate if I'm following what the Book of Mormon and the Bible have in common and only rejecting the things that conflict?"

Rebecca was subdued as she walked home. She was exhausted by the turmoil that was going on inside of her. Now nothing else seemed important. She dragged herself into the house, ate bread and milk and fell heavily into bed.

Darkness was settling across the mountain valley. A fresh breeze chased dust from the air. She could hear the creek tumbling across rocks in its rush downhill, away from Pinto.

A phrase moved into her thoughts as she listened to the creek churning on its way. She quoted the words, "Consider the kindness of God—it leads to repentance."

She was still feeling the curious flattening of her emotions, the unexpected reaction to Cora's indifference. Had she expected Cora to agree with her?

In recalling the conversation of the afternoon, Rebecca was struck by the brash statements that she had made. Jesus Christ is God. Would that knowledge be enough to sustain her in her next move? She had said she would consider throwing everything out and believing only the Bible. Where would that lead her? What would Andrew think? They wouldn't understand; they would label it apostasy.

"I'm not an apostate," she whispered into the darkness. "I don't want to leave, but this new understanding is important. It's like Sister Ellis said, I have a knowledge and it's important. I want desperately to tell the others about it."

She sighed and turned. There was a nagging feeling of something left undone. Suddenly she realized how seldom she prayed. Wasn't this something to pray about?

She sat up and watched the moon disappear behind the trees, and then she tried to pray. "Our Father in heaven." She stopped and sighed. Approaching God seemed impossible. Would He understand all she had been thinking and feeling?

As she listened to the crickets chirping on her steps, she was remembering that Jesus talked about calling His disciples friends. He said they were friends if they did as He commanded them. What would it be like to be a friend of Jesus?

Could she get His attention? If He was God. . . . "Jesus Christ—God." She paused. There was that picture which had been growing in her mind since she had read the crucifixion story. Those steady eyes watched her.

"Please, I want to thank You for being willing to become a man and then for dying for my sins. I believe the things in the Bible, and I want You to know I don't believe the other about having to keep rules and work for salvation. I don't understand much about You, but I'm sure clinging to the knowledge that You died on the cross so that we can be free from all our sins." She gulped and took a deep breath. "All our sins. I don't have to do anything about them."

She tilted her head and thought: There was that verse, " 'If we confess our sins, he is faithful and just to forgive'—that He is You, Jesus Christ. Please forgive my sins and let me have Your atonement."

The sobs burst from Rebecca, and the years of fear and aching separation slipped away from her. Much later she wiped her eyes and whispered, "There really is a glory. Joshua, you were right about the Whitmans. The glory's a down-inside thing that can't be known except by the one who has it."

There was another verse nudging at her thoughts. She went to light a candle and open her mother's Bible. In the seventeenth chapter of John she read, " ' . . . the glory which thou gavest me I have given them.' "

Again she knelt beside the bed. "Jesus Christ, I adore You. You are Truth. I feel like I've been rejecting so much, and now all that's left is You. I'm making up my mind to no longer believe anything that leaves You out. Finally I can rest easy inside, believing You really are God and Your powerful sacrifice for sin takes care of everything. I'm knowing down inside that I don't need anything else."

When she went to Cora the next day she announced, "I'll never be fearful again. I was so afraid when I started telling Him all about my sins, even though I knew it wasn't anything new to Him. Cora, I felt like He moved right through me, forgiving it all. It was the most exciting thing that's ever happened to me."

"Because you feel so good?" She was shaking her head. "I feel good every time I go to meeting and sing those blessed songs. If it's a good feeling you want, why didn't you say so? I could have helped you long ago."

"No, not feeling. It's knowing I'm no longer fighting what's in the Bible. See, I've been knowing God's talking in this Book and He's talking to me." She paused, "Cora, you don't understand, do you? I guess you've got to be so hungry for Jesus you'll do your own searching. Then you'll discover who He really is."

"They'll call you apostate."

"I'm not aiming to be a troublemaker. I want to stay here and help others see this better way to live." Rebecca put her hand on Cora's shoulder, "Remember, you said you'd pray for me to know the truth."

"But I didn't mean this. I meant the way we understand truth."

"Two truths in conflict means that one of them isn't truth."

28

....

$\mathcal{R}$ebecca tapped on the doorpost of Cora's cabin. "Cora, stir yourself. Relief Society will take up in another fifteen minutes."

"Come in." Cora's voice was dispirited. As Rebecca entered the house, she rose slowly from her chair.

"Ah, Cora, you're feeling poorly, aren't you?"

"Just seems like the world's a-setting on my shoulders today."

"The Mister? The young'uns look fine. Is it Jessie again?"

"No. We haven't heard another thing since she hightailed it to Great Salt Lake. There'll be plenty of talk at Relief Society." As they stepped out into the bright July sunshine, Cora glanced sharply at Rebecca.

"What's the matter?" Rebecca asked, patting her hair.

" 'Tisn't your hair. I was just wondering . . ." her voice trailed into silence.

"You're looking to see if I still mean all those things I said. Cora, I do. The rightness of it all is growing on me."

"You'd better be quiet about this. If they don't think you're apostate, they'll think you're crazy."

Rebecca turned and squeezed Cora. "Oh, Cora, I wish I could help you see it. Like today. Somehow these worries don't touch me the same."

"Well, they'd better. They'll touch when you have to tuck that little baby under your arm and run before Buchanan's troops."

"It's getting worse."

She sighed, "Sometimes I just wish Brother Brigham would use a little more discretion and not do so much talking, especially to Washington."

"What's he said now?"

"Oh, he's riled because of all these reports that've been hitting Washington. Now he's saying if Washington sends troops in here, we'll slay them."

"But we're still only a territory and under Washington's control."

"You go remind Brother Brigham of that! And to cap it all, I hear that Brother Kimball's promised to fight until he doesn't have a drop of blood left."

" 'Tis a pity these federal men had to spread gossip." Rebecca searched her friend's face, noting the lines that deepened day by day. The pity welled up in Rebecca, and she wanted to bundle up her new joy and dump it on Cora. Instead she said, "I don't think you should fret. You know there's been a heap of talk all winter, and it's come to naught."

They reached the Gardners and Cora said, "Just the same, I can feel something in the air."

The quilt frame was set up, and the women clustered around it. The quilting was moving toward the outer edges, and those like Rebecca and Granny with mounding waistlines or arthritic backs could sit comfortably.

It was a poor quilt Rebecca admitted. Its worn fabric and uneven filling had been salvaged from bits and pieces the women contributed. She could also admit the value of the quilt lay not in the promise of warmth, but instead in the stitching together of the lives of the women in the room.

Margaret moved down the bench to make room for Rebecca. "You're looking mighty fine for it being the end of July and you carrying that load. You just wait, come the seventh or eighth young'un, you won't be so proud of it all."

"My, as hard as I had to work to get this one, I doubt there'll be that many."

"Could be. There won't be enough of that man to go around the way he's marryin'."

"Now, Margaret," Cora chided hastily, "he hasn't taken any since Alma."

"No, but he's casting sheep's eyes at Linda Seelands."

"So's every man in the territory. Never you mind what she says, Becky."

Wondering what gossip had escaped her, Rebecca said, "Well, if he's planning on taking more, he'll have to work harder on that house he's building. Seems the building isn't keeping up with the marrying."

"You'll be moving to Harmony?"

Rebecca sighed, "I'm afraid so. But not if I'm allowed to have my say."

"Law, girl, I'll have to teach you how to give a man a scotch blessing. There's ways to get them to wantin' what you want."

"Well, with this new trouble with the army, I suppose all the men'll have more pressing things to do 'sides marrying."

"Oh, Sister Gardner, you have news?"

"Well"—she settled herself back in the chair and folded her hands—"seems most of Great Salt Lake City as well as people clear down to the Utah Lake were up in the mountains, camping out and having a big time celebrating."

"Why in the mountains?"

"Heat. Been terrible there this summer. No wonder people's tempers are short."

"What they celebrating?"

"Oh, law, how could you forget? It's the tenth anniversary since Brigham Young came into the valley and said, 'This is the place.' "

"I wish he'd slept through that part of the trip 'til they hit California."

"Now don't you say that," Granny chided. " 'Twas the place the Lord showed."

"Well, you never mind," Mrs. Gardner said impatiently, "That's water under the bridge. You're ruining my story. Well, they just got set into having a good time when a bunch rode up from the city, coming like their coattails were afire. In no time Brother Brigham announced President Buchanan had dispatched troops from Fort Leavenworth, Kansas. Well, that ended the celebrating. Brother Brigham took action in a hurry. He's sent the Legion across the mountains to raid the army. Those fellows are taking this mighty serious, thanks to Brother Brigham."

"And then—" She was prompted from the far side of the quilt.

"The Saints went back to Great Salt Lake City and got busy."

"Oh, law!" came the anguished wail from the other end of the quilt. "We can't fight them, that's—"

"Treason?"

"Then you'd better believe the Legion'll come up with an idea in a hurry."

"Well," Mrs. Gardner continued, "right now they're busy. They've moved all the important documents south. All the women, children, and the livestock have gone, too. The men took straw and stuffed the houses full of it. When Buchanan's troops move in to take over, they're going to see the whole city go up in smoke."

During the weeks that followed, the indignation and anger shared at the Relief Society meeting became the growing mood of the whole community.

In August, Apostle Richards sent word to the men serving under him in the Nauvoo Legion that they were to report without delay any person found to be either wasting grain or allowing it to pass into the hands of Gentiles passing through the territory. By mid August every able-bodied man in the militia was taking part in daily drills.

Rebecca was seeing Andrew more often now, although his visits were quick stops as he moved between his farm in Fort Harmony and Cedar City where most of his men lived. Most often he arrived late at night, tired and short-tempered, wanting only rest and food. His answers to her questions were short and terse.

One morning he faced her across the table and said, "Look, Rebecca, this is getting to be very serious. You are in no condition to be alone. Either you settle things between you and Priscilla and have her here, or I'll hog-tie the two of you and take you to Fort Harmony. You can stay in the barn if you can't tolerate living with the others."

"Andrew," she swallowed, "you wouldn't—"

"There's whispers also," he continued, forcing her to look at him. "I've heard mention your name and the word apostate. What's the link?"

"Apostate." Her thoughts flew to Cora. She had said that word. She had warned Rebecca to be careful. Those women at Relief Society? "Andrew," she faced him squarely, "Cora warned that people would think me strange, but, honestly, I'm not rebelling. I'm simply living my religion to the fullest"—her voice deepened as she stressed the word—"just the way Joseph Smith explained it."

"What are you saying?"

She took a deep breath. "Shall I show you the passages in the Book of Mormon?"

"No, only tell me what you mean. I trust you'll not distort his words."

"He says that there's only one God, and that Jesus Christ is our God, come to earth to die for our sins. He says there's no other way to obtain salvation except through Jesus Christ."

He studied her face. "Why should that rate you the name of apostate?"

"Don't you see what it means? Jesus Christ is God, He is our atonement—the great and only atonement. He is also High Priest forever, giving out that atonement to us. He forgives us every sin we commit if we ask. He says He will be our friend if we obey His commandment to love." She smiled and lifted her hands, "Andrew, I'm not finding that hard!"

He was frowning. "Go on."

"You sense that isn't all?" She clasped her trembling hands together and said, "This atonement delivers us from the wrath of God forever. Now you understand, don't you? Joseph Smith said we're damned if we don't live by the everlasting covenant once we hear about it. Brother Brigham said there are sins that the blood of Christ can never atone. According to what Brother Joseph Smith said first and according to the Bible, that's not so."

Moving impatiently, he said, "You've forgotten, Rebecca. Brother Brigham has clearly stated that God's revelation is a changing revelation. We must live by the very last revelation that we have received, and all these things you've been saying are replaced by later revelations."

She was frankly trembling. "Andrew, in the writings of Joseph Smith, it says God is unchangeable. If Jesus Christ is God, the power of His atonement can't be less than the everlasting covenant of marriage." He was staring at her, but his eyes seemed to focus beyond her.

"That means," she continued softly, "that we are free—free from fear of damnation and wrath through Him. We're free from—" She couldn't finish the statement. It would break everything that bound her to this man. He was turning away from her, unseeing, unhearing.

In the days that followed, while the trouble swirled about the territory, the word *freedom* captured Rebecca and claimed her attention. While she sewed and baked and scrubbed, while she attended Sabbath worship and listened to the storm of war talk, the word moved through her being with a cadence of its own.

"Free," her mind called, while the words from the pulpit reminded the people they were to avenge God of His enemies; Zion must stand against the world.

Now more often there were Indians in the streets of Pinto. Rebecca was hearing them called "the battle-axe of the Lord." Rumor was that Brother Brigham was saying the Indians would have to help the Mormons or the United States would kill them all. And in the midst of it, Rebecca recalled that Jesus had talked about loving our enemies.

Enemies. Into the turmoil of her thoughts came a new thought: Priscilla.

Shame flooded her as she recalled the words she had flung at Priscilla. As quickly as she stuffed the troublesome thoughts from her, they returned to haunt her.

On one of the days that Rebecca escaped to Cora's busy household to avoid her own troublesome thoughts, Cora dragged out their bone of contention.

"I've been doing lots of thinking about all the things you've said. You can't be right. There's all the things that prove God's with us."

"Like what?"

"God's proved He's been helping us right along. There's the miracles, the healings. Surely that proves we're right. There's the seagulls helping when the crickets got the wheat. Now, Rebecca, what'll you say to that?"

"Those things stopped me for a long time. And then with this churning around inside, I finally had to admit what I was reading. It was like God was drawing His finger under the words.

"Cora, you judge the dress by the whole, not by the fancied-up parts. No matter what, it's all got to start out right. You have to have something to measure truth by. More than ever I'm convinced it's Jesus. If you don't understand about Him—about His being God and being down here for just one reason and that was being the Lamb for our atonement—well, then, nothing else in God's Word falls into place. It's nothing, it's empty, without God's power.

"I couldn't get anywhere thinking He was just an elder brother. The Bible doesn't support that." Cora was shaking her head, but Rebecca went on, "You can't see Jesus in heaven, being our High Priest, serving before the altar that's stained with His own blood? You can't see Him really loving you and caring about what happens to you and helping you live like He wants? Then I'll have to do what you did for me."

"What's that?"

"Pray that God will help you find the truth."

———

The beginning of September saw Rebecca's harvest doing well. The corn and potatoes and onions were nearly ready. The beans were drying on the vines. She would dig carrots while it was still possible to bend that far.

Her little house was being prepared for winter and its small new occupant. She had the cradle brought from the barn and scrubbed it until it was white. In her chest there was a pile of little clothes. A shelf held folded diapers, old but soft.

Andrew surveyed her preparations without comment, but he brought her a sack of flour, and she sighed with relief. Could this battle be counted as won? Would she be allowed to stay? The lines about his eyes were taut. She thought he looked thin, bowed; she busied herself caring for him.

But when he was gone, she came up against that softly whispered name in her conscience. Finally she threw her hands wide in surrender and asked, "Jesus, what are You wanting me to do about Priscilla?"

There it was out, admitted, and the relief was great. The words welled up in her memory: "If your brother has ought—" These were Jesus' words. She whispered, "I suppose that means 'sister' too?"

It was a fine, clear day when she went to Cora with her request.

"Horse? You want to borrow my horse?" Cora cried, "Rebecca, you are out of your mind for sure. You in nearly your last month and wanting to ride a horse. Where do you want to take her that you can't just walk?"

"Cedar."

"Oh, glory be." She groaned, and Rebecca was feeling like a six-year-old. But explanations wouldn't do. Then Cora would know most certainly that she was crazy.

In the end, the horse was lent, and after collecting her shawl and a ripe melon from the garden, Rebecca set out.

The horse was old and inclined to take life easy. But then Rebecca was inclined to take life easy, especially today. The brilliance of the early autumn day was just a beginning hint of the month to come. She saw a touch of yellow in the cottonwoods along the creek.

Turning onto the road leading to Cedar City, she murmured, "I'd forgotten the brilliance of the coral hills against the blue sky and dusty cedars. It's a glory, most certainly. Jesus Christ, You made it."

Not a cloud marred the sky; not a soul moved on the barren plains. For once she appreciated the wide scope of the desert. Not even an Indian could hide in that barren waste.

29

· · · · · · · · · · · · · · · · · · ·

$\mathcal{I}$n the middle of the afternoon, Rebecca's horse reached Cedar City. As if now aware of a need to look smart, he cantered briskly through the streets. As she turned toward the Morgans' new cabin, Rebecca was seeing how the community had grown. It was spilling away from the fort like chicks bent on adventure, not safety.

She was looping the reins over the fence in front of the Morgans' house when Sister Morgan flew out the door. "Rebecca! I'd recognize that hair anywhere, but not the shape you're in." She hugged her and said, "Come in. You've had a long ride from Pinto. I've some buttermilk chilling and a bit of light bread."

Rebecca looked around the silent house. "Where's everyone?"

The look Mrs. Morgan gave Rebecca was long and hard. "It's the troubles. Aren't they laying you out with the sermons? Well, the men are in the fields working their heads off to get the crops in. The young'uns are right 'long side."

"Well, the talk's been pretty strong."

She nodded and answered, "Brother George Smith's been preaching to scorch us all."

"The men need to be prepared to protect us. Who knows what Washington—"

"Yes, but he don't need to get them riled up like a band of avenging angels." She studied Rebecca, "Do you know his other one's living in the fort? I hear you two don't get along."

"I suppose she's told it all." Mrs. Morgan was nodding, and Rebecca confessed, "Well, I have to go make it right. I can't live with myself."

"She's bound to notice that you're worse off than she is," Sister Morgan said dryly. "These slips of the lip are hard to live with. Child,

I don't expect much of a welcome for you. Better come back here for the night. The afternoon's well spent, and 'tisn't safe to be abroad after dark these days."

She was silent for a moment while she refilled Rebecca's cup. "I recall some stories. You and Priscilla aren't the only scrapping females in Zion."

The milk was refreshing and Rebecca was loath to move. "What did you hear?"

"Fellow over by Parawan took a second one against the wishes of the first, and did the first wife have a time! She wouldn't have them in the house, so she found a dinky little place and just moved their stuff in while they were gone. They had to come home late at night and set up the bedstead before they could go to bed. She keeps her eyes on them, though. If they don't get up early 'nough in the morning to suit her, she throws rocks at their roof."

At last Rebecca could no longer delay. She bid Sister Morgan a reluctant farewell and walked toward the fort.

"Sure, we know where Mrs. Jacobson lives." The trio of little boys marching in the center of the fort were carrying sticks over their shoulders. They halted their maneuvers long enough to point the way, and then they followed her.

"Priscilla, I've come—" Rebecca hesitated and studied the closed face of the woman facing her. She had changed almost beyond recognition, and Rebecca's heart squeezed with pity even as she was wondering if the principle were making a sharp-faced old woman out of her also. Priscilla pushed the disheveled hair away from her face and shifted the toddler to the other hip. Her soiled frock was straining across her middle and Rebecca was guessing five months were gone on her.

"If you've come looking for Andrew, he's not here. He's been back and forth, but he's too busy training these men to have any time for woman problems."

"No, it's you I've come to see."

Priscilla looked at the trio of miniature soldiers. Silently she stepped back and allowed Rebecca to enter the house.

Age hadn't improved the poor fort. Fallen chinking admitted the sunlight in bars across the table and the bed. She saw the floor was uneven and splintery. Now Rebecca understood why the child was crying. There was a festering sliver in his leg. "Do you want me to help you?" She pointed to the leg.

Priscilla looked surprised. "I'd be obliged. I tried to get it out yesterday."

"Needs a good scrub with lye soap." Rebecca pressed while the child screamed.

"I'd never expected you to be doing this after what you said."

"Priscilla, I'm sorry. God has guilted me with that scene so many times. Now I see the real me, and I squirm with embarrassment and shame. Please forgive me?"

"Andrew didn't make you come?"

"He doesn't tell me what to do—not much."

"You're brave risking it all with a few hot words." She was sober.

"Well, aren't you doing the same?"

She shook her head. "Not no more. Andrew laid it to me and made me see how's otherwise I couldn't expect to have an eternity except as his or somebody's slave. Rebecca, no woman can make it without her husband's say so." There were dark shadows in her eyes, and impulsively Rebecca took her arm.

"Listen, Priscilla, that isn't so, and I want you to know about it. Please, will you move to Fort Harmony when Andrew finishes the house? I know it won't be pleasant living with the other wives. I know, because I've gone through it. But I want you to know there's a hope that doesn't have anything to do with the principle. I see the fear in your eyes, and it's just like the fear I was feeling until this summer."

There was a sound behind Rebecca, and she was suddenly conscious that the doorway had been darkened for some time. Andrew stepped across the threshold.

"I never expected to see the two of you together." He lifted the child while his eyes pierced Rebecca. "What are you doing here?"

"I've come to see Priscilla."

"She's sorry for calling Andy a bastard. That's good, isn't it?"

Andrew's eyes shifted to Priscilla, and Rebecca watched her shrink away. "I guess you'll be wanting supper, won't you?"

He looked at Rebecca. "That the only reason you've come? Isn't it a risk this late in your time? Where are you staying tonight?"

"Mrs. Morgan has asked me to stay with them."

"I heard you say you'd move to Fort Harmony."

She glanced at Priscilla, wondering how much more he had heard. "Yes, Andrew, I'll come as soon as you're ready for me." From outside came the sound of laughter and the clanging of metal.

Andrew glanced toward the door. "The fellows are gathering for drill."

"They're going to put a hole in that water bucket if they don't leave it alone," Priscilla said heavily as she took the child from Andrew.

"Come, I'll take you to the Morgans." Andrew got to his feet and Rebecca nodded.

They were walking toward the gate of the fort when Andrew cocked his head. "Someone's riding a horse awful hard," he muttered.

A cry came from the street, "Is Brother Jacobson around?" Rebecca hurried to keep up with Andrew. A red-faced man jumped off his horse.

There was a sharp edge of anger in the man's voice which revealed more than his muffled words. As they reached him, he said, "They're heading this way. They're bound for California, and it sounds like Hamblin had given them permission to graze in Mountain Meadows. What's the matter with him? Let's speed them on their way."

Andrew's voice cut in. "Calm down and tell me what's going on."

"It's a bunch called the Fancher party. Gentiles from Missouri way." There was a low growl, and Rebecca thought of the play she had seen.

A chill touched her as she heard, "There's no way we can sell them grain or anything without Brother Brigham gettin' down on us."

Another voice cried, "Well, the train's come through every town looking for grain and grazing. The Saints are keeping them moving right sharp."

"Tell Jacobson about them namin' their oxen Brigham Young and Heber C. Kimball."

"Maybe our prayers are about to be answered."

"What do you mean?"

"Haven't we been asking for the Lord to avenge the blood of the Prophet?"

"But these are emigrants!" Rebecca cried out; "they didn't have anything to do with the Prophet's death." The men turned to look at her, and there was silence.

The rider spoke up. "Don't be too sure. They said they're from Missouri. Some's boasting about being around when the Prophet was murdered."

"I heard a guy over the other side of the mountains gave a bunch of onions to one of them, and a brother took a board to the side of his head for doin' it."

"We gotta listen to council. Brother Brigham says he'd rather see the grasshoppers get the grain than the Gentiles."

Rebecca turned and walked away from the fort. When she reached the cabin, Sister Morgan exclaimed, "Law, girl, you look as if you've seen a ghost!"

While Rebecca rested, she told all she had heard, slowly concluding, "I've never seen men like this. It was like they were building up to a frenzy."

"Rebecca, 'tis a fever and there's no calming a man when he's in it."

"How do you get them to stop and understand how those people must feel?"

"Rebecca, you best be quiet and not say another word about it. There's been enough going on around the territory. If there's the slightest whisper of people not being together—" She awkwardly patted Rebecca's shoulder.

Rebecca was thinking about Andrew, remembering the tender moments, the tender touch. "He can't do it," she whispered. "It isn't in Andrew to be harsh with anybody."

"You don't know what's in a man when he must live his religion."

"Living his religion! There's all those things that's been whispered—"

"Blood atonement? avenging the Prophet?"

"They've got to be made to think."

Mrs. Morgan took Rebecca's arm. "I'll not let you waste yourself—that's what you'd be doing. Stay here and we'll take care of that little babe."

Rebecca's arms circled the roundness. "You're right. I must think of my baby. I've risked him too much today."

"Besides, they'll be out in the fields with their guns; then they'll be at the ward listening to more talk. Just stay out of it, Rebecca, or you'll get us all in trouble."

Later that last sentence drifted through her thoughts before Rebecca slipped into sleep, tucked securely under a soft quilt in the far corner of the Morgans' loft.

When the rumble of voices from the street below awakened Rebecca, it was very late. She lay listening. A thin, angry voice rose above the others.

"I've been shoved from my home for the last time. I'm suspicious of anything that smells Gentile, and I don't feel inclined to sit around and wait. We know the army's moving this way. How do we know this bunch isn't sent to feel out the country and see how we're prepared?"

"I say let's sic the Indians on 'em," came another voice. "They've been spoiling for a good fight, and all they'll want is the cattle." The voices dropped to a whisper.

Now there was the sound of boots moving down the boardwalk. Rebecca had just turned to sleep when she heard, "I don't think Irving's with us. Too much a Gentile lover."

"There's ways to bring him in line."

"I've my doubts, too. Don't know's I've got the knowledge of it yet. But I know I can't go against the council. I'll have to let them be my conscience for me."

"Brother, you're seeing right." More steps rang against the boards. Beneath her a door closed, and the floor squeaked under Brother Morgan's weight.

Sleep was gone. While the moon moved slowly, Rebecca found it impossible to silence her mind. There was the picture of the wagon train, those innocent faces and cracking whips. Heber and Brigham. Hasty words, wasted lives.

While she shuddered against the straw tick and wished for daylight, new thoughts widened in their circles, overlapping the first thoughts and painting smooth lines of responsibility against the outer edges of her being.

She nearly regretted the Word of God which she had fed into her mind with tireless efficiency. Twisting her head against the pillow, a moment's bitterness questioned, *Did you ever guess that, once placed, the Word would never leave you? To ignore it now, after having taken of that grace eagerly with both hands wide and grasping is to ignore not only responsibility but it is to ignore God—that God with the searching eyes and the loving touch. Jesus with the scars on face and hands.*

"There is a glory," she whispered, contemplating that face. The words of Jesus came through her lips. "The glory thou gavest me, I have given them." She took a deep breath and whispered, "Jesus, I can't risk losing that glory. Now I think I know how the Whitmans felt."

At breakfast the next morning Brother Morgan said sharply, "Sister Jacobson, you've picked at the problem of the wagon train with more appetite than you've hit your porridge. Can't you get it through that pretty little blonde head that you're not to fuss yourself about this? You just leave it to the men to get council from their leaders and handle the whole situation."

Mrs. Morgan served her another scrap of bacon. "What's gotten into you that you can't leave this to the men?"

"I keep thinking about those people."

"What about Haun's Mill?" Brother Morgan wiped his mouth and shook his finger at Rebecca. "One of the men gunned down a little boy, saying 'nits make lice.'"

"I know," she whispered, "I know we've been wronged, but another wrong won't make it right."

"We've vowed to avenge the Prophet's blood," Sister Morgan said simply.

"But if we do it on the innocent, won't that make us worse than them?"

"We won't—the innocent will be saved." He bent his head to the bowl while the shock of his words spread through Rebecca.

Last night she had comforted herself, believing her imagination was running wild. Now she watched Brother Morgan calmly eat his breakfast while the horror built inside of her. Her guesses were confirmed.

There was a tap on the door behind her, and Andrew pushed it open. "Morgan, I'm heading for Pinto. I'll be back by nightfall. Rebecca, finish your breakfast and come along. I'll take you home. What did you do about the cow?"

"Cora's milking her. I told her to keep the milk in return. Andrew," she took a deep breath, and her resolve hardened, "I'm not going back with you."

"Yes, you are. You're in no condition to tarry this far from home."

"Andrew, all those things I said to you. I meant them all. I'm convinced this Jesus Christ isn't just a brother to us. He's God. Telling Him I believed that brought Him close to me. I find myself in the position of having to oppose you. I'm sorry, Andrew. I must listen to Him first of all."

"Rebecca," Mrs. Morgan said slowly, "I'd never expect you to rebel against your husband. You're mighty close to being an apostate."

Apostate. The word swirled around Rebecca and Andrew. His eyes burned down into her, questioning. She took a step backward, but the word was pressing against her, demanding an answer. Was the word pressing against him also? The anger faded from his eyes. As she continued to study his face, she saw the color fade from his sun-bronzed skin. His lips were a tight white line. For just a moment he closed his eyes. One groping hand nearly touched her.

She forced her eyes away. "I'm not rebelling," she said slowly; "I'm only believing God's Word. It tells me that I'll know I've really passed from death to life by loving the brethren. With all the things

God's pushing into my heart through His Word, I guess I'm having to risk facing your anger and being called apostate. I can't turn my back on Him."

"What are you saying?" Mrs. Morgan persisted while Andrew and Mr. Morgan waited.

"Isaiah says that the grass withers and the flowers fade, but the Word of God lasts forever. Joseph Smith says avenge; God says love. Do I reject the Bible to be a Latter-day Saint?" She faced Andrew and lifted her chin.

"You'll reject the Prophet's revelation just on the basis of a pile of words?"

"It was only a pile of the Prophet's words that I was asked to believe at the beginning of it all."

"There was the manifestation through the spirit."

"Jesus said," Rebecca spoke softly as if she were focusing on words printed on her mind, "that in the end many would approach Him, claiming to have driven out demons and saying they've performed miracles in His name. His reply was that He didn't know them. See, He's requiring more'n what we do in the name of religion—He's wanting our hearts to run along after Him."

"And you'll still risk the wrath of God?"

She opened her eyes wide. "Oh, no. I've accepted the atonement of His blood. There's no greater way to be made right with God than through God's sacrifice for my sins. There's no wrath for me when I'm saved by that blood and wearing the righteousness of Jesus Christ. I don't have to work for my salvation. It's been bought with Christ's blood."

She continued to watch Andrew, and there was a sadness welling up in her. She couldn't think through to the end of all that she was saying to him; she dare not.

The sun was hot and placid when she stood beside Andrew's horse. "Go, Andrew. I'll be back in Pinto by tomorrow night at the latest. There's fresh bread and buttermilk in the spring house. There's plenty of eggs, and there's vegetables in the garden."

She was aching for understanding and acceptance as she pressed against him. The horse moved restlessly under her weight, and she stepped away. One part of her said that he would soon forget her resistance to his will—he always did.

When the dust cloud hid his figure, she sighed and turned. Sister Morgan was watching her with a curiously detached expression. "Now, what'll it be?"

"Why," Rebecca said slowly, only then accepting the burden that was lying heavy upon her, "I'll ride toward Beaver. They'll listen to me." There was a perplexed expression on Mrs. Morgan's face, so she explained, "The wagon train. I'm not a threat, and with this," she gestured toward her pregnancy, "my message will carry a weight that mere words wouldn't give."

30

....

$\mathcal{A}$cross the valley Rebecca could see the wagon train approaching. Heat waves distorted the line of wagons and cattle, making them appear to move more quickly than they did. Rebecca nudged the horse, "Come on, old dear. I know you're tired, but there's no water here, and just standing in the heat won't help at all."

She caught up with the wagons, bisecting the train as she crossed ravines and cedar-covered hills. She wiped the alkaline dust from her face and waited.

A woman sitting beside the driver of the first wagon stared and pointed. Rebecca watched the driver drop from the wagon and come toward her.

"Lost?" She shook her head. He was noting her condition. "Need a midwife?"

"No. I need to talk to someone in charge of the wagon train."

His face darkened. "I take it you're a plural wife running away from home."

"No, no. It isn't that at all, but it is terribly important."

He hesitated and then turned to point to the next wagon approaching. "Charles Fancher's in that wagon. Best talk to him. I'll call him out."

Rebecca watched him lope toward the wagons; then a man on horseback cut toward her. "Lady, Mac says you wanna talk." His dusty face was closed and polite. "I'll ride along beside you and listen to your story."

"I've just come from Cedar," she started slowly. "I think there could be trouble ahead for you."

"What kind?"

"The Indians are—"

"Being riled by the Mormons?"

"It's been a bad year, and they're never above thieving. It's best you get on out of the territory without stopping."

"That's impossible. The livestock have been on short rations and bitter water for a week now. We're just able to keep them moving. We've been given permission to camp on Mountain Meadows until the livestock have enough strength to get them across the desert." He started to turn and then asked, "Where's the nearest water?"

"Another hour or so. You'll need to swing toward the mountains. Most folks just go into Cedar. I wouldn't suggest it."

"Is there grass?"

"A little. Mostly rabbit bush."

"Did you ride out just to meet us?" She nodded, and the man was silent. Finally, "You're welcome to ride along. We haven't been getting too friendly a welcome hereabouts. There's a few hot-heads in our group. They make trouble for us. If you're tired of settin' that horse, my wife would be pleased to have you up with her. Come along and I'll tie your horse to the back of the wagon."

"I'd be glad," Rebecca sighed; "I'm not accustomed to riding a horse."

He halted the wagon long enough to allow Rebecca to climb to the seat. She settled herself and turned to point. "See that bluff? Turn into the trees there. It's a pretty good trail. The men go through there with wagons when they haul wood. Won't be much water," she cautioned, "but there's a pool backed up."

"So we'll be tapping a Mormon reservoir?"

"Won't do no harm; no one's around. Scout it out if you're worried."

"I'm Liz." The woman's lined face was friendly, but her eyes questioned.

Rebecca introduced herself and said, "I'd better explain to you. The more knowing—" She stopped, surprised at the sudden painful tightness in her throat. "I'm sorry, it's just that I'm tired and confused. I can't believe this is really happening, and when I stop to think about it, I'm afraid—"

"You're taking a risk riding out so close to your time," the woman said slowly. "Aren't you afraid of the Indians?" Rebecca shivered and didn't answer. It was Brother Morgan's hard eyes that she was seeing.

"We're a mite tired too," Liz said with a sigh. "This is all much different than we expected. 'Tis so late in the season we decided to turn south and avoid the terrible mountains. You've heard about the Donner party?" Rebecca nodded, and she continued, "We're short of supplies, but we have plenty of money to buy, only no one will sell us a speck of anything. We've offered more'n usual. One woman traded a cheese for one of our bedquilts. Listen to the cattle. They've been lowing like that for a week. The water's brackish. We can't go on like this much longer."

"Your husband said Hamblin's told him to stay in Mountain Meadows. I hear it's good. But with the talk—" her voice trailed away. She noticed the growing curiosity in Liz's face. She took a deep breath. "The Saints are riled. Washington's moving in an army, right into the territory."

"We heard," she said softly.

Rebecca was still apologetic, "It seems to me, with the Indian problems and all that, it would be best to push on through the territory."

"Without water and good grass, we'll never make it." The lined face turned to Rebecca, and the kindly eyes were searching out Rebecca's thoughts. Liz's eyes soon mirrored Rebecca's fears.

As soon as the wagon train turned and headed into the sheltering cedars, the air began to cool and freshen. Now the lowing of the cattle lifted into a bawling demand for water, and the train moved quickly through the trees to the clearing where the Saints had built a dam to catch the spring runoff.

"Better get your water before the cattle muddy it," Rebecca cautioned. "There's no flow at this time of the year."

Rebecca stood apart and watched the wagons drawing into their tight circle. Fires blazed, and cooking pots were filled. Still she hesitated, confused by her fatigue and uncertainty.

Charles Fancher approached. "As soon as we can get the men together, I'd like you to tell us all that you've told me. We need to ask you questions. I feel there's more to the story." Before he turned away he said, "Have your supper with us. There's plenty of bedding."

The cattle were contented, although the grazing was poor. The children were bedded, and the fires sank to coals. While the women moved about their tasks, the men gathered to the Fancher wagon for Rebecca's story.

She briefly described the scene in Cedar. "It's a feeling more'n anything. For a long time there's been the whispered words, the riled feelings. The men have been drilling their battalions since spring. There's been so much talk. You sense the wound-tight emotions, the anger underneath it all. The Indians are stirring, and no Gentile is welcome. As long as there's all this fuss about the army moving into the territory, they'll trust no one."

"I heard the Mormons have vowed to avenge the deaths of Joseph Smith and his brother. Is that true?" She nodded. "Even on the innocent?"

"It's rumored some of you are from Missouri, and even some of you were there when they were killed." There was a soft curse.

Someone spoke, "That's the Marshall brothers foolin'. You fellows, see what your smart talkin's doin'?"

Charles Fancher stood up. "Maybe it would do to talk to the—" he hesitated over the word—"the Saints in Cedar City."

Rebecca was shaking her head. "I'm fearing it's too late. Besides, there's just not much you can do to turn off the Indians once they're stirred."

"You think it'll only be Indians?"

"I—I'm hoping so."

From the back of the crowd came a voice. "Charles, you know the livestock can't take pushing. Hamblin told us there's no place else for grazing, no other good green grass until we get across Nevada. There's lots of desert before then. We'll never make it."

"If we're running for our lives, it'd be smart to sell the cattle."

"I don't think you'd raise a cent," Rebecca said flatly. "The Saints don't have money for buying, and the Indians take what they want." The murmur of voices rose, and Rebecca could only watch and wait. These people were being pushed to the wall, but their fighting spirit wasn't gone.

Finally a man spoke up from the group. "I'm in favor of sticking to the original plan. Many thanks to the little lady. We'll be on guard, but we'll push ahead."

The men drifted off to their wagons, dark shadows moving into darkness. She heard Fancher ordering the men to take double guard, and then he came back to her. She was standing beside the fire, feeling its warmth touch the chill that was making her tremble.

"I reckon," he said slowly, "they know what you've done today." She nodded. "Won't this put a lid on your going back to them?"

She thought for a minute and then slowly said, "I wasn't thinking about one day ahead of today. I suppose it's going to make it hard."

"What will you do?"

"Tomorrow we head through the mountains into Pinto." She shrugged.

"You live at Pinto?"

She nodded. "That's down close to the ironworks. Through the mountains. The road goes through Pinto, and the mountains snug up pretty close to the road."

"And that's going to be bad." He was watching her face.

"I'd guess."

He was silent while the last embers of the fire were popping and blinking out. She could hear the soft lowing of the cows.

Nearby was the clank of harness and the click of hooves against stone. "Seems to me," he said slowly, "there's still more underneath what you've said. There's more you're fearing, or you wouldn't have taken the risk to ride out. I'm guessing you won't be the least bit welcome at home right now."

She thought of Andrew's stony face. Suddenly it was as if her heart were being shredded from her. She closed her eyes against the pain. The splintery edge of the wagon pressed against her face. "I wasn't thinking," she whispered; "I wasn't seeing the whole of it until this moment. It's like a wall I've built, isn't it? There's no room to change anything, and they'll never understand. What will they do to Andrew once they find out? They'll never believe I haven't betrayed them. I've only tried to protect—" she raised her head, "and even that hasn't worked."

From a moment of silence, he said, "I have an idea. Ride along with us to Mountain Meadows. You can hide in the wagon as we pass through Pinto. Stay with us until we reach Nevada, and then we'll send you back with a rider. He can say that we've taken you hostage for our safe passage. In that way you can be delivered home, free of blame."

Rebecca nodded and with growing eagerness, exclaimed, "Oh, yes, that's very good." But even as she spoke the words, she felt she was grasping a straw bridge. There were those words she must push out of her mind, the picture of an open grave.

The next day the train avoided Cedar City, cutting a new trail across the flatlands, heading for the distant cut that marked the mountain valley through which they must pass.

Mountain Meadows was all that Hamblin had promised it to be. When Rebecca opened her eyes that Sabbath morning, the early sun was slanting pale light through the morning mists rising from the deep gorge sheltering the river. Although it was September, the grass was still green and full of life. The cottonwoods and willows clustered along the edge of the gorge were tipped with gold, but the meadows seemed a forever summer land. Rebecca could hear the frogs croaking with the background music of swiftly moving water.

Lying in the little tent, concentrating on the sounds and smells of this spot, even while the strange ache of the future leaned heavily upon her, a thought occurred to her. Could she give herself to the enjoyment of this day and this place without entertaining thoughts of all that might lie ahead? Could she trust God with the future? It seemed a divine challenge, and she felt her heart lifting in response. The baby was stirring within her, and she pressed her hands against him. "My little one, how glad I will be to see you! But today is today, and while we are one, we'll give ourselves to this moment."

Mrs. Fancher was standing beside the wagon. With head lifted, she was breathing deeply of the freshness of the morning. "Ah, Rebecca, how wonderful it is! It's a spot where a body could be content to stay forever."

"There's all that's necessary—the water, the sun and grass. The frogs and birds seem most content."

"But they've no need to seek their fortune. How blessed they are. After breakfast, we'll be having a Sabbath worship." She paused with bucket on hip. "Would you be inclined to worship with us or—"

"Oh!" Rebecca cried, hardly daring to hope, "do you believe Jesus is God and that the Bible is God's Word—truly believe?"

"Why, of course. I grant, some of us live it better than others; but we have a good preacher right here, and he's an encouragement."

There was a question on her face. Rebecca confessed, while she poked her toe in the damp soil. "I've been reading my mother's Bible. I choose to believe Jesus is God and that the Bible is God's Word. I believe in the atonement of Christ."

It seemed as if there was a holy hush spreading across the meadow as the people gathered on the grass, facing the darksuited man. The Reverend Harper was holding a large blackbound book. As Rebecca studied him, his eyes met hers. *He's feeling a heavy load*, she thought.

Now the Book was opened to words that had grown precious to her. Like gentle drops of rain they fell: "the trial of your faith . . . more precious than gold . . . hope to the end for grace. . . ."

———

On Monday, the Indians began their attack. The first line of washing had been strung between the wagons, and the women were bending together over the steaming tubs. They were chatting merrily.

When Rebecca straightened to rub her back, she saw the cloud of dust. Mute, she pointed, and at that moment the war cries echoed across the meadow. While women's screams filled the air, Rebecca hung motionless, her arm still lifted. The heavy shouting of the men broke the spell, and she became a part of the mass that raced to the wagons, burrowing deep into the sheltering depths.

Through a slit in the canvas Rebecca watched the men take their positions behind that mounding bank of dirt that stood between the wagons and the river. Rebecca was seeing it all as sharply as if it were being etched eternally on the crystal of her mind.

Dust puffed from the dirt bank, and she realized the menace was rifles, not bows and arrows. Now bullets cut across the chasm, showering the wagons, the horses, the cattle, and the men. They were drawing a steel curtain between the wagon train and the river lying just down that steep slope.

As a bullet tore into the canvas above Rebecca's head, hands forced her down. "What are you doing," Mrs. Fancher gasped, "sitting up there with the bullets a-flyin'?"

"Why," Rebecca said slowly, speaking out of the shock that wouldn't release her to move and think and feel, "why, they've cut off our water." The silence in the wagon reached the smallest child, and dismay swept across the faces.

It was Mrs. Fancher's brisk voice that broke the spell. "There's no call to fret. The men'll send the Indians a-packin'. 'Tisn't the first Indian raid we've had."

Throughout the day, the Indians continued to make their swooping attacks on the wagons. Inside the circle of wagons, while one group of men crouched to return their fire, the others were digging an entrenchment.

Warm bodies, tiny limbs pressed against Rebecca. A breath touched her cheek. "Miz Jacobson, why don't the Indians go home so we can sleep in our own wagon. I'm thirsty."

The sun rose higher and seared the moisture from the grass. A sip of water was shared, a bit of bread. Children were hushed and babies nursed. Still the women and children huddled close, trying to read courage and hope in each other's faces. But Rebecca had to turn away, fighting the night-time thoughts that shadowed her.

Liz Fancher was speaking, "It's certain we can't go another day without water. There's not a speck left in this jug, and the bucket's been empty since yesterday. We need water for the wounded."

Another woman whispered, "They're working now to send out children with a white flag to get water. They don't shoot children."

"No!" Rebecca cried, "no, they mustn't—" Liz's eyes warned, and she dared say no more.

As the day passed slowly, Rebecca recalled the words that had drifted up to her as she lay in the Morgans' loft. Was it possible that she had really heard those words? *Avenge. Let the Indians do it, so's there's no blood guilt about the women and children. Listen to council.*

Live your religion. Avenge the Prophet.

Blood atonement. Sharp and clear came the picture of Brother Johnson. She could hear his shovel strike the stones as he lifted the earth from his own grave. Andrew. There was that question again.

Timmy's mother was comforting him. "Never you mind. Those people in Cedar, like as not, have heard about this, and they'll come rescue us. There's lots of people around here; they'll help."

The words burst from Rebecca, "You don't know—" All eyes focused on her. The children were hanging on her words. Trusting. She was silent now, turning away.

The days were losing significance. The sun went down, and the coolness eased the thirst; fretful sleep eased the hunger.

Silent shadows slipped close to the wagon. "Are you safe? Many's been shot; a number won't make it. There's no way we can slip down for water. Be brave; help'll come."

Morning came and Rebecca must hide her face, stifle her fears. "God, Jesus," she whispered against the canvas. "Please, the children are so young."

An edge of desperation was moving through the company. The last of the water was carried to the wounded.

Rebecca shook her head sadly as the three men prepared to slip out of the camp. They were going to Cedar for help. "It's a waste," she mourned as she cuddled little Annie Barker against her. Annie's father had been wounded yesterday. Now Timmy's father had been shot. Rebecca reached down to pat the shoulder of the little boy huddled miserably against her while the babe within her stirred against her ribs.

"Timmy, how would you like to hear a story?" His expression was blank as he turned his head toward the sounds of battle.

Dusk was deepening as the Reverend Harper crawled between the wagons, whispering encouragement to the women and children. Rebecca asked, "What's become of the men who went to Cedar?" He avoided her eyes. As she started to speak, he hastily interrupted.

"Mrs. Evans sent this bit of bread for the children. Be brave, sister."

Behind Rebecca there was a muffled sob, but she didn't turn. She leaned wearily against the rib of the wagon, and little Timmy reminded, "Pa says stay down."

When the sun was gone a cool wind swept across the meadow, whistling through the trees. Rebecca could hear the gurgling water, and she licked her parched lips.

"Rebecca," Liz Fancher was speaking cautiously, "doesn't it seem to you that it's been a long time since we've heard the Indians?"

"Yes, it does." She sighed with relief, but tried to conquer hope.

She was dozing when she heard the babble of voices. A call swept across the meadow with its answering chorus. "It's help! Someone's coming with a flag."

Timmy hugged Rebecca, and they crowded to the end of the wagon to see. There were two men, three. The darkness wasn't revealing all, but a shadowy figure was led into the circle of wagons. The elation seemed to still, die. The voices deepened.

A man left the group and came to the wagon. It was Mr. Fancher. "These men are from Cedar. They say the only way we can safely get past the Indians is to leave everything here except enough necessities to see us through and then walk the thirty miles back to Cedar. We're to go unarmed, marching with the women and children in front. There'll be wagons carrying the babies and the wounded."

"Charles, that doesn't sound like a wise thing to do. How'll we last through such a long walk with so many little ones?"

"Who are the men?" Rebecca asked in a low voice. "Might be I should talk to 'em."

"No," he said sharply. "For now it's better if they don't know about you."

He turned to his wife, speaking softly and shaking his head, "It doesn't sound smart at all; but I've been outvoted, and we'll go."

"The risk is worse than staying," Rebecca said heavily. "You don't—"

He cut through her words, "The only thing we have left is hope, Rebecca; don't snatch that from us."

In the darkness wagons creaked, and terrified horses snorted. There was the sharp cry of the wounded as they were lifted into the first wagon. Children and babies were taken from their mothers. Whimpering with fright, they were bundled into the wagon along with supplies. The creaking of the wagon was fading as the silent lines of women and older children took their places.

Now it was their turn. As they fumbled their way down the trail, back through the cut, walking past trees and bushes, Rebecca became conscious of dark shadows joining them. She pressed her knuckles against her lips to quiet their trembling.

From the sounds of heels striking stone, Rebecca guessed a multitude was behind her, but she dared not look. Her heart was pounding with a heavy, slow beat. The pale gleam of moonlight brightened

the scene, revealing shapes. She brushed at the perspiration damp-
ening her face and tried to calm herself.

Suddenly there was a shout: "Do your duty!"

The shadows erupted into life. Dark forms ran from the trees and
bushes. From behind her shots rang out, and the meadow was filled
with screams of terror. "No, oh, no! Please!"

Dark forms streaked toward her. Rebecca plunged away from
the trail, running desperately. Behind her, screams were becoming
cries of agony. The thudding of hooves approached in the darkness
ahead of her. Suddenly a horse glistened in the moonlight. A rider
scrambled from the saddle, and the light touched his face.

"Andrew! Oh, Andrew!" At the moment of recognition she was
seeing him turn and kneel. Moonlight touched the muzzle of his
rifle, and she stopped. Her hands had been outstretched. Now they
reached instinctively for her breast. With a sigh she dropped her
hands and waited. How could she have expected anything else?

The rifle kicked backward as a knife of light leaped from its
muzzle and the noise of a shot carommed among the trees. A
hammer-like blow against her right ribs jerked Rebecca backward.
She stumbled and fell face-first on the rocky ground.

The man stared for a moment, then fumbled to reload. Finished,
he began to raise the rifle to his shoulder, but Rebecca's body was
limp and quiet. Satisfied that his mission was complete, he stood
and reached for his horse.

————————

The lone rider was heading westward. In front of him the mountains' dark peaks funneled off to the south. He reined his horse and
listened to the raucous cry of a crow echo through the morning air.
Joshua's breath had frosted his beard, and his hands were stiff with
cold.

Autumn color had faded into the gray and dismal browns of
November. Today bare branches whipped the frosty air. Narrowing
his eyes against the sun, he studied the clouds sweeping north along
the edge of the mountains. He touched his horse's neck. "Old girl,
we'll avoid that storm by cutting west here, but I don't reckon I know
where this road leads." He absently patted her as his eyes continued
to scan the countryside. "It appears to be a meadow, and if it just
keeps rolling gentlelike, clear to Nevada, we've an easy trip ahead."
The horse responded to his nudge and turned down the narrow
trail.

Joshua knew he shared the trail a moment before the horseman appeared. He pulled aside and waited. The man approaching was dark. His broad shoulders were covered by a great coat as dark as the beard that touched it.

As he rode slowly toward Joshua, he pushed his hat away from his face. His blue eyes were watchful, measuring. He stopped his tall roan in the middle of the trail. As the horse pawed restlessly, he said, "I thought I was seeing things for a minute. That's a nice looking buckskin you're riding. Did you buy her to match your britches and your hair?" His grin was an even slash of white in the dark beard.

Joshua tensed and frowned. The man's friendly manner struck an uneasy response from him. He tilted his hat a shade closer to the bridge of his nose. "I don't rightly guess I gave it any more thought than you did when you picked your coat."

There was a pause, and the man's grin vanished. When he spoke his voice was heavy. "You lost? Not many ride this way."

"I'm looking for a shortcut west." He gestured toward the dark clouds. "Straight south I'll run into snow."

"Could be. But this road dead-ends at Mountain Meadows." He paused, and wary eyes searched Joshua's face. The years of traveling had taught Joshua to keep his thoughts to himself. The muscle along his jawline tightened as he ducked his head.

"Then point me on my way. I want the fastest road out of Utah."

"Better head south for the Clara, then west." The eyes were still wary. "What brings you this way?"

Joshua hesitated, and tension crept through him. Despite the warning every instinct gave, he couldn't resist one last try. He shoved his hat back and admitted, "I'm looking for a friend. When I pass through the territory I always ask. Just a friend, but I like to keep track of my friends."

"What's his name?"

"Her—her maiden name was Wolstone. I don't know the married name. Rebecca Wolstone from Illinois. Ever hear of her?"

The blue eyes darkened and his mouth twitched fleetingly. Slowly, the man raised his hat and smoothed his hair. "Yes," he paused, "I've heard of Rebecca Wolstone. You can quit looking for her. She's dead." His eyes were emotionless, but as the man continued to talk his eyes held Joshua's. His voice was flat, low. "Rebecca wasn't one of the sturdy Saints. It's unfortunate, but the kind heavenly Father knows best." He paused, and when he spoke again his voice was heavy as if he spoke almost against his will. "We Saints don't fight the will of the Lord, although at times we reckon it to be harsh, harsh as the land we call Zion."

He nudged his horse, and the restless beast moved closer to Joshua. The man pointed. "Just head toward that cut in the mountains. The trail's easy to spot, and it'll take you direct to Clara."

Joshua slumped in the saddle. As he rode he was scarcely conscious of the lowering clouds, the swirling flakes, and the bite of cold.

The horse picked her way along the mountain road, as aimlessly as if she no longer carried the rider on her back. It was late in the afternoon when Joshua's emotions reached the depths, and once again he was becoming aware of life and deepening cold when he heard the horse behind him.

This time it was an Indian pony. The blanket-swathed figure moved close to Joshua and halted. The blanket was dropped and the bronze figure straightened and peered through the snow. "Mormonee lost?"

"No, I'm heading for the Clara. I think I'm on the right trail. I'm not a Mormon." The Indian was studying him.

"Cold. Bad." He pointed to the darkening sky; then he beckoned, gestured, as he reached to tug at the buckskin's reins. "Come." He motioned toward the sky again, and pulling the blanket close, he walked his horse ahead. Now Joshua realized the Indian was offering to lead him.

"I'm obliged!" he shouted; "just point the way. I don't—"

The Indian was moving ahead, and Joshua followed. Within an hour his guide turned off the road and started up the mountain. Joshua halted and shouted, "No! I go to the Clara." The Indian came back and twitched the horse's reins. Now Joshua was beginning to sense the urgency in the Indian's actions, and reluctantly he fell in behind the Indian pony. As the trail narrowed and the pony slowed on the slippery slope, Joshua became aware of his surroundings. The trees were becoming taller and the undergrowth heavier. When the timber formed a canopy against the blizzard, Joshua caught the scent of wood smoke.

They broke into a clearing. Snow-covered cones dotted the area, and Joshua realized they were in an Indian village.

They led their horses to shelter under the trees. Joshua shook snow from his clothes and removed his snow-laden hat to wipe the moisture from his face. The Indian was untying bundles, lifting them from his pony, and Joshua went to help.

"Sun." There was awe in the Indian's voice. Joshua realized he was staring at his hair and beard. "Sun child," he said again, this time with understanding. He nodded and grinned. "Mormonee sun child, too."

"No, I'm not Mormon," Joshua said, "I'm—" The Indian was unwrapping the bundle and Joshua caught his breath. With a quick step he moved and touched the little leather trunk. "Where did you get this?"

The Indian seemed surprised, "Mormonee sun child." He frowned and hesitated while his dark eyes studied him again. He said, "Come, sun child." Bewildered, Joshua followed the Indian through the snow to one of the huts. He stooped and staggered through the opening. In the dark, smoky room he stood waiting for his eyes to adjust to the dimness.

One of the women turned from the fire. Her braids were long and as yellow as new-ripened wheat. His lips were stiff, unbelieving, but he must try the name. "Rebecca?" She was much taller than he remembered and much too thin.

It was a long moment before she moved, and whispered, "Joshua, is it really you?"

"Mormonee sun child."

"Like children of light," said the woman standing beside Rebecca. Joshua stepped closer to Rebecca and looked into her face. There were pain-filled shadows in her eyes. Looking at the thin, pale cheeks, he ached for her suffering.

Gently, as if he were touching a wounded child, he reached for her. A sigh escaped her lips as she leaned against his shoulder. He felt tears against his neck.

The Indian woman stepped close to them, saying simply, "You two belong." She touched their hair. "I not believe Eagle's story about woman on mountain with hair like light. Now two of you."

There was compassion in her eyes as she said, "Sun child very ill. Fever from gun wound; baby born dead."

Joshua felt Rebecca's trembling and sensed the deep, silent sobbing. Alarmed he said, "Rebecca, don't. You are safe now. I'll make certain of that."

When she could talk, she raised her head, "Why did you think I wasn't safe?"

He shook his head slowly. "I don't know. But there was nothing in me except the constant need to find you. The feeling wouldn't let me rest." Was he sensing her shrinking away from him? "Rebecca, I'm asking nothing except, will you please let me take you home to

Ma? You don't need to say one thing about what's happened. Just come with me. Let the past go."

The room emptied slowly, and Rebecca said, "I think it will be best forgotten if I tell you all first." They sat down beside the fire. The Indian woman, Solali, touched Rebecca's shoulder before she left. Rebecca explained, "Solali was a plural wife too. She wasn't happy and returned to her own people. That's why she speaks English. She also understands why I can't return to them."

Joshua watched the sadness creep across Rebecca's face as she stared into the fire. Finally, she roused herself and began her story.

The embers dulled and grayed before new wood was added. A fresh log flared and glowed, but the embers were dying again before her story reached that night on Mountain Meadows.

Watching her face, knowing now where the story was leading, Joshua said, "As soon as I rode into the territory I knew something was afoot. I've never been aware of such emotions, and they were everywhere as I rode the trails and looked in the towns."

"Looking for me?"

He nodded. They were silent for a long time, but when she spoke again, he sensed an easing of the tension between them.

Rebecca whispered, "When we started the march back to Cedar City, it seemed the very air was alive with something evil and frightening. My knees would scarce hold me as we walked. And I was sensing them moving out of the darkness. When the shouting began and the screams and gunfire, I ran. Then I saw Andrew." She swallowed and shook her head. Grief bowed her double. Joshua stirred the fire and waited.

" 'Twas the Lord. I am sure of it. It was His blessed faithfulness, not a quirk of fate that sent this Indian to me. You've heard them say he recognized me by my hair." Her voice was low and husky. "I don't know what significance he saw in it, but he hid me in the bushes and later carried me to this village. You've been told the rest."

Out of a long silence she spoke, "It's the blood atonement. 'Tis written in the Doctrine and Covenants. I read it for myself. Says that if a man in the priesthood has a wife who sins against the new and everlasting covenant, she is to be destroyed in the flesh. Do you understand, Joshua?

"When I told Andrew I was trusting in the atonement of Jesus Christ for my salvation, this meant I was rejecting the new and everlasting covenant. He was obligated." She trembled and held her hands to the fire. It was a long time before she whispered, " 'Tis his religion that makes him into this. So far as he knows, I'm dead. For him to know otherwise means he'll have the job to do over again."

"Then there's no way you can return to him," Joshua said slowly. "Your choice of Christ's atonement was a denial of the new and everlasting covenant. To return to him means death. Rebecca, you know I'm obliged to carry you out of here."

It was his turn to be silent and then his words were tentative, as if he sensed he was probing a sore spot. "You know these plural marriages aren't recognized by the government of the United States. And he didn't tell you he already had a wife when you married him. Nowhere else in the country will he have any legal hold on you."

For a moment Rebecca's expression became hopeful; then fear crept into her eyes. " 'Tis so. But I'm still here. Under the covenant, he's obliged to destroy me if he really loves me. They teach 'tis the only way I'd make it to the highest glory."

"Then you must flee for your life. Rebecca, I'm taking you home with me." As if he sensed her questions, he raised his hand. "Rebecca, I'm asking nothing. Only let me take you home. For us both, that is enough for now."

When Joshua moved again, it was with the motion of casting off a burden. He asked, "Were there survivors?"

Rebecca shook her head. "I had Solali ask Eagle. He said that all the emigrants were killed except the smallest children. Seventeen of them were taken to the Saints. That means there were one hundred and twenty older children, men and women who were killed. Eagle admitted the Indians had been given the task of murdering the women and children. Oh, Joshua, I still can't believe it. The stories were so horrible. Eagle said the wolves got the bodies; they had been poorly buried. When I remember those kind people. . . ." She turned away with her grief. Her voice muffled, she said, "I'll never forget that I failed."

The fire died and they could hear the wind and feel the press of cold. Joshua rose to kindle it afresh. In the light of leaping flames, Rebecca stirred and straightened. The lines were still on her face and the shadows in her eyes, but she lifted her chin and her hands were moving, touching the world around her.

"I made these people realize I must never return to my home. But there was one thing from the past I wanted. When I explained it to Solali, she sent Eagle to Pinto for it."

"The wedding dress?"

"My mother's Bible. Before I left Pinto I felt the strong need to hide the Book. It had become too precious to risk. I placed it in the trunk where it belongs and shoved it back under the bed. I couldn't tell Eagle to bring just the Book, because there was another black book there. I dared not run the risk of having him bring the wrong book, so I asked for the trunk."

"But the dress?"

"It's in there. But, Joshua, the dress wasn't the important thing. It was the Bible. My mother was trying to tell me that the Holy Bible was my only hope. I'm sure of that now. How blind I was to think a marriage was what she had in mind. How blind I was to think anything could supplant what God has given in His Word."

In another moment she moved again. This time there was a new expression on her face. Even in the shadowed room he could see the sad lines ease as her eyes were touched with new light.

"My friend," she whispered, "my dear faithful friend. I can't begin to understand the sacrifice you've made for me. Will I ever be worthy of this care, this concern?"

He took her hand and squeezed it, clasping it between his two. "Rebecca, seems I don't know much about God, but I remember how I felt first off—unworthy. I couldn't lift my face to Him. When I finally could understand what He was saying to me in His Word, I knew He was wanting me to be thinking now about His love, not my unworthiness. If He doesn't want those feelings of not being worthy between me and Him, I sure can't imagine Him thinking it's good between a man and a woman."

There were shadows moving back into her eyes, and he guessed her thoughts were on the past again. His own heart ached, but he could only watch helplessly.

Suddenly she took a deep breath and leaned forward. "Joshua, can you be patient?" She raised a trembling hand, but as she pressed it against his shoulder and then lifted it to his face, the trembling ceased.

With the other hand she brushed her hair away from her eyes and met his steadily. He smiled down at her. "Patience? It's faith, Becky. Everything's going to be all right."

With
This Ring

Preface

The preceding story, *The Wedding Dress*, centers around Rebecca Wolstone's early years. In 1831, the same year the Church of Jesus Christ of Latter-Day Saints was organized, she was born in New York. Rebecca's earliest memories were of life on the mud flats of the Mississippi River, near a community that was soon to become the Mormon city of Nauvoo, Illinois.

Those mud flats robbed Rebecca of her family. The Wolstones, along with many of their neighbors, fell victim to the swift and deadly cholera. Like many of the other children left orphaned that year, Rebecca was taken into one of the neighboring homes in the community. The Smyths were kind to the young girl, but she never forgot that she was one more mouth to feed in a poor, hungry family of young ones. Neither quite a family member nor a comfortable guest, Rebecca grew up without really having a sense of belonging.

In 1844, the year of Rebecca's thirteenth birthday, two events profoundly touched and changed her life. That spring seventeen-year-old Joshua Smyth, the eldest son in the family and Rebecca's dearest friend, left Illinois to find a niche for himself (and, eventually, the rest of his family) in Oregon Territory. When he left, his eyes promised Rebecca what his words dared not say, and Rebecca was filled with both desolation and hope.

Meanwhile, the Mormon Church had from the beginning faced persecution and rejection. In Nauvoo, no less than any other place, the Saints were living an uneasy existence.

When Joseph Smith, founder and president of the church, and his brother Hyrum were murdered just miles from Nauvoo, Rebecca Wolstone's attention and sympathies were captured. And when the

Saints left Illinois for the Great Basin in the far West, Rebecca was numbered among them.

Great Salt Lake City became Rebecca's new home. Under the watchful eye of Brigham Young, subject to the doctrines of the Mormon Church, Rebecca struggled to be a good schoolteacher and to learn to conform to the church. But her "rebellious" ways merited her the discipline of a move south to the frontier town of Cedar City.

For Rebecca had balked at becoming a plural wife. In this "doctrine," the church declared, God had revealed His highest plan for His people: only through "celestial marriage" could a man achieve the highest heaven. This doctrine, including plural marriage and blood atonement, is still found in the DOCTRINE AND COVENANTS.

The Principle, as the doctrine of plural marriage was called, had been practiced covertly from the earliest days of the church. Only after the Saints had moved to the Great Basin did the church leaders feel secure enough to reveal to the world that doctrine which they had been denying publicly from the very beginning. To the federal government, plural marriage was illegal, and any children of such unions had no legal rights in the nation or as heirs. No wonder, then, that few women had accepted Brigham Young's generous offer of "freedom," extended that October conference of 1856. Outside the Territory they would have been considered prostitutes with illegitimate children.

Brigham Young's unhappy wife number twenty-seven, Ann Eliza, divorced him and tried to sue for an enormous settlement. While recognizing that the United States courts gave no legal recognition to polygamy, he made a magnanimous offer of $200,000 in settlement of the suit, with the provision that the courts must legitimatize all Mormon plural marriages by declaring his marriage to Ann Eliza legal. The court was unwilling and unable to do so.

The accepted practice among the Saints was to include the first wife as a participant in subsequent marriage ceremonies. But occasionally, as in Rebecca's case, the marriages were made without informing the women of the existence of other wives.

Rebecca, caught in such a marriage, eventually rebelled despite her original resolve to conform and accept the teaching of the church. In the midst of her struggle, Rebecca began to search for God, a search which led her away from Mormon teachings and nearly cost her life.

In an Indian camp, Joshua Smyth found Rebecca recovering

from a near-fatal gunshot wound inflicted by her Mormon husband, and planned to take her with him back to Oregon. Throughout the years, he had demonstrated his faithful friendship as well as a deep sense of responsibility for Rebecca's welfare.

With This Ring takes up the story of Rebecca's new life. As she leaves the desert country of Southern Utah, she begins the move from barrenness to hope. But will she ever be truly beyond the reach of her former church?

1

· · · · · · · · · · · · · · · · · · ·

$\mathcal{R}$ebecca could smell the pungent smoke of the pine and sage fire. Bitter cold won out over its feeble warmth, and she buried her nose in the rabbit-skin robe. Snuggling deeper into the robe, she felt sleep claiming her again.

The resinous pine snapped like gunfire and, with a cry of terror, she struggled against the blackness of the dream trying to suck her downward. Even as she fought against its fearful scenes, part of her mind reminded her that it was only a dream, the same one repeated endlessly throughout the days of her illness. But even now that she had strength to contend with the terror of memory, there was still only one escape.

Fighting off the heavy robes and blankets, Rebecca threw herself from her bed mat. Solali, crouched beside the fire, turned with a concerned frown to watch Rebecca. Shivering now, Rebecca pushed aside the heavy mass of blond hair from her face and knelt beside the Indian woman. She wiped the perspiration from her face while Solali's troubled eyes studied her. " 'Tis the dream?"

Rebecca nodded tremulously and held her hands toward the blaze. "That cracklin' log did it. Seemed like rifle fire, and—and I was back there, livin' it over." She was trembling now and Solali reached for the blanket.

More cold air struck Rebecca at the same time she heard Joshua whispering from the doorway. "Solali, I've got to talk to Rebecca." As she turned, the deerskin curtain covering the doorway of the hut was pulled aside as Joshua stepped through the opening and saw her. "You're up early this cold morning. Did you feel the touch of snow in the air?"

Still caught in the terror of the dream, she whispered dully, "Snow?"

It was Solali who saw his worried eyes fixed on Rebecca and moved closer. "Eagle?" she asked. He hesitated for a moment and then turned to the Indian woman.

"Solali, we've got to get out of here," he murmured. "There's trouble a'brewing but plenty."

"Where's Eagle?" she asked again.

"He's here, just come back. That's why—"

Rebecca moved slowly. Turning from the fire, still shivering, she clutched the blanket about her, but she lifted her chin and said, "It's bad, and I might as well know about it. You two have been whispering behind my back for long enough. 'Tis time I start livin' again." Her voice caught; she took two quick nervous steps toward the door and then returned to the fire.

She faced Joshua and, for the first time, saw the lines of fatigue on his face. As she studied those lines, wondering at their meaning, Eagle came into the hut. Moving to the other side of the fire, he squatted and held his hands toward the warmth.

Joshua knelt beside him, and while the two men spoke in low, hurried tones, Rebecca watched Eagle. She was still frowning at what she saw when Joshua got to his feet and came back to her. "Eagle's tired," she said, "and I know he's been gone someplace." She faced Joshua. "You look like something's pressing upon you."

The curtain swung softly into place again as Eagle left the hut. Joshua's worried frown was still on his face as he turned, and pulling off his hat, tossed it to the stack of robes. Though dressed like a native American, his golden hair and beard caught the light and sharpened the contrast between the Indians and himself. Rebecca thought of the strange picture she, too, created. Her heavy blonde hair was braided Indian-style and she was wearing the typical Paiute woman's dress. A tentative smile curved her lips.

Joshua bent down beside her and looked into her face. His smile reflected not so much amusement or joy but simply relief at her softened expression. Knowing why, Rebecca stretched out her hand in mute apology. Joshua squeezed her hand but said abruptly, "Becky, I want you to get your things together right now. We're leaving as soon as we can get packs on the horses."

"Leaving!" Jumping to her feet and spinning away from the fire, she looked wildly about the smoke-filled hut. From the soft couch of rabbit-skin robes which had been her sanctuary since Eagle had carried her unconscious and wounded to the Indian village, to the mounds of pelts for barter and the storage baskets holding their winter provisions of food, this humble hut had been home. She reached out to stroke the curved walls, saplings woven into protection against the elements.

"Leave," she whispered again, her voice reflecting disbelief. She trembled to think of that world beyond the confines of the village. "No!" Her voice out of control, she pressed her knuckles against her lips and tried to calm herself.

"Becky, Rebecca," Joshua pleaded, his voice both placating and firm. "There's to be no arguing. I didn't ask. I'm tellin'. I'd be obliged if you'd ask no questions. There isn't time. Just get your things together." He turned to Solali, "Please—"

"I go too." Shaking her head, Rebecca tried to grasp the Indian woman's arm. Ignoring Rebecca, Solali continued, "You need help."

"I do, more than—" He swallowed hard. Abruptly he got to his feet and reached for his hat. As he left the hut Solali followed him out into the crisp morning air.

Flakes of snow were beginning to obscure the sky. Joshua watched them swirl about and turned to Solali. " 'Tis terrible weather for anybody to be startin' a journey. I'm wondering if Rebecca will make it. If you'll be telling me no, well, I'll be settin' my mind to some other solution."

For a moment Solali stared up at him. Her reply was simple. "Indians don't stay in the mountains during the cold times. Soon the Saints will be wondering why the village has not moved down to the warm, dry desert. Then they will visit the village, and they will find your Becky."

For a long moment Joshua was silent; then slowly and deliberately he spoke. "She's thin and frail. That whiteness and the terrible stillness inside scares me, but I'd rather have her die in my arms halfway to Oregon than to have them get their hands on her."

"Then we go."

They both heard the gasp and turned. Rebecca was standing in the doorway, clutching the deerskin curtain with both hands.

Joshua moved toward her. "Becky, you'll need to hear me out. Go back inside; you'll freeze out here." He pushed at her motionless form and beckoned to Solali.

Inside, on the bed of coals, the pot of water was boiling. Solali moved past Rebecca and Joshua. They watched her kneel beside the fire and stir meal into the pot.

Now Rebecca was aware of Joshua's scrutiny; reluctantly she turned to face him. Speaking slowly as he studied her face, he said,

"Eagle's come with news. You've got to understand, Becky, this isn't my own idea. I'd be willin' to stay here 'til warm weather, but 'tisn't safe."

He paused to pace the tiny circle around the fire before adding, "The dear Lord knows I'm worried about the trip and a'wishin' there would be a spot in the Territory where you'd be safe." He deliberately stopped in front of her and stared intently down at her. "You understand what I'm saying, don't you?"

With a sigh she turned away. A touch of bitterness colored her voice as she replied, "I'm knowin' well."

For a moment he measured her fear and bitterness against what he must say. Trying to soften the impact, he touched her shoulder. "Now you'll hear me out. Eagle's been riding the Territory these past weeks, doing the scouting I dare not do." She looked up with a surprised frown and he explained, "You need to know, Brigham Young has cracked down on every stranger in the Territory. He's issuin' permits to all the travelers hereabouts. I'm understanding, from all that's been told me, that it bodes no good for the man without one. That's another reason we must leave, and quickly. Every day we wait, we stand a greater chance of being challenged by one of his men when we *do* try to go."

Restlessly he paced to the door. "I wish Eagle would come back. I sent him to round up some horses." When he returned to the fire, he saw Rebecca's face lifted to him, the face of a bewildered, lost child.

"Another reason?" she whispered. "Then there's more bad news you've had."

Nodding curtly he faced her and said, "You know since last summer President Buchanan has had federal troops moving this way. They say it's nothing to be feared, it's only the normal thing, and I believed it so. Oregon Territory was right proud to have the troops and the colors on its home ground. Makes a body feel protected. Seems here it was taken all wrong."

Rebecca agreed, her tone dark, " 'Tis *all* taken wrong. Everything the government has done rubs them the wrong way. Brigham's fought it all, saying he'll be governor regardless. Why don't they just leave the man alone for the sake of peace?"

Joshua hesitated and peered at Rebecca. When he answered her his voice was flat, low, "Seems you've been whipped beyond reason."

"I've not," she replied, astonished.

"You're not understandin'. I'm thinkin' you've been beaten down more than you know." After a moment he continued, "Hear me out. Brigham's Nauvoo Legion has been standing off the troops. It's bad enough that he's plugged up Echo Canyon with them, but now Eagle says Young's had them harassing the army all winter. First the Mormons burned the supply trains. When Johnston tried to enter Utah by way of the Soda Springs road, they ran off cattle and blocked his way. Then the weather settled in. While he was hightailing back to Fort Bridger, he lost a goodly share of his stock. Now I'm hearin' that five hundred head of oxen and fifty-seven head of mules and horses froze to death on the Sweetwater. Another five hundred head froze before they made it back to their winter quarters."

He hesitated, then said dryly, "I'm not thinkin' all that stock came along just for the trip. Seems the resistance is a pretty drastic step to take against the whole United States government. There's bound to be problems. I hear the Mormons have burned out Fort Bridger long ago, so that's meanin' the troops spent a miserable winter up there. Now Eagle's sayin' there's new rumbles. In Great Salt Lake City they were getting all ready to start celebrating the spring victory in advance when they heard there's troops a'movin' up the Colorado River."

"Joshua," Rebecca gasped, "that's nearly in our backyard!"

He nodded. "And it's more'n a rumor. I don't know who they are, and I'm not so sure they're troops, but Eagle has spotted them. He followed a scouting party up the Colorado. Says they're gettin' mighty close to the Virgin River."

"Do the Saints know?"

"Yes. Eagle said Hamblin's men were moseyin' right along behind them."

Joshua watched Rebecca as she stared into the flickering fire. Slowly her hand crept to her throat. "What are you thinkin'?" he asked quietly.

"I'm feeling so sorry for all those people—my neighbors and friends." She shook her head wearily. "The good people, the followers. It's just like before. Like Ohio and Missouri and Illinois. I'm guessing how badly they're feeling this—the upset and the fear. Now they'll be pressed to the wall again." She sighed and shook her head, "That proud angry man! Last summer Brigham had them ready to set fire to their homes and destroy everything they've slaved to accomplish—all rather than to settle back and obey the laws of the country. They'll run always. For the rest of their lives they'll run if someone doesn't talk sense into that man."

"I'm not understandin' why the people stand for it," Joshua said slowly, his voice rough with worry. "These are free people. Why don't they rise up for their own good and fight for their rights?"

"Free?" Rebecca's voice was scornful. "They aren't free. They've been taught to obey or they'll be damned." She waved her hand. "See, just like Heber Kimball said, Brigham Young is god to them. And Joseph Smith was god to the people while he was alive."

"Rebecca," Joshua was speaking carefully. "Do you understand? They're coming this way." He hesitated, watching Rebecca as she began to comprehend it all.

"You're meaning them all. The people in Great Salt Lake City and Brigham Young and the twelve. All of them."

He added, "With troops moving up the rivers and pressing in from the east, this Territory will be overrun."

She was whispering as if even now they could hear her. "Where will they go? The only place left is to run to the desert. Those people, all the people, from all those towns—Provo, even Cedar, Parowan, Pinto, Harmony." She pressed trembling hands against her cheeks. Her eyes were darkening as she fought to take deep, calm breaths. As he saw how pale her face was becoming, he found himself doubly determined to leave immediately.

At his shoulder Solali whispered, "Bad as the dreams, it is." He looked at her dark, brooding face.

She said, "I go, too."

He stepped closer to Rebecca. "It's only February, there's snow and cold. It'll be fearsome until we reach the Willamette. The dear Lord knows I intended to wait until spring—now we dare not. Becky, we must leave *now*."

She roused herself and shook her head. She was looking as if she had just awakened, her eyes widening.

"Joshua, I'll never make it. You go, you'll be running for your life. I mustn't hold you back."

"Rebecca," he bent over her. "I didn't come this far just to give up now. No matter how weak you are, you must go. I'll get you through. One thing I know, every hour we delay cuts our chances of making it safely."

With that face so close, those eyes demanding, Rebecca merely nodded as she dabbed at the weak tears on her cheeks. He remained close and, in the chill of the hut, she was aware of his warmth, feeling the strength of him pressing through her coldness and fear to give her hope.

Solali repeated, "I go, too." Rebecca lifted her head and shook it but Solali insisted. "I fear, too. Remember last year and the reformation, the blood atonement. There's danger still." Her dark eyes were flashing as she whispered, "Not any of us rebellious ones will be safe. What happened can happen again."

Rebecca faced Solali and thoughtfully studied the woman. Without a doubt Solali, another former plural wife, was in as much danger as she was. They were both rebellious ones. "Yes," Rebecca put into words her thoughts and again the bitterness came through. "An Indian, raised and educated by the Saints. Privileged to be a plural wife, and now you're choosing to deny it all—at the risk of your life."

Rebecca's eyes widened with growing fear for the woman as she thought about Solali's history.

Orphaned in early youth, the Indian girl had been sold to the Mormons as a slave. But the Saints, in accordance with their beliefs, had raised her as a member of the family until she was old enough to become a plural wife.

Now Rebecca must ask the question that had been on her mind for some time. "Do you miss it, Solali?" she whispered. "Do you miss the other life?"

Slowly Solali turned, and with a puzzled frown she studied Rebecca's face before saying, "The snug cabins and the milk and yeasty bread, I do. I liked caring for the gardens and chickens and cows. But I didn't like the other."

"Say it," Rebecca demanded.

"I didn't like being one of many wives. I didn't like—" She gestured wordlessly and Rebecca finished for her.

"You've said it before. Sharing a man, being scorned because there was no child. You said it was like having a string tied around you, being jerked at will, knowing only that life was a set of rules."

Now Solali added, "They told me I must not forget my past. I must be good so that I would turn white and pure. I must follow the prophet or be damned.'"

"And you want to live like this again?" Rebecca gestured toward the simple shelter.

She nodded, "And I'm remembering you left, too," Solali whispered. Rebecca felt herself writhing away from the memories, but the Indian woman persisted. "You won't go back. You had Eagle bring the trunk. You touch the Book with faraway eyes. But I see much fear. Is that a good thing in exchange? If it were only fear keeping me here, I could not stay."

While they had been talking, Eagle slipped back into the hut. Rebecca glanced at him, wondering how much he understood. This silent Indian with the serene eyes seemed to always be there. Twice within the past year he had saved her life. Yet in the depths of his stoic face there was nothing to reveal his thoughts or feelings. As she studied him, briefly their eyes met and he turned away. She bit her lip, wanting desperately to say to him what she was feeling so deeply, the gratitude.

Looking around the hut, thinking of the people who had touched her life in this place, Rebecca was conscious of a wrenching, a feeling of saying good-bye to all that had been her life for the past months. It was the leaving-home feeling. Wordlessly she stretched her hand toward Eagle, wondering how she would ever repay his kindness.

Joshua got to his feet. He sighed, then with an attempt at lightness, said, "Tuck that Bible back in the trunk with the wedding dress and be ready to leave when the sun clears the trees."

2

· · · · · · · · · · · · · · · · · ·

*J*oshua, aware that Solali had followed him out of the hut, waited until Eagle strode out of sight before turning to her.

She was shaking her head. "Joshua, it's a fearsome thing you're asking of her."

"She's far from well." He shook his head in frustration.

"More than that," Solali insisted anxiously, "there are deep shadows in her spirit. She thinks I don't see, but I've watched her with the Book. Such sadness. Almost—almost, I think she doesn't believe the words now."

A shaft of pale sunlight pierced the trees and Joshua moved impatiently. "Solali, we must go. I'm obliged to you for coming with us." She was nodding as she started back to the hut. He added, "Eagle is going to travel with us too." Her outstretched hand clutched the deerskin curtain. He noticed and asked, "That troubles you?"

Without facing him, she replied, "No. But I do wish to see him forget me." She disappeared behind the curtain. Joshua stood for a moment longer, pondering her reaction to the handsome young Indian.

In the few short months since he had come to the Indian village, Joshua had learned to trust and respect the young man with the deep, expressive eyes. His quiet presence managed to communicate to Joshua a loyal friendship that he was coming to depend upon with increasing gratitude. Although the words between them were few because of Eagle's limited English, both of them were beginning to sense the spirit of the other. As time went on, Joshua was realizing how really unnecessary words were.

Solali paused just inside the hut and looked at Rebecca standing beside the fire with tears rolling down her cheeks. She was pressing her hands against her thin waist.

"You are in pain?" Solali whispered as she watched Rebecca move the fingers of her left hand slowly down her right side. Even as Rebecca shook her head, Solali said, "The wound was bad; that angry red scar will be with you forever."

Rebecca rubbed her hands across her tear-streaked cheeks and in a voice thick with grief said, "I was just remembering. Seems I must remind myself every day. When I don't, I catch myself reaching to feel my baby, and finding only the emptiness and the scar." Now she turned quickly as if to throw off the darkness that gripped her. "Solali, I'm not once forgetting the way you've taken care of me. I guess those bad times will always be with me, but I try, I really do, to think of you instead and the way you were always there when I cried or when the dream came." Rebecca reached toward the Indian woman.

Solali hesitated and then in a low voice said, "You remind me that I am Indian, that I don't hug and kiss like the Saints." She reached out and patted Rebecca's face and while Rebecca clung to her hand, she promised, "I'll still be there when you need me. I don't know why it must be, but I cannot let you go alone."

It was past midday when the six horses left the mountain trail and headed north. Joshua knew that soon the road they followed would wind past the trail cutting down into Mountain Meadows. Would Becky recognize it?

The memory of all that Joshua had heard about the massacre struck him, and he caught his breath as the images filled his thoughts and set him trembling with anger.

Wheeling his horse back to Rebecca's mount, he leaned forward, but she turned her anguished face away from him. He hunched down in the saddle, helplessly at loss for the right words. "This is the first time you've been back here since ... isn't it?" he asked in a troubled voice, thinking of Eagle carrying her to the Indian village, wounded and about to deliver her child.

As he continued to study her, Joshua realized he had been so concerned about her weak body that he hadn't considered the emotional impact of the familiar miles upon her.

Solali pulled her horse even with them and with a relieved sigh, Joshua dropped back. When Rebecca briefly raised her head, he saw the shine of moisture on her cheeks.

He caught Eagle's quick glance, and although Joshua knew the man probably didn't understand him, he said, "Somehow I'm not much good at these women problems."

They were well on the other side of the trail, moving west, when Rebecca broke the long silence. "I'm thinking I must look very strange dressed in this manner."

"You're wanting to wear that calico dress?" Joshua tried for a light touch as he referred to the garment he had previously purchased for Rebecca from an Indian in the village.

"You look like a young Indian boy from a distance," Solali said and added, "We must keep you that way."

There was a thoughtful expression in Rebecca's eyes. She said, "Then it's no accident you've chosen this dark hunk of fur to cover my hair. It's no accident it hangs nearly to my nose. I was guessing it was to keep me warm. Now I understand." The chill in her voice made Joshua almost frantic with despair.

"Becky"—Joshua's tone was impatient, ragged—"it's only in case. You're safe now. Besides, most travelers have enough gumption to stay at home in weather like this." He squinted at the leaden sky as a few more flakes of snow landed in his beard.

"It's a lonesome road we're setting out on," she whispered. "All because of me, my friends must suffer."

"And me," Solali added. "You forget, I've as much reason to leave as you."

"And me," Joshua said, forcing a twisted grin. "With Brigham's crackdown on every stranger in the Territory, and with whispers coming up the Colorado, we're smart to hightail out of the Territory as fast as we can go."

"All except Eagle." Rebecca turned to study the impassive face of the bronzed man who had first come into her life long ago when he rescued her and her milk cow from the mountains near Pinto. "Only Eagle has no reason to run with the rest."

The Indian glanced at her, and a tiny smile tugged at his gentle face. She found herself wondering again how much of the conversation he really understood.

"I think we'd better hurry along." Joshua's words interrupted her thoughts. "This snow is going to be a good storm yet. Even with the best of luck, we'll be spending the night under the sagebrush."

Rebecca shivered and pulled the rabbit-skin robe over the buckskin pants and shirt she wore. "Well, no matter, dressing like a little Indian boy is warmer than struggling with the calico, no matter how pretty it is."

"We'll be hard pressed to explain you once we hit civilization."

"There's people living out this way?" Rebecca asked slowly.

He nodded. Watching the play of expression on her face, he realized she had not thought about the journey that lay ahead of them. "We'll be traveling in Utah Territory for a piece. I've gone the route many a time, taking this trail up toward the Oregon cutoff. I've traveled the Salt Lake–California cutoff too."

"If there's settlements out this way, and this is Utah Territory, then—"

"You're wrong," he cut through her words, guessing the direction her thoughts were carrying her. "This isn't farming land we'll be crossing. It's desert. Except for trading posts and way stations for the freighters, there's scarcely a cabin. You're thinking of Mormon Station. That's snugged up against the Sierras, and we'll go nowhere close to it."

"It's a lonesome land." She glanced quickly at their two companions, remembering the Indian stories she had heard. Would Eagle's and Solali's presence assure their safe passage?

"That's not so. The land's been crisscrossed with trails since the late twenties. You can't feel too lonesome when you find a trail and then see a discarded barrel or even a piece of furniture, though that's not likely. Most of the discards end up being used for firewood."

"What about water?"

"In the summer you best stick to the main routes and hope your animals last between water holes and grass. Winter isn't too bad if you find forage. Winter, there's water holes that never exist in the summer. It's the clay in the soil. It collects and holds the water from runoff."

The snow ended and the sky cleared. They rode across land sparsely covered with sage and salt grass. Occasional sandy hills nurtured struggling plant life in their sheltering clasp, but across the open desert, crimped by distant jagged peaks, they moved in the full blast of the sandy wind.

Their diagonal journey, marked on a northwestern slant toward Oregon, seemed to be a dream of unyielding dimensions. The clumps of sage and infrequent juniper stands were approached and left behind, but the distant mountains seemed ever retreating.

On the third day they saw the first trading post. The tiny log structure, backed by a crude barn and corrals, sprang unexpectedly into view beside a stream and cluster of trees. Contrasted with the days of bleak travel, it was more than civilization. Poor though it was, it was comfort and warmth in contrast to the nights of cold when they had slept sheltered by animal skins and curled around their tiny fire.

Joshua pulled his horse ahead of them. "I'll see if they'll have us for the night." They trailed slowly after him, watching him dismount and stride toward the building.

As Rebecca reluctantly followed, she was realizing that this was the first cabin she had seen since leaving Cedar City. The sight of the log structure threw fearful memories at her.

A fat man in greasy buckskins stood in the doorway listening to Joshua. Spitting a stream of tobacco juice and shifting the plug in his mouth, he said, "Don't 'low no Injuns in the place. If'n you buddy with them, you and yer little fella can sleep in the barn with 'em."

Rebecca's quick intake of breath occasioned a hard, quick glance from Joshua before he said, "That's not right charitable."

" 'Tis." The man smote the doorjamb with his clenched fist. "I aim to be friendly. Ain't I trustin' 'em Redskins with my horses?"

Rebecca was sputtering with righteous indignation as Joshua hurried them out to the barn. There was a touch of amusement in Solali's eyes as she ran after Rebecca. "Never you mind. 'Tis common what he's saying. We hear it often." The amusement turned to tenderness. " 'Tis good to see you ruffle your feathers like a sage hen."

The following day they traveled into a snowstorm. Although the storm started with light flakes merely veiling the rolling hills and clumps of sage, the wind rose and whipped the snow into hedges of misery. They spent the day struggling through drifts that blanketed their legs in bone-chilling cold.

As the afternoon passed slowly, Rebecca knew she had reached her limit of endurance. Her numb hands could no longer master the pony, and she clung to her rabbit-skin robe and wished for her misery to end.

She was beyond caring when the trail broadened into a road and they were curving westward. When there were trees and corrals snugged beside a long adobe building, her pony stopped beside the others.

Briefly she was aware of Joshua's blue eyes heavy with concern. There were his arms to lift her down. Later she remembered the shock of his warmth, the thud of his heart, and the bite of a cold circle pressing against her cheek. Now she knew only Solali's poking, whispering, guiding and pushing.

There was a rush mattress, and the two of them collapsed

together while strange hands stripped snow-encrusted garments from them. Hot liquid was pressed to their lips, and then the blessed quietness of sleep.

When Rebecca was next aware of Joshua, he was bending close, speaking while his anxious eyes studied her face. "Becka," he said urgently, "we won't be leaving. They'll let us stay until the snow is gone. You are safe. There's nothing to harm you here."

"When you call me 'Becka' you sound like Jamie," she murmured. She reached, trying to touch him with a hand which was stone heavy.

"We'll see Jamie soon, just as soon as the willows are green and the water runs free. Rebecca, the worst is over. The fearsome things are gone. Please, just get well—strong." The urgency of his concern for her made her gaze into his shadowed face. Seeing the lines of weariness again, she wondered what she had said during those bad hours.

The way station to which the group had come during the snow-storm was on the Goose Creek Trail, the main east-west emigrant trail crossing Utah Territory into California. They were told it was an extension of the Central Overland Trail between St. Louis and Salt Lake City. On this trail, goods were carried to the mines in California, while mail and passengers traveled eastward. During the winter months it was used chiefly by freighters moving their ponderous wagons north and south, east and west.

While the spring storms continued to pile snow along the route, the flow of travelers continued. Rebecca and Solali quickly found themselves pressed into service, and the adobe way station seemed to expand and contract with people. Lonely, defeated miners trickled eastward; brawny freighters, cheered by their own success, moved westward.

Life centered around the yawning fireplace in the main room. The plank tables beside the fire were laden with the freighters' beans and flour, transformed into hearty meals by Rebecca and Solali. They carried steaming pots of stew and platters of venison while they listened to the men talk.

Discouraged miners lifted their foaming tankards while the freighters lifted their voices. "You mark my words. In a couple a' years there'll be stagecoaches crossin' this land ever' day. There'll be folks movin' faster'n they ever moved before. And it won't just be the miners. This country is a curious place to them back east. Folks all just waitin' to visit the wild west. There's fellas achin' to shoot themselves a buffalo, and ladies dyin' to see what a plural wife looks like and whether Brigham Young has two heads."

There was news. The gold fields in California were about exhausted, but there was talk of gold in Oregon. Rebecca's eyes sought Joshua's, remembering the letters from his youth. Those letters had been filled with hope and then despair. Would he be tempted again by the tantalizing tales? His blue eyes answered with a steady gaze which told her nothing.

The weeks passed. Between snowstorms they could see the hills were greening, and the trees, too, were fluffed with a cloud of green.

While Joshua and Eagle paced restlessly between the inn and the corrals, waiting for the storms to cease, Rebecca was discovering the blessing of this new interlude. With the constant pressure of hungry men to be fed, she was being pressed into service each day with just one more task than it seemed her strength would allow. But through the fatigue she was feeling a new challenge. When she wanted nothing more than surcease, there was one more task. And then there were Joshua's eyes.

In the beginning, when she had first taken over the task of baking bread, while she handled the dough with clumsy hands, attempting to spare the tortured muscles on her wounded side, Joshua had watched her. She had seen him and recognized when his lips whitened in response to the pain she couldn't conceal. In these days she felt the tiny nudge of that old spirited Rebecca who would not be beholden to anyone. She forced her smile and gritted her teeth. It was a glad surprise when she discovered the agony paid in dividends of strength and new freedom from pain.

Late one evening she was alone, resting beside the fire in the main room of the inn. The guests had moved to their rooms, and she was nodding in her cozy spot when Joshua came through the room, hesitated, then joined her.

She listened to the quiet rumble of his voice for a while and then with a yawn said, "That's a patter of nothing talk; why aren't you going to bed like the others?" She rubbed her heavy eyes and peered at him.

"And why aren't you?"

"Guess I'm too tired to face the task of getting there."

Abruptly he squatted beside her and lifted her right arm. She winced as he straightened the arm and lifted it, forcing it past the stretching pain. Now he folded it back into her lap. "Where were you injured?" he asked softly as his eyes continued to search her face.

Silently she raised her left hand and drew a line extending down her right side from under her arm to the edge of her ribs. "It—I must have moved because it was only a flesh wound."

" 'Must have moved'—dear God!" he murmured. She watched his eyes darken. Abruptly he got to his feet and left the room.

3

●●●●●●●●●●●●●●●●●●●

𝒥t was March when the lone rider came in from Great Salt Lake City. That night the stranger was the only guest, and he was full of talk as he sat at the long table between Joshua and the proprietor of the station, Hank Walker.

Rebecca studied the man as she listened. He was marked with a great weariness, but his clothing and gear indicated he was not one of the defeated ones. Obviously he was a traveler with a purpose. When asked about his destination he showed a hint of bitterness. "California."

"Why didn't you wait for the weather to break?" Hank asked.

"I'd had all of Utah I could stomach." He turned to Joshua. "You said you'd be traveling on in a few weeks. Don't take that cut going through the City of Rocks. You'll never make it."

"Why, what's going on?" Joshua asked in surprise.

"Highwaymen. They hole up in a hideout on Goose Creek. A little bunch like yours would be easy pickings."

Joshua studied the man before asking, "You had trouble?"

"No. I'd been warned by those who had. I'm just passing the word along. Seems the best way."

"Obliged, but we're heading the other direction."

"Well, it's a good thing. You know there's bound to be more trouble in Utah Territory. Washington's sent spies up the Colorado. They wouldn't do that unless they had something serious up their sleeves. The Saints are just too big a handful for Washington."

"What makes you think they're spies?" Walker asked.

"Everybody is saying. Besides, what else'd they be? Amasa Lyman thinks a big attack is planned for up the river. He's sent word to Brigham, and now he's at Cedar organizing men. There's rumor he's planning to look for a place to hole up over in the Pyramid Canyon area. I hear tell they're going to call the missionaries and settlers in from all over, places like Las Vegas."

Joshua stabbed at the venison on his plate. "Is Young still planning on moving his people south?"

"You'd better believe he is! President Buchanan's trying to bring in a Gentile governor along with the troops. They're determined to keep peace and make a good little Territory out a' Utah. Brigham Young is just as determined that he'll conquer. He's got a thousand fighting men ready to go." The man stopped to take a big swallow of hot coffee before continuing.

"Last fall, just before I got to the Territory, ol' Brig preached a sermon that set the people back on their heels. He made no bones about how he saw the whole situation. He said that he would be President of the United States, Heber C. Kimball would be Vice-President, and Brother Wells, Secretary of the Interior. But until that came about, the Saints would go to hell, just as surely as they stood there listening to him, if they ever deposed him as governor." He returned to his supper.

Curiously Rebecca watched Joshua. He seemed to be having trouble controlling his feelings. Finally he asked, "How do the people feel about all this?"

"They're behind him; leastwise, he's outfitted men with money from the tithing office. Seems like approval to me. They say they're ready for action right now."

Later Solali detained Joshua with a timid hand on his sleeve. They paused to watch Rebecca carry the empty platters into the kitchen; then Solali whispered, "Do you see it? The Saints will be coming this way. They must—there's no other place to run."

Joshua turned and paced restlessly to the fireplace. On his second trip he stopped to kick at a protruding log. "Solali," he said, "I nearly killed her getting her this far. I'm afraid to move on."

"I know what you heard and saw when the fever came up," Solali said, "But now there's new strength in her."

He nodded. "I know. I've watched her forcing her body, making it gain strength. I know it hasn't been easy. But that journey was so bad, I'm fearful. I can't risk more right now." He stopped and cleared his throat. The haunted eyes of Rebecca never ceased overlapping his memory of a laughing, happy girl.

"She's like a wounded bird," Solali whispered, "but she will fly again. When the sun breaks through and the air is soft, just watch her spirit soar."

"Please, God," he whispered. "But until that day—"

It was the middle of March now. While the sun brightened and warmed the earth, the wind softened, but Joshua lingered on. And while he was lingering, the wagon train arrived.

When the three wagons pulled by weary, overloaded oxen crept into the station, Joshua had been watching them for an hour. They were coming down the trail from the west—that should have settled his worries. When he saw the load of household goods bulging from the wagon, he decided the occupants were gold miners returning east. As soon as the woman climbed down, carrying a crying infant and shooing the toddler before her, he went to help with the teams.

Rebecca was in the kitchen when she heard the infant cry. With a puzzled frown she turned to Solali. "A wagon train just came in," Solali murmured as she continued to stir the simmering stew.

The baby was newborn. Rebecca settled the woman in a rocking chair close to the cookstove, then hovered over the pair with painful fascination.

Solali came in with a piece of bread for the wide-eyed boy while the infant began to nurse. The young woman sighed and leaned back in the chair. "Aw, it's good to have the world quit movin' for a time. I'm Katie Martin. We've come from Genoa. Movin' back to the Territory." She settled herself more comfortably. "This is a new place. Weren't nothin' 'long this stretch.three years ago when we moved to Genoa."

Abruptly Solali spoke, "Genoa. Used to be called Mormon Station, didn't it? It's over Pyramid Mountain area, isn't it?"

The woman nodded. "You're Indian, but you surely do speak good English." She said nothing more, but when Rebecca turned from the stove, she saw her intently studying Solali. There was a slight frown on her face, but she asked no questions.

Briskly Rebecca said, "These biscuits are done. Suppose we start serving the menfolk now." She ducked her head toward Katie. "You stay if you wish and we'll get things going out there."

"My husband will be a'wonderin' what's become of me."

"I'll tell him." Rebecca picked up the platter of meat and followed Solali into the big room.

Rebecca placed the platter on the table and Solali rapped a tin cup against a plate to signal dinner.

"Miss?" The man's voice questioned behind her.

"Oh, yes, I was to tell you—" with a smile Rebecca turned. She caught her breath and backed against the table, trying desperately to hang on to her composure.

The eldest son of Bishop Martin stared at her. "I know you, don't I? Wasn't it, ah—"

"Your wife—" Rebecca hastily interrupted, "she's with the young'uns in the kitchen. She says eat with the men. She'll—"

"Oh, yes," he smiled, and then the puzzled look returned. "I know you from somewhere, don't I?"

She dared not remind him of Cedar City, of Andrew, of her old school just outside the fort. But, then, he had been her student only a brief time before his long legs and restless energy had carried him on his way. Genoa—Mormon Station it had been. Why hadn't she remembered he had been sent there? The silence was lengthening.

"Why," she said slowly, "seems I always remind folks of the last towhead they knew." With a shrug he settled himself at the table and she sighed with relief.

Passing to and fro throughout the evening, carrying the loaded platters and returning the empty ones, Rebecca once again found Steven Martin's puzzled frown following her.

Later she saw the measuring glance that moved between her blondness and Joshua's. As she walked away from the table, she heard him ask Joshua. "Where you headed—California?"

She waited in the doorway, holding her breath and desperately willing Joshua to silence. But there was his answer, "No. Oregon. I have a place in the Willamette Valley, up near where the Willamette and the McKenzie rivers join."

"Been there long?"

"Long enough to get me a good piece of land in the richest farming country you've ever seen."

Hank Walker, curious, was watching Rebecca. Quickly she moved to take his empty plate and return to the room with the coffeepot.

Joshua had been watching Rebecca, too. When her hand had trembled against his coffee cup, he had wondered. As Rebecca returned to the kitchen, Katie Martin came into the room and spoke to her husband.

He got to his feet. "I'll go check on Sanders and the team. Let him get some supper."

After a moment, Joshua picked up his coffee cup and headed for the kitchen. "More of that Java?" he inquired, sticking his head around the doorjamb.

Rebecca was bent over the dishpan and merely nodded. Solali lifted the pot, murmuring, "I think Eagle's come back. I thought I saw him through the window."

"I'll mosey out to the corrals," Joshua said. He drained the cup and slipped it into the dishpan. Crossing the kitchen, he let himself out the back door. The light from the window laid a rectangular path of brightness pointing the direction to the corral. He started down the path and felt a detaining hand on his arm.

It was Eagle. A quick hand touched his lips and a tug took him off the path and against the side of the barn. Eagle's hand still held him silent. There was a conversation taking place on the other side of the wall and words drifted through.

Joshua moved impatiently. The men were talking about moving east, not west. Now a word caught his attention. *Towhead.* He heard, "She wouldn't admit she recognized me, and that makes me wonder. I'll bet you fifty she's Andrew Jacobson's wife. Can't help thinkin' he'd like to know that."

Joshua's chest ached with the pain of holding his breath. Eagle's hand guided him away from the wall. They circled the inn and stopped. Eagle's face was grim. "Pinto, Cedar men."

Joshua was beginning to get himself under control. He took a deep breath. "So you recognized them. I'm guessing it isn't a good idea to stick around here any longer." He clasped the shoulder of the Indian and said, "Go to the kitchen and get some grub in you and give me a chance to think about this."

Rebecca heard the light tap on the door. With her hands still submerged in suds, she watched Solali open the door and stand aside. Eagle spoke to Solali in Paiute, his words urgent and low.

Solali went to fill a plate for him. "He's been to the Indian villages south of here and says there's a bad feeling. It's because Brigham's made promises he can't keep."

"How's that?"

"Like being a battle-axe of the Lord—that means no Indian will be killed while he's fighting for Brigham Young. We know that isn't so, and the Indians are murmuring against the white men now. Also they are being forced deeper into the desert where there's nothing to feed their families."

Eagle finished his supper and went into the main room of the inn. Rebecca hung her towels and watched Solali go to their tiny room behind the stairs. Through the doorway she could see Eagle and Joshua still standing beside the fireplace.

Nighttime sounds were claiming the inn. Overhead the floor timbers creaked and a child whimpered.

The voices beside the fire dropped, and the flames crackled as the backlog was positioned for the night. The stairs creaked again.

From her station by the door, Rebecca could see that Joshua stood alone. Still wondering what she should tell him about the Martins, she slipped out to stand beside him.

Now she saw that he was holding a black-bound book. "Ah," she whispered, "is that the Bible you bought in California?"

He nodded and pulled a bench close to the fire. "Lately I've not spent much time with it, searching out what it has to say."

"Do you think that's important?"

"Becky, I'm knowin' the Lord's approval every time I open the pages, but more, I'm knowin' it's a real guiding hand."

She sat down beside him and plucked at the threadbare calico she wore. "Seems I'm losing my hankering for it. I was trying to live up to it for a long time, but lately my faith's like this old dress— about to give out on me."

"Are you back to thinkin' you have to earn the blessings of the Lord?" he asked.

Her head snapped up and she looked at him. "That's the way it appears, doesn't it? I guess I've been watching the ground for so long I'm afraid to look up."

"You've been sick and weak. Now—" his voice faltered and she glanced at him, surprised to catch the frown, the lines pressing his lips hard. Unexpectedly a tiny hard knot in her heart loosened.

She whispered, "Joshua, you've been such a wonderful friend. How can I ever repay you?"

There was only silence. She watched his hands tighten on the Book. Finally he fumbled with the pages and his voice was low. As he read to her, she became conscious of the center of her being becoming tender, sore. He was repeating words that had been familiar and dear to her the previous year. But now they were making her realize there was a threat within her. It seemed the words were trying to break down a wall she had built, stone by stone.

She jumped to her feet. Pressing her hand against her throat she whispered, " 'He's come to give me life,' 'trust in the Father,' 'trust in Him.' Joshua, right now I'm fearful to listen to the words. Someday—" She brushed past him and rushed to the kitchen.

"Rebecca." She stood waiting with her back to him. Out of the silence he spoke in an even voice. "I'm sorry. I don't understand. One of these days when you feel like talking your heart feelings, I'd be glad to listen."

But Rebecca was busy remembering the words he had read. The thoughts circled through her mind, demanding an entrance deep inside, but she wanted only to shut out the words. Yet they were there and they couldn't be denied. She pressed her hands against her cold cheeks.

Now more words were coming into her mind. " 'I will not leave you comfortless . . . my peace I give unto you . . .' " Such words couldn't be ignored; they must be accepted or disproved. But there was another thing she was seeing for the first time: Jesus' words had become Joshua's words. She looked at him uneasily, wondering how she had missed that before and what it would mean now.

Suddenly he spoke urgently. "Rebecca, we must go. Tomorrow. I'm sorry, but it must be." He turned and took the stairs two at a time. Astonished, she watched him. Now she was realizing that she hadn't told him about Steven Martin. For a moment she hesitated and then shrugged. No matter. They would soon be gone and it wouldn't be important. After tomorrow it would not be a thing to fret about.

4

· · · · · · · · · · · · · · · · · · ·

 $\mathcal{I}$ t was good to be back on the road—even Rebecca was feeling it. They were moving away from Utah Territory and steadily working their way toward Oregon.

At times the road before them seemed to inch along through the sand and barren bush. The mountains circled around them, remote, with only a dreamlike promise of a fairer land beyond them.

Once again the snow swirled about them, as if the Territory were reluctant to release them without a final thrust of misery. Again the horses walked slowly, bowing their heads to the storm as the people on their backs huddled in misery. But the way stations were clustered along the length of the California trail, and each night they were able to find shelter.

On the day that the sun shone brightly again and the snow disappeared, Joshua said, "Today we'll be headin' north. The Applegate trail is just ahead."

"Applegate," Rebecca repeated dully.

"Or Old South Road as it's known back home," Joshua explained. " 'Twas cut through soon after the terrible trips in '44 and '45 down the Columbia. The Applegates lost a couple of children when they were shipping down the river. The rapids just about make the trip impossible."

"I don't understand," Solali said. "We've heard about the Oregon Trail; what's this road?"

"The Oregon Trail cuts straight north through the Territory. From Fort Boise, where we were, the trail jogs west first and then north, clear to the river."

"The Columbia?" Rebecca questioned, sitting straighter in the saddle now.

"Yes, then it goes west only to The Dalles."

"If the rapids on the river are so bad, why don't they cut a trail?"

"There's no place to hang it on those bluffs," Joshua said ruefully. "Portage is so bad there'd be a road down the river if it were in man's power to build one."

He continued, "There's the pass through the Cascade Mountains now. Barlow cut it through in '45. It's south out of The Dalles and goes west over the mountains. The Applegate road joins with it in the valley. In the beginning the Old South Road was cut to give better access to the Willamette Valley. That's enough—we've only one road to contend with now. Right soon we'll ride up north across the end of California and drop down through the mountains into Oregon."

He was quiet for a long time. Finally he spoke again, reluctantly. "This next section of road cuts through lava beds and mighty thirsty land before it reaches Oregon. We've had a heap of Indian trouble along the road 'til '56. But then, I guess, we'd really been askin' for it ever since the land was settled." He paused to slant an apologetic glance at Solali and Eagle.

"Guess hindsight is better than foresight," he commented. "Leastwise, now we can see where we've gone wrong. That is," he qualified, "some of us are seein' and wonderin' how to rectify the situation." He turned to study Rebecca's face. "Pushing the tribes out of their homes doesn't make more sense than their pushing back. Don't you forget, Oregon's just as raw as Utah. Maybe our troubles are a shade easier to handle, but they still need settlin'. You'll not expect a heaven on earth, I hope."

She lifted her head and frowned at him. "I reckon I'd not given it much thought. You're saying there's scrapping to be done before things are settled. I recall your letters lent that air."

"Then you remember about the Whitmans?" He waited for her nod before adding. "They're the doctor and his wife murdered by the Indians. Well, from that time on till last year, '56, there's been trouble."

"That's been nearly ten years." Her voice was low as she tried to hide the dismay rising in her heart. She closed her eyes briefly against the dark thoughts.

As if guessing, he hurried on, "You've got to understand the situation. For the Whitmans, the climax came when the Indians around their mission were hit by a measles epidemic. 'Twas bad enough on the white man, but they'd been hardened to such disease. The red man hasn't. The whole lot of Indians demanded

Whitman cure their disease, and when he couldn't, they saw it as conspiracy since the white men were recovering. To compound the problem, the red man took to his steam house to try his own cure. That made matters worse."

They rode in silence as Rebecca recalled the story Joshua had written in one of his letters. After years of ministering to the Indians, the doctor and his wife were murdered in their home. Before the end, others had died also.

"Like I said," he murmured, "hindsight. If we'd just learn to respect their ways, let them live like always, we could've been neighbors, peaceable."

Joshua was quiet for a long time and then he chuckled and shook his head. "There was one good story that came out of the mess about an Indian who refused to take part in the killings. Seems maybe the Whitmans did manage to convert one Indian. I heard this story old Joel Palmer told on himself. Said he met an Indian chief and the fellow asked him if he was a Christian. Old Palmer said yes, and that seemed to be the end of the matter until the chief caught him playin' cards. Joel said by the time the chief finished with him, his jaw was hanging to his knees. This supposedly wild and unlearned savage, twenty-five hundred miles from civilization, was tellin' him how to live right before the Lord. Made quite an impression, and Palmer determined he'd leave the card playin' alone forever." His voice dropped to a musing note. "Imagine, one Indian completely converted. A totally changed life. Proves it can happen." Rebecca wondered at the note of awe in his voice.

The next day as they walked their horses up a rocky cut, Rebecca asked, "What's Oregon like?"

"Like everything you've ever seen. Green and fertile with rolling hills like Illinois. Barren in spots like the desert we've ridden. I've traveled the Oregon Trail from one end to the other twice now. I've been down California way and crossed back to Utah Territory three times now. But it's Oregon for me."

Rebecca pondered his words. She knew of the times he had entered Utah Territory looking for her. *What if* . . . Suppose he had found her on that first trip? She knew a moment of bitterness as she forced her thoughts away from those shadowy pictures her mind threw at her. Still, *what if?*

His words cutting through her thoughts were gentle now. Perhaps he too was handling the *what ifs*. "The Willamette Valley where Pa and I have taken land is as fair a place as you could ask for."

He slanted an easy grin at her. "The Donation Land Act Congress passed in 1850 gives every man 320 acres. If he has a wife, she gets 320 acres too. Pa and I had a nice piece of the valley, snugged up together with plenty of water. It's rollin' hills backed by timbered acres. Just back of it all, the mountains rear pretty sharp-like. There's neighbors, but even Pa can wiggle his elbows without gettin' them in somebody's soup."

Later as they rode their horses across the corner of California, he said, "There's trees and rivers and mountains. And fir marches right up the side of the mountain. There's lumber for houses and pasture for livestock. There's soil achin' for the plow and there's room for everybody who wants to come, and for the passel of young'uns he'll raise.

"Down Salem way you can hear the sawmills screechin' and the riverboats tootin'. That's progress. Matt's farming down there now. It's wheat country, and they're shipping it out fast as they can raise it." For a while he was busy with his own thoughts; then, "Salem's the capital of the Territory now. Things are rolling there. If you want to see action, you go to Salem."

Again he slumped in the saddle, his voice dreamy. "Oregon's a right pretty place. When the woodsmoke curls around through the wet trees, a log cabin feels mighty good. Makes a man feel snug and warm, right at home. You plant wheat in the autumn and sit and wait for the winter rains to nourish it along. Come summer you cut the wheat, thresh the grain, grind it into flour. Then you put it on a ship and send it to California. We exchange our gold for theirs. But we'll never run out like they will. We don't dig it, we plant it."

Rebecca's mind ran on with his words, drawing mental pictures of her own. She was replacing, transplanting the old with the prom- ise of new. His words seemed to make a spell, enticing and luring her on. She could almost forget the shadows of the past.

Now he straightened in the saddle. Ahead of them were the mountains, drifting blue-green with the misty rain. They climbed through gentle air, soft with the wind-borne scents of Oregon. Still dreamy with Joshua's talk, Rebecca thought she was catching a scent of Salem's woodsmoke in the midst of the pine.

Here in the mountains she was seeing moss growing thick on the north side of the delicate trees, woven into a mist of fairy lace. Was that trunk a spindle resting against the sky?

On the day the mountain began to slant downward, Joshua grinned at her and said, "Becky, welcome to Oregon Territory. You're home."

Home! She turned away to hide the tears. The word slashed

through the hardened dreams and splintered fences she had gathered to hide her soul.

They rounded that last sharp promontory, and Oregon rolled gently out before her like folds of green velvet. Joshua was watching her. After her first stunned surprise, she moved, looking about with delight. "This is Oregon." It wasn't a question; she was affirming it. She was accepting it with a stirring of senses she thought had been gone forever.

As Solali's horse grazed her way even with Rebecca, the Indian woman studied first the scenery and then Rebecca's face. "It's like a picture book, isn't it?" she whispered. "Like as if you turn the page, it's gone." A shadow touched her face and Rebecca wondered at the sadness.

Hastily Joshua said, "But this picture won't disappear; it'll be better. Welcome to the fairest section of the country. Oregon Territory, soon to become a state."

Rebecca's indrawn breath was ragged, nearly tearful, and Joshua's voice deepened as he expressed what now could be pulled out of the back of their thoughts and faced. "Just as sure as we rode out of that Territory and lived to tell it, we've come into new life. It's different here, Rebecca. The past is over forever; you can forget it now."

The silence of the peaceful land seemed to flow into them and they lingered. It was Joshua who moved first. He pushed his dusty hat away from his face. Rebecca turned to face him.

"You say it's over, that this is all new life." Her voice was low. For a moment she couldn't bring her eyes up to meet Joshua's, but when she did, forcing a brave smile, she pleaded, "Please, may it really be so?" Across the space that separated them she saw him frown. "Joshua, may I bind you to secrecy?" Now her voice was cold, hard, as she said, "My past must never be mentioned again if I am truly to live a new life."

"You know Ma and Pa'll find that hard." Joshua would have much rather promised her the silence she requested. But he went on, "They know where you've been; don't they have a right to know?" Shaking her head, she pressed her lips and reached for the reins. He stretched a staying hand. "Becky, I'm still not touching the real girl, am I? I'm sorry." He was shaking his head. As he turned his horse, he said, "I'm feelin' this way deep down inside of me. Becky, this secret is wrong. It's a mistake." But to her retreating back he said, "I'll respect your wishes."

He moved ahead and led the way down the mountain to the

green valley. When the rocks were behind them and they rode side by side through the meadows, Joshua said, "We've still a fair piece before we reach home. We'll head up Jacksonville way for now. I want to see Scotty MacLennan. I've heard scarce a word about the Territory since I've been gone."

"Is Jacksonville a goodly town?" Solali asked.

"Fair. They've been mining for gold hereabouts since '51. Here and the Josephine."

"You have?" Rebecca's quick question drew a glance from him, and Eagle turned to look at them.

"Nope. I recovered from my spot of gold fever right sharp and haven't been drawn since. Didn't take much gawkin' over the top of the dredge to convince me that the ladies doing the laundry were richer than we were. No mining for me; I'll take my riches the hard way."

The day was far spent when they turned west to follow the creek along the edge of the mountain. Joshua let his horse mosey along until Rebecca caught up with him. She noticed the taut lines on his face had relaxed into a pleasant half-grin.

"It's good to be back, to be free to settle in and start livin'." Shooting a quick look her way he said, "I'm not complaining about the past; I'm trying to explain how I feel now."

"Joshua"—she could only bring her voice up to a whisper—"I'll never be forgetting how you've put yourself out just for me. I'm guessing you've never half settled in here because of me and that land would be nearly fallow if it weren't for your folks and Jamie."

He nodded, adding, "We're not wanting you to feel beholdin', not a one of us. I've explained why I've gone lookin'. It was a need bigger than myself. The need's satisfied now. No matter how you make your life from here on in, the need's satisfied; that satisfies me." His glance slid sideways as if gauging her response. With a sigh she accepted this newest gift. He was holding her in an easy grip, not demanding.

Now a startling thought made her straighten in the saddle. If the grip was loosening, could it mean he no longer wanted her? What about those letters? Were they merely a part of the past that must be forgotten? Those promises were only the promises of youth. She looked down at her hands; ragged, weathered and well-used, they belonged to a different Rebecca. The woman riding beside this Joshua was not the girl he had left in Illinois.

"We've been through a bad place in the road together," he said softly. "But that's no reason to keep you beholden to me for the rest of your life. I sure don't want it that way."

He settled his hat against the slanting rays of the sun and continued, "Life's a hard enough patch to hoe without havin' the blamed rocks in the way."

Later, when they were entering the outskirts of Jacksonville, Rebecca realized their journey along the cabin-spiked trail hadn't prepared her for this. Her mind was still filled with the memory of log cabins guarded by squawking chickens and spotted bovines as they rode through Jacksonville's tree-lined streets. White picket fences and milled lumber houses painted white and pooled in brilliant flower gardens marked their way.

The hitching post where Joshua tied her horse belonged to the white clapboard house. Its wide verandas were bedecked with wicker furniture and scarlet geraniums in clay pots.

"Joshua, I can't," Rebecca whispered. "Not dressed like this, I can't." She touched her trail-stained buckskin pants and shrank back.

"This isn't the governor's mansion. This is just Scotty's." He was still wearing that pleased grin.

Slowly she followed Joshua's eager strides. "Scott!" he bellowed, heading around the house toward the barn. With a crash and a cloud of dust, the barn door banged against the building.

Rebecca was still watching the dust rise and the wall vibrate when the man burst through the door with a shout of glee. Towering above them, wearing clothing as tattered and stained as theirs, carrying a pitchfork, he rubbed his tousled red hair and roared, "Joshua, me lad! You've returned to the promised land. And have ye settled your brothers so's that you ken claim your inheritance?" He thumped Joshua's shoulder and wheeled around. "Aw, a fair one you've brought, and these are your Indian friends." Even Eagle's face relaxed as the Scotsman pumped his hand.

They settled on the veranda and drank buttermilk frosted with coolness. When the sun had dipped behind the last hill and Rebecca's teeth began to chatter, she was rescued by an Indian woman and swooped into the kitchen for hot tea. Scotty's introductions trailed after them. This was his wife, Matilda.

There was no time to explain—the chatters were more nerves than cold. In the kitchen Rebecca was immediately surrounded. She saw two more dusky-hued women and a dark-eyed child. As Rebecca was settled in a chair beside the cookstove, the women were introduced. The child was Ross and his mother was Star,

Matilda's sister. Tika was her friend, and all three were from the Klamath tribe.

Scotty had come into the kitchen to introduce the women. With his arm about Matilda, he addressed Solali. "I suppose you'll be able to talk their lingo. Seems no matter what tribe, you manage to understand each other."

Matilda, dressed in a demure calico dress with a spotless white apron, wore her lustrous hair coiled against her neck in a decidedly un-Indian fashion. She spoke with a gentle Scottish burr. "It is the tie of blood and earth, not language, because there is a difference." She patted his arm and gave him a gentle push toward the door. "Now, off with those muddy boots if you're to set one foot beyond this kitchen."

5

. . . .

While the woman heaped the serving platters, Scotty waved his guests toward the door across the kitchen. Matilda led the way into the dining room.

Rebecca's eyes took in a table, round and bedecked with snowy white to match their hostess' apron. The plates and platters were china—matching china. "This is Oregon Territory," she murmured in a wondering voice. "I'd guess me back east, not the farthest end of civilization."

They finished the venison roast and the fried chicken with the heaps of garden vegetables. There had been tender light bread and delicate preserves too.

Big wedges of dried apple pie were being pushed across the table before Rebecca could take her eyes off the marvel of the room. She poked her fork into the pie. These people and their homes were telling a story far more clearly than words. And the story was a sharp contrast to all Rebecca had known before.

She looked at the shiny, dark sideboard. The brilliant mirror above it reflected the sparkle of crystal and the glow of lamplight. These people were part of a community that was well established, secure. There was money enough for houses, which were more than mere crude shelters against bullets, fire, and weather.

She found herself acknowledging it all with a slight nodding of her head. *People don't import fancy furniture like this if they're wondering whether the Indians will leave it alone,* she mused. *You don't have china and crystal if your stomach is gnawing from poor and scanty victuals.* And, furthermore, she noted that a carpet like the one under her feet wasn't designed for muddy boots. Yet Scotty looked like he could have been transported from Utah.

With a start, Rebecca became aware of the conversation tossed back and forth between Joshua and Scotty. She glanced at Joshua and saw the yearning on his face. She turned to Scotty, wondering at his power to bring out that expression. The red-haired giant was hunched across the table, rumbling the china and silver as his fist punctuated each phrase with a thump on the table.

"Scotty," Joshua answered, "quit guiltin' me with leaving the Territory last August just before the constitutional convention. Just tell me what I missed. You knew I couldn't wait forever! I explained—" He hesitated and quickly glanced at Rebecca.

Scotty nodded and said, "Well, first off, you know as well as I do that circumstances made it so as everything pointed to stoppin' the squabbling and gettin' with it to become a state. The squabbling's been going on since '56, so you know all about it."

"It's about like two brothers scrapping."

"Right. It goes on and on, with matters just gettin' worse. But let an outsider stick his neck in and—"

"That's all it takes to get things settled in a hurry. Differences don't matter anymore."

"On our part," Scotty murmured contentedly, "the Dred Scott decision was a blessing. Leastways, it finally spurred us on to get with the issue of becoming a state."

"Dred Scott," Rebecca ventured timidly, "does that have anything to do with you?"

"Naw, he's no kinfolk of mine." Scotty was laughing now. "I came by my name through the back door. Weren't born with it."

"It's a handle," Joshua explained. "He's a native-born son of Scotland. The hair and the brogue stuck before his name did. Scotty's easier to remember than MacLennan."

"Dred Scott," Scotty came back to her question, "was a black man, trying to gain his freedom in a legal way. He said since he'd lived in a free state, he was free."

"Free state," Rebecca repeated. "That's one that didn't hold with having slaves?"

He nodded. "The country's been fightin' this thing since Thomas Jefferson's time. Mark my words, the rumbling's gettin' worse. There's going to be big trouble before the issue's settled." He stopped and sighed. Now facing Rebecca he explained, "When this all started the Union had settled on something they called the Missouri Compromise."

"I've heard about it," Rebecca said. "But the Dred Scott thing, what is that?"

"Happened about a year ago." Scotty settled back in his chair. "The decision. Dred Scott was a slave belonging to a Dr. Emerson, an army surgeon. In the progress of moving about, Scott was forced to spend two years in a non-slave state. Later he was returned to Missouri and his master died. Then he sued for freedom, sayin' that his living in a non-slave state actually made him a free man. Well, there was some shenanigans that went on, desperate man that he was, but finally his case reached the Supreme Court. The gist of the ruling handed down said that Negroes couldn't be citizens, the Missouri Compromise was unconstitutional, and Congress had no power to restrict slavery in the territories.

Rebecca pondered, trying to understand. Finally she spoke. "I know the Missouri Compromise sets limits on which states could be slave states, and says the northern part of the Louisiana Purchase would be free."

"At the time," Joshua explained, "this meant there would be twelve slave states and twelve free. Also it denied Congress the right to set restrictions on slavery in new territories seeking admission to the Union."

"But it was repealed by the Kansas-Nebraska Act," Scotty reminded them. "The part we're most concerned about's called 'popular sovereignty.' This is meanin' that the territories have the right to decide whether or not they will allow slavery in their states. At the time of admission, their constitution's to be written for or against slavery."

"And this is affecting Oregon?"

"The Territorial Constitution said no slavery. The Dred Scott Act said Congress had no right to restrict slavery in the territories. This was our chance. The blamed Territory has been draggin' its heels for years. Now was the time to settle down and get some serious business done."

Scotty paused to laugh gleefully. "I'll tell you, things have been hot around here ever since! Washington rumbles had it that Oregon would be another slave state. True, there were plenty casting their votes that way, and since then there's been many secessionist ideas circulated. But we fooled them all!

"In the end, when we got around to votin' on the constitution as a whole, there were only three items on the ballot for ratification. They were: do ya vote for the constitution, do ya vote for slavery in Oregon, and do ya vote for free Negroes?"

"Lane's the Territorial delegate to Congress, and he's soft for the South," Joshua warned.

"And he's bound he'll be the state's first senator." Scotty sat up straight and shook his finger at Joshua. "Josh, me lad, you need to start pushin' right now."

Joshua was shaking his head. "I'm too young."

"Oregon's young. Your next protest is that you're only a frontiersman. Everybody in the Territory falls in the same cast. Not a one of the bunch is a professional statesman. You stand as good a chance as the next man."

Rebecca's head was whirling from pivoting back and forth between the two men. She heard Joshua's protest again and Scotty's retort, "A man can't hold back for any feeble excuse, or we'll lose the state to the pro-slavery forces."

"You're puttin' the pressure on me."

"And I will until I'm assured you'll be at the Republican Convention." He paused for a moment and then added. "Wouldn't hurt you a mite to become a Republican."

"I've no choice," Joshua stated bluntly. "The Democratic party is splittin' apart over slavery."

During the conversation, Matilda motioned to Star and Tika. The two rose and began to clear the table. Solali joined them. When the table had been emptied down to the snowy cloth, Tika closed the kitchen door.

Scotty shoved his chair closer to Rebecca and rested his arms on the table. "My dear Miss Rebecca, if you're going to be a part of this new place, it's important you understand all of this."

With a mock reproving glance at Joshua, he added, "I can't imagine why you've failed to acquaint the young lady with the goings on in the Territory. I'm guessin' you thought you had better things to talk about. But there'll be no harboring an ignorant one here. Every man and woman in the Territory has got to come and settle himself down to being concerned about it all."

"But slavery?" Rebecca questioned. "Law, I'd heard it was dying out."

"Well, it ain't. It's a device of the devil himself to pass the rumors that make a man complacent."

Matilda stirred and stretched a gentle hand toward her husband. Rebecca still marveled at the soft burr coming from the Indian lips. "Scotty, it can't be *all* politics. Miss Rebecca will be fearin' that's all we are—politicians."

She turned to Rebecca. "You know we have a stagecoach comin' most days, least when the mud's not hub deep. It travels up from Portland. There's talk it'll be going clear to Sacramento in California, maybe next year."

"Jacksonville seems a right nice place," Rebecca said wistfully. "I saw shops. There's many a house like yours—milled lumber."

" 'Tis nice. Since the Territory's expandin' this way our little Jacksonville is growin' and smartin' up real nice."

"Gold mines help," Scotty interjected. "Not all this affluence comes from farming. That's still poor man's work."

"And many of us still fit that shoe," Joshua added ruefully.

"Never you mind." Scotty pointed a finger at him. "It's your choice—now stick with it and be happy."

"I'm not complaining"—Joshua glanced at Rebecca—"least not for myself. I could've joined the miners on the Josephine, but I'd have let the farm go beyond recovery."

"My boy," Scotty's deep voice interrupted again, "it's clear you're cut from better stuff than the hard rock ones. You're edging straight toward politics, plain as the nose on your face."

"You've just been listenin' to Jesse Applegate again."

He nodded and settled back with a pleased grin. "Talkin' and plannin'. Jess and me know the size of our influence. We lack the gumption to stick with what it takes to be political. You don't. Men are starting to talk and listen. I hear your name. Especially last August." His heavy brows furrowed and his eyes flashed.

"If you'd been there, we might have decided to send you to Congress instead of that soft-centered Joe Lane."

Joshua threw his head back and laughed. Wiping his eyes, still shaking his head, he said, "That's a joke! Me against Lane? Want me to look like a whipped puppy? Besides, I couldn't sit around forever. You and I both know every political faction in the Territory has been on again, off again. First they wanted to call a convention, but when not enough on their side would rally, it was off again. It's been goin' on like that for years."

Scotty was nodding his agreement and Joshua continued, "You can't get together a state government that people will accept when you can't get the people together to begin with, and then they won't agree on what's important. There's too much fightin' and pulling different directions."

"But that's all settled and done." Scotty thumped his chair to the floor. "Man, it's settled. Now just go be our senator."

Joshua was shaking his head. "Maybe later."

"Don't think you have enough influence? You could have gone in there and pushed railroads. That'll swing plenty of votes."

"We need one, that's certain. The farmers will never make it without. The whole Willamette Valley is a paradise for growing things, but with no market within reach, why plant? Seems the market in California is drying up—they're decidin' down there that plantin's more sure than diggin' gold. We're going to have to range farther afield to peddle our crops."

While Scotty was nodding his agreement, Matilda stirred restlessly. She whispered to Rebecca, "There's a woolen mill in Salem. A machine does it all except what the sheep does."

Scotty turned to his wife. " 'Tain't so. There's a little strippin' of the sheep that takes place before the machinery takes over."

Matilda ignored him. "Later I'll show you some of the goods. Beautiful." She slanted her eyes toward her husband. "Better'n Scotland and Ireland put together."

He looked at her and chuckled. "Scotland and Ireland put together explodes. And quit your teasin'; we'll have our politics, or you ladies will never have your railroads."

In the morning it was raining. For three days they lingered on at Jacksonville while Scotty and Joshua argued politics.

During the three days, Solali and Rebecca learned their way around the MacLennan kitchen, while Eagle roamed the countryside and the men moved between barn and kitchen talking, oblivious to the world around them.

As Solali kneaded bread and stirred the simmering pot of stewed apples, she admitted, "I'd forgotten the pleasure of living like this." Rebecca, tongue-tied with the picture of their past, caught Matilda's curious glance. But Solali's feeble explanation erased the picture of the Indian village from Rebecca's thoughts. She had simply said, "We've been cookin' beside the trail over a poor sagebrush fire for too many days."

Now Rebecca added, "It's the food. You know, Matilda, I'd been eating Solali's lumpy mush for—" she gulped and added, "for a long time before—before I found out the lumps were *roasted grasshoppers!*"

There was Matilda's amused glance at Solali, sharing that intimacy which gently scorned white ways. "You did survive, didn't you?" And when Rebecca wrinkled her nose even Solali laughed with Matilda.

After dinner on that final day, Rebecca was able to ask Scotty some of the questions which had been nagging at her. "What else happened at the convention that Joshua missed last August?"

"Well, young lady, how much do you know about making a state?"

"Little."

"It goes this way. First you gotta be a territory. See, when you get a bunch of people livin' together in a spot 'o land, there gets to be problems. Sooner or later there's the question of whose army ya yell for when the goin' gets rough. Rough it was, with the Indians. Seems like you have to do something pretty concrete to get to belong. Like this bunch settin' up constitution."

"And—" Rebecca was becoming impatient with Scotty's teasing.

Joshua looked at him and said, "Scotty, you'd better be careful with your joshin'; she's been a schoolteacher."

"Oh, beggin' your pardon, lady. All this time I figured you were leadin' me along just to make a good impression. In that case, I'll not only inform you, I'll appoint you his campaign manager—all you have to do is put enough gumption into him to make him see his value and be willin' to put a little knuckle behind his beliefs."

"Fight? Mercy, I don't want Joshua to do that!"

He turned to Joshua. "I'm seein' you have a big job to do. You take her home and educate her all about politics."

"What about the Constitution?" Rebecca asked.

With a chuckle, Scotty settled back in his chair. Joshua's eyes were seeking hers, and then he answered, "Do you remember I told you about this in a letter? Oregon became a territory in '49." As Rebecca looked at him, meeting his eyes, the letters from out of the past became a link, binding them together in a kinship she had nearly forgotten. As Scotty took up the lesson, his voice rumbled in the background as she let the tender memory of those letters circle through her thoughts.

"Applegate." Scotty's voice rose as if to capture her thoughts. "Old man Applegate was in on this from the beginning. He helped write the Territorial Constitution. But Joe Lane was appointed the first Territorial governor."

"And you think Joshua could beat Lane for the senate seat?" Rebecca's voice reflected the awe she was feeling as she looked from one man to the other.

"Scotty's dreamin'," Joshua muttered.

Ignoring him, Scotty said, "You know, there's nothing that makes a man appreciate his country more'n to be out from under it, all by his lonesome. A body likes to feel secure." He pointed his finger at Rebecca. "I know you're going to say constitution again. That came later. When it did, it gave every man 320 acres. They voted to exclude slavery from the Territory, but they wouldn't allow any free Negroes." His piercing gaze centered on Rebecca. "You see, young lady, there's no place on God's earth that's perfect. If you're going to live in Oregon, you'll have to be a scrapper like the rest of us."

Rebecca stared up at him. Her thoughts tumbled with emotion. He was inviting her to fight, to have an opinion. In the past, how badly she had wanted to raise her voice in protest, how she had suffered with the agony of holding her tongue. She looked at Joshua smiling at her. A new feeling rose in her, hope taking wings.

6

· · · · · · · · · · · · · · · · · · · ·

"'Tis all downhill, all the way home," Joshua had announced when they reached the summit of the final mountain pass.

Since leaving the MacLennan's in Jacksonville, even the horses found it impossible to move quickly. This was home and they all knew it. Now they meandered the woods and valleys slowly, savoring the belonging. As they rode down the length of the Willamette, marveling at its crashing descent, the river gorge widened and gentled, and the valley spread before them.

The rolling meadows and rounded hills with their crowns of fir and hemlock seemed groomed, disciplined into civilization. It was nearly impossible to believe that the distant field had always been meadow green, that the clump of wild plum was there by happenstance, not design. That curve of hill and windbreak of pine seemed deliberately cultivated to surround the distant log cabin.

As they wandered down the valley, curious eyes and friendly faces met them at every door, demanding that they stop. While Rebecca probed the ways of life in the valley and studied the cabins and their occupants, Joshua and the men talked. Bending over split-rail fences, they analyzed the August convention and the new Constitution. "Politics, politics," her hostesses would say, smiling.

More likely than not, Rebecca was discovering, Joshua was well known by all the people they greeted.

As Rebecca shared tea and chatter, she recognized the authority and influence that seemed to come through all Joshua's conversations. The faces tilted upward, hanging on his words.

Later as they rode, he brooded, "Up the valley there's bad feelings. Seems people are sidin' up with the South and muttering about needin' slaves if we're to progress. That's the hook they used in the South." He turned to look at her. "See, in the beginning the southerners were in favor of abolition. Then came the surge in cotton production. The growing market made them change their minds. Said they'd never make it without slaves."

"They could have hired," Rebecca objected.

"That cuts the profits," Joshua said, adding, " 'Tis hard to be charitable when there's such an easy way to get rich."

The next day they rode off the trail to stop at a farmhouse. "I know it's a delay," Joshua said, "but these are people I want you to meet."

At first approach, the cabin looked like all the others they had passed. But as the horses reached the fence, Rebecca changed her mind. *There's a certain neatness,* she thought; *seems like these folks are really proud of their place.* She was still noticing that not a weed or stick of wood marred the scene of order when Joshua cupped his hands around his mouth and shouted. People poured from the tiny cabin.

Rebecca hadn't time for astonishment, even when she saw the people were Indian. She had been in their presence only a few minutes when she realized they were Christians.

When they finally moved on again, Joshua told her about them, and his respect for them was evident in his words. "You saw them. Their life is a testimony just like that Indian Palmer met. God changes men for the good, no matter what their past has been. Every red man in the Territory must be given a chance like these people." The passion of his feelings came through and Solali turned to look at Joshua. Her eyes were still wide with wonder at all she had seen. Now a smile touched her lips, but she rode on without speaking.

When they finally turned east into the valley Joshua called home, Rebecca found herself hanging back, suddenly timid. Joshua pulled his horse in close to her and studied her face. "We're leavin' the Willamette River," he turned to point. "See, she's continuing on north while we're headed east up the McKenzie. That's our river," he explained again. "Pa and I have land just the other side of it."

Rebecca was trying to listen, but her thoughts were full of Joshua's mother, Cynthia, and that old feeling. From out of the past the words welled up in her memory: *Cynthia doesn't want me.* Her eyes sought Joshua's. But she remembered, too, those things he had said just before they arrived at Jacksonville. He didn't want her beholden; maybe he didn't want her either.

Now she saw his eyes wary, full of the unsaid things. "Becky"—

he bent close and his eyes begged her to understand—"you've made me promise silence, and I'm fearful. Pa and Ma are bad enough, but the others—they'll deal with you harshly. I know my neighbors. There's a kinship around these parts that makes secrets hard to keep. They think they've got to know everything about a body."

He dropped his hand; she was still shaking her head.

"Don't worry." There was just a touch of impatience in his voice. "I'll not be the one to say it. I hear you, and I promise I'll not say a thing to them. But you'll have to live with it."

Rebecca straightened and stared at him. A retort burned on her lips, but suddenly she was caught. The idea was liberation, freedom. He was guessing, and a smile touched his lips as his words echoed her thoughts. "From this day on, the past is gone. Bury it, just like it never existed." He took a deep breath: "Becky, for me that's how it is. I hold you that way—please."

Quietly she folded her hands across the saddle and the tears rolled down her cheeks. "Buried, done," she whispered. She guided her horse down the hill after him as he moved to catch up with Solali and Eagle.

At the very end of the little caravan, even behind the pack animals led by Eagle, Rebecca rode into her new life, conscious of new thoughts. Joshua's words, including all the unsaid ones, made Rebecca realize just what this journey was meaning. "It's past, gone," she whispered to herself as she took a deep breath. But she couldn't forget she was still ignoring that small dead spot in her heart.

At the bottom of the hill the road flattened out. Now they rode into a narrow valley, bowled between rolling hills wooded with hemlock and fir. They passed plowed fields and pastures filled with cattle. Houses and barns marked the farms. Now there was a line of fence and the military parade of young fruit trees.

The McKenzie River caught up with them and twisted past one farm after another as it plunged downward to meet the Willamette. Crashing over lips of tumbled stone fringed with fern, the river took on character. Rebecca felt its force, its energy as it plunged down the mountainside in front of them.

As they traveled, the day which had begun damp and cool began to mellow and warm. The sun was wringing sweetly scented mists from the earth. With each step that Rebecca's horse took, she felt a new thrust to life. There was an underlying excitement, a stir toward delight; but her troubled senses scarcely dared trust the urge.

The sun was setting when their road narrowed and the McKenzie quieted. Joshua dropped back to ride with her. "We'll be there soon," he reported. "In a bit we'll be passing through Waltstown. There's a general store, a blacksmith shop, a school, and a church. Not much else, but it's a start."

"What kind of a church?" she asked curiously.

"Kind?" he echoed, looking surprised. "I don't reckon it has a tag. Seems around here people aren't too fussy." He frowned. " 'Tis not like what you've known in the past."

As he urged his horse forward, Rebecca thoughtfully studied his back, wondering how Joshua really felt about her past. There was that stigma. Even in Utah Territory it was well known how those outside the Territory regarded plural wives. Rebecca sighed, and the ever-present burden on her heart claimed her attention.

Blue shadows were piling up under the fir and hemlock when, with a shout, Joshua cut in front of the pack animals and headed down the twin ruts winding through meadow grass. "This way!" his call drifted back to them.

Briefly Rebecca reined her mount and watched Eagle cut through the grass to join Joshua. They had left the road mounting the slope to the foothills; their path, moving at right angles to the road, was heading along the valley through meadows lush and green. Between their trail and the mountains the McKenzie River churned toward them.

Rebecca allowed her horse to follow the group, and Solali hung back to ride with her. "This is my home," she stated flatly. Rebecca glanced at her, wondering if she were disappointed that the journey was nearly ended. Solali was looking around now with interest, and Rebecca dismissed the thought with a shrug.

It was a peaceful ride through tall bushes clumped close to the water and the scattering of evergreens that lined the road. Just ahead a stream of smoke announced a cabin. But Joshua didn't slow. He gave a quick wave of his hat to the distant figure by the barn and hurried on. Now they plunged down a grassy slope and at the far reach of the valley, snugged near the upslope of the mountains, was another cabin. There were the soft greens and white of young fruit trees nearby. Behind them there were corrals and a barn. A line of fence drew her eyes to the brilliance of green-gold. "That's grain," Solali remarked, and then added, "This must be Joshua's farm." This time her voice had a happy lilt. Rebecca turned her attention to the house.

As they walked their horses slowly toward it, she could see that it was much larger than the homes they had been seeing down Waltstown way. It was built of logs. The late afternoon sun flooded the house with light, warming the varied brown of the logs and giving a sparkle to the windows that flanked the door. While they continued to ride toward it, Rebecca sensed the natural fitness of the gentle brown structure with the rolling hills around it. It was in harmony with the land. From spreading veranda to the massive chimney of river stones, she felt the peace of it. And she was knowing how well it fit the man who was riding toward it.

Rebecca pulled on the reins. There was a spot of color on the veranda. That would be Cynthia. As the woman moved down the path, Rebecca's hand stole to her throat. The cord biting into her neck reminded her. Quickly she snatched the black furry hood from her shoulders and stuffed it under the rabbitskin robe. Her trembling fingers rubbed at the grimy buckskin and tugged at the worn fringe.

"Oh dear, I look so terrible," Rebecca mourned. Solali grinned at her and Rebecca reached for her. "Solali, I'm so glad that you've come with us. I don't think I could face this alone." She hesitated a moment and then spoke quickly, fearful of how Solali would take it all. "Solali, I've asked Joshua to say nothing about our past. You know and I know—" Her voice trailed away. Solali's eyes widened as she looked at Rebecca, but before there was time for an answer, Cynthia was beside Rebecca.

The woman's hair was gray now and her face was lined. Held in the clasp of her arms, Rebecca discovered that her body was soft and warm. For a moment there was that old yearning for mother love, and then she was realizing how long it had been since those long ago days beside the Mississippi.

But when Cynthia held her off to study her face, Rebecca was even more deeply conscious of the passage of time. There were more hugs and pats and warm welcoming words. But in Rebecca's mind lingered Cynthia's shocked expression and the way that expression had included dark questions. But her arm around Rebecca as they walked toward the house was warm and firm. Cynthia was doing the talking, placing Rebecca back into the circle of their lives. "Pa's up the way, a'workin' at buildin' us our own little house. Matt's married and livin' down close to Salem. His Amy is a right pretty girl, delicate like a little posy." She added, "They're expecting their first young'un soon. Jamie's been hirin' out down at the wharfs at Champoeg. There's a lot of shipping goin' on down there." Now she sighed and said, "Course, Prue's still back in Illinois. Just think, if they'd come, then we'd all be here together, just like old times." Rebecca was thinking that her voice didn't carry the message her words did, but she dismissed the thought as Cynthia went back to her conversation. "All along the way here, they're raisin' grain. Then they're a'shippin' it down the Willamette to the Columbia, then out to the ocean."

Her voice was filled with awe, "Land, it seems strange to be thinkin' of the foreigners eating bread made outta our grain. Even the Russians are buying it." Now she focused on Rebecca again. "He's making a good living down there and he's sparking a girl, my Jamie is. She's part Indian." She sighed, "Women are scarce around here. But," she added quickly, "there's no call to fuss about her being Indian." She slanted a glance toward Solali.

"Jamie," Rebecca marveled, "little Jamie grown and courtin'!" They had moved across the veranda and through the open door and Rebecca stopped to look around. The room they entered was large and bright with light from the big windows on each side of the door. A stone fireplace filled the end wall. To her left an open door revealed a bedroom. Cozied between the end of the fireplace and another door on the right was a stairway angling upward.

On the right Rebecca could see the big kitchen. A shiny black stove dominated the center of the room.

"See," Joshua was explaining as he waved toward the kitchen, "in the beginning, the kitchen was my cabin and the rest of the house just grew from it."

"Joshua and his pa hauled all those river stones up and dumped them outside the door to the cabin." Cynthia pointed to the fireplace. "I declare, they didn't want to move them again, so they just built the fireplace where they dropped them."

Joshua laughed and picked up Rebecca's trunk. Cynthia looked at it and then cocked her head at Rebecca. "So, it did finally catch up with you," she remarked slowly. Again she looked at Rebecca with those questions in her eyes. "I didn't have much faith in that stage when I sent it off."

Rebecca caught her breath and bit her tongue to keep from spilling a torrent of questions about the trunk. How badly she wanted to know just when it had reached Great Salt Lake City. With a sigh she turned to follow Joshua up the stairs. As she climbed the stairs, she muttered to herself, "I guess turnabout's fair." If Cynthia's questions must remain unasked, then Rebecca dare not admit her own.

Beyond the shining windowpanes of the cozy room she and Solali were to share, Rebecca could see the barn and corral. An apple tree outside the window was making promises with its show of blossoms. As memories of her favorite apple tree back in Illinois flooded over her, Rebecca realized with a start, her birthday had just passed.

Joshua said, "Shall I place the trunk under the window so you can lean on it and smell the apple blossoms?" She was both pleased and dismayed that he would remember the thirteen-year-old girl of so long ago leaning on her window sill and peering through the apple-tree branches at him.

"Joshua"—there was a painful pressure around her heart from the old memories—"life doesn't go back. Some things just can't happen again."

"Yes, they do, Becka. If there's hope enough, they can happen again." Abruptly he leaned across the trunk and pushed the window open.

"Joshua," Rebecca warned, "you'll fall out."

"No, I won't." He plucked a branch and backed into the room. "There. Until apple time, this must do." He held out the branch of delicate blooms and slowly Rebecca reached for it. She tried desperately to hide her tears in the blossoms as she hunted for words.

"Just tell me that you won't go running off to Oregon this time," she finally managed.

"I cross my heart," he said. "No more running. We've both had enough to last a lifetime. Besides, we're here! This is Oregon, and now life begins. It's all new." His eyes were reminding her there was no past.

She ducked her head and he touched her chin. "No more tears, ever," he said gently, "but may I have just one smile?"

She turned away and sniffed appealingly. "I'd be obliged if you'd just let me owe it to you."

Joshua walked slowly down the stairs. His mother was waiting below. She stood hesitant, awkward and he reached out to give her a quick hug. "Don't look like that. Everything will be just fine. Give her time. Just, please, don't question her. The past is mighty painful." His eyes were demanding and for a moment she couldn't move beyond them.

"She's so—" her voice faltered.

"Old?" He brought the blunt word out. "Mother, Rebecca is twenty-seven years old. You haven't seen her for eleven years. I haven't seen her since she was a scrawny little girl of thirteen, all big blue eyes and mounds of taffy hair. We all change, even you." He bent over to pinch her rosy cheek. More gently now he said, "Me thinks it would be best to forget about tying links to the past and be content with helping her build a new life."

"You're talking brave, like saying so makes the years already gone by as if they never were."

He was lifting his stubborn chin toward his mother in a way he hadn't done since he was a lad. He delivered the flat statement, "They weren't."

Her eyes met his again and he saw the decision being made. For now the dark questions were being pushed aside. She blinked and patted his arm.

"Thanks, Ma."

7

· ·

$\mathcal{R}$ebecca, leaning over the kitchen table, moved her lips silently as she read the newspaper spread before her. It was almost more than she could grasp. She mouthed the words again. The back door opened and Joshua came into the kitchen carrying a basket filled with greens, peas, and early beets.

"Joshua," Rebecca said as she marked the spot, "will you come here, please? I can't believe the terrible things this paper says. Is this man foolin'? Why, that's terrible language to be using about somebody!"

"You're reading the *Statesman*," Joshua replied. "Editor Bush is a mighty powerful voice in the Territory."

"I don't like the way he's speaking," Rebecca muttered, turning back to the paper.

" 'Tis frontier talk. There's no sweetness and light about the Oregonians. No man with a gentle voice is likely to be heard about here," Joshua continued as he dumped his load into the washtub. "Good politics involves a little swingin' of the fists."

"But talk like that? Sounds like he's not too fond of the delegate to Congress. Isn't that General Joseph Lane, and isn't he the man you said was governor at one time?"

"Yes to both."

"Why's Bush sliding around and giving him a fictitious name if everybody's guessing it's Lane anyway?"

He shrugged. "That's part of the game. Seems to add to the excitement if you're having to dig through the garbage and the funny names to figure out who it'd be. Seems a body stands a better chance of getting a man's attention if the words aren't plain old grammar-school words." Rebecca turned back to the newspaper.

After a moment Joshua said, "The *Statesman* was the voice of Oregon for a long time. Don't know how much longer Bush'll be able to hang on to the hat. It's about broke him. Had the job of printing the Territorial laws. They wanted five hundred copies. Also had the job of printin' up the Territorial legislature session laws back in '54 or '55. All that printed material plus his new press was lost at sea when the ship carrying it sank.

"He never did recover his money or his good humor after that. Lane's still trying to get hold of some money back in Washington to pay for the printing of the laws of the Territory. He's also trying to get Congress to foot the bill for the Indian wars."

Joshua took time to lift a dipper of water to his lips. "Ah, that's good. It's getting hot out there." He continued, "About the money for the Indian wars: General Wool wasn't too impressed with the claims Washington and Oregon Territories set forth, and the money is mighty slow comin'. Could explain why everybody's taking it out on Lane. Now there's rumblin' among his own party. They're saying that Lane's responsible for delaying the statehood bill."

"Why ever would he do that?"

"He isn't. Out here, Oregon way, it's kinda hard to believe that the most important work on the docket in Washington isn't gettin' the bid for Oregon's statehood approved."

"You sound as if you know what's going on back there."

Joshua shrugged. "Any man with a reasonable head on his shoulders agrees that Lane's doing right."

"If that's so, why's Scotty unhappy with the man?"

"You got to understand—Scotty's radically opposed to slavery. Doesn't sound like much to say that. Seems at least half the Territory's that way, but Jacksonville and most of the southern part of the Territory is in favor of slavery."

"But they wrote 'no slavery' in the Constitution, didn't they? Doesn't that mean the matter's settled?"

Joshua straightened and turned to Rebecca. Slowly he said, "This nation is being torn apart over the slavery issue. Sooner or later men are going to take sides and it will be more than fists a'flying before it's all over."

Rebecca looked down at the paper. The cruel words seemed to leap out at her. The insinuations and veiled threats became more than childish indignities. Slowly her hand crept to her throat.

"Rebecca, don't—take it like that," Joshua begged. He was standing close to her, looking down. The bright light of the midday sun touched his face and she looked into his troubled eyes. She took her hand from her throat, hesitated a moment and then, taking a step nearer, she dropped her hand across his shoulder and peered at him.

"Why, Joshua," she said with surprise. "I've just now realized it. Your eyes have flecks of green in them. *That's* why I think of sunlit forests when I think of you!"

His eyes were changing, darkening. Ducking his head, he pressed his bearded face against the hand resting lightly on his shoulder. "Remember," his voice was muffled, "Scotty said I was to be educating you. You best be quiet and listen."

The moment that should have been captured in lighthearted laughter stretched and flattened. A fly buzzed against the window. Slowly Rebecca moved, her hand dropped and she sighed.

Turning from the table, she said, "Seems at times I still have a difficulty fastening my thoughts on a subject and keeping them there." She looked apologetically at him, wanting desperately to pour out her feelings, begging him to have patience for just a little longer.

Matter-of-factly he turned back to his task. As he poured cold water into the tub he said, "The corn's not much good around here. I knew it wouldn't be; there's just not enough of the good hot weather here, but I can't help hankerin' for the roasting ears we grew back home. There's a spot up the side of the hill, surrounded by rocks and facing south. Come next year. I'll try my luck plantin' up there."

In less than a week it would be June. Almost six weeks had passed since Rebecca had arrived in Oregon. Today as she stood in the doorway of Joshua's house looking down the valley toward Waltstown, she mused over the changes that she had seen taking place.

It seemed she and Solali were being accepted into the community with little fuss. She was feeling the acceptance and even now beginning to relax into it. If there were undercurrents of question, she was unaware of it.

Without having willed it, she knew life was picking a new pattern, and she was knowing how she must live in order to keep settled forever the dust of her past.

Because she had determined she would not acknowledge that past, she found she must demand of herself a new discipline. There must be no fragment of living or thought to point to the life behind. She must ignore the weak arm and force it to behave like its

companion. Without a hesitation in her step, she must move as if
her serene woman-life had never been interrupted.

But there were those moments when the past would tumble into
her thoughts, even though she was learning how to catch herself
quickly. She knew that when the dark pictures and heavy moods
threatened her, they could sweep from her mind everything, even
the knowledge of the next ingredient for the bread she was mixing.

If there was primary satisfaction in these beginning days in
Oregon, she found it in thinking that Cynthia never guessed her
deepest feelings or sensed the despair life had heaped upon her.

Joshua's household had also accepted Solali as easily as a stone
slipping into a quiet pool. If Cynthia questioned the presence of a
woman whom she and her neighbors had considered savage, her
placid face never revealed it. But then, it was easy to overlook Solali. Her hands were busy at the right time and her quiet efficiency
kept her beyond even Cynthia's reproach.

Eagle was another problem.

From his dress to his stoic silence, Eagle was decidedly Indian.
The braids and the buckskin didn't give way to overalls and boots,
even when Solali assumed the dress of the white woman. Fortu-
nately for all concerned, Eagle's restless energy wouldn't harbor the
stricture of house and farm. When Rebecca saw Cynthia's reaction
to the man, she was relieved to see him go, knowing it would be
easier for Cynthia to accept the gentle Solali when Eagle wasn't
around to remind them of the differences. And increasingly, Rebecca needed Solali's quiet presence there.

Now Rebecca was thinking about the scene late one afternoon
last week. It still made her uneasy. Rebecca had been sitting alone
and quiet beside the cold fireplace when Cynthia walked into the
house carrying a bolt of dark blue calico sprigged with pink roses.

As Rebecca stood up, Cynthia held the cloth up to her. "Right
pretty, being you're a towhead. You're gettin' pink in your cheeks
again and the roses will help."

"That's nice." They turned. Joshua stood in the doorway watching, with an admiring, questioning look.

Solali came in behind him, and her wistfulness was revealed in
her face and fingers as she bent to touch the cloth. "Oh, it's beautiful!"

Cynthia frowned when Solali spoke, questioning, Rebecca knew,
how an Indian woman could speak English as easily as a white
woman.

Cynthia's only comment was, "Rebecca needs a new dress. I

spotted this at the store last week and knew 'twas made for her."

"It takes me back in time," Rebecca whispered with a catch in her voice. "You telling me to hold still, then shaking your head because I'm getting tall."

"Now you're such a little thing."

"But she *is* getting pink in her cheeks." Joshua took the milk pails from Solali and left the house. After lingering a moment, Solali followed him. The touch of sadness on the woman's face etched the scene on Rebecca's mind.

One of the biggest adjustments for Rebecca was the Sunday worship services. True, the women wore calico, just as they had back there. True, they carried their dinners to church and shared them under the trees; but there the similarities ended.

From the hymns to the prayer: *Dear Heavenly Father—in Jesus' name*; from the sermon out of the Book marked Holy Bible, it was different. No longer was she hearing the Prophet's words expounded. Rebecca's mind drank in the truth like a thirsty stallion.

She was hearing the words she had read in secret and learned to love. The promises which had fearfully trembled on her own lips now tumbled in thundering affirmation from the lips of Parson Williams. It was life underlined and emphasized; meanwhile Rebecca must sit primly, not giving way to the wide-eyed wonder she felt.

On these Sabbaths, serenely, quietly, as if it had always been this pattern in the past, she donned Cynthia's extra dress and followed her to church. But never must she allow herself to forget that she was working out a new pattern of living. Sometimes it would all seem easy and natural; at other times she would catch that shadowed look in Joshua's eyes or see Solali's questioning glance.

Sometimes community acceptance could be easy as Katy Horton's sliding down the pew and offering the hymnal. But sometimes, particularly after church when the congregation met under the trees for dinner, she had to work hard to fit herself into the new way of life. Now she found herself timidly reaching out, daring to express her thoughts and feelings.

Sometimes, while the women spread their fried chicken and apple pies across the tables set up under the trees, the men would cluster around a new horse and hotly discuss the latest news from Washington. When their voices rose and the gossip about Lane or his buddy, Asahel Bush, turned to politics, Rebecca would find herself inching toward them.

Scotty MacLennan had whetted her political appetite and challenged her mind. Now as the high tide of emotion erupted from the men, she found herself strangely drawn. Sometimes she dared ask a question. "At the Constitutional Convention, was there more'n just the Democrats there?"

Impatiently—after all, she was a woman—"Yes, only about two-thirds of them were Democrats. There was a Republican there. Don't know his name. There were two Whigs and a handful of independents. 'Twas a bunch of different ones too, includin' some Free Soilers."

Others added their voice. "I'd like to see Dryer—he's the editor of *The Oregonian*—head for the Republican side."

"Aw, he's got his head in the sand. He'll never admit the Whigs are done, washed up. It was the slavery issue that done 'em in way back in '53."

"Jesse Applegate was there. Still hanging in there as an independent. Shrewd, huh? Waiting to see which way the ball bounces. . . ." And they were off again, forgetting her.

Joshua was standing beside her now, and Rebecca whispered, "More'n one party and no one telling them how to vote. Think of that!" Joshua threw her a sharp glance and the concern she saw reminded her of their secret. This was Oregon. She turned back to the tables.

As she helped lift the baskets and spread the tablecloth, she was fussing at herself. What a slippery thing the tongue was! How easy it was to trip up herself. Joshua had been more careful than she. One more word and surely these people would know. They would recognize that the only place hereabouts where there was only one party and one voice would be Utah Territory. Or did they even know?

Over fried apple pies, the arguments erupted again. "I'll tell you why Asahel Bush's Clique is losing out. It's his fault as much as anyone. He's been tryin' to run the Democratic party since '55. He don't care what the doctrine of the party is; he's just for it. You'd think a body who isn't a Democrat is ignorant. He's sayin' right now that there ain't to be a public office for that other bunch, the Nothings. I tell you, one of these days he'll get his up-and-comin's. And I hope the Republicans give it to 'im."

"You Republican?"

"Naw, I'm a good Democrat, but—"

"Well, the Republicans'll never make it if they don't get a bunch to rally 'round the flag pretty soon."

"Had a good start in the November '56 Convention. A Republican was elected enrolling clerk."

"Some think that's no honor." And with that flat statement, the group broke apart. A few returned to the table for another fried pie while a game of horseshoes ended the politics and the women sighed at the mess left behind.

The days of nearly constant rain gave way to sun and warmth. The garden brimmed with produce and on the hillside behind the house the wild berries were ripening.

The sight of the wild blackberries sent Rebecca into the house that June afternoon searching out Solali to help her pick the fruit. As Rebecca walked through the house and up the stairs, she sensed the quietness, feeling it fasten its claim upon her. She also felt a waiting in the quietness—but for what? She sighed.

The door of the room she shared with Solali was closed. Without thought, she turned the knob and entered. Solali was on her knees before the trunk, holding Rebecca's Bible. In the seconds before the woman moved, Rebecca saw first the Book and then the dress that Solali wore. The dark blue calico with the pink roses fit Solali as if it had been made for her.

"I do believe you look better in it!" Rebecca said, recovering quickly.

Slowly Solali stood to her feet. She closed the Bible and placed it on the bed. When she turned the mixture of emotion on her face touched Rebecca. "Oh, Solali, don't be embarrassed. I don't mind that you wear the dress."

"But *she* would."

"Yes," Rebecca said thoughtfully, sensing the undercurrents that Solali had noticed in the household. "But Cynthia is that way. Do you know that I am an outsider, too? Always, even back when she took me into their home as a little girl. She was kind to me, always, but I never forgot that I was the outsider."

"It is different with me." She looked down at the dress and carefully spread its folds. "It is beautifully made, but when I put it on I feel the lack in me. The Indian dress fits me. Then I feel at home."

"At one time you dressed like this. You were raised to calico, not the Indian dress."

She was nodding. "This has been good, this time here. I wanted to see if I could wear the dress, be the white woman again."

"You're wanting to live like this."

While her fingers fumbled with the buttons on the dress, she nodded. "I don't know how to explain it. Rebecca, until you came to the village of my people, I was content. Joyfully I had slipped back into their ways." Fingering the buttons she sighed, "I had nearly forgotten the past, the log cabin and Mormon quilts, the milk and eggs and fresh bread. In smelling the woodsmoke and tanning skins and drying meat—in mixing and baking our bread made from rice grass seeds and the pollen of cattails for the little ones, I was forgetting."

She turned to gesture toward the Book. "Can you understand? I turned my back on the teachings of the Mormons and tried to pick up again the ways of my people. I would have been content to forget the reading of white man's books if you hadn't brought this one. The first ten summers I had lived with my people had grown dim. The next eight summers with the Mormons I knew I must push from my thoughts. But now." She stopped and pulled off the dress and reached for her own frock. Smoothing her hair and fastening the buttons she said. "I kept thinking the clothes and the Book could change me."

"Why do you want to change?" Rebecca frowned as she asked the question.

"I'm not certain why. When you first came to the village you talked about the Book."

"When I was sick?" Rebecca asked in a low voice.

"Yes, in the worst of the time you begged for it. It was almost as if it was a charm you believed in, that you must touch it."

"Not magic, Solali," Rebecca said. She was trying desperately to forget about the time of her illness and to bring back all those thoughts and remember the words. How could she explain the ideas that made the Book so important?

"When Eagle first brought the Book to the village, you clung to it as if you were afraid to let it out of your sight. Since we've come here, you seem to—well, isn't it important anymore? Is it because Joshua is with you now? Why have you changed?"

Rebecca couldn't answer. She was busy with her own painful thoughts. Now Solali said, "I'm nagged by the Book. I want to discover what is important about it all. And, then, I want to become a part of all this new way to live."

"But you won't even go to church with us on the Sabbath."

Solali looked bewildered, "But that's what the Mormons do. Is there really a difference?"

Shocked, Rebecca stared at Solali. In her mind the differences began lining up. But even as she contemplated them, Solali's bewildered expression informed her of her failure.

Rebecca dropped her head, whispering, "Solali, I'm sorry. I've taken and taken of your kindness and I haven't given you a thing. In spite of how it has seemed, this really is the most important part of my life." She touched the Book, continuing, "Please forgive me, and right now I'll change it all." She stepped toward Solali and hugged her. "Come help me pick berries, and I'll tell you about Jesus."

The berries plunked slowly into the pails. But that was all right; Rebecca was explaining some very important truths, and she needed both arms to gesture, threatening the loaded bushes and half-empty pail. Words were so limiting. She had explained about sin and the righteous God. She tried to detail the story of the covenants and give life and passion to the picture of God, and then create a clear picture of a loving Savior in Jesus Christ. She quoted John 3:16 and the Romans passages telling of man's sin.

"There's just no hope without Jesus. God said it in the Old Testament, and the Apostles repeated it in the New. Jesus said He was the way and the truth and life." In frustration her tired arms dropped.

And Solali spoke around her puzzled frown. "You are thinking to persuade me? You are so passionate to convince me that you are right. Rebecca, if the Book is true, if it shows the right way, why can't I read it myself and discover what I must believe?"

Slowly Rebecca sat down on a rock. "You mean I don't have to convince you that you must throw out Mormonism and accept this?"

"I have already thrown out Mormonism. It did nothing for the dark inside of me, the fear. You see, you forget that no matter the color of the skin, down underneath, we are the same. I don't have to be persuaded to be fearful of God. It is there. Rebecca, I didn't leave the Mormon way because they were mean to me. I left because I must find peace, and it wasn't in the Mormon faith. Now you say it is all in this Book. Let me read it. I take it slowly, with much thought, anything that is given to me. Will your God be patient with me while I learn to listen to Him?"

"Yes, Solali," Rebecca whispered, humbled, torn by her wild emotions and Solali's quiet, rational statement. "Yes, and I guess I can quit yelling that He loves you."

Her eyes widened thoughtfully. After a moment she nodded, saying, "But yes. It is all a pathway of love, isn't it? From the beginning until the end. Why, if that is so, and if the way gives such peace, is it so difficult?" Now she turned a stern glance down on Rebecca. "And why do you forget the love?"

"Have I?" she mourned. "Oh, Solali, have I forgotten it?"

"Could it be there's more to His love than you know?" Again Solali's eyes were wide with questions, and there was a beginning excitement in them.

8

....

$\mathcal{I}$t was July. In the fields beyond the house the winter wheat was a blaze of yellow, moving gently to the touch of wind. Today Solali, Rebecca, and Cynthia sat on the veranda where they could feel the same breeze that moved the wheat. Each held a piece of calico generously patterned with vivid flowers.

As Rebecca's needle reluctantly poked in and out of the fabric she held, she was watching the wheat. While it bent in gentle waves, she was feeling a dreamy contentment wrap her. "Here in this place it is so peaceful and good, it's terribly hard to think of pain and fear and sorrow," hardly realizing she spoke aloud.

She saw Cynthia's eyebrows arch in surprise and Solali glanced quickly at her. Hastily Rebecca said, "I'm thinking of Mrs. Hanson. I heard tell her mentioning the journey into Oregon Territory—the troubles," she babbled on. "It's hard to believe people can come through that and be at peace once again." There was silence while the needles moved rapidly through the cloth.

Cynthia sighed and said, "A time back I said I'd be content forever if I could get me a cookstove. You remember me sayin' that, don't you, Rebecca?" She nodded without taking her eyes off the sewing. Cynthia continued, "Well, now I'm thinking how nice it'd be to have one of those sewing machines. Mrs. Collins has a picture of one. Seems a body could get one shipped around for a wee price. Seems they might even have one or two in San Francisco looking to be sold."

"Now, Cynthia," Rebecca murmured, "why do you want a sewing machine? There's scarcely any calico to be had in the stores in Waltstown. If Mrs. Collins hadn't been willing to part with this piece, Solali would have waited until spring for a dress."

"Things are better in Salem and Portland. When we first came, nothin' was to be had from the States. Seems they were losing ships all too often. It was hard—everything had to come around first off. Before then, they didn't even have flour mills, and the flour was shipped around. Now look, we're shippin' it all over, even as far as Hawaii. Lands a'livin', they talked about wearing animal skins and carving plates out of wood. Things are easy now, compared." Cynthia shifted and sighed.

Rebecca was nodding. "Mrs. Hanson was telling me about those times. She came to the Territory with the Applegate bunch. Her telling me about the trip down the Columbia was enough to scare the wits out of me! No wonder they worked so hard to get in this cutoff up from California way."

" 'Tis better," Cynthia added, "but there's still no wagon road along the Columbia. There's just not enough room along the canyon to make it safe for families to go over. They've taken cattle along the road since first off, but they've lost a sizable bunch, too."

Rebecca was still shaking her head. "Seems it couldn't be worse than the river. Mrs. Hanson says the Applegate family lost two boys when their boat went over. Law, when I think of those wild currents and the falls and all—"

"Leastwise," Cynthia interrupted, "it would have taken you weeks longer to get here. That's why this area didn't start settling right off. The richest land in the whole Territory was the hardest to get to until the Applegates cut through here."

She stood up. "Well, I guess I should take some water to Joshua. I'd expected his pa to be by this afternoon early, but I guess he's so caught up in buildin' that house he can't be bothered."

"It's going to be a pretty place." Solali lifted her face from the sewing. "All that milled lumber makes it fancy. Heard him tell Joshua he'll paint it white just like the places in town."

" 'Nother year and these log places will be out of style," Cynthia said comfortably. "That new mill in Eugene is sure turning out the lumber."

"I love this place." Rebecca glanced up at the mellowed logs of Joshua's house. "Inside, with the planed walls, it's as neat as any of the fancy clapboard houses." She got to her feet. "Here, I'll take water to Joshua. I'm so tired of sitting I'm about to stab myself with that needle. You like sitting, and Solali has a heart to finish her dress; let me go." Cynthia nodded and settled back with a sigh.

Rebecca filled the little tin jug at the well and set off across the fields toward the distant line of trees and the ring of the axe. Just beyond them she knew Joshua was cutting wood. The water sloshed against her skirt and the coldness was a shock measured by the heat of the day. She walked quickly, glad to be free of the sewing.

Trudging along the edge of the wheatfield, Rebecca mused on the changes that were taking place in Solali. It was obvious that she was responding to the Book and the story of Christ, but it was puzzling to watch the evidence of struggle going on in her. At times the Indian woman seemed content, but there were those unguarded moments when the sadness in her eyes betrayed other feelings. Rebecca noticed that when Eagle returned from his mysterious forays, Solali seemed more determined than ever to adapt to the white man's way of life.

Rebecca reached the edge of the evergreens and paused to listen. Again she heard the ring of the axe and she headed up the hill.

As she reached the clearing, Joshua dropped his axe and stepped back to watch the towering tree slowly lean. With a mighty crack, it fell, crashing to the ground with broken branches flying.

"Bravo!" Rebecca called as she walked across to him. He turned to wave and she was suddenly shy. He had removed his shirt. Chest heaving, he wiped his sweating face and waited for the water she was carrying.

"Just in time," He grinned down at her and reached for the jug.

"Don't drink too much," she cautioned. "Your face is as red as fire."

"You've bright cheeks too. Come sit in the shade with me." She followed him to the felled log. "It's old; there won't be fresh pitch," he said as she poked at it with an exploring toe.

"It's nice up here—the piney fresh-cut wood smell. I love it." She turned to smile at him and noticed the leather thong about his neck. From it dangled a gold ring. She ducked her head, recalling that snowy night in Utah Territory when he had carried her from the horse to the wayside inn. Through her slipping consciousness she remembered there had been the sharp cut of cold metal against her colder cheek. It must have been the ring.

"You've noticed the ring," he said. "It's from the gold I mined in California." His voice teased lightly, "I must prove I've been there."

"But why don't you wear it?" She could have bitten her tongue. It was obvious.

"It's too small." Still the teasing note, "There was only enough gold to make a ring this big. Wanna try it for size?"

And now there was the echo of a long-ago letter: *"Becky, it's you*

and me for the green forests of Oregon. I think I'd better snatch you
before someone else does."

She turned away, desperately trying to find a safer subject. "This
is a pleasant spot. It's pretty well cleared. You planning on building
here?"

"No, not unless you and Solali won't let me stay at the house. It's
cleared only for the timber." He hesitated and then added, "You
know, Pa's building on his land and the house is about done."

The thought swung between them like the ring on its thong, and
there was nothing she could find to say. Rebecca's hand drifted toward her throat. He reached for it. "You needn't do that."

"What?"

"I've noticed that when someone backs you into the corner, you
grab for your throat. I'm not pressuring you, Becky. I'm content to
wait."

She turned. "I—I've got to be getting back to my sewing." He
walked through the trees with her.

"I wish Eagle would put in an appearance right now. I could sure
use a little help with the wheat." There was a touch of curiosity in
his eyes as he looked down at her.

"I'm sure I don't understand why he comes and goes so myste-
riously," she murmured.

"It's Solali. Haven't you guessed?"

"I'd wondered." She turned. "Joshua, I feel her wanting to break
with the Indian life. After all, she spent nearly half of her life with
white people and it's bound to make a difference in how she feels."

"Yet she left them."

"It was the plural marriage. She hasn't said too much, but I know
how she feels."

Joshua's face was thoughtful. "Do you? Sometime I wish you
would make me understand how *you* feel."

She caught her breath and studied his open, troubled face. It
was too much. Those things were too much for her to share. He
would never be able to accept it all. She turned and walked slowly
down the hill, deeply conscious of her sore heart.

Would it ever be possible to bare her soul of all the time of hurt
and loneliness—especially to him? "Please, God," she whispered,
"that mustn't be. 'Tis bad enough to think back through it all. 'Tis
impossible to consider talkin' it out." It felt good to be talking to her
Father again.

Even as she was whispering the words, there was a busy part of
her mind wondering what it would be like—sharing with another

human being all the deep parts of her heart. Was it possible someone could help her understand the turmoil going on inside? There were those thoughts connected with God and how He fit into the whole scheme of things. "There's this feeling," she murmured as she walked back along the field of grain. "I'm having the picture of a great big curtain hanging in my life. On one side's me and on the other there's God. 'Tis all right if that's the way it should be, but why am I feeling otherwise?"

There was Solali's question. Was it possible that God's love could penetrate the curtain?

9

....

$\mathcal{R}$ebecca, beside the table in the kitchen, was steadying the chair on top of it. Cynthia was standing on the chair, leaning toward the cobwebs with broom in hand. The back door swung open. Rebecca could see it all as it began to happen.

Just as Joshua walked through the door with a basket in his arms, the broom descended crashing to his shoulders.

Rebecca laughed. Standing in the middle of the kitchen full of the smell of rising bread and stewing apples, she laughed. While the midmorning sun slanted through the window and pooled brightness like a flood on that scene, she leaned helplessly against the table, still laughing. Now weak, she felt her hands slipping from her station at the table and tried to signal her powerlessness. Joshua shoved the broom off his shoulders and ran to rescue his mother.

Cynthia sputtered indignantly, "No call to carry on like that." She straightened her apron and allowed Joshua to lift her off the table.

Joshua's face was a study of perplexity. "First time I've been took for an Indian. How's come you didn't go for Pa's gun?"

"Oh, Joshua," Rebecca gasped. "Your face when she hit you with the broom!"

Joshua was chuckling now. " 'Tis many a year since my ma took the broom to me. But I don't recollect getting it in the head before."

With Cynthia's dignity rescued, she too began to smile. " 'Tis silly. It weren't ever that funny. There's cobwebs above the door. I put the chair on the table in order to reach them with the broom. Now if you menfolk had just made this kitchen with nice planed wood like the rest of the house walls, I'd have never been at it like that."

Rebecca was still laughing. "It wasn't you on the table; it was Joshua getting the broom in the face as he walked through the door.

And me, not able to think whether to yell or leave the chair."

"Well, we'll do it every day if it'll make you laugh like that." Joshua was smiling down at her.

She caught her breath at the expression in his eyes. "It's every-thing—" she whispered; "the beautiful day with the sun shining through the window. Even the apples and bread. I—I guess I'm find-ing it's good to be alive."

"About time, young lady, to be celebrating the Lord's goodness." Joshua's voice was teasing, but the underlying message was there.

He started for the door and paused. Shifting the empty basket, he said, "I've a mind to do like the visiting parson suggested last week." While Rebecca's thoughts fled back to the Sabbath message, he continued. "With Pa gone so much, I'm guessing I'll be the man around here and start family devotions and reading out of the Bible. Every evening."

He disappeared and Cynthia's astonishment kept her silent for a moment before she said, "Well, I declare! I never know what to ex-pect from that young'un." Rebecca was tempted to remind Cynthia that her "young'un" was past thirty years of age.

Cynthia went back to shucking corn, pausing to say, "He's right, this corn's nothing." After a moment she grumbled on, "Since we've been here he's been right sharp about preaching to us about our responsibility to the Lord. Insistent he is about Sabbath worship. It takes a body back. He's not been raised to think goin' to church is important. I'll not take the lip of my own son measuring my life and telling me I'm a'lackin'. Now this is his own land and his own home. We've decided that from the beginning. He was here first, and this place is his choice." She paused and cast a glance toward Rebecca.

"Anyways, it's his place and he's to do as he pleases and we'll all cooperate." Again the sharp glance. While Rebecca was busy won-dering why Cynthia would rebel at the Bible reading, she began to understand. Cynthia was expecting Rebecca to rebel, too.

Cynthia dumped the corn into the bucket and continued, "I'll be a mite more content with it all when Pa and I get settled in our own little place. This house is bigger'n a barn. The two of us don't need room like this. That young man looks to be counting on a passel of young'uns."

Rebecca's hand stole to her throat as she fought the memory of that tiny, lonely grave. Cynthia gathered the corn husks and headed for the door. As the door slammed behind her, Rebecca found the bright happy kitchen suddenly a prison, holding thoughts from which she could not escape. She turned and ran toward the stairs.

That evening Joshua kept his promise. At the end of a warm day, past dusk, when the last chore had been done, Joshua carried the lamp to the middle of the kitchen table. "Ma, Becky, Solali," he called.

They settled in their chairs and he opened the Book and began to read. Rebecca watched his strong fingers supporting the Bible, turning the pages. She was lost to the words as she studied him. The lamplight touched his sun-darkened face and brightened his hair. Briefly his eyes caught hers and she concentrated on the words, hearing him read, " 'He restoreth my soul: he leadeth me in the paths of righteousness for his name's sake. Yea, though I walk through the valley of the shadow of death, I will fear no evil: for thou *art* with me; thy rod and thy staff, they comfort me.' " Rebecca felt her lips twist with bitterness and for a moment her mind went dark. Then she heard, " 'Surely goodness and mercy shall follow me all the days of my life: and I will dwell in the house of the Lord for ever.' "

Later, as she started up the stairs behind Solali, Joshua said, "Becky, wait up." The tiny circle of light didn't reach his face, and she was grateful for the shadows that surrounded her.

"I'm sorry that my reading hurt you." The words of denial rose to Rebecca's lips, but before she could speak, he continued, "I read some more and I couldn't help thinking about you. Please, will you come back to the kitchen for a while and let me read them to you?"

With a sigh of resignation she followed him into the kitchen. They sat down together, and the pale light drew them closer as he opened the Bible. His voice was quiet, meant only for her ears. Again she tried to concentrate on the gentle, deep tones, shutting out the words. But they were compelling and she knew she must listen.

"Rebecca, I don't know how much you believe of all this, but I'm feeling the power in His words. I'm wanting them, like a prayer, for you. Listen and let them in."

"Let them in," she repeated wonderingly.

"Yes. I'm wanting them to become a part of you. They must in order to do their work."

"Joshua, you're talking strange."

"Because I believe there's power in God's Word? He says His word won't come back without doing what it's supposed to do."

The retort was forced from her lips, "Even if I don't want it?"

"But you do. You haven't come this far for nothing. You want all the beauty heaped on you."

It took a long moment for the answer. She was trembling as she said, "Yes, I do."

Tenderly he began, " 'Behold, thou desirest truth in the inward parts: and in the hidden *part* thou shalt make me to know wisdom. Purge me with hyssop, and I shall be clean: wash me, and I shall be whiter than snow. . . . Create in me a clean heart, O God; and renew a right spirit within me. . . . Restore unto me the joy of thy salvation.' "

The words hit Rebecca, twisting through her being, flaming with distorted meaning. She was hearing a long-ago voice. For a moment she pressed her fingers against her forehead, remembering. That woman at the ball in Great Salt Lake City—she had blackened plural marriage with the words given by the Gentiles. "Fallen woman."

Rebecca leaned across the table to face Joshua. "Now tell me," she whispered the angry words so that her shame would not be spread beyond the room. "Tell me that you must change me until I am worthy of you!"

"Rebecca!" He jumped to his feet and reached for her, but she was gone, flying through the hall and up the stairs.

Rebecca had just begun to dish up the eggs and bacon the next morning when Joshua and his friend Scotty came into the kitchen. "Throw on another plate," Joshua called, "Scott's here."

"I'm back from Salem way," Scotty announced. "And since I didn't find the young, honorable Mr. Smyth down that a'way, I decided to see if he were still livin'." He took the cup of coffee and settled himself at the table.

"The said honorable was busy a'fussin' over his wheat crop," Joshua declared shortly. "Now, tell me what happened."

"Not much. Actually, you'd a'wasted your time goin'. The Republicans had already washed out. They'd nominated candidates, but the whole lot of them threw in the towel. Said the party lacked organization. I've my feelings." He paused to attack the plate in front of him. Later he added, "I've come to the conclusion these fellas were lookin' for an easy win, not a hard fight and a loss. Seems the gumption had gone out of them. 'Course they wouldn't win a seat, but they still needed to get their names in there. You don't become a household name before the next election by hiding out in the barn come this one."

When he returned to the plate of bacon and eggs, Rebecca asked, "And how is Matilda? I enjoyed getting to know her, and I find myself pining for her company."

Scotty began to answer, but Joshua interrupted eagerly, "Tell me what did get accomplished."

"Well, Lane, Smith, and Grover are headed for Washington. I'm hopin' this'll be Lane's last. There's just too much dissatisfaction with the man. Heard tell that he said he doubted a man could be a good Democrat and vote against slavery in Oregon. From a fella who's reluctant to name his side of the fence, that's just too pro-slavery. Trouble is, Lane's just awful political."

"Heard any more about the bill for statehood?" Joshua asked.

"Well, we know it's passed the Senate, but now it's hung up in the House of Representatives. 'Tisn't all Lane's fault. The southern faction in both the Senate and the House are really buckin' the anti-slavery clause."

"I suppose that's causing a lot of rumbles through the whole Territory, but particularly down your way."

"Right you are. The softs have given themselves a new name. They call themselves the National Democratic Party. This whole showdown has them steamin' like a brand-new engine. I expect they'll be spouting off hot air for a long time after we get to be a state."

"Particularly if this thing in Washington comes to a head and splits the country wide open," Joshua added bitterly.

"Now you're not to be saying that," Scotty said soberly. He finished his coffee and held his cup toward Solali. "Gotta admit, Jesse Applegate's about sick over it all. He's been riding the southern part of the Territory and he says the mood's really bad. Some's been tearin' down the flag in parts. Other places there's more fists a'flyin' than words. Didn't expect to see this much restlessness apart from the Indian troubles."

"Does Lane know what's goin' on?"

"Naw. He and Bush aren't even communicatin' now. Bush's gone so soft all he can spout now's Stephen A. Douglas and Popular Sovereignty."

"Well, Lane asked for it, sneakin' around behind Bush's back and trying to get another newspaper to toddy to him, buyin' in at the back door."

"There's been such bad stuff in the papers," Rebeccca ventured, "I've just about quit reading it. I sure can't understand it. Such name-callin'! I can't understand how Christians can get by the Almighty with such carryin'-ons and name-callin'."

"Where'd you get the idea they're good Christians?" Joshua asked.

She turned from the stove. "Why, that's easy to see. Just look at the fine houses and rich lands. They're all prosperous. With the Lord just blessing in that way, you know they're mighty pleasing to Him."

Scotty looked blankly at Joshua. "You been teaching her theology, too?"

"Not me." He turned. "Rebecca, that's about the most foolish thing I've heard you say. Fat cows and fine farms don't tell a mite about what's going on in a man's heart. Bein' in good relationship with the Lord touches the heart, not the pocketbook. I could give you a whole list of names that you'd recognize as being rich but on no account Christian. For starters, how about all those in China and India and Egypt who've never heard of the Lord?"

"Josh, me lad," Scotty drawled, "I'm a'thinkin' you'll make a much better politician than preacher. Which reminds me"— he heaved himself to his feet and reached for his hat—"mighty nice to meet you, ma'am," he bowed toward Cynthia and addressed Rebecca. "Either he ain't teachin' or you're not listenin', my dear. I'll be checking on the two of you later." Joshua followed him out the door.

Outside the pair strode rapidly toward the barn with Scotty talking all the way. "I'm serious, me lad. I'm also more'n a mite concerned. Oregon's splitting into statehood at the most difficult point in this nation's history. We need every decent, thinkin' man we can get if we're to survive in an honorable way."

Joshua took a deep breath and rounded on Scotty MacLennan. "I hear you, but man, you don't understand. I love this Territory, and my heart's a'quakin' in me over the problems, but Rebecca comes first."

"Do I hear you right?"

He nodded. "She's the most important part of my life right now. When I know her to be strong and—well, then I'll be more'n eager to stick my nose into the political machinery." For a long, silent minute, Scotty was studying Joshua's face.

Slowly he said, "I get you, friend. I'm almost envying those feelings you're having. But one thing's certain"—his voice was gruff with unusual emotion—"if you can feel that way about a woman, you'll be the most compassionate governor we'll ever get." He flung himself on the horse and touched his hat.

When Joshua returned to the house, Eagle was with him, and Joshua's shout reached Rebecca and Solali in the kitchen. "Got another plate? Eagle's back."

Just as silently as he had slipped away, Eagle had returned. And as usual, he moved in and out of the house on quiet moccasined feet. So silent and impassive was he that he seemed to Rebecca like a bronzed shadow come to life. And always his quiet, steady eyes watched Solali. Still feeling the emotion of Joshua's revelation concerning his feelings about her, using the Scripture to dig at her past, Rebecca gladly fled to Solali's problems.

First there must be a confrontation. Later, standing in their bedroom, she faced the Indian woman. "Solali, why doesn't Eagle return to his people?"

"Because he will not listen to me."

"He loves you, doesn't he? Then what are your feelings about it all?"

She turned and Rebecca was reminded that although Solali's quiet strength and even temperament seemed to belong to an older woman, she was still really only a girl.

Tormented by Joshua's words when he had, in reading the passage from Psalms, unwittingly revealed his true attitude toward her, Rebecca was conscious of the need to handle Solali's problem gently. "I don't know how your people feel about your plural marriage, but—"

Solali turned away shaking her head, "It isn't that." Then she turned back to Rebecca, frowning. "I've been reading about Jesus. He is different from the Mormon god and I am confused. They said I had to be baptized and join the church. They said I must marry a man who already had three wives. They said I must have children. I didn't have children and they were angry. Did they think I had *willed* my body to have no child?"

"But that is in the past," Rebecca said slowly. "You must put it all behind."

She shook her head. "I'm wondering what your God will demand. I—"

"Oh, no!" A cry of anguish ripped through the silent house. Momentarily Solali and Rebecca hung transfixed by the sound before Solali dashed from the room to the stairwell, with Rebecca right behind her. Together they stared down at the scene. There was Matthew. Beside him stood Cynthia holding a feebly whimpering bundle.

10

· · · · · · · · · · · · · · · · · · ·

*R*ebecca looked down on the stark white face of Matthew and understanding slowly flooded through her. She threw herself down the stairs and into Matthew's arms. Holding her childhood friend close, her tears mingled with his in shared agony.

Joshua came in from the field and Cynthia sent him down the road for Mrs. Chambers. While she rocked the tiny infant, Cynthia explained, "The Chambers have a tyke but a few months old; she'll be able to take this one on."

The story was all too familiar; no explanations were asked or given. Cynthia rocked her grandbaby while Rebecca led Matthew into the kitchen.

She knew words were impossible—for her and for him. The shock was too new. She offered only tea and embraces, a pat and more tea, this time with bread. And through it all, Rebecca was knowing herself plunged backward, thrust into a sickness of soul that she had believed impossible. Through the dull haze she bitterly assailed her false security. It was the house, Oregon, Joshua's cheerful face which had done it all. She had thought herself escaped from hell and floated to heaven—a real heaven, with no danger of hell catching up.

In the shifting patterns demanded by frontier life—the patterns that Rebecca in her emotional turmoil refused to acknowledge as ordinary life, hard and real—the household was moving quickly, adjusting. A wooden-faced Matthew took his place in the fields with the men. Motivated by hard work with the companionship of his father, brother, and the silent Indian, he was forced to live, to lay to rest the wife and companion whose body now lay beneath the soil.

During the daytime hours, Solali carried the wee one down the road to Mrs. Chambers to nurse.

The harvest was finished, the grain had been threshed, and Matthew accompanied Joshua to the Umpqua River where the grain would be ground into flour and shipped downstream to the coast.

Again Eagle disappeared, quietly, without a word. But this time his absence was brief. When he returned there was a young Indian mother and her papoose with him. His explanations were brief, and Solali interpreted with a relieved smile. "This is Kalli," she pointed to the woman. "She will stay here until Matthew's baby is weaned."

Again the household shifted. Now the commodious house seemed cramped.

When Matthew and Joshua returned, they stayed only briefly. But before they left, Joshua followed Rebecca out one evening as she carried kitchen scraps to the chickens.

Tagging along after her, he implored, "Becky, will you hear me out?" She was shaking her head. "You've refused even a word with me for the past month. Must I force you to listen? I'm just wanting to beg your pardon. But you did misunderstand me."

"You've said you wouldn't pressure me, Joshua. Keep your word."

"So be it," he muttered, and then he added, "Matthew and I will take Eagle and go up to Pa's place. He's been there alone working at that house. I suspect he'll need some help getting the roof on before the rain starts."

"Are they planning on moving before winter?"

"Yes. Could be this house will split at the seams if they don't."

"Has Matthew decided to stay?"

"Yes. When he buried his Amy he left the place for good. Says he'll never go back. Can't say that I blame him, and he's sure welcome here."

"Ah, he's about to make himself ill with it all," Rebecca said slowly, suffering over Matthew's tortured life and the tiny, motherless baby. "It would be the best thing that could happen if he would find another wife to help him with that baby." Still shaking her head, she went to toss scraps to the chickens.

"Rebecca." She heard the helpless note in his voice but shook her head. To her back he said, "Well, I'll return soon, and then you *must* listen."

She watched him walk back to the house. His square shoulders and rapid stride seemed to cancel the wistful words. There was an ache growing in her throat and she rubbed it as she watched the door close behind him. In a moment she could see a small spot of light shining through the kitchen window. He had moved the lamp in there. It was time for the Bible reading.

She sighed heavily. Why should those words Joshua had read from the Psalms matter so much to her? She lingered, taking time to scatter a handful of grain for the chickens.

When she returned to the house, she entered by the front door. Quietly she crossed the room and climbed the stairs. She dared not stay downstairs with Joshua and Matthew and the Bible reading tonight.

In the bedroom Solali was bending over the child in her lap. She gave Rebecca only a brief glance as she continued to croon to the baby as she bathed him and dressed him in clean clothing.

"What is it that you are singing to him?" Rebecca asked.

" 'Tis a Paiute lullaby, about the wind and the trees and a mother's love. Do you suppose Matthew would mind?"

"No, it's as soft as the wind itself, and the baby's nearly asleep. You really enjoy caring for little Thomas, don't you?" Solali nodded and Rebecca found herself comparing her reluctance to touch the child with Solali's obvious adoration. Solali wrapped a light blanket around the baby and lifted him to her shoulder. Rebecca followed; from the doorway of the bedroom she watched her go down the stairs, crooning and patting.

What a good mother Solali would be, even to a motherless infant! Wanting to watch that tender scene a little longer, Rebecca walked to the head of the stairs.

The stairway followed the kitchen wall down a short six steps and then turned at right angles for another six steps along the fireplace wall. The last three steps turned and bordered the massive stone fireplace. As Rebecca leaned over the railing to watch Solali, she saw Eagle waiting on the last flight of steps.

He had been leaning against the stone of the fireplace and now he stepped into Solali's path. The lamp on the mantel illuminated Eagle's face. Solali hesitated; his expression arrested Rebecca's retreat. His soft words were Paiute, and after a moment Solali answered him in his language.

Although Rebecca had no idea what the conversation was about, she still was caught by Eagle's expression. Momentarily open, tender, it was changing as Solali spoke. In the next instant, Rebecca caught her breath. If ever she had seen a man's soul on its knees, it was now. He waited, then Solali took a backward step. Her arms about the baby tightened and her head snapped backward. There was one sharp word from her. Rebecca watched Eagle's face harden as he moved away from the light. His answer was brief, angry. Solali slipped down the stairs away from him and entered the kitchen.

Rebecca found she was holding her breath, hands clasped to her throat. The dark shadow below her moved and was gone.

Early the following morning the three of them left. Matthew and Joshua rode across the hills to their father's parcel of land. Eagle turned his horse downriver, away from them all.

Rebecca thought she was alone as she stood in the doorway and watched them ride away, but when she turned, she discovered Solali, still as ice, with her face pressed against the window.

Cynthia came from the kitchen, wiping her hands on her apron. "Are they all gone? With no menfolk to cook for today, I'm of a mind to go into town. Rebecca, you come along with me. Solali and Kalli can handle the little that needs to be done." She was removing her apron and patting her hair. "There's sewing going on at the Depoes. It's been a long time since I've had much time to gad about. I've a spot of crocheting to do, and Lettie has promised me a new pattern. You can always work on the tuckin' on that new dress." Rebecca sighed with surrender and saw Solali's amused smile as she ducked into the kitchen.

But after all was said and done, Rebecca thought, settling herself in the Depoes' parlor, it wasn't too much of a burden to poke the silly needle in and out when you had the lady-folk to take your mind off it all.

The Hanson bride was "showing" now, and for a while the talk was of babies and little knitted garments.

Mrs. Hanson, the mother-in-law of Betty Hanson, was sitting beside Rebecca. As she knitted rapidly, the pile of pink in her lap grew. "Miz Hanson," someone commented, "you know that son of yours'll have a fit when he sees that pink shawl."

"It'll not be the first boy to be wrapped in pink," she answered comfortably. "Long as the child's healthy and happy, who can complain? 'Sides, this was the only yarn I could buy. Seems everybody else hit the bunch of blue before I could get there."

"There's a pretty good crop of young'uns coming on up and down the McKenzie." The parson's wife paused to thread her needle. "And you mark my words, that's a good sign. Shows the Almighty's blessin' us all with peace and prosperity."

"Well, I'm not too certain about that." Mrs. Hanson pursed her lips. "I remember a pretty good crop being produced in the most unlikely spots. We had a bunch spread from here to there comin' across in '44. That wasn't a peace and prosperity time."

"Oh, no, it weren't," tiny Mrs. Crocket shivered. "Suffering like I'd never have believed! Comin' across I got out scot free, without losing a soul of my family, but let me tell you, that wasn't common. And 'twas but the grace of God that brought us through. If it weren't the cholera being bad enough, there was the running short of supplies. Them days there weren't no Barlow Pass or South Road to travel. We went up the Oregon Trail the whole way. When we got to The Dalles we all bunched up together in one spot. Like pourin' grain out of a narrow-necked jug, it was."

"You're talking about waiting for boats?"

Mrs. Crocket nodded. "In them days there weren't no fancy carts on railroad tracks to be pulled by mules, like they got along the river now. No sir. We had to wait to get floated down the river, and dangerous it was."

"Why were you waiting?" Rebecca asked curiously.

"Weren't enough boats to carry people," Mrs. Hanson answered.

"But the worst part of it all," Mrs. Crocket continued, "was that everybody had run out of food. We'd been livin' on mighty short rations for weeks and then there was nothing until they shipped some in from downriver."

There was a long silence in the room broken only by the occasional creak of a rocking chair. The air in the room was stifling and Rebecca rubbed at her throat.

Mrs. Crocket spoke again. "When they finally brought in supplies, some died from the shock of it."

"I don't understand," Rebecca said.

"Well, for instance, in the family camped next to us, one fella couldn't wait to cook his potatoes. He cramped up something awful and before the sun went down that night, he was dead. You can't go without food to the brink of starvation and then stuff the body without paying the consequences. No matter how hungry, you feed slow and careful or it'll do you in."

"What a terrible trick of—" Rebecca stopped. She couldn't say the word. Fate? What did that impersonal title mean? God? She dared not blame Him, yet the churning feelings were there.

During the rest of the afternoon, while the conversation shifted to a lighter tone, Rebecca found herself seething with emotion as the old questions tried to surface in her mind, tried to burst past her determination to trust God.

She found herself studying the faces of the older women. Across the room sat Mrs. Dunsberry. She had scarcely spoken all afternoon. Rebecca watched her bend over her needlework. Of all the women in the room, only she held a bright swatch of material covered with an intricate design of delicate stitchery. The other women were working on mending—repairing tiny worn garments or patching coarse homespun. Some held calico being shaped into new garments or woolen yarn being furiously knit in a race against winter.

Rebecca's attention was drawn back to Marsella Dunsberry. She studied her face, her dainty dress, and the carefully coiffed hair. It was like looking at a china doll with very sad features. Cynthia leaned close and whispered, "She's a strange one, but there's reasons. Lost her husband and two children movin' west. Most strange it is that she stays."

Briefly Mrs. Dunsberry lifted her head and looked at Rebecca. When she picked up her needlework again, not a flicker of expression had marred her face.

Wonderingly, Rebecca turned to study Mrs. Hanson and Mrs. Crocket. Their tales had given the somber note to the afternoon, and Mrs. Hanson didn't conceal her heartache but had talked freely about the loss of two of her children. Yet both women were serene of face and composure. The little Mrs. Crocket seemed impossibly small and frail, but she had talked about wrestling the oxen and heavy wagon across the desert while her sick husband tossed with fever. Even now, her face was as smooth as if she had never experienced a worry in her life. Watching her laugh and smile as she mended torn trousers, Rebecca couldn't help sighing as she picked up her own sewing.

Mrs. Hanson was watching her, and Rebecca's words tumbled out. "I'm begging the sense to understand all this. Seems the trials you and Mrs. Crocket have lived through would have beat you under, but you're acting and talking as if it was all to be expected."

Mrs. Hanson frowned, "But it *was*." She shifted the yarn and said thoughtfully, "Not a one of us really believed in our hearts when we left home that we'd follow our men clear across those plains without suffering. Sure, we loved them, and sure, there were many more good days than bad. I suppose that's what kept us going."

"The love for your husbands?"

"No, more'n that." She paused and her brow wrinkled again. "My, I don't suppose I've ever paused long enough in my whole life to try to put it all into words. But, then, the feeling's the important thing. Even if you can't understand the pain being served up when you've set your heart on nothing but good, you're still believing that the Almighty loves you and is sittin' right there with His eyes on you, ready and willin' to help you. It's that kind of knowing that gets you through, not all the questions that you can drag up that there's no answer for."

11

••••••••••••••••••••

"The Lord *is* my shepherd.' " The words seemed as dry as dust, but Rebecca read doggedly. While Solali held the baby close, Cynthia curiously studied them both.

It was impulse that had prompted Rebecca to carry her Bible down the stairs this evening, the first evening since the men had all departed. At the time the impulse had seemed right. But now as she closed the Book and folded her hands for prayer, her courage faltered.

"Seems a body gets enough of that at church every Sunday without having to spend time at it during the week." Cynthia got to her feet with a snort. Reaching for the baby she said, "Here, I'll carry him to Kalli and then tuck him in." Solali surrendered him reluctantly.

Her parting shot was delivered from the door. "And you, Solali, ought to be getting your own babies. Like Kalli. I'm seein' how you hunger after my grandson."

Solali's eyes widened as Cynthia headed for the stairs. Hastily Rebecca said, "Don't mind her, Solali. Age has sharpened her tongue somewhat."

" 'Tis no wonder Kalli spends most of her time upstairs."

Rebecca was still fingering the Bible when Cynthia came back into the room. The woman watched Solali get to her feet and leave before she turned to Rebecca. "And you, young lady, I've seen the way my son looks at you. I'm guessing he'll not be content until you marry him. But I'm also thinking that things will be better for us all when we come right out and say what's on our minds."

"Cynthia," Rebecca whispered, guessing the questions she wanted to ask, those which had darkened and narrowed her eyes for months. "I can't talk about it, please."

"I know." Briefly compassion gentled her voice, and when Rebecca looked up, she watched the dark questioning in Cynthia's eyes lift—just for a moment. But Rebecca knew those eyes were really seeing her, looking beyond the surface as she said, "I'm as sharp as any old biddy, trying to guess all the details. Before God and man, can you say that my son knows what he's getting into?"

She could only nod, but the hand at her throat felt the heavy beat of her pulse.

Cynthia released her breath in an explosion of sound. "I won't pretend that I don't have my doubts and my questions, but I'll give you a fair chance. You know there's plenty of talk that's come out of *that* place." She waited and when Rebecca didn't answer, she said, "Seein' he's made up his mind, well, then, the sooner the better."

"Cynthia, I'm not ready. I'm not certain that ever—" She pressed her hand against her mouth and swallowed hard. The word had been *again*. Now the word swirled through her mind, searing with all its implications. Little did Cynthia know the real thrust of Joshua's thoughts or her own.

There were those other words of King David, the ones after Psalm 23, reminding Rebecca of Joshua's true feelings, of how he really saw her. "Purge me with hyssop, and I shall be clean . . ." and, "Thou shalt not . . ." Did Joshua really think the hyssop would take away the thrust of those other thoughts? *Adultery. Fallen woman.*

She watched Cynthia move about the kitchen, making the nighttime preparations for the next day that were so familiar. She set the crushed wheat to soak and stirred flour into her bread sponge. Lifting the clean dish towels, she folded them and placed them on the shelf beside the stove. She took the dipper from the pail and drank deeply of the water. Now with a brisk nod to Rebecca, she murmured, "Good night."

Rebecca was still staring at the blue bowl on the table when she heard the whisper of Solali's moccasins. She walked into the circle of light and sat down at the table.

As Rebecca studied the Indian woman, a strange mixture of feelings went through her. At one moment she saw her as Indian and completely without understanding of the white man's way of life, then she was caught in a moment when their spirits seemed linked, when they were filled with the common memories of the past. At those times she knew Solali wiser than herself. There was that serene acceptance of life, at least outwardly, when Rebecca knew so little serenity.

She must probe. "Solali, about the Bible. Do you understand now that I must follow Jesus?"

A tiny frown marred her forehead. "You say this Jesus is God come to live among us and to die for us to satisfy the demands of an angry God." She waved her hand in frustration, "No, no, that's all wrong. I still struggle. I know the Mormon god is angry, he punishes disobedience and withholds good so that we will obey him. Never will we be good enough, because he blesses with good and plenty when we are righteous enough. And we are poor—that means . . ." she paused, shrugged, and then said, "Most of the Indian gods are angry too. They must be appeased. They say there are good gods, but I don't know any. Now this Book tells me about the death of the good man who was really God and what He does is not to please an angry God but instead to clear the path to a righteous God." She stopped and sighed. "It is too heavy for my mind. I cannot understand it all."

Rebecca was whispering but her thoughts were not so much for Solali as for herself. She said, " 'For God so loved the world, that he gave his only begotten Son, that whosoever believeth in him should not perish, but have everlasting life.' "

"Then God is—" Solali shivered, a puzzled expression in her eyes, as she tried to explain her feelings. "It's so far beyond what I've heard. I think I need to read more in the Book. It is so hard to remember it all."

"That's why Joshua wants us to read every night."

"The words"—now it was Solali who was whispering—"they are holy, if they are from the Great Father, as you say. If so, we dare not forget one of them." She lifted her hands, cupped in supplication. For one brief moment, Rebecca caught the awe Solali was feeling. She felt her heart respond and lift in adoration. Then silence dropped into her soul. She sighed and stood up.

The two left the kitchen together and walked up the stairs to their bedroom. From across the hall came the sleepy whimper of Matthew's baby and the answering murmur from Kalli.

As Rebecca settled herself to sleep, she said, " 'Tis a lonely house without the menfolk. I'm glad we have neighbors close enough to run to."

"You're thinking Indians?"

Reluctantly, "Doesn't the mind go that way when one's alone?"

Through the silence of the night, Solali said slowly, "They call us savages and say we must learn the white man's ways. If I follow your God, then I best marry a white man, isn't that so?"

Rebecca raised herself to one elbow and stared over at the dusky face. "Solali, I don't recollect reading anything in the Bible that leads me to think that way. Why do you?" The dark head moved restlessly on the pillow but there was no answer.

Ten days later, as Rebecca worked alone in the garden, she reflected on the activities that occupied the women's time while the men were gone. Despite the busy hours, there was an emptiness, a waiting. Suddenly a scream pierced her lonely thoughts. Rebecca pitched her armload of weeds and ran toward the house.

The screaming was coming from the kitchen, from Kalli's child. She burst through the kitchen door and stopped in amazement. Solali was holding a frothing mass of flying arms and legs, trying to submerge it in the washtub. Hair tumbled, soaked, Solali lifted her face. "Rebecca, help! This child thinks I'm trying to drown him."

Kalli stood beside the stove. Her dark eyes were filled with apprehension as she looked from Rebecca to the child, but she made no move to rescue her frantic son. Reluctantly Rebecca knelt beside the tub and tried to grasp the thrashing arms.

"Ho, ho!" the booming voice filled the room and the thrashing ceased. It was Matthew filling the doorway. Kalli flew to him and Solali settled back on her heels and pushed the hair out of her eyes.

"Oh, Matthew," Rebecca jumped to her feet and embraced him. "You're back."

"And just in time. What are you two trying to do to the young man?" He picked up the towel and lifted the child. "There, young fella. This always happens when the women outrank us men." While his jovial voice rumbled contentedly, the child cuddled against him.

Matthew continued to rub the child and Rebecca studied his face. The lines of unhappiness seemed to have lifted. "You're bone thin," she accused; "I suppose you've all been working yourselves night and day and living on scraps."

He nodded. "Need to get the place finished before the rains start. Josh stayed to help Pa finish up. He'll be along next week." Matthew reached for the little clothes Kalli held out.

With an exasperated sigh, Solali ruefully surveyed the messy scene and said, "Law, it sure would help to talk whatever language she speaks."

Matthew put the tot on his feet and turned to lift the tub of water. "If you ladies had just turned him loose in the crick, he'd have got almost as clean and there'd be no call for the fussin'." His voice was still the contented rumble, and he followed Solali out the door with the tub.

Cynthia came into the kitchen with an armload of freshly dried sheets. Shaking her head at the rumpled towel and the pool of water on the floor, she dumped her load on the table and reached for a dry towel. She nodded toward the door. "I'm beginning to think that Matthew's gone soft on Solali. Just my lot to have a flock of Indians for grandbabies."

Surprised, Rebecca turned to look through the open door. Matthew and Solali stood beside the garden patch talking earnestly. Slowly Rebecca said, "I think you're jumping to conclusions." But she remembered that statement Solali had made, and Eagle's face. His tenderness had changed to bitter disappointment in response to Solali's words.

Just after supper that evening, the wind gusted through the valley bringing cool air and a swirl of rain. While the women were finishing the dishes, Matthew knelt beside the fireplace and said, "Let's have a fire and read the Bible here."

Rebecca came to the doorway to look at him. Her thoughts were busy with pictures of Matthew at Bible-reading time in the past. His disinterest and sorrow seemed to leave no room to hear and respond to the words of comfort and help which Joshua had chosen to read.

The fire was blazing. Matthew crossed the big room and entered Joshua's bedroom. When he returned he was carrying Joshua's Bible.

"Oh," Solali said slowly. She was standing in the doorway to the kitchen holding Rebecca's Bible. "Then you won't need this one." She came to sit on the settle with Rebecca. Kalli came into the room carrying the baby. She hesitated, then sat on a stool close to the fire and cuddled the child.

A wistful expression crept across Matthew's countenance as he looked down into his son's face. "I'd be obliged if he favors his ma," he said slowly.

His hand was trembling as he opened the Bible. "I guess I'd better tell you that I've made my peace with God." His voice was self-conscious and he fumbled with the Book. "Josh made me see, no matter what, the most important thing isn't understanding but *trusting* God." A quick finger rubbed at his eyes and a folded paper slipped from the pages of the Book.

Rebecca picked up the paper and shoved it into her Bible. Her heart was heavy with its answer to Matthew's sorrow. "Ah, Matt, we know. 'Tis a sorry lot trying to outguess God."

When the others had slipped away to their beds, Rebecca continued to sit beside the fire.

Matthew's confessions had released the tide of thought which she kept dammed up in the back of her mind. Now the dark clouds of memory surfaced and set her hands trembling and dabbing at the tears. Impatiently she moved quickly and opened her Bible, seeking the solace of the words. The familiar ones, the comforting ones.

Instead, she found the paper from Joshua's Bible. She started up with it, then realized that Matthew had carried Joshua's Bible back into the room with him. The door was closed and the house silent with sleeping people.

While her fingers fumbled with the paper, she realized it was a letter addressed to her. "Dear Rebecca," she read. "Seems I express myself best on paper. I've no call to apologize, for I was offering you the best from my heart with the insights His Spirit gave me. That I've hurt you, there is no doubt, and for that I apologize. It seems I was bringing out thoughts from His Word that were new to you. I was never guessing that you didn't see what seemed both natural and clear to me. I'm understanding now. I've been hearing men talk about God's Word truly and honestly. I'm convinced that the loving Heavenly Father has provided everything for us that we need through the blessed atonement of Jesus Christ. Now I'm guessing you've not seen how far His loving care goes in restoring us to himself."

Rebecca dropped the letter to her lap. Joshua's tender words unleashed a torrent, and she began recalling the words Joshua had read to her. " 'Restore unto me the joy of thy salvation.' " Even as she whispered the words, she wondered what they really meant.

She went back to the letter. "Little Becky," she read, "I've been seeing you moving into a darkness of spirit, and His words burn through me. I'm not understanding it all, but I read in the Bible that those lashes the Romans put on Him counted for something. In Isaiah it says that by His stripes we are healed. I can't help remembering the way He touched the people while He walked this earth, healing them from one end of the fellow to the other. I've been praying for that poor, injured side of yours. One of these days, I'm going to tell you what I'll be doing about that wound. Right now I count it a blessing when I see you kneading the bread and using the broom, even while I know it hurts. But isn't it right to think He can take away all those black memories you have?"

She dropped the letter to her lap again and stared into the dying fire. Her fingers crept to her side and traced the tender furrow of scar tissue. As the wind lashed the trees and drove the rain against the house, Rebecca's thoughts drifted.

On a long-ago night, in her lonesomeness, she had wished for the kind of soul-deep communication that Joshua was now offering to her. She winced, feeling again the pain his quote from David had brought, the picture of shame they had drawn.

"Times like these," she muttered, "makes a body want to fly back to where there's no taint." She stopped, stunned by a sudden realization. "Just like the children of Israel," she whispered, "things get bad, and you're yearning for the leeks and garlic of Egypt."

She shivered and poked another stick on the fire. With the need to defend herself, she muttered, "Well, 'tis a barren land where people see you different than you are." Now she picked up her Bible. "Might as well read; there's no sleeping on a lonesome night like this." Briefly her thoughts dwelt on Joshua. Was he sheltered from the rain? Was he eating enough?

Moving restlessly on the hard wooden settle that bordered the fireplace, Rebecca slowly turned the pages of the Bible. Occasionally she paused to read, snatching at words which now caught her attention and then became lost as the storm outside grew in intensity.

She started up from her seat. Almost she thought her mind was playing fancies, that there had been a voice and the sound of hooves against stone. Now above the pounding of the rain there was the unmistakable crash of the barn door. She ran to the kitchen window. At the moment she caught sight of movement outside and as she turned to shout for Matthew, the door crashed inward. Joshua and his father stumbled into the room.

Clutching her throat, she stared at their dripping figures. "It's raining up the way," Joshua explained, reaching for towels. "Pa and I decided we'd come home for some hot grub." Around the towel, beyond the lightness of his words, his eyes were full of concern. While Mr. Smyth rubbed his head and started for the stairs, Joshua asked, "You all right?"

She sighed and dropped her hand. Turning abruptly she poked kindling into the stove. He touched her shoulder, "I've frightened you. Becky, I'm sorry. Seems everything I do goes awry."

"It's just—" she gulped, fighting the feeling which had sent her heart to pounding. Her hands trembled against the towels. "I hadn't expected you."

"I was getting uneasy, thinking of the things that needed to be done here. When the rain started, Pa and I decided to come. There's no likelihood of getting shingling done in this weather."

She watched him cross the parlor to the bedroom where Matthew was sleeping. Still conscious of the new rush of warmth and life his coming had brought, she began taking down plates and cups. She was lifting bacon and eggs from the frying pan and stacking buttered toast on its warming plate when the two men came into the kitchen. Wearing dry clothes but still shivering, they sat down while she poured tea into their cups.

"We'd a' had the place completely shingled if the weather'd held," Mr. Smyth said as he took his cup and gulped the hot liquid.

Looking at the food, Joshua added, "Yes, but we'd a' starved to death beforehand."

Rebecca was finishing up the dishes and setting the kitchen in order when she heard the stairs creak. She looked to the door and Mr. Smyth said, "Night, Becky, and thanks." She nodded. In the parlor Joshua was pushing a log into the cracking fire. She turned back to the kitchen. The rain still pounded at the window. Slowly she wiped the table and hung the wet towels.

From the doorway Joshua said, "I see you found my letter."

"It fell out of the Bible when Matt was getting ready to read. It had my name on it so—"

"Don't get your back up. I intended for you to see it some time. Will you listen to me now?"

His broad shoulders filled the doorway. There would be no pushing past him. She clung to the back of the chair, filled with a new consciousness of him. The times he had held her, helped her, carried her; feeding, touching, urging life back into her at the worst of it as they had fled across Utah Territory.

Now she realized that, trusting as a child, she had known only a child's emotional response to him. But it was changing. At what moment had it happened? What thought or need, what event, plunged her toward this understanding? Was it the feeling of unending vigilance as he had cared for her? Was it his strength, surrounding her, demanding response and life when life seemed impossible? Was it that man on the mountain, the woodcutter, stripped of his shirt, revealing the gold ring shining against his golden body? Rebecca shook her head—slowly, wearily, unknowing and confused.

"Why? Will you run forever?" She tried to reply and the words were lost, but the theme of them was in her thoughts: unworthy.

He lifted her hand from the back of the chair and led her to the settle, saying, in that gentle, companionable way of his, "Upstairs we've a heap of feathers just waiting to be made into cushions for this thing."

He leaned against the fireplace and gazed down into the crackling fire. "About that from Psalms. At the time I read those words to you, Becky, I'd no idea you'd see me as judging you. Rebecca, you've told me yourself how you're trusting in the atonement of Jesus Christ, saying you've accepted His forgiveness for—" the word hung unsaid. Now he added, "Then do you think I'd *dare* judge you? I was trying to say to you the words I've heard preached a good many times, how a person must *let* God. He'll not only forgive sins forever, but He'll begin changing him into a new person." He stopped to take a deep breath before saying, "He wants you to be rid of the past and able to live the future with love for everyone."

"Love!" Rebecca cried, her mind spiraling down into that black pool of memory. "You mean that I am to love—" With a quick movement Joshua was beside her, his fingers pressed against her lips.

"Don't say it," he demanded sternly. "I'm seeing you changed now. Listen." He released her and settled back on his heels beside the fireplace. Slowly quoting Isaiah he said, " ' . . . he hath sent me to bind up the brokenhearted, to proclaim liberty to the captives, and the opening of the prison to them that are bound . . . to comfort all that mourn . . . to give unto them beauty for ashes, the oil of joy for mourning, the garment of praise for the spirit of heaviness . . . that he might be glorified.' Rebecca." He was whispering now. "Those verses are talking about Jesus Christ and what He wants to do in people's lives. That's what I'm wanting for you."

12

••••••••••••••••••••

$\mathcal{B}$eauty for ashes. The little white church was quiet, waiting. Slowly the congregation filed in. In the Smyth family pew Rebecca was seated beside Solali, who was in church for the first time. Rebecca kept looking at her, admiring the new calico dress and the smooth cap of dark hair, fashioned like Rebecca's sunlit locks. Matthew was sitting beside her holding his infant son. The brooding expression on his face told his story. Beside him sat Cynthia, and her straying fingers straightened the blanket, touched the baby's downy head. Mr. Smyth was beside his wife. While the years had softened her figure and sharpened her tongue, the years on Mr. Smyth had served only to wither and warp. Next were Jamie and his intended, Eva, whose adoring eyes were fixed on the slight man beside her.

Rebecca watched the pair. This was the first time Jamie had been home since Becky had arrived in Oregon. She seemed unable to fill her eyes with enough of the young man who was a smaller version of Joshua. He caught her eye and smiled. Beauty for ashes. This was beauty.

The young man in cutaways strode across the platform and seated himself at the organ. There were the opening chords and the nod of his head. The congregation stood and sang: "Praise God, from whom all blessings flow—Praise Him, all creatures . . ."

The sun streamed through the high, bare windows. She could see clouds and sky, branches and birds. Beauty.

The jangle of harness and the creak of a wagon wheel momentarily overwhelmed the Parson's voice. Beauty.

Beauty was the present, ashes the past. The ashes still lay heavy upon Rebecca's heart, stirred now and again as a sensation of life tried to creep beyond the pain of the past.

She was wishing she could remember all those other words Joshua had read to her. She clung to the Book in her lap and wished she dared to search for the words now.

After the meeting, the grounds were dotted with tables and benches and friendly groups. As before, during the summer months, the valley dwellers had carried their dinner to church. While the afternoon slipped away, the best of the settlement's cooking was shared.

Today Rebecca sat at the picnic table and listened to the chatter about her. Did these people know their lives were being cemented as surely as the icing held Mrs. Hanson's cake together?

She saw Kalli sitting under a tree nursing the baby and watched her dark eyes shift from one group to another. Her impassive face didn't reflect a single thought or hint of emotion. She seemed unaware of the tiny blond boy at her breast. What magic had Eagle worked to bring this timid creature into Matthew's life to serve as wet nurse for his child?

But Kalli was a woman, like Rebecca. She was separated by culture and language and surrounded by strangeness, unable to communicate with those around her; Rebecca was seeing her as another pattern of herself.

In the merrymaking about the tables, Kalli was forgotten. A feeling of helplessness turned Rebecca restless in the presence of those dark eyes. Jumping to her feet, Rebecca selected a piece of fried chicken from the platter and went toward Kalli.

Kneeling beside the woman, she saw Kalli's son curled on the corner of his mother's robe. He was asleep, a piece of bread clutched in his hand, his cheeks streaked with dust and tears.

Kalli nodded as she took the chicken and nibbled at it. Rebecca's feelings were spilling over. "Oh, Kalli," she whispered, knowing the woman didn't understand, "I wish I could help; yet you came voluntarily."

A calico skirt stopped beside Rebecca and Solali folded her legs under the billowing skirt and sat beside Kalli. "It's a fearsome feeling to not be able to say the words," she said. "I know. I can no more speak her language than you. Eagle says her husband is dead and she was unhappy in the lodge of her husband's family. I'm feeling in time she'll become one of us."

Rebecca studied Solali's troubled face. "Are you meaning someone like yourself who has chosen a new life?" Solali nodded and turned her face away.

The woman sat in silence until finally, with a sigh of futility, Rebecca started to rise. Softly Solali said, "If I could speak to her, I would make her realize it is worse to belong to two worlds. The heart never leaves home."

Rebecca paused. "Why don't you have Eagle tell her this?" Startled, Solali's head snapped backward and she stared up at Rebecca. The movement reminded Rebecca of the scene at the bottom of the stairs when in just this way Solali had looked up at Eagle. Solali's eyes were pools of misery. Slowly she shook her head.

Rebecca walked back to the table while the two Indian women continued to sit under the tree. It was the first time, Rebecca realized, as she watched Solali, that she had seen her friend choose to act in a manner contrary to the image of the white woman.

A yellow leaf dropped from the tree overhead and landed on Rebecca's plate. Nettie Morgan said, "September's snuggin' close. Then comes winter and the rains begin. 'Tis a good season for the women to go a'visitin'. You come." For a moment curiosity gleamed in her eyes. "You know, for all the time you've been here, we scarcely know you. Cynthia's told us a little about how she came to know you and all, but she's pretty close-mouthed. Almost mysterious-like. Seems to think if there's to be any gettin' acquainted, you best be informing us. Says you've been a schoolteacher." There was a pause and then, "Seems there's always a call for good teachers around about. Now, when we get to be a state and there's aid from Washington, there'll be more call for teachers and new schools."

Now she turned to watch Solali get to her feet. "Think that Indian will be marrying Matthew?"

Rebecca pointed to the next table where Cynthia and a young woman were talking. "I'm thinking Cynthia has other ideas. That girl's a pretty little thing, but she doesn't look more'n fourteen." The woman was still watching Solali, and Rebecca was remembering the phrase, *the heart never leaves home.*

Rebecca turned slowly, "This Waltstown is a nice little place. Seems every time I look there's a new store or house being built."

"Have you been in Madame Tuchey's shop? It's advertised in the newpapers even. Says she does dressmakin' and hats. But I'm a'guessing she'll have to find another occupation to keep goin' in backwoods country like this."

The woman snickered and Rebecca looked at her. "You're implying she's not nice." Rebecca saw her smirk and bite her lip before adding, "You're just guessing?"

The woman flushed, "Pretty obvious, ain't it? Us frontier women haven't the money to support the likes of a hat shop."

"But there's a new organ in the church. I'm thinking it's short supply that limits the people more'n money." Rebecca continued to study the woman and her thoughts were busy, placing her own name under the innuendo. Abruptly Nettie got to her feet and began gathering her dishes. Her cheeks were red as she impatiently settled her basket and called her daughter.

"Mrs. Morgan," Rebecca began with a sinking heart.

"Not now!" she snapped. "I'll be talkin' to you later." Her skirt swished as she marched off.

Cynthia handed Rebecca a basket. "Take this to the wagon. And, Becky, I'd be of a mind to step softly around Nettie Morgan. Maybe 'tis gossip, but you haven't a call to sweeten her tongue."

Rebecca's ears were still burning as she crawled into the wagon and turned to watch Solali and Kalli. Solali's unhappy face made it clear there was only one thing to do. "That Eagle," she muttered, "I do wish he would learn to speak and *understand* English."

Joshua looked down at her and said, "Maybe he knows more English than you've guessed, and maybe he knows the best way to avoid woman chatter is by pretendin' otherwise." His eyes were dancing and she guessed that he had heard the whole silly conversation with Mrs. Morgan.

Cynthia heaved herself into the wagon and said, "Joshua, I'd be inclined to use your wagon tomorrow. Rebecca and Solali could be takin' a load up to the house. Now the roof's tight there's no reason we can't be movin' things slow and easy-like."

"Ma, I've never seen you do anything slow and easy-like," Joshua teased, "and I'm thinking you want to jaw Pa about finishing up the place. He's hurryin'."

The next day Rebecca and Solali took the wagon and team up the road to the elder Smyth's section. The trip in the ponderous wagon, behind the plodding horses, took all of the forenoon. But, then, the precarious load didn't lend itself to faster travel. There was the chest of quilts and cases of dishes and canning jars. Mrs. Smyth's rocking chair insisted on rocking, and the little footstool and the tall clothes horse kept colliding. Solali played referee and grumbled.

" 'Tis a pity she couldn't wait for the men to pack this wagon properly. They'd have been through with plowing that section by evening."

"But isn't this a lark!" Rebecca exclaimed.

"Lark?" Solali asked suspiciously.

"A—a happiness," Rebecca scrambled for words. Once in a

while she hit a snag in Solali's understanding and then she was doubly conscious of her friend's Indian heritage. Looking at Solali, she asked, "Did Eagle say when he would be back?"

There was the lifted chin. "No, and I didn't encourage him to return at all."

They turned off the road and wound down the trail to the house. The Smyths' new house sat in the sprawl of older buildings and corrals which had been constructed years before when the section was first claimed under the Donation Land Act.

When Solali pointed to the older buildings with a frown, Rebecca explained, "At the time Joshua brought his family to Oregon Territory, his pa made his claim up here and worked the land, but they built Joshua's large home and all lived there together."

"And the ma and pa are moving because of us?"

"No, Joshua said they'd already decided to make this move. Two years ago. It's taken that long to get the house built, with helping Joshua and all." Her voice trailed away. Again she was deeply conscious of the sacrifice Joshua had made in order to find her. Now she saw how his search had affected the whole family.

The trail ended in front of the little house. The aroma of newness and fresh lumber still clung to it, and the planed wood shone bright and clean. " 'Tis almost too pretty to cover up with white paint," Rebecca said, pointing to the golden wood.

"Those windowpanes are in need of a good scrubbing," Solali observed.

"Oh, that'll wait. It's the push to get the roof completed and the paint on before the rains start."

"After the desert country it seems a marvel to worry about a whole season of rain, doesn't it?" Solali slid down from the wagon seat and turned to Rebecca. "Are you hurting? I was hard pressed to not complain about her sending you off like this when I was guessing your poor side screamed with pain."

"It did hurt," Rebecca admitted as she went to turn the horses loose to graze. "I've just got to act otherwise. Cynthia would have been full of questions if a big strapping girl like me couldn't heft a little chest of drawers like this without complaining."

"Just the same"—Solali gave Rebecca a push—"you let me do the lifting now and you just ease it to the ground. I 'spect Joshua will fuss when he finds what she's put you through today."

"He'll not say a word," Rebecca said shortly.

It was on the return trip that Rebecca accepted the changes in her life. Solali had been talking about how Cynthia's furnishings would fit into the little home, when Rebecca began thinking of the gaps that were being created in Joshua's home.

She was standing in the parlor later, looking around at the empty spaces in Joshua's house when Cynthia came into the room. "It does look bare without my rocker and the fancy work around. I 'spect you'll get yourself busy with such things this winter. The women visit around with their fancy work and they'll be asking you to join. I don't know about Solali. But if she's going to be a white man's wife, she'll need to be learnin' too."

Solali was hesitating in the doorway to the kitchen. Her face was troubled and she turned away. Rebecca was so full of wondering about that expression that Cynthia's words didn't immediately catch her attention.

But now Cynthia was addressing her. "What about you? It's going to be a bad spot you'll be in if he marries her and they all move back up Salem way. He'll be needing Kalli for another year, so that leaves you and Joshua here."

She marched past Rebecca and entered Joshua's bedroom. Rebecca went to the kitchen to find Solali. "Did you hear her? Is that what you intend?"

Solali was standing beside the table and she turned, puzzled. "Rebecca, I—"

Cynthia came back into the room. "I saw these old newspapers in a stack in Joshua's room. They're just the thing I need to wrap these jars of fruit."

"Oh." Rebecca looked down at the table. "I'd not noticed you'd been cleaning out the fruit closet while we were gone."

"The menfolk'll be going up that way soon and if I've packed a box or two real good with these newspapers around the jars, well, then they can carry the batch without breaking 'em."

Rebecca pulled the wooden crate close to the table and said, "We'd better be at it. 'Tis getting close to suppertime."

Solali picked up a newspaper and shook out the folds while Cynthia immediately went back to her former topic. "Now, Becky, folks are asking about your intentions already. What's a body to say with Josh tellin' me to keep my words to myself?"

Solali lowered the paper. There was a touch of strain in her voice as she asked, "Where did you get these papers?"

"In Joshua's bedroom. They's old ones."

Solali glanced quickly at Rebecca and said, "I'm a'wondering if he'll want you to use them—there's, well—" she stopped and looked imploringly at Rebecca.

Mystified, Rebecca reached for a paper, "What is it, Solali?" But Solali held the paper away from Rebecca. As she opened her mouth to speak, Cynthia snatched one of the papers from the stack and turned to the window.

"Oh, oh," she muttered, "this 'uns got an article in it that bodes no good for the Mormons. I don't read too good, but leastwise I can understand this."

"Joshua's been saving these for a purpose; we'd best put them back," Rebecca said hastily.

"No, not until I've read a bit more." Cynthia's voice was full of suspicion, and the glance she threw Rebecca's way made her heart sink. Now Solali gasped and Cynthia reached for her paper. "Read it to me or I'll figure it out for myself." Solali was shaking her head. Backing away from Cynthia, she tried to hold the paper away from her.

The back door flew open and Joshua came through. His easy grin disappeared as he looked from his mother to the jars and the newspapers and then to Solali's outstretched arm.

"I see you've found my newspapers," he said slowly as he looked at his mother.

"Just a bunch of old ones, I thought. I'd have never believed otherwise since I don't read well, but Solali here was gasping over them like they's pretty good. So's I'll just be reading them for myself if I can't get Solali to read them for me."

Slowly Solali lowered her arm and held the newspaper toward Joshua. With a sigh, Joshua took the paper and placed it back on the stack. When Cynthia reached for it, he said, "No, Ma. If you insist, I'll tell you what they have to say. And I expect when I'm done, you'll be none the happier or the wiser."

"Then why've you been hangin' onto them all this time?" Cynthia snapped. "I already saw they're old. Some's from California and there's more from Oregon, but they came out in the year 1852. We weren't even here then. How come you have them?"

"I've made it a point to keep up on the things going on in Utah Territory. These are the tales that have come out of there."

"But are they truth?" Solali asked softly.

Joshua turned toward her. "Only the good Lord knows for certain, Solali, but I'm certain there's a pretty good basis for the stories, otherwise they wouldn't keep a'flowin' out of the Territory."

"What do they say?" Cynthia demanded.

Joshua picked up the paper Solali had returned to him. "This fellow is quoting an emigrant who had the misfortune of hesistating too long in Mormon country. A great deal of this is reprinted from a pamphlet, probably written by either a Mr. Slater or a Mr. Goodell. At the beginning the fella is quoting a judge in Utah Territory. It's his remarks to the Gentiles during a trial. He says that he is thanking God that in the time not far distant he'll have the authority to pass sentence of life and death upon the Gentiles, and that he intends to have their heads snatched like a chicken being readied for the pot. Then the fella writing goes on to repeat a few words from Brigham Young. The gentleman quotes Brigham Young as saying that if a Gentile says anything against the Mormons, they'll take off their heads—in spite of all the emigrants and the United States and all hell, that'll be done."

He lowered the paper. "Now, Ma, you any wiser or happier?"

"Wiser," she muttered slowly, looking at Rebecca. "But read the rest; I want to know it all."

"No, Ma. You can see there's a fair stack here. Some's letters written to the newspapers by overlanders who've suffered at the hands of the people of Utah Territory, and it's not going to do you a bit of good to hear it all. I had to know what was going on until I could get Rebecca out of the place." His voice softened. "She's here. Now's the time to help her rebuild a life that's been hurt terrible by those years in the Territory. Ma, your place is just to love Rebecca. She's safe; let her forget about the place."

Cynthia lifted her chin. "Leastwise, how do I know she's not here to spread their ways?" Rebecca gave a weak cry of protest, but Joshua's hand was restraining her.

"No more, Ma. You have no idea what Rebecca's suffered through and it'll be her secret forever. You've no right to pry. Rebecca's no more a threat to you than I am. We both serve the same Lord. Now, please, hush forever about it all."

Cynthia hesitated and Rebecca saw her tightly pursed lips. Her heart sank even more as she saw Joshua relax and smile at his mother. With a shrug Cynthia slowly reached for the papers. "Well, no call to waste them; I'll just use them to wrap the jars like I intended all along."

"No, Ma." Joshua was still smiling as he scooped up the papers. He stuffed them into the stove and struck a match. In silence they stood in the kitchen and listened to the roar of flames.

"I wish the matter could be settled forever with so little fuss," Solali said slowly as she turned and walked from the room.

13

· · · · · · · · · · · · · · · · · · ·

𝒯he next evening, after supper, Joshua said, "Matt and I'll be leaving in the morning. I've cut the last of the hay and mended the barn. There's enough wood to do for a time. Now we'll get Pa's place tight for the winter. A week up there ought to finish it all."

"Then you'll come get the rest of my furniture," Cynthia said with satisfaction.

"And I'll be facing a pretty bare house," Joshua remarked. "About time I take Rebecca and Solali up Salem way to buy some furniture for this place."

The baby fretted, and words were passed around the table as casually as the pot of stew. Rebecca realized she was staring at Joshua and she tried to force her attention back to her plate. But the thought of traveling to Salem, going into those big shops and selecting furniture for this house—Joshua's house—filled her mind. She was seeing wood—polished, carved, just like the MacLennans'. A table, chairs, a sideboard materialized in her thoughts. She felt Joshua's silence and glanced at him.

His presence across the table from her was overwhelming. The open neck of his shirt revealed the slender rawhide thong. She watched the muscles across his shoulders ripple as he passed the pitcher of milk. Now he looked up at her and the force of his blue eyes was boring into hers, demanding an answer for a question not yet asked. He would never be like his pa, shooed with the broom of a busy housewife, relegated to his corner, used impatiently, tolerated. Joshua was not to be ignored.

Her hand slipped upward to her throat and she was remembering the way he had looked that night before the fireplace. While the rain had battered the house, she had felt his eyes boring into her soul. Could he see into the very bottom of her thoughts? Would a man whose strength and wisdom stemmed from the God whose black Book he held be a presence she could live with for the rest of her life? She trembled.

Joshua looked at the hand gripping her throat, and she saw the questions in his eyes.

Later, after supper, Solali was alone in the kitchen. The dishes had been washed and dried. She was hanging the towels when Matthew came into the kitchen. She felt his constraint before he said, "Solali, come walk down to the river with me. It's a pretty night and Josh said the fish are jumpin'." Her fingers slowly stroked the towels.

When she finally turned to look into his face, all the easy answers she had dreamed of saying fled away. "Yes, Matthew, I'll go if you want."

They walked toward the McKenzie. Here the river tumbled out of the mountains and the force of it had created a hard bed for the cataracts. In giant steps it plunged down the valley as it rushed to join the twisting Willamette, combining to wash through the valley toward the Columbia River.

As Matthew and Solali walked through the thickets of berry bushes and willow on a path cut by others, Solali was thinking of the young married couples in the valley, those who had obviously used this path to good advantage in the past. There was a sadness beginning in her heart, and she knew now was the time to face herself honestly. Life would be much different than what she had dreamed of since coming to the Oregon Territory. One look at Matthew's face tonight had revealed this.

Matthew's words interrupted her thoughts. "You like the little tyke, don't you? I've been watching you. My little fella needs a mother."

"I am Indian."

"But different than Kalli. We don't even speak her language."

"She will learn."

"Solali, you've been raised by white people." He stopped and then said, "Aw, Solali, it doesn't even matter if you have two heads. I want to marry you."

She faced him in the dusk. "Until this evening I wanted to marry you. But—" How could she ignore all his yearning face revealed, and how could she hurt him by admitting the lack in herself that only she recognized? "You know I've been married."

"Joshua has made me understand. He says that you were married to a Mormon, and he also said those marriages aren't legal.

None of the territories or states recognize them except Utah. Fact, he said in a lot of places they crack down pretty hard on the guy caught living in plural marriage. Jail and such."

"Matthew—" She was feeling the pressure. "You deserve better than me, than this kind of marriage."

In his stillness she felt his awareness. Although it was dark now, she wondered if he were seeing into her thoughts as he spoke slowly, "I understand. Have you forgotten that I was married too? I don't expect it to be like it was with Amy. Josh says there's just no way to recapture the past. I guess I know what I'm asking. It's just that we have the chance to help each other and share life together." His voice was flat now. "We both need a partner."

Finally she promised to consider his proposal. They linked hands as they walked back up the path in the darkness, but Solali's heart was heavy. Before they parted she dared bring out one more problem. "You said something about making peace with your God. I still struggle with your God."

Rebecca was asleep when Solali entered their bedroom. She tiptoed across the room in the dark and leaned against the cool window. The moon was rising now, the kind of moon that spoke much to her people. It warned of the seasons to come. Its gentle brightness urged them to hurry on to new harvest fields. Soon it would be time for the gathering of nuts from the pine trees.

She closed her eyes and felt the life of her people possessing her, filling her with yearning. And there was Eagle. The cold, the days of hunger no longer worried her. But, she admitted as she leaned against the window frame, if there were no Eagle, then life with Matthew would be possible. It might even seem the best way. She watched the moon progress across the sky.

It was late and she moved restlessly. Fearful of disturbing Rebecca, she moved slowly across the room. Now at the door she paused, looking toward the quiet form of her friend. Thinking of the times in the past when Rebecca had awakened during the night, weeping and tearing at her pillow, she hesitated, holding her breath. When she had satisfied herself, listening to the deep, regular breathing, she slipped through the door.

From the head of the stairs, she saw a tiny fire glowing on the hearth. Joshua's bright head was bent over a book and after a second, she slipped down the stairs.

He looked up. The expectancy on his face disappeared as she moved into the light. "Hello, Solali. You can't sleep either?"

She shook her head and sat down opposite him. "The Bible?"

He nodded. "Don't like carrying the Book up the valley. It could get wet, and then where'd I be?"

"Rebecca has one." A shadow crossed his face and she added, "But I'm thinking you need the words very much."

He was staring into the fire and he replied soberly, "I'm beginning to think I need them more than anything else in my life." Glancing up he said, "But how about you? Rebecca's told me about the struggles she had trying to make you understand the difference between how you were taught concerning the Mormon god and about the true God."

Solali nodded and admitted, "Seems to only confuse. What I've learned keeps getting mixed up."

"Maybe you'd do well to read it for yourself."

"I have been—but I don't read well."

"You speak English very well, and you could learn to read better."

He moved to sit on the settle beside her. Placing the open Bible on her lap, he said, "I'll explain to you just what you can expect to find in the different parts. You get Rebecca to help you read. Any time you want you can use my Bible, just be careful with it."

Solali bent over the Book and her fingers pointed out the words just as Mrs. Tomkins at the school had taught her. Joshua gently moved her fingers down the page. She read, " 'For God so loved—' " She looked up. "That's what Rebecca says. She says that's the difference between the two gods. I don't know what she means about obeying. How can you obey a god? She says that we're to not be fearing this God. I don't understand how you can follow just love."

"Love must pull more strongly than fear." As Solali listened to Joshua, she was remembering the way Cynthia had shaken her head over Joshua's many trips into Utah Territory searching for Rebecca. Cynthia didn't understand love, either.

Solali turned her head to study the strong features of the man bending over the Book. She looked at the golden glow of his hair and skin. "Children of light. You really do belong together." A feeling tinged with envy touched her. "You do love Rebecca, don't you? It isn't because you are almost her brother, but it is more. It didn't take those newspapers and their fearful tales to make you go after her, did it?"

A muscle in Joshua's face twitched. For a second he looked at Solali, allowing her to see his eyes as they darkened, tortured into an expression very near the way Eagle had looked. Slowly she said, "I don't think I know what love is, either."

"Love," he said thoughtfully, as if wondering himself, "is it like a quiet river, bending and slowly changing? Or is it the cataracts crashing down with power, life—" he stopped.

Quickly he took up the Book and began to turn the pages. Now his hands were still. "I—I don't know where to turn. Solali, it nearly takes a lifetime of reading before you catch it all. Seems like it did with me."

"All of what?"

"The picture of God's love and patience with mankind. How He provided a way to rescue His people even when they didn't know they needed to be rescued. Reconciling—it's in there. It means to bring back to Him. All this is in there, but you'll have to read it for yourself."

"Joshua," she whispered, "I need something now. Isn't it possible? How do I compact a lifetime of reading to help me now?"

Joshua dropped to his knees beside Solali. Still holding the Book he studied her face. Neither of them heard the whisper of footsteps on the stairs. Footsteps that started, hesitated, then retreated. Joshua was speaking softly. "Solali, I do believe you really are wanting—do you believe the story about Jesus?"

"That he was God come to live here and to die?" She nodded.

"You know," he said, studying her with those intense blue eyes. "Solali, you know all the thinking about it isn't going to do you any good. Christianity is an invitation from God to you. You have to take up His offer. Do you really want to make this Jesus Christ your Savior forever? Remember, He's God. If you're saying that you want to belong to Him, remember, that means you'll be making Him the most important part of your life. You'll be giving Him the right to do anything He wants with your life. I doubt you understand what that means."

Her eyes were wide with excitement. "Joshua, I'm only full of yearning. I feel like Cynthia's little chicks trying to burst my shell."

"I think you must pray. Shall I say the words for you to repeat?"

She nodded and they bent their heads together. "I believe the Holy Lord Jesus Christ came to this earth and died for me. I accept that atonement, Lord Jesus. Because of your love, because you died, I ask you to forgive my sins and allow me to become your child. I want to live my life for you. I want you to be my God." Her words were breathy echoes of his. Now she blinked and smiled up at him.

"Look, there's something I want to read to you. And it's yours forever." He opened the Bible and found the place. " 'He came unto his own, and his own received him not. But as many as received him, to them gave he power to become the sons of God, *even* to them that believe on his name.' "

In the half-light of dawn Rebecca slipped from the bed, dressed and crept down the stairs. Taking Cynthia's old shawl from behind the kitchen door she wrapped it about her shoulders and slipped through the door.

The late summer dew was heavy on the grass and Rebecca's dress wiped a furrow through the meadow as she wandered. She knew the hem of her dress was becoming heavy with moisture, but she tightened the shawl around her arms and continued to walk.

At the edge of the trees where Joshua cut firewood, she hesitated and looked down the valley toward the house. In sleeplessness, with her mind churning beyond rational thought, she had felt the house pressing in upon her. Now alien, foe, not friend. But this morning it was simply there, unmoving, unthreatening. It wasn't the house pressing in upon her last night, but the people it held. How deeply she was aware of those people with their emotions, hidden thoughts, even fears; was there no escape?

She studied the place and fought to calm her rage. If only those people would leave her alone! Where was quietness and peace to be found? There was no real peace. She had to accept it. That scene last night—she must accept it too. But she could not deny the jealousy, the surging anger she had felt last night, when by the glow of the fire she had seen Solali and Joshua with their heads together.

"Oh, my God!" she cried. The dew cascaded off the tips of the fir branches splattering her face, but even the wetness didn't cool her anger. Rebecca turned bitterly from the sight of the house. "It's happening again. 'Tis the same old sick feelings, the same betrayal. God, do You have no man on this earth who will be true to one woman? Is that what I get for trusting a man?" There was no answer, only the heaviness of her own heart.

She tightened the shawl around her and plunged into the trees, wanting only to be hidden from the view of the farm nestled peacefully below.

She followed the trail cut by Joshua's wagon to the clearing, still full of the bruised fragrance of freshly cut wood. She chose a stump. Now shivering, she pulled her feet under her and prepared to wait for the dawn and for the sound of the wagon and team going down that road, carrying Joshua, Matthew, and Mr. Smyth away from the farm.

Cynthia was preparing breakfast when Joshua and Matthew came into the kitchen. Eager to share the news with Rebecca, Joshua looked around the room. "Where's Becky?" Cynthia shrugged and continued slicing bread. Solali came into the room and her eyes met Joshua's. He saw they were still filled with wonder. Impatiently he asked, "When's Becky coming? I want her to be the first to know."

"Oh," Solali blinked and looked around. "Isn't she here?"

Now Cynthia paused and waved the knife. "I 'spect she's gone out somewhere; my shawl's missing." The coffeepot began to boil over and Joshua snatched it up.

Matthew said, "I'm guessin' she's gone for a walk. There's a trace through the field and heading up to the trees."

"I'm not wanting to head for Pa's until I speak to her," Joshua said. He carefully set the coffeepot on the back of the stove and continued, "You have your breakfast and I'll go fetch her."

Rebecca was still sitting on the stump when the sun began to touch the trees with light. She stayed motionless when she heard the twig snap, waiting until the sun brightened his hair before she acknowledged his presence. Her voice was flat. "I expected you to be on your way by now."

"That means you've planned to avoid me?"

"I didn't sleep too well, needed the fresh air. Besides, I didn't think I'd be missed."

"And I'm to go without a hot breakfast."

"Cynthia's there. And Solali."

His eyes brightened. "Then you know about Solali? Did she tell you all that happened last night?"

Brushing off his question, not wanting to admit her ignorance, she jumped to her feet and tried to distract the ache in her heart with chatter. "Seems a waste, this gallivanting off all the time."

"Well, come along, I'll get my job done and be back here. Didn't know you were missing me so."

She tossed her head. "Oh, that's smart talk. Bet you're having a girl in every valley."

"Oh, yes, and I'm shinglin' and courtin' at the same time," he retorted. "Come along; breakfast will be ruined."

"Just think of the time you'd have saved in the running back and forth if you'd only snugged your houses right up together."

"There's an unclaimed section stuck between our places."

"I heard tell about the Donation Land Act. You're lucky the

Mormons didn't hear about that. A Mormon and his passel of wives could take over the whole valley."

"Rebecca, what's got into you?"

"Nothing. But I see I'm going to need to teach Solali a few things. She's sure not much of a cook."

"Well, I know that. Now come along or Ma'll be throwing our breakfast to the chickens."

At a loss for words in the face of his amused calm, silently Rebecca hurried after him.

They were all around the table and the warm room was full of the delicious odor of coffee and bacon and eggs. As Rebecca slowly hung the shawl behind the door, she saw the pleased grin on Joshua's face as he waited beside her chair. When she sat down, he moved behind Solali's chair.

"Now we're all here together, I want to be the one to tell you," he began in his pleased voice. Rebecca saw him touch Solali lightly on the shoulder. Catching her breath, Becky ducked her head and waited. She fought the childish urge to stuff her fingers in her ears. He was speaking again. "This is something wonderful, and I want to tell you all about it." Again he paused and Rebecca looked at Solali, seeing her suddenly shy. "Last night," Joshua said, "Solali became a believer, a child of God."

Rebecca gasped, Matthew's face brightened, and Cynthia passed the eggs. Matthew peered around his mother's arm. "I'm wishin' it could have been me to lead her in the way. But I don't have the easy tongue." He was beaming shyly, possessively.

With a sigh, Rebecca picked up her fork. Her hand was trembling and she pressed the fork against the plate. "Here, have an egg." Joshua shoved the platter at her. She passed the platter and stared at her plate, but she was seeing that nighttime scene from the head of the stairs.

Joshua was finishing his breakfast, draining the last of his coffee. He was looking at her and the questions were still there. "Becky?"

"I—" The fork was moving faster, but she contemplated the lump in her throat and decided it would be best to just mash the egg on the plate.

"Rebecca, I would like a word with you." The row of eyes fastened first on Rebecca, then moved to Joshua.

"Well, I 'spect you'd better speak up so's we'll all hear," Matthew drawled, "Unless you want Ma to weed the garden at six in the morning and me to head down the road and Solali here—"

"Might be a good idea at that," Joshua interrupted. "On the other hand, might be we'll go weed the patch, since Rebecca's already soaked."

"Joshua—" helplessly Rebecca began, then fell silent. His hand was on the back of her chair.

"Oh, pawsh, go in the parlor," Cynthia snorted. "You think a body's all ears? Solali, go fetch Kalli for breakfast." Solali's face brightened and a smile spread across her face as she left the room.

Matthew was in the wagon, waiting at the front door. He flicked the reins along the backs of the team and settled lower on the seat and tilted his hat over his eyes. Rebecca stared through the window at him, ignoring Joshua.

His hand on her shoulder brought her around, gently but firmly. He was shaking his head. "I don't think I'll ever on this earth understand women. I'm getting the idea that everyone's in on a big secret except me. Becky," he paused and shifted from one foot to the other while a perplexed frown creased his forehead. "You tried to slip out without saying good-bye. Why?"

She shook her head. "Rebecca Wolstone, I'm waiting." She jerked her head up to meet his eyes. Wolstone, not Jacobson—and she could see he meant it. He wasn't thinking of the past or anything else. Her hand slipped toward her throat and he reached for it.

"Why do you look like that? Are you fearing me? You know I said I wouldn't pressure you." He hesitated while he continued to study her face; then slowly he reached for her. Trembling, Rebecca came, conscious of him with all her mind and body.

His arm held her close as his left hand lifted her chin. She was filled with the glory of him, the light in his eyes and the smile behind his golden beard. "Children of light," she murmured Solali's words. Slowly his arm tightened, bringing her closer, measuring her response. She closed her eyes, suddenly weighted, shy. In the moment he held her close before touching her lips, she felt the gold ring pressing against her face.

"My Becky," he whispered. "Always and forever you've been mine, but do you realize, through all these years I've never held you like this, and I've never kissed you?" Now Rebecca opened her eyes. With her two hands she wiped away the tears from her eyes before she wrapped her arms around his neck.

14

•••••••••••••••••••

In the days that followed it seemed to Rebecca that she was wrapped with the essence of Joshua. And while she ached with loneliness, his touch and his presence informed her that she would never again be unloved.

But even in the lonely hours she found that life must go on. There was work to do. Tasks waited.

It was Rebecca's secret; the very air was golden because of him. At least she thought it her secret. Finally Cynthia rescued the half-pared apples, the pan and knife.

Turning to Solali she demanded, "Find her something to do that takes only a half a mind. Where the rest of hers has fled, I don't know. But I do believe we'll need to be having a weddin' before Pa and I can move up to the house."

Rebecca moved. "Wedding? Oh—but that's—well, maybe."

She tried to separate herself from the dream, but she continued to hang suspended, useless, knowing only the counting of time until he would return. Beyond Cynthia's ever-questioning look was So-lali's wistful expression. Rebecca tried to reason with herself, tried to grasp reality and found it only added substance to her dreams.

On the day Joshua was to return, Matthew came alone. "Pa's hurt," he reported. "Nothing too serious. He slipped from the roof and wrenched his back. Joshua made him go to bed and stay there and he's sent me to fetch Ma. We've got things pretty cozy right now. I can go back and stay until he's feeling better, then—" He paused to study Solali's face before adding, "I'm of a mind to move back down to Salem before the rain starts. We've had a pack of trouble with squatters anyway."

Rebecca saw the exchange of glances between Solali and

Matthew. Now she picked up the word. "Squatters—what's that?"

"Them who walk in and take over. If they're let to stay long enough, it's nigh on to impossible to prove you've had honest intentions toward the land in the first place."

Matthew moved restlessly around the kitchen and Cynthia got to her feet. "I 'spect we might as well get that wagon loaded and head out. Don't like to be caught on the road after dark. Mortons tell that the Indians have been causing problems down by Jackson Creek. The thieving bunch, they want the grub without working for it."

Rebecca saw Solali wince. She hesitated, wondering what she could say to remove the sting of the woman's words. But after a moment Becky shrugged and, turning to Cynthia, said, "I'll help you gather up the things you want to take this trip. Do you want Matt to load in the little chest too?" She saw that Cynthia was still muttering as she went up the stairs.

"Becky, don't," Solali said softly. "It doesn't matter." She gave her a push toward the stairs.

Rebecca went to carry down a bundle of quilts. When she passed the kitchen door with her load, she saw Matthew and Solali facing each other across the table.

Settling her bundle beside the front door, Rebecca turned just as Solali spoke. Her voice was low, meant only for Matthew, but the earnestness of her tone had Rebecca's attention. "You see, Matthew, much as I like you and respect you, much as I want to raise your little Thomas, I can't marry you."

On her way upstairs, Rebecca was opposite the kitchen door, seeing Solali with her head bowed. Her softly spoken words were indistinct, but Rebecca heard, "Not fair—it's wrong. Eagle has my heart."

"But Eagle has left," Matthew said and then waited. Suddenly realizing that she was eavesdropping, Rebecca ran up the stairs. Behind her came Matthew's heavy voice saying, "If you change your mind, ever, Solali, I'll be waiting."

Solali, Rebecca, and Kalli watched the wagon rumble down the lane. The loneliness and the regret pressed in upon Rebecca and she wondered what the two Indian women were feeling. Kalli's wide eyes studied Solali as she turned toward the kitchen.

That evening, after Rebecca and Solali had milked the cows and fed the chickens and pigs, they closed the house against the evening chill and nighttime sounds.

Although it was only dusk, Solali put the lamp in the middle of the kitchen table. With no men to cook for and with Cynthia's hearty appetite gone, they scrambled eggs and browned bread on the hospitable warmth of the stove.

Kalli was a small chunk of silence at the end of the table as she fed the child. Solali still persisted in her attempts to teach Kalli English. "Bread," she held up the slice; now, pointing to the stove, she said, "Toast."

Kalli's face was blank. Solali shrugged and reached for the butter. After she had spread the toast with the butter, she handed it to the little boy. "Baby," said Kalli beaming.

Rebecca sat down across the table from Solali and handed the eggs to Kalli. "One thing," she said, "we'll not have to worry about Cynthia hearing our conversation secondhand."

"How long will you keep your silence with her?" Solali asked. "I see the questions big in her eyes. It's not good." She was shaking her head as she ladled jam onto her plate.

Rebecca sighed, "It makes a strain. I feel it constantly and I see the questions too. Whatever Joshua said to her to make her keep her silence must have been strong. She's always been prone to speak her mind." She raised her hands helplessly. "But what am I to do? Solali—I am so fearful. You saw how she was with the newspapers."

Solali picked at her eggs, and Rebecca was conscious of her brooding expression as she looked at her. Finally she placed her fork on the table and leaned forward. "Solali, I'm feeling *your* questions too. I have for weeks now. We've no vow of silence."

She nodded, "True, except the vows our minds hold."

"What do you mean?"

"Rebecca, I'm fearful for you. Since that—all this time since it happened. That, back there at the Meadows." Her words were choppy and her eyes were begging for Rebecca's understanding.

She took a deep breath and started again. "Please. You have been frozen away from the feelings. I must speak. My people weep and talk. You have done neither. There's just been those terrible dreams at night and then you push them away. I thought time would heal but as it has passed, I've seen you become hard like the lake in January. Is that good? Will it ever cease to be, just by your pretending? Is this really the way of the white man? I hear them say to stiffen your back and don't complain. I heard that much while I was a Mormon. Is that all your God can do for you? I wonder, because I cannot see any good in this way. Like a wound hidden, there is no healing."

"I am not certain I understand you." Rebecca was breaking her toast into neat little squares which she then carefully spread with apple jelly.

"Then look at me; you are using the toast to hide away again."

Rebecca looked and was surprised at the hint of mockery in her voice as she said, "I'm looking and I see a young Indian maiden telling an older woman how to face life."

For an instant Solali's face became closed and then she said softly, "Can you not let your heart be open? Joshua has been teaching me about Jesus and I have been reading the Book. Please, Rebecca, I am trying to understand too. And I see this way you live as a—" She hesitated for a long moment while her brow furrowed in frustration. Finally she straightened and held out her hands with forefingers extended. "See, like this." Slowly she crossed the fingers at right angles.

When Solali dropped her hands, her face was troubled. "I must understand how to believe and trust in this Jesus, since He is my God. The Book shows that while Jesus lived among men, He was touching them, loving them, and healing them. Joshua says He is alive, in heaven praying for us before the Father."

She hesitated again and then softly said, "When I look at you, I don't see Him alive. I don't see Him touching you and healing you." The silence in the room grew and the darkness settled.

When the silence was impossible to bear, Kalli stood up and began carefully stacking the dishes. Now that she had their attention, she smiled with satisfaction and marched to the nail on the wall which held the dishpan. Dropping a chunk of brown soap into the pan, she reached for the teakettle and poured a stream of hot water on the soap. She was smiling with delight at their attention. Carefully she stretched her hand toward the steaming dishpan.

"No, Kalli!" Rebecca jumped to her feet and ran for the dipper of cold water. With a gasp of relief, she poured and tested. "Now, Kalli, you wash."

She sat down and they watched Kalli add the dishes to the pan and pick up the dishcloth. Rebecca felt as if she had been stretched to the breaking point; now the tension was dissolving as completely as the soap melting in the pan.

She leaned her elbows on the table and tried to sort through the emotional jumble of her feelings. Solali's words had stripped bare something she had been hiding—hiding so completely that she didn't know it existed. Solali was watching her.

"It's all right," she whispered. "Solali, I'm sorry I snapped. It's just—well, please say no more now."

And the next day, while the sun was bright and Kalli was busy with the dishpan again, Solali held Thomas and brought out the words once again.

She said, "I've read the story of Jesus and that woman at the well. You know, the one who had been living with a man who wasn't her husband. It was like Jesus had been reading my thoughts and suddenly He was saying: 'I know what you are wondering, Solali; I say go and sin no more.' "

"And what *were* you thinking?" Rebecca whispered.

"I was feeling the belonging to Jesus Christ, and knowing that I must be holy. Then I wondered about my past—the years I lived as a plural wife and my rebellion and running away from it all. I guess everything was making me feel like a sinful woman."

"Is that why you told Matthew you wouldn't marry him?"

Solali waited for a moment before she answered, "No. Seeing you with Joshua changed everything for me. But that was only the end of it. It was Joshua who helped me see the beginning, and that started to change my thinking. First, I was thinking that your God would want me to marry a white man, just like the Mormons required me to marry a man with two other wives. But that was all wrong. Joshua showed me in the Bible that Jesus Christ is the atonement for sins for *everyone*. He died to give me all that I was trying to earn for myself by being a good person and doing what I was told to do."

"Yes, I know all that."

"I understand now, it's a gift, this salvation. Joshua called it being reconciled to God, being able to call Him Father just like Jesus did. Joshua said I didn't have to do anything to deserve it. I just had to take it. When I knelt down and told Jesus Christ I was sorry for my sins and that I wanted to have His atonement, then I knew I didn't have to marry Matthew to be a Christian. But later, I was thinking about how things are going. Those things Cynthia said about Jackson Creek."

Rebecca leaned across the table. "Solali, you're thinking about how the white man has pushed the Indians off their land. How they've made promises and then haven't kept them. You know I am ashamed of all this."

"But they will continue to do it. We are weak people. Soon we won't exist. I can see how I would have a better life by marrying a white man. Remember, I know what it's like to go to school and live in a warm house in the winter and dig a garden patch instead of living in a willow hut and following the harvest of nature. At one time it was a good life. Now the white people are making it very hard for us to live as our fathers lived. I chose to escape. I would marry Matthew."

"But you've told him no. Why?"

She lifted her head and her dark eyes were dreamy. "I saw you and Joshua. I understand that you belong together and that there is a great love."

Rebecca took an unsteady breath and whispered, "Yes, there is. I'm almost afraid to think about it. Seems like a wind will blow it away."

Solali was studying her face and Rebecca pressed her hands against her warm cheeks. Solali said, "You look as if you aren't quite awake, as if you are afraid to face the dawn." She was silent now, and a dark shadow seemed to move across her face.

"Don't look like that. I'll pray you and Eagle will have the same love."

She was shaking her head. "I wasn't thinking about that. It's you. Rebecca, how can you be happy when you haven't cried?"

"Solali!" Rebecca jumped to her feet. "You're digging at me. You don't understand white people. We don't believe in letting out all the dark thoughts."

Solali rested her hands on the tabletop and leaned toward Rebecca. Her eyes demanded Rebecca's attention. "And you will go through life pretending those things didn't really happen? Rebecca, I heard your screams while the fever gripped you. You relived that night over and over. I heard you cry, 'Please, don't kill the children!' And then you cried, 'Timmy, Timmy!' Who was Timmy? And when your baby was born—do you remember what you said?"

Rebecca's hands clasped her throat. "Solali," she whispered, "you'll kill me, don't . . ."

"Rebecca, I know enough about Jesus—"

"Solali!" she screamed and the sound tore through the kitchen. Now whirling and pressing her hands to her ears, she ran from the room, crying, "Don't ever say it again. Now leave me alone!" She ran across the parlor and into the room shared by Matthew and Joshua.

Dimly she remembered that when her sobbing ceased, Solali crept into the room and pulled the quilt over her shoulders.

When Joshua came, it was Solali who met him as he led his horse to the corral. His smile faded when he saw her haggard face. "It's Rebecca," she said with a weary sigh. "Please stay here and let me tell you about it before you see her. I am to be blamed for it all, and it is much worse than I thought. I knew she must mourn, but I didn't understand the—the darkness of it all."

Slowly Joshua pitched hay to his horse and then picked up a towel. As Solali continued to bring out the painful words, he rubbed down the sweating horse.

"You've ridden her hard," Solali paused to reflect.

"Yes, I was anxious to see Becky." He faced Solali. "Your words aren't making too much sense. A dream, a nightmare? Becky is a healthy, normal woman. She'll get over it."

"You'll have to see," Solali whispered. "Joshua, I didn't understand. I thought only that she needed to cry over that baby before she could come alive again."

Joshua frowned. "I think I'm beginning to see. You're saying you see things I don't. That her quietness and then her laughter was telling you her problem. Yes, I've seen it's from one to the other she has moved. Now I'm seeing more. There's a fence about her heart. I was ready to accept that as the grown-up Becky, but you're saying it shows her hurt." He paced back and forth in the barn as Solali talked on.

"I listened to her during the bad time when she first came to our village. There was fear and anger in her. I saw the wild expression in her eyes and heard the screams. I don't know how she can hold it in. Sometimes during the night hours, it haunts me." Solali caught up with Joshua and looked into his face. "Does Jesus still heal?"

Joshua stopped and stared at her. Slowly he said, "Solali, Jesus Christ is alive. The Bible says He's the same, and He did it then. I remember a verse that goes like this: 'Who his own self bare our sins in his own body on the tree, that we, being dead to sins, should live unto righteousness: by whose stripes ye were healed.' "

Now he sighed with relief and smiled down at Solali. "It isn't hopeless. We have a kind heavenly Father who has given us all things in Jesus Christ. Solali, we must pray for Rebecca."

As he walked rapidly toward the house, Solali ran to keep up with him, crying, "But you don't understand—"

"But I believe." As he reached for the door, he patted her shoulder. "I've the faith to believe that Jesus Christ can handle Rebecca's problems. He has so far."

He found her at the stove. Without looking up she continued to slice potatoes into the frying pan. When she finished, she turned her head and he saw her eyes were shadowed, remote. "Joshua, you're back. How nice." He leaned to kiss her and she moved away. "How's your pa? Is it serious?"

"Naw, a stiff back for a couple of days. He's still tough. He and Ma'll be back down here next week. Then, they're saying, if there's any visitin' to be done, we'll have to come see them."

"Why are they coming back?" He knew Rebecca was making conversation.

"Pa's going to take Ma into Salem and they're going to have a shoppin' spree before the rains begin. We got a good price for the wheat and the money's burnin' a hole in Pa's pocket."

"Just like always." Rebecca's voice was sharp.

"Just like always," Joshua echoed, more caught by the sharpness in Rebecca's voice than he was by the memory of his father's past spending habits.

Kalli came into the kitchen carrying Matthew's baby. Her child ran to Joshua and lifted his arms.

"Hello, big guy." Joshua swung him high.

"Hello," the child mimicked, giggling as he nestled against Joshua's arm.

Clasping the child close, Joshua whispered, "Hey, I'd like to keep you forever. You're a good young'un." He addressed Solali. "Matt's serious about leaving for Salem. May go next week."

"Is he angry with me?" she answered.

"No, I think he understands. Matt was pretty wrapped up in his Amy."

"Eagle?"

He shook his head. "I haven't seen any more of him. He sure wasn't talkin' when he left here, so I don't know what—" Solali turned away with a sigh.

"Hey!" Joshua was watching Kalli with a pleased grin. She had given the baby to Solali and now she was busy carrying plates and forks to the table. She brought bread to the table and skillfully sliced it. "Lady, you're doing fine." Joshua reached awkwardly around his armload of child to pat Kalli's shoulder.

"Fine," the child echoed, swinging from Joshua's neck. "Fine," echoed again from Kalli, an uncharacteristic glitter of expression in her eye. Silently Rebecca brushed past carrying the platter of meat.

After supper Joshua took Rebecca's hand. "Let's leave Solali and Kalli with the clean-up. Seems that young lady is taking pride in what she's learning to do."

"Eagle seemed to think she would be content staying here forever," Solali said as she got to her feet. "Yes, Rebecca, go on. You need the fresh air." Addressing Joshua, she said, "She's scarcely been out of the house for a week now."

Rebecca hesitated and Joshua nudged her toward the door. With Kalli's child swooping around their heels, they headed through the autumn-bare fields. "Soon it's frost and scorch, that's the autumn weather here; then comes the rain." Joshua picked a stalk of dried grass to nibble. "Some say it looks dead then when it's picked clean. It just reminds me of the work that's been done. Week after next I aim to plow the wheat field and get ready for the winter rains to do my work, keepin' the little wheat seeds happy 'til summer."

Still she was silent. "Guess I'll cut us some more firewood tomorrow," he reflected, then, "Rebecca, after Matt collects his household and heads for home, how's about us and Solali going to Salem? You know it's the capital of the Territory. There's always something going on there. Right now things are moving swift toward our getting statehood. It'll be exciting for you. How about it?"

"Joshua." They had reached the corrals and she turned to back against the log fence. He watched her take a deep breath and then she said, "I can't marry you. I'm sorry. It just won't work."

He stepped close and bent down to look into her eyes. "Seems to me you've changed your mind awful fast. Mind tellin' me why?"

She moved her head wearily. "I've a heart to try my hand at school teaching."

"That's strange. First time I've heard you mention it since we've come home."

"Joshua, leave me be. You said you wouldn't pressure me and I'm holding you to that."

"Mind kissin' me and then telling me that again?"

"No." He saw she was breathless and he pressed again.

"Solali's said you've had a rough time of it while I was gone. Rebecca, I know what I'm getting. It's you I want and I'm willing to handle the problems. Let's forget about the past and just work at building a life together. I need you as much—maybe more'n you need me."

She stood tall and ramrod stiff. "I'm not making myself understood. Joshua, I *can't* marry you."

"You're not married." Her eyes were darkening and he pushed the brutal words at her. "You've lived with a man. You've been misused and tortured. I take it you can't face the risk of it happening again. Becky, I can't tell you I'll never disappoint you; but *hurt you* deliberately? That won't happen. If you're fearin' me, then that's something I can't control. You've seen me for what I am. I'm not pretending and you know that. From the outside of me clear through to the heart, you see me as I am. If that isn't good enough, well say so and I'll not bother you again."

"Oh, Joshua," her voice broke. "It isn't that. You're beautiful all the way through, and you're deserving of so much better."

"After spending years hunting for you, are you trying to tell me I don't know my own mind?"

She was shaking her head. "Don't pressure me. I've made my decision and there'll be no changing it now."

He stepped close to her and clasped her forearms in his warm hands. "Don't you think you owe a body enough to come clean and say the real reason?"

For a moment she was motionless, her head cocked as if listening and then she moved. Jerking herself free, she turned and ran to the house.

Joshua followed slowly, knowing suddenly how futile, even powerless his efforts were. His shoulders sagged and then straightened. In the past, in the black days, he had known only the burden and the prayers.

15

· · · · · · · · · · · · · · · · · · · ·

*B*ehind the house, under the low eaves, the stack of firewood was growing. Matthew came and left, taking with him his son and Kalli with her child. He would find someone else to live with them to keep the tongues from wagging. The oak and apple trees held a hint of autumn color.

Again Rebecca refused to go to Salem, but the pain in her eyes when Joshua asked was enough to give him heart.

He was waiting patiently and he knew that Rebecca was aware of it. While he bided his time, he was seeing Rebecca grow thin and pale.

One night Joshua awakened to a whisper of sound from the parlor. As he lay in the darkness, he recognized the familiar sound, one that had penetrated his sleep often during the past days. Knowing now what he would find, he dressed and quietly crossed the darkened house. In the shelter of the high-backed settle, Rebecca crouched, shivering.

One glance confirmed his guesses: the dreams Solali had talked about. In her white, tear-stained face and shivering form, lighted only by the dying embers of the fire, he saw her undisguised despair.

Going back to his room he took the quilt from the bed and brought it to Rebecca. She allowed him to wrap her in it and tuck it about her feet. He poked at the fire and added wood before he sat down on the stool.

"Don't say it." Her voice was thick and weary. "It's simply that I can't sleep and I didn't want to disturb Solali."

"Forget the—all else." His voice was rough. "I only want to help you now and I can't do that until you'll allow it."

"Just dreams." She shivered and pulled the quilt close. "By morning I forget."

"Tell me about them." Her stony face gave him his answer. "Would you like tea?" She shook her head. He kept the silence, wondering what to do when words failed.

Finally she stirred. "Joshua, leave me to sort things out. Before, when I kissed you, I honestly didn't realize—" More silence and then she continued with a controlled sob. "There's such ugliness inside. I thought I was whole, mending. I'm thinking God's telling me how unfit I am to even dream of a—of life again."

He poked at the wood and waited, constrained in a way he couldn't understand.

Out of a long silence she spoke, almost dreamily, and her words chilled him. "I know that Jesus Christ has redeemed me for all eternity through His precious blood—" For a moment there were ragged sobs, revealing an anguish he hadn't guessed. "But I can't bear the burden of the past. Why will He not release me now to go to Him? It would have been better—my baby. Why must I live on in the torture of the past? I yearn so for release."

It was much later when he said wearily, "Becky." He was fingering the gold ring strung on rawhide about his neck. "If I hadn't gone to California, if I'd come straight to Utah, then this—" He dropped the ring and looked up at her. "I guess I'm sayin' it's just as much my fault as yours."

The fire died, winking out in its final glow. Now the kitchen window lightened and the rooster crowed. When Joshua got to his feet, still wordless, Rebecca's face was only a pale shadow. His hands hung helplessly by his side as he walked back to his bedroom.

And the next night, when she would have followed Solali up the stairs, he stopped her. "I've been thinking, Rebecca. Come listen."

"Joshua, no, please."

His voice was ragged with weariness, cutting in on her protest. "You're thinking God has brought you this far and that now He will abandon you. Don't you think He is your *Father*, that He wants you to have happiness and the fulfillment of all that a woman holds dear?"

She moved restlessly and he forced his words quickly, trying to prevent her retreat. "I don't see God as being like that. Is it possible that the years of teaching by that other church has left fragments in your thoughts that aren't thoughts from God?"

"I don't understand."

"You make me think of something the apostle Paul wrote—it

went like this. He said, 'You foolish Galatians, are you bewitched? You started with the Spirit; are you trying to do it all on your own now?' "

"Say it, Joshua."

"You're giving up on following Jesus Christ. You started just the way you were supposed to start, but now you're handling the reins. Just like a young filly throwing herself into the race and forgetting who's the rider."

"No, you've got it all wrong. I'm knowing I'll never be fit to be a wife and mother. I accept this as being from God."

"Why are you talking like this?"

"It's before me, the facts. I know how I am inside."

"If you're saying you're afraid you'll never bear another child, Rebecca, that's not why I'm wanting you. I love you for yourself. If there's never a child, it won't change how I feel about you."

She burst away from him, away from the tenderness in his voice and said impatiently, "You don't understand."

"Yes, I do. I understand that you've problems you won't air to me." She was shaking her head and desperately he said, "Solali told me about all she lived through with you when you were so badly wounded and ill with the fever. And then she told me how it was when the baby was born. Rebecca, other women live through these bad times and recover to live normal lives."

"I know!" She was shouting while the tears streamed down her face. "I've been treated to their stories since I've been here. I'm not saying I've had it worse."

He held out his arms. "My little Becky. Don't you see that I love you? How I wish you'd let me share the load with you."

She avoided his arms. "No, you don't." She paused and wiped at the tears. Now wearily she added, "And you'll force it from me, won't you? Joshua, I'd soil you with my ugliness." In a moment her tears were dried and her eyes were flashing. She drew herself up and her face contorted with rage. Leaning close to him, she hissed, "You would never carry this load. You see, *I hate that man on the Meadow.* I've lived a long time with the burden, but now I see he didn't have the right to take my life from me because I disobeyed him. There was no divine redemption in killing me. That man is not my god and never has been. No longer do I accept Brigham Young as ruler of my life and eternity. Not one thing he says can send me to hell, but together those two men stripped me of the only thing I had left in this world—my baby.

"Don't look so shocked, Joshua. You don't think I can hate like this because I lost a child? How can you judge what a baby can mean until you've desperately wanted a child and then to have cuddled him in your body those long months, only to have him denied life and stripped from you?"

"Rebecca—" Joshua's voice pleaded.

"Those men did it. Andrew, because he was obeying counsel; and Brigham Young, because he raised himself up as god and dictated with the power of life and death. He chose death for me." She paused only briefly and then lashed out again.

"And don't tell me I'm to forgive if I will be forgiven. I'm not forgetting that I was in all those difficulties because I was minding a God who knew and cared. He could have at least allowed me to have my baby. The rest I believe I could learn to live with, but this I cannot."

Joshua's eyes sought hers, but she looked away and pushed his hands from her.

"Yes, you might say I tried to bargain with God. I obey if He gives me my baby. Even on that hot ride across the desert when I tried to save those people's lives, I was expecting God to treat me like I was something special."

"And you're complaining," Joshua said slowly, "because God didn't act in the manner you chose for Him to act?"

Slowly he turned and sat down on the stool in front of the fire. For a long time he gazed into the glowing coals, watching them change from fire and warmth to a feeble glow and then dull ash. The things that he thought he would never admit surfaced in his thoughts, and they roamed through his mind, troubling him.

It was one thing to pray and feel sweet release, but it was quite another to pray and feel increased agony, especially when that agony must remain faceless, unnamed.

He was still pondering the significance of the words the Lord had burned into his thoughts when his only reason for living had been to find Rebecca. And, thinking back to those days, he found himself finally admitting his dark moment.

It was his groping, trusting, blind instincts which had led him on that final trip into Utah Territory. But even in the worst of times, he had felt a sureness, a sense of direction, moving through him. Until that last day.

Once again he felt the total desolation of that moment when he had been informed of Rebecca's death. There on that wind-battered mountain, confronted by the nameless stranger with the cold eyes, dealt that message, Joshua's faith shattered.

For hours as he wandered, his God was dead. Even at this minute Joshua's heart was wrenching as he remembered his moment of abandoned faith.

With a sigh he straightened and turned to Rebecca. "I guess it isn't in us to ever know God so completely that we don't sometimes stagger under the load. Rebecca, you're thinking my faith's always been nigh perfect. It isn't.

"If Eagle hadn't rescued me out of that snowstorm and brought me to you, I'd a plum walked off the edge of the earth without an upward glance. And all that, heaped upon the encouraging things the Spirit had been saying to me for months."

He saw a spark of interest on her face. "The Spirit," she whispered leaning forward. "What did He say?"

"You need to understand how I was feeling. I was plain tuckered out with praying and hoping and trying to understand the load He was putting on me to keep looking for you. I'd been at it for years, and I couldn't understand it. The thought kept comin' through to me that He was trying to offer you a chance to escape. I didn't know what you must escape, but I prayed the words. Then I hit the bottom. It seemed I couldn't say the words one more time. Seems then I was hearing Him say new words to me, and I was hearing them as a promise."

He gestured toward the dying fire. "I've never wanted to say them to you, mostly because I didn't like the thrust of them, and I wasn't sure of the reason why He must work this way when He had the power to rattle Utah Territory until you dropped out." He tried to grin but knew it was without humor. Rebecca's eyes were still dark in the pale oval of her face. She waited.

"It was the words God used through the prophet Amos."

"What were they?"

" '. . . and ye were as a firebrand plucked out of the burning.' "

She slowly backed into the corner of the settle and he could no longer see her eyes. After a long time he said, "Rebecca?" There was no answer, nothing more to be said.

Joshua got to his feet and began pacing the room, moving between the fireplace and the front windows. He was no longer restraining Rebecca, demanding an audience with her, but she continued to sit, watching him pace.

The fire had died, leaving the room in shadows. He stopped in front of her. "I honestly believe that if God through Jesus Christ is able to rescue us from the judgment fires, He is equally able to rescue us from ourselves. I keep seeing those lashes across His back.

For every one of them, He's won our healing. And the healing isn't complete until it goes clear through to the mind. Body, soul, and mind, we belong to Him; we must."

Now Rebecca jumped to her feet and headed for the stairs. He was saying, "Ask, Rebecca."

She paused at the top of the stairs and said, "But you see, don't you? You see the hate that I am inside. I will not allow you to live your life with this burden."

"It isn't necessary. Ask, Rebecca."

The room was barely light with dawn when Solali slipped from the bed and left the room. Rebecca lay straining to understand every whisper of sound that came from below. Joshua would be leaving today for one last trip up the mountain to his pa's house. Would he insist on seeing her again before he left? Her heavy heart trembled away from contact with him.

The sky was pink when she heard a gentle nicker from his horse. Creeping to the window, she knelt with her elbows on the trunk. Joshua and Solali stood beside the horse for a moment more and then he mounted. Did his last glance toward the house search out her window? She shrank back.

When Rebecca finally dressed and went downstairs, Solali was busy in the kitchen. Rebecca's guilty conscience reminded her that if Joshua had told Solali about last night, it wasn't evident in her easy manner. She glanced up. "Sleepyhead. Joshua has left for his pa's section. Said to tell you good-bye."

Briefly there was curiosity in her eyes and Rebecca turned away. Solali reminded, "Today is the day the women get together at the Nortons' for sewing. Are we going?"

Rebecca nodded with a wry smile. She helped herself to the cracked wheat warming on the back of the stove. "I suppose so. There's not much else to do. I don't believe we can dry another batch of apples; there's too much moisture in the air."

" 'Tis true. It's not like the desert country. Even the clothes take forever to dry here."

16

••••••••••••••••••

That afternoon Solali and Rebecca saddled horses and went into Waltstown. Solali remarked as they rode along, "Don't know that I want sitting all afternoon with a dab of needlework, but I like the ride." Then she added, "Besides, I want to see their houses. Seems the people aren't as poor about here as the Saints were."

"Solali," Rebecca said in a panic, "don't mention the Saints to these women."

"You know I won't. I'm hearkening to what you've said, though I know not why we should worry so. Seems a body would adjust to the idea we've left the church and now are following Jesus Christ."

"I'm still so fearful; I dare not let it slip out we were one of them."

"Is it fearful? I'm shunning their questions."

Rebecca didn't answer. There were those deeply buried thoughts burning in her. She tried to fasten her attention on the beauty around them. They crossed the McKenzie River as it slipped down through the little valley before slanting north to join the Willamette. Just before it entered Waltstown, it gentled and meandered quietly through the village.

The foliage along the road was touched with the colors of autumn and the annual grasses were drying. But the lush greenness of Oregon was still evident in the hemlock and fir as well as the meadow grass and the bushes and undergrowth along the river.

"Do you suppose this country will ever have the dead brown we had back there? At this time of year even the evergreens looked tired and dusty."

They had reached the outskirts of town and both women fell silent. The town clustered about one long main street. Down the length of the street were scattered the shops. There was a lawyer's office now, tucked in between the hat shop and the blacksmith's shop. The hardware store and the grocery shared a common roof and canopy. Across the way was the church, neat with white clapboard and a small, square belfry. As if in deference to its importance, the grounds of the church spread out like ample skirts, offering grass and shade to all.

Rebecca pointed. "If this were back east, they'd call it the town square. Here it's not quite big enough or square enough. It's just plain old folksy church grounds." She lowered her voice now as if afraid her thoughts would slip through. "What's different here is the planed board houses. Not a one adobe, and not too many log cabins here."

Solali chuckled. "Adobe, in this rainy country? You'd wake up some morning to find your house had melted away during the night. There you'd be in the middle of a mud puddle, in bed while the neighbors watched."

They passed the store, the blacksmith shop, and the schoolhouse. "I think the Nortons' is that place with the blue shutters. Oh, my, aren't they pretty?"

The house was small and lined with women dressed in their best calico. Knitting needles flashed and the crotchet thread unrolled; while the fancy bits of stitchery were admired, the conversation shifted lightly about the room.

Rebecca looked around, trying to spot some of the women she had met at the last sewing bee. There was the tiny Mrs. Crocket. She smiled and nodded. Once again Rebecca searched the woman's face as she wondered about the stories she had been told of her experiences on the overland trip to Oregon.

After Rebecca and Solali had studied every detail of the parlor and the kitchen beyond, and then listened to the conversation, their eyes met with amusement. Solali whispered, "Adobe not withstanding, womenfolk are the same everywhere."

But there was Solali. While Betty Hanson talked about her layette and the new cradle her husband was making, Rebecca watched her friend. She was interested in the women, their dress, their homes, but there was a difference. Long before the tea and cake was served, Rebecca saw the faraway expression in her eyes. The stitches she poked in the pillow cover came slower, the thread tugged with indifference.

Later as they rode home, Rebecca said, "You didn't enjoy yourself?"

Solali looked startled. She waited until they had left Waltstown behind and then she said, "I guess I'm just now accepting it." She glanced quickly toward Rebecca. "This life just isn't the life for me."

Rebecca wanted to mention Eagle, but the unhappy droop to Solali's lips kept her silent.

Evening was well upon them before they turned down their own lane. The dark shadows filled Rebecca with uneasiness. As she and Solali took their milk pails and went to the barn, Rebecca reached out to touch Solali. "I'm glad more than I can say that you're here with me. It's a lonesome place after dark."

There was Solali's quick look and even in the twilight Rebecca saw the concern. Before she had finished milking her cows, the brooding shadows were back upon her spirit. She tried to brush them away as they walked to the house. "Seems a good time to start some cheese. We'll never use all this milk with Joshua gone."

Solali set her pail inside the house. "Mr. Evans at the store said he'd buy butter. Joshua ought to get more pigs to fatten." She turned away. "I'm going to pick some tomatoes."

Rebecca entered the house. The silence of the place swept about her and she was conscious of every sound. The wind brushed a branch against the kitchen window and wood in the box beside the stove slipped as Solali entered and slammed the door. When Solali stood just inside the door, caught in an attitude of listening, Rebecca knew she felt it too.

"Seems strange," Rebecca said slowly, "the place was burstin' with life one minute and now there's just the two of us." Solali's dark eyes were wary, waiting. Rebecca moved quickly, trying to shake off the mood. "We're a bunch of silly ones. What's there to be afraid of in Oregon?"

Solali didn't answer and after a moment Rebecca went to shove kindling into the stove. "Would you like a pancake for supper?" Solali nodded and went to sit at the table.

"Rebecca," she said slowly, "do you ever think about—well, about things that happened back there and wonder? About the beliefs of the church. Would those—those things reach out this far?"

Very carefully Rebecca set the skillet on the stove. Unbidden, a face rose in her mind—the face of the son of Bishop Martin, the man at the way station. She turned to study Solali's troubled features. It was some minutes before she could force the words past her stiff lips. When she did, they lacked the humor she tried to put in them. "Solali, are you trying to borrow trouble?"

Solali moistened her lips. "I'm just a'feeling your troubles, wanting to know what you're thinking. Seems, lately, about the time the sun goes down I feel the heaviness starting in you."

Rebecca admitted. "I'm dreading the night. Even on the nights I don't dream, I toss and turn." She brought the pancakes to the table and pushed the sliced tomatoes and honey toward Solali.

"Would it help to ask the Father to take away the dreams?"

When Rebecca could meet Solali's eyes squarely, she said, "Would it? I don't think so."

"Why?" She couldn't answer. There was only Joshua's "Ask!" moving through her being, and she knew he didn't mean to ask for the fear to be gone.

Later as she was finishing the dishes, Solali came in with Joshua's Bible in her hands. "Rebecca, I don't understand these words." She placed the Book in front of Rebecca and touched the verse.

Rebecca read, " 'Whereby are given unto us exceeding great and precious promises: that by these ye might be partakers of the divine nature, having escaped the corruption that is in the world through lust.' " She closed the Book. "Partakers of the divine nature."

"Promises," Solali whispered. "God promising something to us." There was wonder in her voice, for a moment words seemed to fail her, then thoughtfully, "But how can a promise do that?"

Joshua's word was forced out. It was impossible to deny. "Ask."

"It's to be had just for asking? Free?"

"Free." Rebecca's fingers were busy in the pages. She found the place and read it to Solali, but it was really for her own benefit. " 'He that spared not his own Son but delivered him up for us all, how shall he not with him also freely give us all things?' "

"All things."

Could that possibly mean those kinds of things Joshua had been talking about? Like the church bell tolling out, the words rang through her—body, soul, and mind. Like the body, the soul must be free before the mind can be.

There was that blackness inside and Rebecca hugged her arms close, feeling the pull of that one complaining muscle in her shoulder. "It's cold, Solali. I'm going up to bed."

Solali was reading the Bible and there was only the briefest of nods from her.

Once in bed the words returned, *All things, freely, body, soul, mind*. Rebecca tossed restlessly.

And in the morning Solali found her beside the stove, huddled over a cup of tea.

"The dreams?"

She shook her head. Solali poured tea for herself and sat down facing Rebecca. "What is it?"

She felt her grin twist. "I just couldn't sleep."

And after breakfast, Rebecca took a deep breath and knew her resolve was complete. "Solali. I'm going upstairs. Please let me alone. I must settle it—all this—in my mind." Relief blazed through Solali's eyes. Rebecca hesitated. "Do you care? There's washing to be done."

Solali pushed, "No, now go."

Upstairs Rebecca spread the open Bible on the trunk sitting under the window. She knelt beside it. Through the window she could see the road. A gentle rain had polished the trees and bushes beside it, but in its emptiness, the road looked lonely. It triggered the emotion in her. Far down the way, just tipping the trees, she saw a puff of smoke. That would be the Chambers' home.

She visualized their breakfast table. There would be little Aaron with his tangle of curls dripping porridge down his chin. And Martha. Children. The blackness crept in upon her. Closing her eyes she let it sweep over her. The Bible slipped off the trunk and her weary arms tried to support her head. "Oh, God, why, why?"

The rain ceased and the feeble sunlight touched her. She bent over the Bible and misery kept her thumbing through the pages. Now she remembered the agony of spirit that had sent her into this Book in the beginning. Her wandering fingers found the fifth chapter of Galatians and she read the beginning. " 'Stand fast therefore in the liberty wherewith Christ hath made us free, and be not entangled again with the yoke of bondage.' " Her heart melted as her finger moved down the page and stopped. She read, " 'Ye did run well; who did hinder you that ye should not obey the truth? This persuasion cometh not of him that calleth you.' "

Rebecca's sobs broke into laughter and then ended in tears. "Oh, my kind Lord," she said wiping at the tears. "It's as if you're sitting here beside me, telling me those very words. I'd forgotten how good it is to talk to you, listen to you—these are the very words of God, and I hear you speaking them to me.

"I don't know why I've allowed myself to be led astray, why I've forgotten how good it is to know your closeness." Abruptly she was silent, and the sure understanding of it all sank in upon her.

The emotions tumbled in. She was caught up in bitterness, loss; she was now twisted beyond reason, captured by rebellion in a dark tunnel of her own making. "It was the moment I blamed You for snatching away my baby. I thought my child was due me. All I did for You, trying to rescue those people. I thought You at least owed me the life of my child."

While she sobbed, prone on the floor with the scrap of rag rug catching her tears, a word moved through her sore mind. "Oh, God, how can I escape?" Escape, a chance to escape. Those were Joshua's words. He had written them in a letter. Then night before last, he had given them back to her. The letter? She hadn't re-read the words, the letter had disappeared. Had it been burned? Burn. A firebrand—plucked not from a fire but—the scene filled her mind.

There was that one moment of unbelievable horror before the silence and blackness had claimed her. Plucked.

Rebecca shivered against the rug and feebly tried to force herself up, away from the floor, away from the memory of that scene. "Oh, God, what are You trying to do to me?" *Ask*. With her face buried in the bedquilt, she whispered, "What is it?"

In waiting she felt the quietness creeping into her, stilling her pounding heart, soothing her aching head. She waited; now cradled, upheld, sheltered, and then released.

At that moment she was remembering another scene from the past. It was lighted by a shaft of light pushing through the tent and touching the books on her lap. Outside the willow leaves had fingered the tent like a gentle, inquisitive spirit. A peaceful scene, but there was turmoil inside. Inside the tent, inside Rebecca.

Clearly she recalled the scene, feeling again the struggles of that young woman as she tried to understand the strange forces that were shaking her. "Oh!" Rebecca cried suddenly, seeing that time with brittle, shining clarity. "I was seeking for truth and my lap was full of Mormon books. Why didn't I have the Bible there? That was my moment for finding and there was nothing to be found because, like a horse with blinders on, all the truth was being held away from me while I concentrated on what was in my lap—all those Mormon books.

"For one moment the door was open—that was the moment I questioned." Rebecca whispered. "If I'd said, 'Jesus, show me the way,' I'd probably have run out into the streets of Salt Lake City and straight into the arms of Joshua, 'cause later Ann told me he was there seeking me."

A brand from the burning.

Much later, when the tears had wrung her into limpness and surrender was total, Rebecca was able to speak to her Lord again. "You don't owe me anything. I owe You everything. You are God. You with the nail-pierced hands and the scarred face." She paused and then said slowly and wonderingly, "By your wounds I am healed. Now my wounds will remind me that you have chosen to rescue me, a brand from the burning. I blamed you for my circumstances. You rescued me."

And then later. "I am healed. I accept you as God, Lord of all of me." She paused. "Now there is my anger." Again she sank beneath the burden. Andrew, Brigham Young. Was it possible to look beyond the hate?

In quietness, she waited. Knowing finally the depths of her hate, seeing the impossibility of escape, knowing her total helplessness, she was wrung into weakness. And then there was hope. She whispered, "Lord Jesus, I need a miracle. That promise. You were delivered up for my death. Now I am dead."

She felt a stirring of life. "You were delivered up for *their* death, too, Andrew's and Brigham Young's, but they don't know it. I know it, I'm *living* in it." Her voice quiet, "I forgive them."

Through her trembling spirit, she stretched out a hand, knowing only total weakness. "The Divine Nature—You. That's the part I need. Fitting me for *life* unto righteousness!"

It was dark when Rebecca walked downstairs. In the kitchen, in the middle of the pool of light from the lamp, Solali sat waiting. Her dark eyes were searching, curious.

Rebecca sat down at the table and spread her hands, palms down. "The blackness is gone. I don't understand how it is possible. It's just simply, totally gone. I'm knowing it is another gift of himself. First He gave me His atonement, now His very life is in me."

Solali whispered, "Is it really possible to live life so close to the Great Spirit that you are held that close, feeling His thoughts, living His love, walking His ways? The Book talks about it here in 1 Corinthians in the second chapter." Now her voice was yearning. "Is it possible this goodness is for anyone who truly searches for it?"

"I think now," Rebecca whispered, "it's all held in that moment when our spirits choose. Do we rebel, or do we live?"

17

· · · · · · · · · · · · · · · · · ·

The following day began calmly enough. Rebecca was still moving in the unbelievable circle of serenity. At times she was almost afraid to take too deep a breath, but then there was Solali's wide-eyed joy to remind her of it all. And inside there was that tremulous assurance of yesterday's healing.

The sun shone, the teakettle merrily spouted steam. The fragrance of coffee and toast still clung to the air. Now, with Solali's hands deep in the dishpan and Rebecca wiping the dishes, Solali said, "I've been putting this all together."

She turned to face Rebecca. "Not so much thoughts as feelings. I'm knowing more and more that I'm wanting to go back to my people. There's a big yearning inside of me to help them find this new way of living—not the white man's way but God's way." She stopped and Rebecca knew she was searching out every line of her face, wondering how she was feeling this morning.

"It's still there," she said gently. "And I've never slept so well as I did last night."

"You didn't hear the storm and the wind crashing branches against the house?"

Rebecca shook her head. Turning the plate she was drying, she watched the design of apple blossoms catch the sun. Solali continued, "Our people have need of this message. They must know that the Creator of the heavens and earth loves them. I know their heartache, and it grows worse. I know their loyalties. When they hear about Jesus Christ, and understand, they will be willing to give their hearts to Him.

"Do you understand, Rebecca? When an Indian tears out his heart and offers it up, that's all there is. There's nothing left for him to own. His life is gone and it will all belong to the great God."

Rebecca dropped her towel and turned to Solali. "What a beautiful way to explain it!" With awe in her voice, she repeated. "What beauty! That's what I did. Solali, I tore out my heart and there's nothing left to own. You've understood that all along, and I've just now really grasped it. I—"

There was a shout from the front of the house and the door banged open. Before they could react, Eagle bounded into the kitchen. "Joshua?"

Rebecca was the first to recover. "Why, Eagle! He's gone."

"Gone." With the word, she was seeing that this was no longer the serene face of the Indian she had first met on the mountain. Bewildered, he echoed the word again, "Gone."

Looking at the lines on his face, seeing his agitated pacing of the room, Rebecca knew she must make him understand. "To his pa's place," she touched his arm, "shingles." Understanding swept over his face and now Solali moved. She took her dripping hands out of the dishpan and slowly wiped them on her apron as she spoke softly in the Paiute tongue. Eagle's face cleared. He was nodding and then shaking his head as she reached for the bread. He spun around and headed out the back door.

Solali explained, "He'll take a fresh horse." They were hearing a final shout and the clatter of hooves on the roadway. "I'll go take care of his horse," Solali said.

Rebecca ran to the front door and watched him disappearing down the road. "What's happened? He's terribly upset and he's riding that horse mighty fast." She turned. "Why didn't he eat? It'll take him a good hour to get there, even riding that fast."

"I don't know," Solali said. "He wouldn't tell me, but then I'm feeling he's still angry with me. He said only that he must see Joshua. I'm sure most of his stomping around was just to show me his anger."

"Oh, Solali, I don't believe that."

"But you don't know Eagle. When he left here, I made sure he didn't have a reason to return." She turned and walked back to the kitchen. Rebecca noticed the discouraged droop to her shoulders and didn't know whether to be sad or happy. There were all those things Solali had said just before Eagle came. And now he was gone without even so much as a friendly glance for her.

It was nearly noon when Eagle's horse galloped into the clearing where the neat little cottage stood. The last shingle had been nailed into place. Mr. Smyth had brushed on the last stroke of white paint and Cynthia had polished her windows and settled her kitchen. Joshua was busy loading the shed with a season's supply of firewood.

When he heard the horse, he rested on his axe and waited for the rider to show himself. Now waving his hat he shouted, "Eagle, my friend! We've finished up here and you've arrived just in time for a little celebrating. Ma's frying up a chicken right now." He stopped. Eagle was off the horse now and his face was flinty.

"Josh, we talk." Abruptly he headed for the barn and Joshua followed.

Mr. Smyth was lifting a ladder as they entered and Joshua said, "Pa, you ought not be fooling with heavy things for a while longer. You know I've come just to save you swinging the axe for a few more months. Now, take it easy while you can."

"Why, Eagle," Mr. Smyth's mild voice showed surprise. "I'd thought you'd left us for good." Eagle replied with only a grunt.

Joshua said, "Tell Ma we'll be in later. If the chicken is done, don't wait dinner for us. Eagle has some talkin' to do."

In slow, carefully chosen words Eagle began. "You see fear? Rebecca."

Joshua's head jerked. "She's hurt?"

He shook his head, "No. I see your heart. I know her pain. I know her man, Mormonee." He made a twisting motion with his hands and before Joshua could understand what he meant, he added an eloquent shrug and smote his chest.

"Are you trying to tell me that you know Rebecca's Mormon man and that you don't know what's going on inside of him?" Eagle nodded.

Now he added, "He comes."

Joshua frowned as he studied the Indian's troubled face. "I'm thinking I don't understand you."

"Here." Eagle's eyes were unwavering.

It was the expression that dropped the fear into Joshua's heart, convincing him of the unthinkable. He rubbed his hands slowly over his face, hoping somehow that his worst nightmare wasn't reality. He paced, then came back to face Eagle. "You're saying that he's coming here. Why?" The dark, inscrutable expression moved across Eagle's face. Joshua was reminded of how little he understood the man. But there was Rebecca, and there were the chiseled features and the cold eyes. There was his obvious fatigue and the winded horse.

"Mormonee come. Bad."

"And I've got to do something about it, but what?" His voice echoed the desperation he was feeling.

Eagle was shaking his head. "Go, take Rebecca."

"Run. You mean he will try to take Rebecca?" Eagle nodded. The lines deepened on his face and slowly he drew his finger across his throat.

"Blood atonement." Horror tightened across Joshua's chest like a paralyzing grip. All of the stories coming out of Utah Territory that he had heard were culminated in Rebecca's terror. He grasped Eagle's shoulders and studied his face. "You're saying this is the man Rebecca lived with. You're saying that he tried to kill her once and that now he comes. Run with Rebecca? Where on God's earth would we run?" He dropped his hands from Eagle's shoulders and paced the barn.

When he stopped before Eagle again, "If he'll follow her clear out here, where would she be safe? We'll spend the rest of our lives running. Do you know what this means? We'll always be knowing that he will yet seek her out and find her."

Again he paced the barn. Disjointed words were tortured out of him. "Eagle, she's nearly out of her mind now. The memories. The nightmares. The hate. I'd hoped she would find the way out. There's this new threat now. He doesn't see—the crazy man doesn't understand that he has no claim on her." Joshua dropped his wildly waving arms and stared at Eagle's impassive face.

"That's it." Joshua stood still. As the realization hit him, he felt calmness sweep over him and he was able to think clearly. "Nowhere in these United States or in these territories is Brigham's doctrine of plural marriage accepted as valid except in the Territory of Utah. In some states the penalty for bigamy is severe. If I could—" He stopped.

The scene of that last night in his own home flashed through his memory. There was Rebecca with the burning, hate-filled eyes, whispering that she would never marry him because of the blackness in her soul. With a groan he turned to pace again. Now his shoulders dropped in defeat.

Eagle's hand fell on Joshua's shoulder. "I kill."

"No." Joshua turned. "Eagle, that's murder and you know it. They'd hunt you down. You'd never escape as long as one man knows what you've done."

"He kill Rebecca." The words were flat. The truth of them was something that Eagle knew as fact. Now Joshua was faced with accepting it.

Joshua walked slowly to the log fence surrounding the manger. He leaned across the logs and scratched the bovine head thrust at him. Through his fear and anger, he felt again the quieting touch. He continued to rub the cow's face and all the impossibilities of the situation began to lose their thrust.

"Seems a body ought to quit trusting his knowledge and let God start directing," he mused. He sucked in his breath and breathed out the prayer. "Father, I believe You're putting this into my mind, and I'm going to have to trust You to work it all out. She's said no pretty strongly. A step at a time. I'll take it and I'll trust You."

He walked back to Eagle. "There's only one way on this earth I can hope to rescue Rebecca from this." Eagle was frowning and Joshua guessed he wasn't understanding all his words. He slowed, speaking carefully. "I'm going to get Rebecca and marry her. He'll have no power on this earth to take her if she's my wife."

"He kill," Eagle warned.

"Will you tell me where he is?"

Eagle nodded and dropped to his knees. With his finger he drew a crude map, showing the trail from Utah. Now lines slashed through the trails, marking the streams and rivers along the route. It was clearly the pattern of rivers and streams cutting out to the Oregon coast. That meant he was in Oregon, working his way up the Applegate trail. Now Eagle touched a spot. "Big settlement."

"City." Joshua said slowly. "Could be Jacksonville, or it could be closer."

"McKenzie."

"He knows the river, the locality," Joshua said slowly. "Have you any idea just where he is now?" Eagle shook his head. "It isn't enough for Rebecca and me to be married right now. She mustn't even be seen by him. For—" He pressed his lips tightly together, thinking now of the effect on her if she were ever to find out that he was in the Territory.

"See," he looked up at Eagle, "we'll have the wedding and everybody around can spread the word that we're married. We'll clear out until he's gone back to Utah."

Eagle frowned. Supposing he didn't understand, Joshua said, "She'll be mine. He'll have no right to her."

Eagle shook his head. "Josh, no understand Mormonee."

Now desperately aware of his need for action, Joshua said, "Eagle, I've got to know just exactly where he is. Will you track him for me?"

He nodded. Bending again to the map, he drew the forks of the

McKenzie and the Willamette rivers. Tapping their confluence he said, "Tomorrow, sundown, we meet. I find Mormonee now."

Joshua got to his feet. "Today is Friday. I'll go home and set plans for the wedding. Sunday we'll be married." He turned to Eagle. "Come, eat and rest." Eagle shook his head but Joshua pushed him toward the house.

When Eagle bit into his first piece of chicken, Joshua said, "Ma, Pa, Rebecca and I will be having a wedding this Sunday. Will you drive into town for it?"

Cynthia turned from the stove. "Wedding," she said slowly. "Well, I suppose so. Should give a body a little time to prepare; I don't have a thing to wear."

It was nearly dark when Joshua rode into his own yard. As he led his mare around the house, he saw Rebecca disappearing into the barn with a milk pail.

The enormity of all that he had planned struck him full force and his heart pounded. "Oh, Lord," he whispered, "You've got to be with me in this. I don't know how I'll handle this. Is it too much to ask that You make her willing?"

Joshua pulled the saddle and bridle from the mare, opened the gate to the corral and slapped her on the rump. He followed Rebecca into the barn.

"Hello, my favorite milkmaid." She straightened and looked over her shoulder. Her face brightened. His heart leaped in response. "If I can talk you into scrambling an egg for me, I'll do the milking. I'm a mite hungry. Only took time for one piece of chicken at noon." She nodded, and he tried to understand the wondering expression in her eyes as she hesitated and then hurried toward the house.

When he entered the kitchen, there were two pairs of eyes to confront. Solali's were nearly as full of questions as Rebecca's. He found himself smoothing his hair self-consciously after he had washed his hands.

When he sat down at the table, Rebecca turned from her task at the stove. "You've caught us short. We didn't expect you home so soon. When there's just the two of us here, we don't do much fussing about what we eat. At least there's a bit of bacon and the bread is fresh."

Solali added, "We're still harvesting tomatoes. This far up the side of the mountain I had been expecting to feel frost long before now. It's still as warm as summer, nearly." She was watching him with that curious expression. Now her question was timid. "Ah—did Eagle see you?"

He nodded. She waited. Rebecca came from the stove, saying, "I've started some dutch cheese. It should be ready to eat by tomorrow." He was still looking at Solali, wondering at her expression. He knew that Eagle's horse had come from here, and now he was guessing that neither Solali nor Rebecca knew his mission. Those were big questions in Solali's eyes, and they were about Eagle.

Solali's eyes met his again and then looked away. "He's fine," Joshua muttered, still wondering whether or not he should confide in her. In the end he decided no conversation was better than the evasion that would be necessary if he were to protect Rebecca.

Solali got to her feet. Leaning across the table, she reached for the dishes. "You two go on," she instructed. "I'll be washing up the dishes and then early to bed. I'm—"

"I can't stay," Joshua interrupted hastily. "I'll have a word with Rebecca and then I must be on my way."

"So soon? Where are you going now?" Rebecca asked with a gasp of surprise. Did she seem to be disappointed?

He forced his emotions to quit talking such nonsense. He followed her into the parlor, wondering how she would react when she found out his destination.

He took his time kindling the small fire on the hearth. "I cut a pile of wood for Ma and Pa," he said. "Pa's back still isn't too strong."

Now the fire was crackling and the smoky pine scented the room. He settled back, still reluctant to bring out the words which must be said. He winced thinking of his earlier bravado. Was it totally impossible to think of another way to handle the situation?

Staring into the fire, going over his conversation with Eagle, the memory of the Indian's seething anger touched him. If their exchange of words was limited and unsatisfactory, the man's face, even now, sent fresh new chills through Joshua's heart.

He straightened and turned. Rebecca was sitting on the settle watching him. Framed against the dark wood, her hair gleamed soft and pale. The thought of having her hurt again sent him to her side. "Rebecca." He stopped, surprised by the expression on her face. Her eyes were wide, studying him with an openness and trust he hadn't seen before.

Slowly her lips parted and she caught her breath. As if suddenly giving in to an earlier resolve, she said, "Joshua—"

"Rebecca," he interrupted roughly. The words must be said and now. The demand must be made before any tenderness would carry him beyond his determination for immediate action. Now. He took a deep breath and met her puzzled expression. "Tomorrow is Saturday. The next day is Sunday—"

"I know." There was that wondering look on her face.

Again he was abrupt, saying, "We're going to be married on Sunday. I've made up my mind and that is how it will be. I love you and you love me. There's no more to be said about the matter. I didn't go all the way to Utah for a sister. I want a wife. Now get that dress out and I'll see you in church on Sunday."

He jumped to his feet and backed toward the door. "I'm sorry. There isn't time to listen to your arguments. Just be there. Ma and Pa are coming down. I'm going now to talk to the parson." His voice was desperate. "Just be there, do you hear?"

"Yes, Joshua."

"What?"

"I said yes, Joshua. I'll be there." He released his breath in an explosion of sound. She frowned and repeated. "Yes. You act like you didn't expect me to say yes."

"I didn't." He stared at her. There was still that open, trusting expression. "You won't change your mind?"

"Do you want me to?"

"No. I just want to be certain that you'll be at the church on Sunday."

"I will."

"Ah, Becky!" He tried to keep the silly grin off his face. She flew to him with her arms open wide. After breathless, silent moments while they clung to each other, Joshua reluctantly released her and started for the door.

"Joshua." Her face was turning upward, now questioning. Her words were whispers. "That letter. Joshua, you said I must ask you what you would do about my wound."

He hesitated, torn, and then there was only that question. Bending over her he cupped her face in his two hands. For a long moment they looked into each other's eyes. In a husky voice, he said, "Becky, my dearest, I will simply kiss the length of that scar, and all the time I'll be thanking the kind Heavenly Father for snatching you and giving you back to me. Always that scar will remind me of how precious your life is to me."

He was nearly to Waltstown before he recovered from his bemused state enough to wonder at the change in Rebecca, and to wonder why he had not thought to ask the reason for it.

Before Joshua had left the parson's home, the town was in an uproar. Best dresses were being hauled to the ironing board. A group of the more accomplished cooks in town were rushed into a hurried conference. Mrs. Norton got out the ham she had been saving for a special occasion.

All heads were bent over the cookbook before Joshua reached the road.

"What's the rush after her puttin' him off all summer?"

"Who said she was?"

"His ma."

"Maybe they caught a young'un a little early."

"Bessie!"

"Well, they have been there alone except for that Indian woman . . ."

"There's no call."

And the next day, just before Joshua reached the fork of the Willamette and the McKenzie, he stopped at the general store. The only new shirt he could find was most certainly a dandy shirt. It was pale blue with tiny dark flowers.

While he eyed it dubiously, the proprietor said, "It's better than a dirty one. Seems to suit you better'n a white one with a collar tighter'n a hangman's noose." He leaned across the counter. "Between you'n me. The missus thinks I can't buy those kind. I'm just guessing I can't sell 'em. But if you really want one, well, Salem's the closest place."

In the end Joshua bought the shirt and let the man talk him into a silk scarf. Then he needed to smell all the soap before he found one that smelled man-like. "Don't want the bees following me," he explained as he paid for the items.

"Only one reason a man would fancy up like that." The proprietor eyed him again. "Too bad I don't have a wedding ring to sell you; bet I could've."

Joshua patted his chest. "I have one of those. About wore it out totin' it around, but it'll do."

When Joshua reached the meeting place, Eagle stepped out of the bushes. His face was still stern. "Mormonee coming this way. Two days, maybe three. They go slow."

"Another day or so and people will know who he's a'looking for," Joshua said, adding bitterly, "And they'll be giving out information, thinkin' he's a long-lost buddy."

Eagle led him through the bushes, away from the pounding water. There he had built a fire. A salmon was impaled on sticks and cooking slowly. He pointed to the bed of skins. "Rest. You go in the morning and I go back to trail."

Joshua nodded. "I've pretty well covered this section. Gentle-like, I've let it be known I'd be obliged if folks were a little tight-lipped about me." With a weary sigh he dropped to the skins. "If I'm out of here by dawn, I'll be to the church in plenty of time."

Eagle's eyes were full of curiosity, and Joshua guessed that his grin was telling him more than the words. "She's going to marry me. Tomorrow morning at the church. The whole town will be there."

Early the next morning, Eagle stood on the bank of the Mc-Kenzie. For once his face was lighted with a grin of pure delight as he watched Joshua.

"Aw!" Joshua split the water howling in misery. " 'Tis mighty cold."

Eagle had the fire going, but he was still shaking his head. "Wedding," he grunted. He studied the shirt before he handed it to Joshua.

"I'll buy you one like it if you'll get married." Joshua was surprised to see the fleeting shadow cross Eagle's face. He turned away as he combed his pale hair, saying casually, "Did you know she sent Matthew a'packin'? I think you've read her wrong." Joshua wasn't certain Eagle understood, but he did see the expression on the man's face soften.

Before Joshua reached the outskirts of Waltstown, he heard the church bell. This was no terse reminder of Sabbath worship. The bell rang loud and long, with a touch of excitement that reached Joshua. He reined his horse on the last rise and watched the wagons moving briskly down the road.

18

· · · · · · · · · · · · · · · · · · ·

$\mathcal{S}$olali reported, "Mr. Chambers says he'll be along to take you into town to the church. The parson told him to come." She followed Rebecca around the house as Rebecca's restless feet carried her from parlor to kitchen. "You've scarce eaten a bite of breakfast; that's no way to begin your wedding day."

"Did you check again to see if we got all the wrinkles out of the wedding dress?"

" 'Tis fine." Solali added wistfully, "A beautiful dress it is. Silk and all, with the beautiful pink flowers on it—it'll be the finest dress seen in this town."

Rebecca turned abruptly and clasped Solali's hands. She was blinking away the tears. "Oh, Solali. I've been so caught up with thinking about Joshua, and being in such a rush to be ready for today, that I've scarce given the dress a thought. Do you know this is the fulfillment of a dream I've had since I was a wee girl? I still remember my mother talking about her wedding. Those memories draw such a beautiful picture. I'm believing that now there'll be an even stronger link between us when I can stand before that parson and marry Joshua wearing her dress. How I thank God now that He didn't let me have the wedding dress before—"

She was silent while the dark thoughts threatened her; then she lifted her head. " 'Tis the love of Jesus wrapping it all, and that's all I'll concentrate on. The love of Jesus making right out of it all."

She moved restlessly. "Do you think I should start dressing now?"

"It's not much past sunup."

"I wonder where Joshua had to go?" Solali could only shake her head. "You're worrying about Eagle, aren't you?"

Solali sighed. " 'Tis strange. Did you notice that it was his horse

Joshua was riding when he left? And Joshua was a mite agitated, not like a man just going a'visiting. I'm feeling Eagle's up to something."

"In trouble or hurt, that's what you're thinking?" Rebecca looked questioningly at Solali, but she turned away with a shrug.

Solali paced to the parlor windows and back. "Seems we best get you into that dress. Those buttons will take all day. I've never seen that many buttons to hold together any kind of dress, not to mention a wedding dress. I 'spect it was a miracle your folks ever managed to have you."

"Oh, Solali!" Rebecca, embarrassed, smiled and shook her head in mock horror. "But you are right, there's lots. I've a buttonhook somewhere; that'll help."

When Solali finished the last button, she turned Rebecca. "Ah, there, you look like an angel. The little pink posies on the bodice are all the flowers you need." She touched the deep lace ruffles at the sleeves and the ones cascading down from the shoulders into a deep V at the waistline.

"Are there spots where I cried all over it?" Rebecca asked anxiously, peering over her shoulder.

"No. But that wad of hair is all wrong. Come, let me brush the curls loose." Lifting Rebecca's hair high, Solali brushed the softly curling locks around her finger and pinned the cascade of curls high off her neck.

There was a shout from the front of the house and Solali dropped the brush. "Oh, it's the Chambers; it's time to leave."

Rebecca stood motionless and Solali reached for her hand. "No, don't even stop to think."

"The Bible. I must have my Bible." She whirled around and picked it up as Solali gathered up their shawls. Together they hurried down the stairs.

When they reached the edge of town, Rebecca's trembling hand touched Mr. Chambers' sleeve. "Please," she pleaded, "Don't go so fast. I—"

"You have cold feet like all the rest. Never you mind, just don't think now." Mrs. Chambers turned to smile at her over the baby's head. "Besides, we're nearly late. Do you want Joshua to think you've changed your mind? He might just choose a lass out of the congregation. When a man makes up his mind to wed, don't you be slowin' him down."

"Whoa." Mr. Chambers was halting the team in front of the little white church. Aaron jumped out and called, "Come on, everybody, let's go to the wedding!"

Slowly Rebecca climbed out of the wagon and followed Solali into the church. Suddenly shy, she clutched the Bible against her. Head down, she walked with reluctant little steps.

The buzz of conversation ceased as she reached the door, but until she reached the first line of pews, she dared not lift her head.

They were all standing and all eyes were studying her. In front of the altar, with the sunshine streaming across his shoulders, Joshua waited. When she met his gaze, he sighed with relief and a grin spread across his face.

Beside Joshua, the song leader, wearing his cutaways, stood on tiptoe and lifted his arm. "Let's sing." The organist crashed down on the chords, and as Rebecca walked toward Joshua the congregation sang, "Praise God, from whom all blessings flow . . ."

Parson Williams stepped forward as the skirts rustled into place in the pews. "Dearly beloved, we are gathered here in the sight of God and man—" Joshua gripped her hand and the words faded as she looked up at him. Now his hand tightened and she heard Parson Williams saying, "I charge you, if either of you know any reason why this marriage should not be solemnized, then confess it now. In the sight of God, you must be lawfully joined together."

And through the silence, he spoke again. "Joshua, will you take this woman to be your wife?"

Rebecca caught her breath as he turned to face her. His voice was deep and clear, "I do. I take you, Rebecca Ann Wolstone, to be my wife."

With a gentle smile, she said, "And I take you, Joshua Smyth. I promise to love, to honor, and obey—"

Now in the final moment, Joshua struggled with the scarf about his neck and the ring on its rawhide thong was awkwardly pulled out. Carefully he got his pocket knife and cut the leather. In a voice raised nearly to a shout of triumph, Joshua said, "Rebecca, with this ring I wed you. For as long as we both shall live, I pledge my love and loyalty to you."

"Joshua," came the chant from the congregation. "You're married; you can kiss the bride."

And in the din, Rebecca turned to the parson. "Please—" she opened her mother's Bible and grasped Joshua's shirt-sleeve— "please, we must write our names here. See the place?" Then she shook back the lace ruffles as Parson Williams brought the pen and bottle of ink. There was her shaky signature and Joshua's firm hand signing beside her.

The church bell began pealing out the news. From hand to hand and kiss to kiss, Rebecca and Joshua were moved toward the door. "The wedding cake. Cut the cake," someone called.

"Now, you just wait," came the answer; "there's chicken and ham first. 'Sides, it isn't your weddin'."

The noonday sun made Rebecca blink. She wiggled her shoulders under its warmth. "Oh, what a beautiful, blessed day for a wedding!"

Down the steps, propelled by the force of the crowd, they moved toward the trees and the picnic tables. Joshua's hand firmly clasped her elbow. "Let's get out of here. Let's leave. With all that food they'll never miss us."

"Joshua, we'll hurt their feelings. Let them have their fun." She tried to understand his frown, but they had reached the table and plates were thrust at them.

And the cake. As she moved around it she noticed Joshua's dogged expression, his hurried glance. Amusement curved her lips into a smile. He was expecting tricks. She captured his hand and guided it with the knife through the cake.

"Get him good, smear that icing!"

She was still smiling at Joshua when she became aware of the growing silence. With a tiny fragment of sticky cake still in her hand, she turned, gasped.

Joshua was pushing her aside, moving in front of her. Her faltering hand flattened the cake against the table and she leaned heavily against Solali. In a distant dream she heard Joshua's demanding, "What brings you here?"

"I've come to claim my wife."

The gasp was collective, the murmur of horror grew as the crowd stepped back. Now there was only Andrew Jacobson facing Joshua Smyth. Even in the pain, Rebecca was aware of the slash of blackness. From frown, to hair, to coat; his darkness was aligned against the brightness of Joshua.

Andrew moved first. His casual glance took in the food, the cake, and then sought the authoritative figure. "Parson," his voice was mocking, "am I seeing a wedding party in progress?" He turned slowly to meet the eyes of those men and women staring at him. "This ought not to be," he said gently but totally in command. Andrew Jacobson, leader of men, was in top form.

He turned to Rebecca. "Rebecca, my dear, surely you remember our wedding. Not as grand as this—but it came first."

Joshua moved, saying impatiently, "Jacobson, you have no legal claim on Rebecca Wolstone. Now, just this day, in the sight of God and man, we were united as husband and wife."

Andrew faced the crowd. Where Joshua's voice was taut with strain, his was soft, even and low. "Now you good people honor God's commandments, don't you?" He glanced up at the steeple on the church, paused and said, "Don't you believe the Constitution of the United States of America guarantees a man the right to practice his religion in freedom, without the government interfering?"

The nods were collective. The eyes still curious, they were fastened on Andrew Jacobson, not Rebecca and Joshua.

"Freedom of religion is one thing, but—"

Jacobson's voice cut through Joshua's. Turning to Rebecca he said kindly. "You can't deny, can you, that a marriage took place and that a divorce never did?" Pressing her trembling hands against her temples, she shook her head. "And how long did you live with me as my wife?" She moistened her lips. Now an edge of impatience in his voice, he demanded, "Speak up."

"Three years," she whispered.

"And did I ever give you grounds to leave that marriage?" She opened her mouth and he snapped, "Within the confines of our religion?"

"Jacobson!" Joshua cried, "you are twisting it—the whole picture! What about last year—what about—"

"You're accusing—" His voice ripped through Joshua's. His face was icy cold as his glance shifted between Rebecca and Joshua. "What about it? Remember, these are accusations. You had better be prepared to provide evidence. If you intend to deliver accusations which will blacken my name, my reputation, you'd better be ready to substantiate them."

Without a pause he wheeled to face the crowd, his coat parting to reveal the gun strapped to his waist. He raised his hand, the crowd hushed and attentive before him. "Whom will you believe, a wronged husband or a conniving debaucher of innocent women— a perverter of marriage and religion? My good people, in the name of all that's holy, whom will you believe?"

Parson Williams' face was ashy. He stepped forward. "Sir, in all good faith I performed this ceremony. That it was conducted in a hasty manner, I can't deny. Joshua assured me that it—it was all on the up and up." He cleared his throat nervously under the righteous gaze bent upon him. "Under the circumstances—" he said weakly.

"Wait!" Joshua cried, taking a hasty step toward the parson. There was a restraining hand on his sleeve and he shook it off. "Will you not hear me out?" he pleaded. "Rebecca was tricked." There was a collective murmur from the people and Joshua's words were lost in the growing uproar as he said, "It was a marriage that wasn't a true marriage."

Jacobson's voice rose above the clamor. "She lived with me, knowing the teachings of our religion and the commands divinely given. She knew that we were obligated to honor our god through this marriage."

"But she left that religion." Joshua's statement was heard as the crowd again quieted.

"She has obtained no divorce."

"There can be no divorce when there has been no marriage."

"Are you besmirching the name of this woman? Are you calling her a prostitute?"

The crowd roared and Joshua shouted, "Defend your claims in court! I say you are wrong. Come back tomorrow and we'll find a lawyer together."

"And leave my wife in your hands?" The heads were shifting from one man to the other. Beside Rebecca, Solali gasped. Rebecca raised her face. The expressions turned toward her were hostile. An angry hiss rose.

"No!" Joshua shouted. "I will not allow you to leave here with Rebecca."

"My good man," the parson spoke slowly. "It seems to me that this gentleman has a prior claim. I suggest you not fight his rights. In the name of good religion, and all that's holy, if you must have her, be just and fair. Let him have his day in court."

Joshua moved quickly, but more quickly came the words, "Grab him!" Horror filled Rebecca as she watched Joshua slump under the blow. Now Andrew's hand was reaching toward her.

He passed his gentle smile around the circle and then addressed her. "Come, my dear. All's forgiven. We'll see these good people later."

"I'll not go with you." She raised her chin and stepped backward. Glancing quickly around, she begged, "Please help me." Solali tried to hold her but strong arms were hindering her. Rebecca saw the mood of the crowd and crumpled. "There's no one who will believe?"

She looked from face to face and saw the bewilderment, the pursed lips, the veiled glances. She met Cynthia's eyes and watched her turn away. "My poor son!" she cried, hiding her face against her trembling husband as he bent over Joshua.

"Ma'am," Parson Williams spoke slowly to Rebecca. "You have admitted he is your husband. There is not one thing we legally can do to stop him."

Numbness pricked at Rebecca's face and body. She was barely conscious of Andrew's grasp as he lifted her onto his horse. Parson Williams' words continued to press upon her. They were the only link with consciousness. "Nothing we can do. Sorry."

Andrew's horse was galloping away from the quiet group clustered in the churchyard. Desperately Rebecca clung to the saddle horn in front of her and forced her body away from Jacobson's. His arms tightened about her while the loathing shivered through her.

Chuckling, he said, "Now stop, little one, stop acting like that. You didn't think I would give up once I discovered you were still alive?"

"Steven Martin?" she forced through stiff lips.

"Yes, our dear faithful friend, Steven."

Helpless anger began to well up inside and Rebecca spoke through clenched teeth. "It cannot be love that brings you to Oregon after me. Isn't it more truthful to say you are fearful of what I might reveal, and that your intentions haven't changed in the past year?"

"What is it you're saying?" His voice was mocking. "Why, Rebecca, my darling wife, you don't think I'd allow a rift in my celestial kingdom, do you?"

"Do you really believe that, or is it all just a pretense to which you cling?"

"Hush now. Tell me where you live. We need to get your clothes and a horse for you. Where will we find the baby?"

The strange, twisted scene suddenly became real. The baby was the link. All those hard facts about the baby lay like stones upon her heart. Her silence made him impatient. He hostled her arm. "Speak up. You'll not even consider leaving him behind. After all, he's my son." The gun was pressing against her back, but it was his hand now grasping her arm and painfully forcing it up behind her, twisting her in the saddle until he could meet her eyes, that made her cry out. Through the pain his expression burned life back into her.

"I'll not tell you anything. Let's just see how long this mare will last with the two of us on her."

"We aren't going anywhere until we get my son." The words

rebounded in Rebecca's mind. Her thoughts were full of the picture of Joshua in pursuit and she knew she must stall. She pressed her lips together. He twisted her arm further. "My son."

Now with tears streaming down her face, tears of pain and anger, she cried, "There is no son! Andrew, you killed your child last year. I wish to God that I'd had the wits to say it all to those people. I still can't believe they were so twisted by your half-truths." He jerked her arm and the thrust of pain forced her into silence.

She knew the horse had slowed, but her tortured mind couldn't supply a reason. "My son," again he repeated, this time with a hint of uncertainty. The gun was now pressed against her face.

Terror filled her completely. But with a broken sob, she managed to say, "You'll never believe me, and there's not one thing you can do to prove me wrong or right. You might go back and ask those people. They know there is no child. I challenge you to return. By now they may have their heads." Now with mockery in her voice she cried, "Ah, Andrew, don't I hear their horses?"

For a moment there was uneasiness in his eyes and he released her arm and jerked the horse's reins. " 'Tis a shame, but your precious wedding dress will be a rag before we reach Utah." He cracked his reins across the horse. "Very well, my dear, then you'll have to make the best of the matter." His voice was again smooth and assured.

His arm tightened, cruelly biting into the scar tissue down her side. With the strange detachment shock brings, Rebecca thought of last September and reminded herself it could happen again. Clenching her fist against her throat, she felt the smoothness of the wedding ring and glanced down.

How brightly it gleamed in the sunshine. Did she dare read symbols in that bright circle of light? Was hope possible? She knew with the springing assurance that as certainly as Joshua had sought her and given her the ring, he would not rest until he found her again. Would he find her in time? She shivered and tried to pray.

They had been riding for an hour when Rebecca began to recognize her surroundings. Did he know where he was going? The narrow trail he had been following twisted behind Waltstown up the mountains. They were now directly east of Joshua's section. She knew the area was uncharted and unmarked except for these trails used by the woodcutters. Only crude shelters and high mountains lay before them.

For a moment she toyed with the thought of escape, but how easy it would be to become lost in the dense forest. How treacherous the rocky slopes were with their hidden ravines. How frightening the night and lurking creatures of the dark. She felt that arm fastened around her and was reduced to trembling panic.

But then she took a deep breath and tried to forget the trembling. There was an equal danger. She said, "No man in his right mind would try to cut through this country." Slowly she said, "I've been hearing tales of the cutting of Barlow Pass. That's just north of here; cuts through the Cascades just south of The Dalles. When those folks first crossed the mountains, their very lives depended on slashing their way through. They nearly didn't make it. Half dead when they reached the valley."

He didn't comment. She took his silence as indecision, and hope came newborn. Rebecca found she could pray. She whispered, "Father, O Father, please let Joshua find the way."

When he slowed the horse at the first tangle of bush, she cried, "You realize, don't you, once you get over these mountains you must cross eastern Oregon Territory? The Meekers' train nearly perished, and they had some idea of where they were going."

"And you think I don't?" She was hoping that was uncertainty she was hearing in his voice. They reached another trail and when he turned on it, he spurred the horse confidently.

They were climbing, first east and then north. Now the sun was slanting across the top of the coastal range and Rebecca guessed the afternoon was far spent. Desperate now, she looked around, trying to recall all that she had been told about the area.

That it was densely wooded, she need not be told. They had climbed high above the valley. She did remember that the men felled timber here and snaked it back down to the valley behind their teams. Had Matthew and Joshua come this far to cut wood?

She felt hope die when she reminded herself of the obvious. How would Joshua guess where to look? For that matter, what chance had he of recovering from that blow on the head in time to look before every trace of their passing was covered?

Thinking back to that scene at the church, she remembered the expression on Cynthia's face and, momentarily, bitterness threatened to sweep over her. The stigma was a taint which would follow her the rest of her life.

Now, like an audible command, the words filled her mind: " 'Stand fast in the liberty . . .' " And while bitterness and futility fought for control, there was that command filling her with direction and peace.

She realized Andrew was guiding the horse off the path. He said,

"We're nearly there." Through the trees she saw a tiny log cabin.

As they approached she realized it was very old. When he stopped the horse and slid off, she sat studying it. Its one window was broken and the roof sagged. A twig and mud chimney poked broken remains through the roof.

"Why have you forced me to come with you?" she asked, making herself look at him.

"Because you are mine, part of my kingdom. And also, my dear, you must learn discipline and self-control. You must now earn your right to be part of my household—my eternal household. You will do so by serving the other wives."

She stared at him, studying the familiar face, remembering the hate which had warped her for so long. She rubbed her hands wearily across her face as the disappointment and grief welled up within. How could she possibly endure? Wasn't that hate threatening again? What happened to that sweet peace, the freedom?

"Dear God," she was murmuring in fearful desperation now as she watched him move around the building, examining the ground and checking the sagging fence at the rear of the house. "Please, Father," she pleaded, "I thought I was free of it all—the black things. Now they're coming back more ugly than ever." She thought of a break for freedom on the horse, but remembered the gun in time.

In the quiet moment, while his footsteps receded and the sun-warmed pine scented the air around her, she became conscious of the fearful anxiety loosening its grip. Now set apart, released, she had one glad moment to realize she was fearing not Andrew but the blackness which had previously filled her soul for so long. Now she knew the blackness wasn't inside any more, only outside. And she would not let it in.

In wonder, she sat experiencing the truth while she measured the value of it. She was healed. She was free from the awful, consuming hate. That experience was real, more real than the horror of this present time. The wonder was back in her life as she whispered, "He answered my prayer."

She fell to musing about it. Through surrender to the Spirit, and by asking and accepting, the miracle had happened.

Andrew came around the house and opened the door. Slowly she slid off the horse and followed him into the house. She saw the bundle dangling from the rafters and watched him untie the rope and pull it free. "I see the 'coons and rats couldn't reach my larder. We'll have dinner as soon as you can get it ready." He went to spread the blankets across the shelf bed built into the wall of the cabin.

Turning away from the dismal, dirty room, she went to lean against the doorjamb. Far to the west the sun sparkled on a thread of the McKenzie. "We must be on the top of the mountain," she murmured. The haze of woodsmoke was in the air. It was someone's supper fire far below. Just possibly it could be the Chambers or the Bakers. They would be busy preparing their evening meal, already forgetting the events of the day. Where would Joshua be? And his ma and pa. Her aloneness bit into her, and she squeezed her arms tight against her body, refusing the weakness that demanded tears. Concentrating on taking deep, slow breaths, she pushed the pictures out of her mind and accepted the stretch of the unknown lying just ahead.

A sentence from far out of the past moved into her thoughts. It had been one of those long-ago verses which had carried no meaning until just last night when she had found and read the words.

Aloud now, spurred by the memory-picture Andrew painted when he said "serve the wives," she whispered, " 'Know ye not, that to whom ye yield yourselves servants to obey, his servants ye are? . . .' " Last night she had read those words and rejoiced in her freedom. Tonight—she winced but plunged bravely on with the thought—she *was free*. Jesus Christ had won her freedom.

She lifted her face against the musty, decaying wood and whispered, "I promised to obey you, Lord. Please help me keep that promise." With her eyes still closed she rested and her breathing grew calm and even.

Clearly now, from deep inside, she was thinking and moving deliberately. Surrender to her Lord? Of course. Conscious acceptance that He was here and at work in her, more powerful than herself, than Andrew. Slowly she opened her eyes, saw the moldy wood and heard the crackle of fire behind her.

She turned. On his knees before the pack, having at least momentarily given up on her cooperation, Andrew pulled out the food and dishes and began arranging them on the wooden bench. Now she was seeing his proud figure and arrogant face in a new light. At one time she had thought it impossible to rise above the hate and fear this man inspired; now she was knowing a new fact: She no longer trembled in his presence; he was just a man.

Jesus Christ died for this man, just as surely as He had died for her. Did Andrew know that?

He beckoned. There was a meal to be reckoned with. He fed the fire while she mixed the pancakes and divided the jerky. Strange rite. The old familiar patterns but now changed. It was as if she stood apart, no longer caught in the turmoil of that woman who had been his wife. She held up the apples. "Oregon apples? They're nicer than Utah's."

19
....

Joshua moved and groaned. A cool cloth pressed against his face. Nat Chambers was on his knees beside him. "Sorry, my friend," he was shaking his head regretfully. "How a man can get himself into so much trouble is beyond me! Sometimes a fella needs to be protected from himself."

Joshua's mother pressed the cloth against the lump, her lips pursed into a thin line. "I had a bad feeling about it all along. 'Twer mostly because you were so secret-like."

Solali dropped to her knees beside the two of them and touched Mrs. Smyth's arm. "Please, you're not—"

Mrs. Smyth interrupted her, "Now you just keep quiet. 'Tis easy to see you was stickin' up for her all along. Bet you been pushin' this affair from the beginning."

"Joshua," Solali wailed, "make them understand."

He groaned. "I've tried." He touched his jaw and the lump on the back of his head, struggling to sit up.

Nat said aplogetically, "I think you hit your head on the edge of the table. I aimed only to get your mind off going after that dude. He was wearin' a gun!"

Solali turned to the rim of faces. "Doesn't that tell you something? Don't you see? It's bad, not good. These kinds of marriages. Even the government says so."

"Ya mean the kind Rebecca had with him?" Baker asked slowly, jerking his head toward the empty road.

Joshua pushed himself to a sitting position, cradling his head. "It's illegal. If the same thing happened anywhere else in the country, they'd a' run them outta town."

"That's just what was happening back east. Illinois and New

York." Chris Evans was speaking from the back of the crowd. "Back there they was keepin' those activities mighty secret for fear of the government. But news leaks and that's one of the reasons things were so hot for them."

"No place," Solali added, "recognizes these marriages except Utah Territory."

"I'm not understandin' what you're saying." Mrs. Chambers pushed her way through the group. "What's illegal? What's goin' on?"

Joshua raised his head. "Rebecca married Andrew Jacobson, thinking he was a single man. It turned out that he was already married and had a family. In any place but Utah that's called a bigamous marriage and it's not only illegal but it can cause a heap of trouble for the guy caught in it. The second marriage just plain doesn't exist in the eyes of the law. In Utah these kinds of marriages are not only tolerated, they're encouraged. It's the teachings of the church."

"And just what does all this make Rebecca?" Mrs. Norton's voice was belligerent. "We've no call to be sucked into accepting a bad woman in the town. This is an honest, law-abiding place. We don't want no bad women."

Solali dropped her head. "You don't understand. Rebecca *didn't know* he was already married! And after she found out—well, I— Rebecca and I were both members of the church. When Brigham Young tells you to do something, you aren't allowed to think for yourself; you just do it."

"You're saying you were one, too?" Lettie Depoe whispered. "I'd never have guessed. You seemed to be so nice."

Joshua raised his head. "Mrs. Depoe, if your husband came home and said that Parson here told him that he had to take another wife in order for you all to have a position in the hereafter, would you fight it?"

"I'll say I would!" she said indignantly; then she cocked her head, slowly saying, "You mean that's the way it goes? . . . Maybe I wouldn't, especially if I could see others doing it. You say they believe *God's* putting it up to them?" She settled back on her chair and said, "My, how could that man lead them astray? Why, there's nothing in the good Book to let you think—"

"Might be easy to swallow, if'n you let someone else do the thinking for you." Little Mrs. Crocket was speaking. "I've heard all kinds of tales. Seems a body could get sucked in deeper and deeper. Where do you call an end to taking what they say as gospel?"

Mrs. Hanson spoke up, " 'Tis a danger. Always. A person needs to know just what the good Book says, and then keep on stuffing the words inside him so's he'll never get confused or led astray when someone comes along with a fancy teaching.

Now Clarence Norton demanded, "Yes, but where do we call an end to all this? What does it make this little girl, Rebecca? Did I hear you say that a divorce isn't possible?"

"There's been no legal marriage," Joshua repeated simply. "He was already married to another woman. In the eyes of his church he did no wrong. The church will recognize as many marriages as he wants to make. But let one of these women step outside the Territory, and you know just how society sees her."

"And you knew all this and still wanted to marry her?"

"Where's *your* religion, Norton?" Hollis Evans demanded. "Didn't you hear the Parson's sermon last week? He said we're not to judge. He said we're to forgive and live in love. If that's what Joshua has done, that's what we're to do."

Joshua tried to get to his feet and Cynthia held him down. "Wait a minute, son. If I hear you right, your intentions are to bring a tattered lily into my home, soiled."

"It isn't your home, Ma, it's mine," he said simply without rancor. While they stared at each other, the conversation continued around them.

"What about the story in the New Testament about the woman taken in adultery and Jesus sayin' that the guy without sin could cast the first stone? What of it?"

"Well, I really like Rebecca. Sweet little thing like that! She's had a hard life of it. I'm for sayin' I'd like her to be part of this community and I'd be proud to call her my friend." Mrs. Baker pushed her hair out of her eyes and juggled her toddler.

Joshua got to his feet and stood swaying.

"Where are you going?" Abe demanded.

"I'm going to find my wife. And I'm lookin' until I do, even if I have to track that guy clear to Utah."

"Hey, she really *is* Joshua's wife, isn't she, Parson?"

Cynthia stood beside Joshua. With arms akimbo she said, "Whose idea was it, all this keeping quiet about her past?"

"It doesn't matter now," he said flatly. "But I guessed that this is just what was bound to happen. I knew you all would be judgin' her and pointin' your fingers if you knew. I was hoping the facts would never come out. I hoped that she could recover from the pain of her past and that then we could be married. Now there's this. God only knows the fear and anguish she's feelin' right now." His eyes met Solali's and he read the answering horror in her eyes.

"Then you pushed having the wedding today for a reason," Parson Williams leveled a stern look at Joshua. "I'm guessing you got wind that he was coming." He paced an anxious step back and forth in front of Joshua. "Young man, if you'd told me the whole story, I'd have sent the man packing and you'd have your wife."

As Joshua reached his hand toward the man, the sound of hooves beating on the hard-packed road broke the silence that now held the group. "It's someone coming fast." They surged to the road.

The man was off the horse and racing through the cloud of dust. "Eagle!" Joshua and Solali gasped together.

Joshua could see Eagle's face was lined with fatigue and the panting, snorting animal he rode told more of the story. Now he saw the face Eagle lifted to Joshua was filled with sorrow and his puzzled eyes were searching Joshua's. "Moved last night." He hesitated. There was still that questioning expression as he glanced around at the silent crowd of people. Seeing the ruins of the dinner and the cake with its one missing piece, he turned quickly and his anxious hand grasped Joshua. "She not go—willing?"

"What do you know?" Joshua stepped closer.

"I saw—" he motioned toward the road and then pointed to the mountains—"I follow and—almost I stop them." Now he shrugged.

"Do you know where they are now?" Joshua was speaking intently, slowly, hoping the man was understanding every word. "Can you lead us to them?" Eagle was nodding and Joshua spun around. "Ma, Pa, Solali, I'm going after her."

"Not alone. You stand no chance alone." It was the parson speaking, but Norton and Baker chimed in and other voices were added to the protest.

"We're all going. That's the least—"

"A fresh horse for Eagle!" Joshua was yelling as he ran for his horse. Quickly saddles were thrown on and cinches jerked impatiently. Already Eagle was plunging ahead of the others. "Up the mountain?" Joshua questioned, "Eagle, are you sure?"

There was only that brief nod and the men spurred their horses after him.

Over an hour had passed before Eagle reined in and lifted his hand. "This far I follow."

"There's not much of a trail up this way," Chambers said slowly.

"We're pretty close to the road and we've all cut up this trail just ahead when we've gone to cut wood. Seems off to the north there's a tumble-down cabin. Somewhere just beyond that the trail ends. If they try to cut through to the crest, they'll have a hard time of it. It'll be a fight every inch of the way. One thing, if he's really come this way, there's no hope of their keepin' ahead of us. There's no way he can cut through the bush that fast; the stuff's thicker'n a hedge."

"Likewise," Norton was speaking now, "we'll be bogged down and lose time a'fightin' our way over and all for nothin' if'n he's *not* come this way."

"Aw," Evans added, "why'd a man come this way in the first place?"

"He'd be taking that trail because he didn't know better or else 'cause he's afraid of being chased."

Parson Williams spoke up, "Afraid? That doesn't sound like an honest man." Joshua jerked his reins impatiently, not knowing whether to be glad because the man was seeing light, or angry because he still questioned.

Eagle was off again with Norton riding beside him. The sun was slipping behind the coastal range and the sky flared yellow. "Not much of daylight left." Thane Hanson spoke behind Joshua. The horses slowed to a walk as they fought their way through the tangle of maple vine and huckleberry bushes. Rhododendron and scrub fir bound them like grasping arms. "Seems we ought to stop and make some plans," he continued. "These trails are bad after dark. 'Tis easy even for a good horse to go over the side, bein' he can't see through the bushes either."

"There's time for talk when we know where they are." Joshua's voice was rough. With the press of nighttime, Rebecca's terror-stricken face filled his thoughts.

From the shadows ahead came the night owl's call. "Hold it," Joshua snapped, "that's Eagle. Wait up."

He circled his mount and the men closed in. Now Eagle was in their midst. "Cabin. I smell smoke. Hobble horses, we walk."

"When we get close we'll have to fan out," Joshua muttered. "If we're right about him runnin', we'll never catch him otherwise. Watch your feet; he'll have a sharp ear cocked."

They moved out silently, carefully. When the straight, sharp shadow of the cabin roof was their horizon, they stopped. Norton moved close to Joshua.

"What if he's holdin' a gun on her?"

Joshua turned his face toward the man. Through clenched teeth he muttered, "This is my game now and there'll be no need of words with him." Joshua felt Eagle's hand on his arm and was silent.

"We move around cabin," Eagle whispered; "we wait."

20

· · · · · · · · · · · · · · · · · · · ·

Rebecca paced the tiny cabin; back and forth she went across the broken boards and stretches of packed earth floor. The chill of the mountain air moved in the broken window. But with a curt shake of her head, she rejected the blanket Andrew held toward her.

"That's a right pretty dress," he drawled. "Too bad you didn't see fit to wear it to the ball. Remember the ball?" At her silence he continued, "You'd have been the belle of that ball because of the dress. Even Brigham's wives couldn't have outdone you. Imported lace, huh?" She still didn't answer but turned to pace again. "Might as well sit down; it could be a long, cold night."

"Just what are your plans?"

"East. Just move east even if it's only a mile a day. When we hit the cutoff we'll be safe."

"What do you mean, safe?"

"Well, I'm expecting your fella will be coming out with a gang."

She turned to look at him and caught the brooding expression in his eyes. "You don't really want me, do you?" she whispered. There was no answer and she continued, "Why don't you just let me go? The child would have been the only possible reason for you to come after me and now—" She couldn't go on for a moment and then she whispered, "If you ever did love me, why not allow me to have my happiness now?" He didn't answer and she continued to pace.

When he finally spoke his voice was heavy. "Rebecca, you've wearied me in the past with your rebellion. When will you settle yourself to accept things as they are?" She stared at him, realizing the futility of any thought or reasoning outside of that which he chose to believe.

The fire was burning low and the nighttime chill was creeping into the cabin. Andrew got off the bench and lifted a log toward the fire. "It's a wonder you don't burn the place down," she said. "There's chinking constantly falling into the fire. But then go ahead. About the time the roof catches fire, those down in town will begin to wonder who's up here."

Andrew stopped and looked at her for a moment. A worried frown creased his forehead as he said, "Could be. Might be a good idea to check out that chinking before I shove more wood on."

He dropped to his knees and leaned across the dying fire to peer up the chimney. The gun holster tipped and her attention was caught. Without thought or design, two quick steps put her behind him. Again he leaned and she bent over him. A gentle shove with her left hand and her right hand had the gun.

"What in the name—" Soft ash flew, but he recovered his balance and got to his feet.

Back across the room, Rebecca watched him. Her breath was coming in quick hard gasps, but the gun she held was steady and it pointed at the white spot of his shirt. Even in the dimness of the room, she could see the color leave his face. He started to take a step and then hesitated.

"That *is* a good idea, Andrew," she said. Her voice was very soft, but she knew he heard. "Now, put your hands out so's I don't get nervous."

He tried to laugh but it was strained. "Rebecca, my dear, that gun is loaded, you best—"

"I'd already figured it was loaded, and you would have used it, wouldn't you? I know you would. There's last year to remember." Now she was silent, watching him, seeing the real fear in his eyes. Suddenly there was the sickening terror of last year moving through her. The cries of the children, wide-eyed and clinging, pressing about her. Could she be hearing again the women with ashen faces as their sounds of agony split through the night air? The gun trembled in her hands and she looked down at it, now fully aware of what she had done. She was holding Andrew's gun and if she pulled the trigger, she would kill him.

"Rebecca." His voice was still taut with strain. "Please put that gun down and let's talk."

"Andrew . . ." she hesitated, now caught by more recent memory. There was that one illuminating moment on the day she had prayed for healing. At the moment of discovery had come the sure understanding that now filled her thoughts. It was she who possessed all needed things—light, understanding, truth.

Because God in His gracious giving had given her himself—light. Now she was seeing Andrew groping—blind, weak, bound. That expression on his face—the features were sagging in fear and defeat. Wasn't he spiralling downward, ever deeper, while she was free and her movement was upward? It was Jesus Christ who had given her freedom. And with the freedom? The verse moved into her thoughts, ". . . and we ought to lay down our lives . . ." She sighed and now she was speaking to that Presence, saying, "I have to prove all those things, the forgiveness—my forgiving him and the healing—that I really do walk in love, don't I?"

"What?" Andrew asked, taking a tentative step. She realized the gun was drooping in her hands. She raised it and then laughed. She was knowing it was first irony and then real joy. "You're tetched," he whispered. "All those things that happened to you—"

"Ah, Andrew, 'twas no fault of yours that I wasn't. 'Twas all of God that I am whole and free and alive." The freedom rushed through her and she actually chuckled. "I'm holding this gun now so's you'll listen. See, it was like the Lord Jesus Christ threw a bucket of understanding over me the other day. For a year I'd been hating you, groveling in the ugliness. There was scarcely a day that I didn't remember those horrors and think of my dead baby without wishing I could tear the heart out of you. And then . . . Then there was a moment with God, and all that hate changed."

She looked at him and saw the curiosity in his eyes even as he licked his lips nervously. As she watched, she was accepting the sure knowledge that there was no way she could walk out of the cabin alive. There had to be a death, and hers was already completed— on the cross with her Lord Jesus. It was the only way. In the face of Jesus, the other was unthinkable.

Again the mirth rose in her and she couldn't resist saying, "These are the things I've wanted to say to you, Andrew, since years ago I first began discovering the way. But never did you quite allow me to say it all. I was bound by fear then. Now *you* are bound—by this gun, and you'll have to listen.

"At the moment I told Jesus Christ that I would forgive you and I would love you, there was this pure vision I was seeing. Andrew, you are caught in a web, being pulled down. You must stop it before it is too late. Don't you see? Every moment, every breath you take moves you farther away."

"From you?"

"No, from truth. From the possibility of reaching out and taking that beautiful thing Jesus Christ is extending toward you."

She could see that momentarily he was stunned, intrigued. "And what is it?"

"His salvation. It is *by grace* you are saved, through believing and accepting. You see, it's all a free gift. Salvation is something Jesus Christ has won for you. There's nothing He wants from you except your love and loyalty." She was whispering now, "Could the proud Andrew ever surrender his kingdom and his godhead for the privilege of being a love slave?" There was no longer any laughter in her; it was the ultimate question.

And, seeing something in it all, he whispered again, "What is it?"

"I'm fearing for you," she whispered back. "I never thought in my life I would have a moment's further emotion for you, but now I'm seeing the torture in you and I'm catching a glimpse of how much it will be. Andrew, when you see Him, what will you say?"

He knew who she meant and she saw the wondering in his eyes.

"We don't create our salvation, our righteousness," she whispered; "it's a beautiful gift. All we need do is tell Him that we want it. But you have to be willing to tear your heart out and give it to Him!"

He still hung motionless, unmoving, caught. She glanced down at the gun and took a deep breath. While it was still shivering through her, she turned and tossed the gun out the window. "You don't give with a gun in your hand," she said as she turned back and held out her empty hand.

There was his movement and the sound at the window at the same time. "Hold it, Jacobson, or I'll kill you on the spot."

Men surged into the room while Rebecca and Andrew stood motionless, staring at each other.

And then there was Joshua. His white, strained face came between them. "Rebecca, are you all right?" She must touch him, erase those lines on his face.

She was nodding her head slowly, trying to move her lips while he held her close. "I know," he whispered; "we were listening. It's life after you'd given it up. But it's life, too, for me, my darling wife."

He was still holding her close while she murmured, "It was Jesus, my Lord. He did take care of it all. Oh, Joshua, if this had happened a week ago, I'd have shot him without a second thought!"

Now the jumble of angry words in the room rose and they turned. "You lied." "False pretenses." "An innocent woman."

Joshua released her and stepped forward. Resting his rifle against the broken fireplace, he said to Andrew, "There's only one way to handle this. You're going back to town with us. We'll have you before the judge to tell your story. And then we'll find out what justice is."

For a moment, just a moment, Joshua half turned to look at Rebecca. She heard the shout, the warning, and Joshua was shoved. There was a quick movement in the fading light.

With Joshua's rifle held high, with his left arm circling Joshua's neck, Andrew backed toward the door. Norton, calm and speaking softly said, "But you said you were in the right. You claimed your special hold on heaven gave you the right to plural marriage. You're saying that we poor mortals know nothin' about the right way to live. Seems since you were so certain about it all at noon today, then you'd be *proud* to have your day in court."

They were nearly through the door when Joshua thrust himself against Andrew's extended arm, pinning it against the doorjamb. The rifle clattered to the ground and Joshua lurched across the room directly in the path of the men scrambling for the door.

Rushing against the tide of men, Rebecca threw herself down beside Joshua. Voiceless, her hands moved over his face, now pulling him close, still wordless.

"Oh, Becka, my little Becky—it's all over." He got to his feet, lifting her with him. "Let's get out of here right now. Those fellows will bring him in. You're my responsibility, my only responsibility."

As Rebecca raised her arms, they heard the gunshot. Slowly she lowered them. Joshua moved first, turning toward the door. "Someone's hurt."

There was the sharp thud of hooves and the whinny of a horse. "Must have been Jacobson shooting. He's got away." He looked down at Rebecca and she saw the fear in his eyes.

She clasped his arms, "Joshua, it's for me you're fearing. You think I can't live with knowing he's still out there. That isn't so. If the healing touch Jesus Christ poured out on me this last week wasn't enough to convince me I'll never fear that man again, then most certainly the miracle He's worked in me just this night would be enough. I could have shot that man—it would have been so easy. But I knew, sure as I knew He was right here with me, there was no longer a hate in me." Her eyes were searching his face. "Do you believe in miracles?"

He was blinking his eyes. "Becky, I'm seeing one."

Outside the door a dry branch snapped. Joshua stepped in front of Rebecca and said, "Who's there?"

Eagle stepped through the door, hesitated. They saw blood,

"Eagle!" Rebecca gasped. "You've been shot. Oh, my dear, let me help." She flew at him, seeing the gash in his shirt, the blood flowing.

"He shot you!" Joshua caught the man and led him to the bed of blankets. Carefully he eased him down, saying, "Becky, is there something to bind around him? He's bleedin' pretty bad."

Quickly she looked around, "Oh, Andrew's bundle." She crossed the room, knelt close to the fire and tore open the pack.

Joshua leaned over Eagle and ripped open his shirt, seeing the wound as he leaned closer. "Eagle, that's no gunshot wound," he said. "A knife did that—what happened?"

"He ran into the bushes, no out." His voice was soft and he gestured with his hand, making a downward motion. "He had knife. I had gun."

"Eagle," Joshua interrupted sharply, "that's enough. Say no more." They stared into each other's eyes and then Eagle turned his head with a tired sigh.

"What happened, what is it?" Solali was clinging to the sagging door, staring at Eagle. "Is he dying?" she gasped. Without waiting for an answer she flew across the room and fell to her knees beside the bed. Her voice dropped to a crooning whisper in Paiute.

"Solali," Joshua protested, "how did you get here?" But he stopped immediately when he realized she would come after the two dearest people to her on earth. "He's only been nicked, but he's losing blood. Move back, and let's get this taken care of. Becky, have you found something?"

"Here's a clean shirt." As she crossed the room she was busy tearing it into strips. "Here's water in this bottle."

Solali elbowed Joshua out of the way and reached for the water. Joshua and Rebecca hung over the bed as Solali worked. The pain on Eagle's face eased and a faint smile crept to his lips as Solali continued to croon.

"What's she saying?" Joshua asked Rebecca.

"I don't know, but it sounds about like the crooning she was doing for Matthew's baby, trying to get him to sleep." Joshua chuckled. He turned to the doorway.

Rebecca had heard it, too. The subdued murmur of voices and the crunch of feet on stones. The rest of the men filed into the room.

Their serious faces centered on Eagle. "We'd a'been more on our toes if we'd a'known the Mormon'd be so violent."

Joshua said, "Got away, huh?"

They exchanged sheepish glances. "Fine trackers we are. If Norton here's going to be runnin' for sheriff, we're going to have to take him out and teach him a few things." They shifted uneasily.

"Sure sorry your Indian friend got it. Is it serious? We could fix a sling."

"Naw," Joshua said. "It's not much more'n a good nick. Shouldn't have been standin' in the way."

They exchanged looks. "Well, it weren't our bunch; nary a shot fired here. Never did get close enough. We stuck around the horses, waiting for action there."

"But what has happened to him?" Rebecca asked, looking around the circle.

"I've a feeling he's a hightailing it over the mountains and won't stop until he gets clear to Utah Territory. He sure ain't around here. We did a good job of beatin' the bushes."

Rebecca looked from one man to the other. Norton touched his hat and said, "Ma'am, I'm right sorry. I know it isn't a good feeling to know he's still a'runnin' free, but—"

"No, please. I'm just thanking you for helping. I'm not fearin', and someday I'll be able to talk about it."

Chambers spoke up. "If you're wantin', we can get a posse together tomorrow when it's light."

"Through this brush. The trail would be dead by morning," Joshua said shortly.

"Right you are." The men looked relieved. "Well, if there's no more we can do here, we'd better be gettin' on home. There's milkin' yet to be done. It's a fair piece down the hill."

Rebecca was smiling and blinking at the tears. Milking. "How can I ever thank you enough?" She looked around at the men. They were embarrassed, curious, she could see, but open.

"Aw, ma'am, I reckon if you'd bake us a big cake and put on a pot of coffee one of these cool evenings and invite us over, we'd all consider it even."

The men filed out the door. Joshua turned to Rebecca. "What did you say?"

"I said 'milking.' They're going to home to milk." Her voice caught. "Oh, Joshua, this afternoon when we left the church, I was riding on a high tide of fear and certain death. I was sure I'd never see you again, even while I tried to hope. Now it's back to life as usual. What a strange and wonderful blessing life is! Milking." She took a deep shaky breath.

"While I was hanging on that horse, thinking it was the end of everything important, I kept thinking about the chances I'd missed."

"What do you mean?" he asked in a low voice.

"The times I could have told you how much I love you, how much I've appreciated you down through all these years. And then the way you rescued me—" She stopped, tears choking her, and then she continued, "—rescued me from all that. The thought of not being able to say it because I had delayed—well—" There was another shaky breath and then with a smile she continued, "I'll make it up. You'll see a wife who doesn't hardly let you out of her sight."

For a moment longer Joshua stood looking down at her and she watched the tight lines on his face soften and disappear as a slow smile crept across it. "And I want to hear it all. Maybe we'd better get started."

He turned and walked to the bed. "Solali, can you help get Eagle back down this mountain to the house? Seems the best way is to ride on his horse with him. I don't reckon he's too bad off, but I'd hate for him to faint from loss of blood and pitch off his mount." Rebecca followed Joshua to the bedside. She could see that Eagle's eyes were sparkling in the firelight.

The impulse was impossible to resist. She addressed Solali. "Maybe you'd better be using the time to tell him about how you decided you really want to go home and live among your people." She paused to shake her head ruefully, "Why you'd prefer that to being a white man's wife, I'll never know, but—"

"Rebecca!" Solali gasped.

"What?" Rebecca asked innocently. "He can't understand English, so it's all right. And you can take all the time you want to tell him that you really love him."

"Rebecca," Joshua chided, his voice full of laughter. Rebecca darted a quick look at Eagle. He was grinning up at Solali as he held out his hands to be helped to his feet. When he was up and moving slowly toward the door, Joshua turned. "I'm thinkin' he doesn't need to lean that hard," he drawled.

Now Joshua slipped his arm across Rebecca's shoulder and pulled her close. "Did kissin' fit in with all those regrets?" She laughed up at him as she stood on tiptoe for his kiss.

The last embers of the fire were winking out and Joshua said, "Becky, my dear wife, let's go home."

Outside the moon was riding high in the sky, ready to accompany them down the mountain. "Looks like Solali and Eagle aren't the only ones who'll have to ride double," Joshua said. "There's only one horse left. They've taken the other ones with them."

Rebecca lingered. Moonlight was gilding the fir trees and turning to silver the decaying boards of the old shack. Joshua followed her glance and said, "The old place won't stand more'n another couple of winter snows."

"I'm glad. I don't want to be reminded of the way I felt when I walked into that place." She turned and looked up at him in the moonlight. "It was such a lonesome feeling. I could see the suppertime smoke rising above the trees. The setting sun made me think of all the cozy settling down that needs to be done at night. All those people were snug in their homes with family and I was alone on the mountainside."

"Were you really?"

"No," she whispered. "I know you want me to say I realized my God was here, and I did. But I guess what I'm saying is that until then, I didn't understand how much I really wanted us to be a family. Joshua and Rebecca."

"Then let's get going, Mrs. Smyth. I have a lot of work to do yet tonight."

She stopped in the path. "Work!" she cried in dismay. "Work? Whatever do you have to do tonight?"

"That pretty wedding dress has some drawbacks. I've been countin' all those buttons down the back of it. There's fifty-four of them. That's enough to keep a body busy half the night."

She was laughing as he swung her up on the horse and then settled in the saddle behind her.

As the horse started down the rocky trail, Rebecca sighed deeply. "Now, why that sigh, Mrs. Smyth?" Joshua murmured, pulling her closer.

"I'm conscious of being surrounded with so many good things. Joshua, I really meant it. I'll not be fearin' that man again, ever. But one thing, I'm certain my God can meet any need I have."

"And you'll have many years ahead to prove it."

"I know, my husband. Also I know it won't always be easy. But that's one reason there's marriage, isn't it?" She turned to look up at him and his arms tightened around her.

Notes

The Wedding Dress

Pages 26 and 121

In Nauvoo the doctrine of the New and Everlasting Covenant, which promoted plural marriages, was revealed to many of the leading brethren. Wives were sealed to some of them by President Joseph Smith, and to others under his direction. Not until 1852 was this revelation released to the world. *Essentials In Church History*, by Joseph Fielding Smith, pp. 338–341.

Page 26

Both Joseph Smith and Brigham Young taught that only the one holding the keys of the kingdom, i.e., the president of the church, would receive revelations. *Saints of Sage and Saddle*, by Fife, p. 100.

Page 26

The first and only issue of the *Nauvoo Expositor* was published June 7, 1844. On June 10, Joseph Smith forced the end of the weekly paper. At this time Joseph Smith was mayor of Nauvoo and also lieutenant general of the Nauvoo Legion. *Brigham Young*, by Werner, pp. 165–172. *Isn't One Wife Enough?* recounts the story of June 10th: "The posse [under orders of Mayor Joseph Smith] entered the building, tore out the press, distributed the type, burned the paper and fixtures, and destroyed the remaining copies [of the newspaper]." *Isn't One Wife Enough?*, by Young, p. 318. See pp. 314–324, concerning events in context of the destruction of the *Nauvoo Expositor*, the murder of Joseph Smith, and the Mormons being forced to leave Illinois.

Pages 73 and 176

According to Joseph Smith's *Book of Mormon*, a dark skin is the result of God's displeasure. The righteous ones (Nephites) had white skin, but those who rebelled against God (Lamanites) were cursed with a dark skin. The American Indians living today are referred to as Lamanites. In a suppressed 1831 revelation to Joseph Smith, the Mormons were commanded to marry the Indians to make them a "white" and "delightsome" people. "The *Book of Mormon* stated that when the Lamanites repented of their sins, 'their curse was taken from them, and their skin became white like unto the Nephites' (3 Nephi 2:15)." (p. 208) *The Changing World of Mormonism*, by the Tanners, pp. 207–214. For a detailed history and discussion of plural marriage, see Chapter 9, pp. 204–290.

Page 91

In September 1850, Congress and the U. S. President approved the organization of the Territory of Utah, and Brigham Young was appointed governor along with the appointment of other officials. *Essentials in Church History*, by Joseph Fielding Smith, p. 477.

Page 101

"We believe in the powers and gifts of the everlasting Gospel, viz., the gift of faith, discerning of spirits, prophecy, revelation, visions, healing, tongues, and the interpretation of tongues, wisdom, charity, brotherly love, etc." *Articles of Faith of the Church of Jesus Christ of Latter-Day Saints*, Number 7, Joseph Smith. These gifts or manifestations are included in this story to be true to history and to show that Satan can and does counterfeit, and that truth can't be judged only by outward manifestation.

Pages 113 and 127

In worship service, there was a lack of reverence, especially in administration of the sacrament which was given unceremoniously during the sermon, with water in tin cans or small glass jars. The fast and testimony meetings were held on the first Thursday night each month. They were emotional times with gratitude, rededication and occasional glossolalia. *Essays in Mormon History*, by F. Mark McKiernan, et al., pp. 298–301.

Page 114

"The [Mormon] missionary has acquired a habit of rising and bearing his testimony. If at first he may have had mental reservations, the habit of expressing his conformity to the . . . pattern set for him by the leadership of the church gradually becomes a kind of intuitive knowledge, a 'testimony.' " "Every Saint . . . has heard of miraculous visitations of bearded gentlemen who have come with a testimony to the divinity of Joseph Smith and the *Book of Mormon*." Also reports of many visitations of strangers doing good deeds, giving 'messages' from the dead. 'Returns' (from the dead) were common. *Saints of Sage and Saddle*, by Fife, pp. 11, 229–230, 234–235.

Pages 114 and 203

Sermon by Brigham Young at the Tabernacle on April 9, 1852, concerning Adam, Our Father and Our God: "It is in regard to the character of the well-beloved Son of God, upon which subject the Elders of Israel have conflicting views. Our God and Father in heaven, is a being of tabernacle, or, in other words, He has a body, with parts the same as you and I have. . . . The Holy Ghost is the Spirit of the Lord . . . but *He* is not a person of tabernacle as we are, and as our Father in Heaven and Jesus Christ are. The question . . . is often asked who it was that begat the Son of the Virgin Mary. . . . Our Father begat all the spirits that ever were, or ever will be, upon the earth; and they were born spirits in the eternal world. . . . We were made first spiritual, and afterwards temporal. . . . When our father Adam came into the garden of Eden, he came into it with a *celestial body*, and brought Eve, *one of his wives*, with him. He helped to make and organize this world. . . . He *is our* Father *and our* God, *and the only God with whom* we *have to do*. . . . When Adam and Eve had eaten of the forbidden fruit, their bodies became mortal from *its effects*, and therefore their offspring were mortal. When the Virgin Mary conceived the child Jesus, the Father had begotten him in his own likeness. He was *not* begotten by the Holy Ghost. And who is the Father? He is the first of the human family; and when he took a tabernacle, it was begotten by *his Father* in heaven, after the same manner as the tabernacles of Cain, Abel, and the rest of the sons and daughters of Adam and Eve. . . . Now remember from this time forth, and for ever, that Jesus Christ was not begotten by the Holy Ghost." *Journal of Discourses* , Vol. 1, by G. D. Watt, pp. 50–51.

Page 114

From the *Book of Mormon*: "And he said unto me, Behold the Virgin which thou seest, is the mother of God, after the manner of the flesh. . . . And the angel said unto me, Behold the Lamb of God, yea, even the Eternal Father!" (p. 25) "For if there be no Christ, there be no God; and if there be no God, we are not, for there could have been no creation.—But there is a God, and he is Christ . . ." (p. 86) "And behold, he shall be born of Mary, at Jerusalem, which is the land of our forefathers, she being a Virgin, a precious and chosen vessel, who shall be overshadowed, and conceive by the power of the Holy Ghost, and shall bring forth a son, yea, even the Son of God . . ." (p. 240, Book of Alma.) *Joseph Smith Begins His Work*, Vol. I, by Wood [Volume I, quoted here includes the first (1830) edition of the Book of Mormon, reproduced from uncut sheets in its original form.] See *The Mormon Papers* by Harry L. Ropp, p. 42, for the changes in the 1961 edition of the *Book of Mormon*.

Page 125

"Utah was Brigham Young's community. He was absolute master of its every detail. He knew every Mormon in Salt Lake City, his name and family, his assets and problems. . . . When he ordered a thing to be done, it was done: tabernacle, temple, towns, schools, state buildings, walls, roads, irrigation ditches, theatre, library. . . . The door of his office was always open. If a group wanted to give a ball, his permission had to be obtained, and later his approval of the guest list. . . . Marriages required his consent, and courtship as well. If a man wanted to enter a business or trade, Brigham Young had to approve. When he asked a man to give up his home, his business and his life in Salt Lake to go on a foreign mission, or to any other of the desert communities, that man went on the mission. When he told a man to enter into plural marriage, that man took another wife. Whatever he said was the religion of the Mormons; when he said that a man or group was apostate that man or group was excommunicated."

"If it seemed that the Mormon was not overburdened with personal decisions, Sir Richard Burton, who visited them as a friend in Salt Lake in 1860, said that Brigham Young's policy was based upon: 'The fact that liberty is to mankind in mass, a burden far heavier than slavery.' " *Men to Match My Mountains*, by Irving Stone, p. 265.

Page 127

A revelation through Joseph Smith, April 1830: "Behold, I say unto you that all old covenants have I caused to be done away in this thing; and this is a new and an everlasting covenant, even that which was from the beginning" (v. 1). *Doctrine and Covenants*, by George A. Smith, p. 36, sec. 22.

Page 132

Brigham Young on Indian problems: "Let every man, woman, and child, that can handle a butcher knife, be good for one Indian, and you are safe. . . . 'let us live together until we are a holy and sanctified society.' . . . You will be whipped until *you have the Spirit of the Lord Jesus Christ sufficiently to love your brethren and sisters freely* . . . . There will always be Indians or somebody else to chastise you, until you come to that spot. . . . This very same Indian Walker has a mission upon him, and I do not blame him for what he is now doing: he is helping to do the will of the Lord to this people, he is doing with a chastening rod what I have failed to accomplish with soft words. . . . So the Lord is making brother Walker an instrument to help me. . . . One thing more . . . what was it that preserved us. . . ? It is true, in reality, God did it. But by what means did He keep the mob from destroying us? *It was by means of being well armed with the weapons of death to send them to hell cross-lots.* Just so you have got to do." *Journal of Discourses*, Vol. 1, by G. D. Watt, p.168–171.

Page 132

Joseph Smith's corrections (additions) to the Bible are in *italics*: The King James Bible reads: Matthew 18:9 "And if thine eye offend thee, pluck it out, and cast it from thee; it is better for thee to enter into life with one eye, rather than having two eyes to be cast into hell fire. *And a man's hand is his friend, and his foot, also; and a man's eye are they of his own household.*" Mark 9:43 "And if thy hand offend thee, cut it off: *or if thy brother offend thee and confess not and forsake not, he shall be cut off:* it is better for thee to enter into life maimed, than having two hands to go into hell. *For it is better for thee to enter into life without thy brother, than for thee and thy brother to be cast into hell,* into the fire that never shall be quenched." Mark 9:47–48 "And if thine eye *which seeth for thee, him that is appointed to watch over thee to show thee light, become a transgressor and* offend thee, pluck it out: it is better for thee to enter into the kingdom of God with one eye, than having two eyes to be cast into hell fire: *for it is better that thyself should be saved, then to be cast into hell with thy brother*, Where their worm dieth not, and the fire is not quenched." *Plain and Precious Parts . . .* , by Edvalson, et al.

Page 143

This is part of the secret vows taken during temple rite of celestial marriage—marriage for eternity. Since the temple hadn't been completed, Mrs. Stenhouse's marriage was performed in the Endowment House. "We swore that by every means in our power we would seek to avenge the death of Joseph Smith, the Prophet, upon the Gentiles who had caused his murder, and that we would teach our children to do so; we swore . . . we would implicitly obey the commands of the priesthood in everything. . . . The penalty for breaking this oath . . . was then explained to us. His bowels were—while he was yet living—to be torn from him, his throat was to be cut from ear to ear, and his heart and tongue to be cut out. In the world to come, everlasting damnation would be his portion." *An Englishwoman In Utah*, by Mrs. T. B. H. Stenhouse, p. 197–198. For a fairly complete description of the "Endowments," read all of Chapter XXI, pp. 189–201.

Page 149

Sermon by Brigham Young, March 27, 1853 on apostates: "I want to know if anyone of you who has got the spirit of 'Mormonism' in you, the spirit that Joseph and Hyrum had, or that we have here, would say, Let us hear both sides of the question, let us listen, and prove all things? What do you want to prove?" (Brigham Young continues with tirade against apostates, particularly Gladden Bishop, then tells a dream he had of a confrontation with apostates—one jumped into bed with one of Brigham Young's wives and her children, then he tells of taking his bowie knife and slitting the man's throat—ear to ear.) "I say, rather than that apostates should flourish here, I will unsheath my bowie knife, and conquer or die. [Great commotion in the congregation, and a simultaneous burst of feeling, assenting to the declaration.] Now, you nasty apostates, clear out, or judgment will be put to the line, and righteousness to the plummet. [Voices, generally, "go it, go it"] If you say it is right, raise your hands. [All hands up.] "Let us call upon the Lord to assist us in this and every good work." *Journal of Discourses*, Vol. 1, by G. D. Watt, pp. 82–84.

Page 160

"No! *Principle* is the only thing—there can be no love in Polygamy. If a man loved his wife, do you think he could have the heart to pain her by taking another? On the other hand, it is because of the love which still remains in their hearts, and which they weary themselves to crush out, that so many of the first wives are miserable. . . . Brother Brigham says, 'We have so many whining women in Zion that its quite a reproach.' " *An Englishwoman in Utah*, Mrs. T. B. H. Stenhouse, pp. 203, 205.

Page 165

"And in that day Adam blessed God and was filled, and began to prophesy concerning all the families of the earth, saying: Blessed be the name of God, for because of my transgression my eyes are opened, and in this life I shall have joy, and again in the flesh I shall see God. And Eve, his wife, heard all these things and was glad, saying: Were it not for our transgression we never should have had seed, and never should have known good and evil, and the joy of our redemption, and the eternal life which God giveth unto all the obedient" (Moses 5:10–11). *Pearl of Great Price* George A. Smith, p. 11.

Page 176

J. M. Grant, Bowery, Great Salt Lake City, September 21, 1856: "If the arrows of the Almighty ought to be thrown at you we want to do it. . . . These are abominable characters that we have in our midst . . . they have no faith in the holy Priesthood. . . . I say, that there are men and women that I would advise to go to the President immediately, and ask him to appoint a committee to attend to their case; and then let a place be selected and let that committee shed their blood. We have those amongst us that are full of all manner of abominations, those who need to have their blood shed, for water will not do, their sins are of too deep a dye. You may think that I am not teaching you Bible doctrine, but what says the apostle Paul. . . ? They are a perfect nuisance, and I want them cut off, and the sooner it is done the better. . . . And we have women here who like anything but the celestial law of God; and if they could break asunder the cable of the Church of Christ, there is scarcely a mother in Israel but would do it this day. And they talk it to their husbands, to their daughters, and to their neighbors, and say that they have not seen a week's happiness since they became acquainted with that law, or since their husbands took a second wife. They want to break up the Church of God, and to break it from their husbands and from their family connections . . . and you need to be baptized. . . . You have got to cleanse yourselves from corruption. . . . Brethren and sisters, we want you to repent and forsake your sins. And you who have committed sins that cannot be forgiven through baptism, let your blood be shed, and let the smoke ascend, that the incense thereof may come up before God as an atonement for your sins, and that the sinners in Zion may be afraid." *Journal of Discourses*, Vol. 4, by G. D. Watt, pp. 49–51.

Page 177

President Brigham Young, Bowery, September 21, 1856: "There are sins that men commit for which they cannot receive forgiveness in this world, or in that which is to come, and if they had their eyes open to see their true condition, they would be perfectly willing to have their blood spilled upon the ground, that the smoke thereof might ascend to heaven as an offering for their sins; and the smoking incense would atone for their sins, whereas, if such is not the case, they will stick to them and remain upon them in the spirit world. I know . . . that you consider it is strong doctrine; but it is to save them, not to destroy them. . . . I do know that there are sins committed, of such a nature that if the people did understand the doctrine of salvation, they would tremble because of their situation. And further-more, I know that there are transgressors, who, if they knew themselves, and the only condition upon which they can obtain forgiveness, would beg of their brethren to shed their blood. . . . I will say further; I have had men come to me and offer their lives to atone for their sins. It is true that the blood of the Son of God was shed for sins through the fall and those committed by men, yet men can commit sins which it can never remit. . . . There are sins that can be atoned for by an offering upon an altar, as in the ancient days; and there are sins that the blood of a lamb, of a calf, or of turtle doves, cannot remit, but they must be atoned for by the blood of the man." (pp. 53–54)

This was not the first documentation that laid out the idea of blood atonement. The idea occurs in *Doctrine and Covenants*, section 132, verse 54, pp. 239, 244, 1952 edition—"Revelation given through Joseph Smith, the Prophet, at Nauvoo, Illinois, recorded July 12, 1843 . . ."

In the latter part of this same sermon on Sept. 21, 1856, Brigham Young offers to release all the women and gives them two weeks to decide: to either leave or make up their minds to accept "the principle" and make the best of it without complaining. (p. 57) *Journal of Discourses*, Vol. 4, by G. D. Watt, pp 51–57.

Page 182

Doctrine and Covenants, Sec. 132, ". . . relating to the new and ever-lasting covenant, including the eternity of the marriage covenant, as also plurality of wives." [Only key verses are quoted from this section.] "There-fore, prepare thy heart to receive and obey the instructions which I am about to give unto you; for all those who have this law revealed unto them must obey the same" (v. 3). "For behold, I reveal unto you a new and an everlasting covenant; and if ye abide not that covenant, then are ye damned; for no one can reject this covenant and be permitted to enter into my glory" (v. 4). Verses 7, 15 and 17 state that all covenants, etc, not sealed by the one anointed, having the keys of the priesthood, are of no force after the resurrection, and there is only one holding the keys of the kingdom at a time: The president of the church. Marriage not covenanted by the church isn't valid in eternity and those involved will be only angels instead of gods. "Verily, verily, I say unto you, if a man marry a wife accord-ing to my word, and they are sealed by the Holy Spirit of promise, accord-ing to mine appointment, and if he or she shall commit any sin or trans-gression of the new and everlasting covenant whatever, and all manner of blasphemies, and if they commit no murder wherein they shed innocent blood, yet they shall come forth in the first resurrection, and enter into their exaltation; but they shall be destroyed in the flesh, and shall be deliv-ered unto the buffetings of Satan unto the day of redemption, saith the Lord God" (v. 26). "Go ye, therefore, and do the works of Abraham; enter ye into my law and ye shall be saved" (v. 32). "Abraham received concu-bines, and they bore him children; and it was accounted unto him for righteousness, because they were given unto him, and he abode in my law; as Isaac also and Jacob did none other things than that which they were commanded; and because they did none other things than that which they were commanded, they have entered into their exaltation, according to the promises, and sit upon thrones, and are not angels but are gods" (v. 37). ". . . if a man receiveth a wife in the new and everlasting covenant, and if she be with another man, and I have not appointed unto her by the holy anointing, she hath committed adultery and shall be destroyed" (v. 41). Verses 45–48 talk about the one having keys of the kingdom and the power inherent. ". . . whosesoever sins you remit on earth shall be remitted eternally in the heavens; and whosesoever sins you retain on earth shall be retained in heaven" (v. 46). "And again, verily I say, whomsoever you bless I will bless, and whomsoever you curse I will curse, saith the Lord; for I, the Lord, am thy God" (v. 47). "Verily, if a man be called of my Father, as was Aaron, by mine own voice, and by the voice of him that sent me, and I have endowed him with the keys of the power of this priesthood, if he do anything in my name, and according to my law and by my word, he will not commit sin, and I will justify him" (v. 59). "And again, as pertaining to the law of the priesthood—if any man espouse a virgin, and desire to espouse another, and the first give her consent, and if he espouse the second, and they are virgins, and have vowed to no other man, then is he justified; he cannot commit adultery for they are given unto him; for he cannot commit adultery with that that belongeth unto him and to no one else" (v. 61). "And again, verily, verily, I say unto you, if any man have a wife, who holds the keys of this power, and he teaches unto her the law of my priesthood as pertaining to these things, then shall she believe and administer unto him, or she shall be destroyed, saith the Lord your God; for I will destroy her; for I will magnify my name upon all those who receive and abide in my law" (v. 64). *Doctrine and Covenants*, by George A. Smith, pp. 239–245.

Page 183

". . . Mormon theology put man definitely in the driver's seat. Joseph Smith and his story of the true gospel and priesthood made sure that the male of the species was the center of God's plan. Only man could hold the priesthood. This principle, of course, applied equally to plural wives. . . . How then could God reconcile this masculine dominance with the need for a great many spirits anxious to be born? This was easy: Make every woman's salvation dependent upon her husband in the priesthood. In short, a woman's salvation here and hereafter was completely dependent upon her being married to a man who held the divine keys of admission to heaven. Moreover, since the spirits were pressing to be born, what could be simpler than to provide for them by making it possible for great numbers of them to take their place on earth through the system of plural wives." *Isn't One Wife Enough?*, by Young, p. 33.

Page 190

President J. M. Grant, Tabernacle, Great Salt Lake City, December 17, 1854: "It would be useless for a man to embrace our religion unless he could be satisfied that the first principles thereof are based upon the word of God contained in the holy Scriptures. In relation to our faith, I would say the Gospel as preached by the Apostles, and as contained in the Book of Mormon, is the same, or agrees with the Gospel contained in the Bible. The Gospel preached by Joseph Smith and the revelations of God that have come through him to the Church as contained in the Book of Doctrine and Covenants, fully agree with the Gospel contained in the New Testament." *Journal of Discourses*, Vol. 2, G. D. Watt, pp. 225–226.

Page 200

This section contains the detailed account of Rosmos Anderson's death by blood atonement and the Johnson affair of Cedar City. *The Changing World of Mormonism*, Tanner, pp. 502–503.

Page 201

"That this doctrine of blood atonement created terror of conscience among the Saints and led to self-slaughter in the cause of righteousness, is illustrated by one story told by a former Mormon leader. One of the wives of a Mormon of Salt Lake City was unfaithful to him while he was on a mission in foreign lands. When he returned, the Church was in the throes of the Reformation, and his wife believed that she was doomed to lose the right to those children she had borne her husband in lawful wedlock, and that she would be separated from him and from them in eternity. She told her husband of her fears and of her sins, and he agreed with her that the fears were justified and the sin awful. She sat on her husband's knee and embraced him as she had never done before, while, as he returned her kisses, he cut her throat and thereby sent her spirit to the gods in all its former purity." (Quoted from *The Rocky Mountain Saints*, by T. B. H. Stenhouse, pp. 469–470.) *Brigham Young*, by Werner, pp. 404–405.

Page 216

" 'The Mormons look up to Brigham Young, and to him alone for the laws by which they are to be governed; therefore no law of congress is by them considered binding in any manner.' " [Charges filed by William W. Drummond, territorial judge for Utah.] "Drummond accused the Mormons of having a secret organization to resist the laws of the Country; of having a group of men set apart by special order of the Church to take the lives and property of persons who might question the authority of the Church; of insulting and harassing the federal officers of the territory; of traducing the American form of government." *Men to Match My Mountains*, Stone, pp. 218–219.

Page 221

Concerning Adam and Eve's sin: "And now, behold, if Adam had not transgressed, he would not have fallen; but he would have remained in the garden of Eden. . . . And they would have had no children; wherefore, they would have remained in a state of innocence, having no joy, for they knew no misery: doing no good, for they knew no sin. But, behold, all things have been done in the wisdom of Him who knoweth all things. Adam fell, that men might be; and men are, that they might have joy. And the Messiah cometh in the fullness of time, that he might redeem the children of men from the fall. And because that they are redeemed from the fall, they have become free forever, knowing good from evil; to act for themselves, and not to be acted upon, save it be by the punishment of the law, at the great and last day, according to the commandments which God hath given. Wherefore, men are free according to the flesh. . . . And they are free to choose liberty and eternal life, through the great mediation of all men . . ." *Joseph Smith Begins His Work*, Vol. I, by Wood, (1830 Book of Mormon), p. 65.

Pages 221 and 228

"For if there be no Christ, there be no God; and if there be no God, we are not, for there could have been no creation.—But there is a God, and he is Christ . . . that Christ was the God, the Father of all things, and saith that he should take upon him the image of man, and it should be the image after which man was created in the beginning; or in other words, he said that man was created after the image of God, and that God should come down among the children of men, and take upon him flesh and blood . . . There is no other way nor means whereby man can be saved, only in and through Christ." *Joseph Smith Begins His Work*, Vol. I, by Wood, (1830 Book of Mormon), pp. 86, 171, 331.

Page 226

"Also there were Brigham Young's own angry words: 'My power will not be diminished. No man they can send here will have much influence with this community. If they play the same game again [sending in troops], so help me God, we will slay them.'" *Men To Match My Mountains*, by Stone, p. 219.

Page 229

". . . the Father of lights; with whom is no variableness. . . . For I am the Lord, I change not . . . neither does he turn to the right hand or the left, or vary from that which he has said . . . he changes not . . . he is the same from everlasting to everlasting . . . he is a God of truth and cannot lie . . . But it is equally as necessary that men should have the idea that he is a God who changes not, in order to have faith in him." *Joseph Smith Begins His Work*, Vol. II, by Wood, (Doctrine and Covenants), pp. 37–39.

Page 234

An example of an intense emotional response of a first wife toward a second wife, as revealed by a family friend: "I think I have never seen more unadulterated hatred than she shows when speaking of this woman. She tells how she herself had refused to visit her husband on his death bed though her children told her that he had been calling for her all day and begged her to go to him. She boasts that 'I haven't spoken to Annie for thirty years and don't expect to speak to her for thirty more if I live that long.' " *Isn't One Wife Enough?*, by Young, p. 203.

Page 234

A first wife moved the second wife elsewhere: " 'I gave her a little heating stove, and took down the bedstead and sent all that with her clothes and bedding up to the other house. I never saw the house; I think it had one room. An old woman lived there and she died. I don't know what time they got back from the conference. I went to bed early. I guess they had to find the place and set up the bedstead before they could go to sleep. My husband never said a word about this, neither did Elizabeth.' The first wife kept close watch on her husband and his new wife. For example, Myra was in the habit of getting up early and doing her household chores promptly. If she found that Roper and the second wife were still lying abed, she would go over and throw rocks on the roof to awaken them and get them up." *Isn't One Wife Enough?*, by Young, p. 195.

Page 237

Concerning the grasshopper plague, Brigham Young said: "As for myself, I'd rather the grasshoppers would eat the wheat than the accursed Gentiles." From Hamblin's journal, May 20, 1855. *Jacob Hamblin*, by Bailey, (Endnote #74) pp. 126–127.

Page 243 and 249

Isaac Haight, president of Parawan Stake, proposed to Saints at Cedar City "that Indians be mustered in a holy war against the great company of Gentiles then moving south through Utah. The Piedes [Indians] had been promised that none of them would suffer death or injury when they attacked at dawn. . . . The Lord's protection so soberly promised, had not worked, and the Piedes, knew they had been tricked." *Jacob Hamblin*, by Bailey, p. 170–171.

Page 248

Apostle George A. Smith's preaching was inflammatory. Of his visit to Southern Utah and Iron County, he reports he found Iron Battalion organized and the people stirred up. ". . . the spirit seemed to burn in my bones to visit all these settlements in that southern region . . . When I got to Cedar, I found the battalion on parade. On the following day, I addressed saints at their meeting house. I never had greater liberty of speech to proclaim to the people my feelings and views; and in spite of all I could do, I found myself preaching a military discourse . . . That was the same Sabbath Brother Young was preaching the same kind of doctrine . . . let us take hold . . . simply to avenge God of his enemies, and to protect our homes and firesides; but I am perfectly aware that in all the settlements I visited . . . a word is enough to set in motion every man . . ."

Priscilla Leavitt Hamblin saw at Mountain Meadows the sight of putrefying, dismembered women's bodies. One story to come out of the discussions was that evidently one man was to be killed because he wasn't in favor of the killing of the emigrants (he escaped). It had been decided in a meeting held after church that the people "be done away with." Then they decided to write to Brigham Young and ask his advice.

Much of the massacre was done by the Iron County Militia. His communication implied that if the Indians wanted to massacre, let them, it was important to keep on the good side of them. The massacre took place, probably, on Friday, September 11, 1857. On Monday or Tuesday before the 11th, Indians attacked the wagon train. ". . . the decision was made that the emigrants, all who were old enough to talk, must be 'put out of the way' . . . and a detachment of the military was sent to assist in carrying out the order . . . each member of the militia was to be responsible for the dispatch of one emigrant man, and the Indians were to take their revenge upon women and children. Thus, they reasoned, no Mormon would be forced to shed innocent blood." Indians fell upon women and children with knives and hatchets. The wounded were killed and dumped. The very young children were taken to Mormons to be cared for. "The wagons and their loads, even bloody clothes, were taken to Cedar City, stored in the tithing office, and later sold at auction." Some of the children reportedly recognized clothing and knives as belonging to their parents. The Francher party had 120 massacred with 17 children saved (maybe 18, with one being killed later because of his age). *The Mountain Meadows Massacre*, by Brooks, pp. 35, 38–39, 43, 55, 73, 86. (For a detailed discussion of the massacre and its immediate background, see chapters 3–5, pp. 31–96.)

Annotated Bibliography
The Wedding Dress

Bach, Marcus. *Faith and My Friends*. Indianapolis: The Bobbs-Merrill Company, 1951. Chapter 7, "The Mormon," pp. 243–292. [Explores the beliefs and practices of six religions and how faith functions in the lives of its believers.]

Bailey, Paul Dayton. *Jacob Hamblin, Buckskin Apostle*. Los Angeles: Westernlore Press, 1947. 1961 Reprint. [Mormon apostle to the Indians in southern Utah, peacemaker among the tribes, Indian agent; he traveled unarmed among the tribes, teaching, preaching, and endeavoring to lift them up from ignorance and poverty. Much material is taken from Hamblin's extensive journals, including his investigation of the Mountain Meadows Massacre.]

Brooks, Juanita. *The Mountain Meadows Massacre*. Norman, Ok: University of Oklahoma Press, 1962. [Copyright 1950 Stanford University; new edition 1962, 1970, by the University of Oklahoma Press, Norman. First paperback printing, 1991. Brooks, a Mormon in good standing, has done the most definitive study of the massacre; completely objective throughout.]

Clark, James R., comp. *Messages of the First Presidency of the Church of Jesus Christ of Latter-Day Saints, 1833–1964*, vol. II, introduction, notes and index. Salt Lake City: Bookcraft, 1965. [Contains official statements of the first presidency of the LDS church during the administrations of Brigham Young, John Taylor, and Wilford Woodruff.]

Edvalson, Fredrick M., Jr. and William V. Smith, comp. *Plain and Precious Parts: Joseph Smith's Biblical Corrections. A Companion of the King James Bible*. Provo: Seventy's Mission Bookstore, 1977. [Internal title: Inspired Version Study Guide—A Key to the Significant Changes]

Fife, Austin and Alta Fife. *Saints of Sage and Saddle: Folklore Among the Mormons*. Published by Peter Smith, Gloucester, Ma. 1966. [Copyright 1956 by Indiana University Press. "This book seeks the authenticity not of history but of folklore of Mormons, to seek out and describe that which has been most typical and most tenacious of Mormon folk."]

Journal of Discourses. Volumes 1 and 2: Reported by G. D. Watt, published by F. D. Richards, London, 1855; Volume 3: Reported by G. D. Watt, edited and published by Orson Pratt, London, 1856; Volume 4: Reported by G. D. Watt, edited and published by S. W. Richards, London, 1857; Volume 7: Reported by G. D. Watt, J. V. Long, and others, edited and published by Amasa Lyman, London, 1860. [From the beginning in Utah Territory, all sermons by Brigham Young and future presidents as well as the apostles' sermons were recorded and published as the *Journal of Discourses*, 26 volumes. Some of the sermons were the original, unrevised, and unedited.]

McKiernan, F. Mark, Alma R. Blair, and Paul M. Edward. *The Restoration Movement: Essays in Mormon History*. Lawrence, Ks: Coronado Press, 1973. [Contains thirteen essays by authors currently writing in Latter Day Saints history.]

Mullen, Robert. *The Latter-Day Saints: The Mormons Yesterday and Today*. Garden City, NY: Doubleday & Company, 1966. [The story of the first 136 years of the Mormon Church, told in terms of the people who founded the Church and brought it to its position of eminence, worldwide.]

Ropp, Harry L. *The Mormon Papers: Are the Mormon Scriptures Reliable?*, Downers Grove, Il: InterVarsity Press, 1977. [Mormon teachings on God, Christ, salvation and the Bible; evidence and theories for the origin of the *Book of Mormon*.]

Smith, George Albert. *Doctrine and Covenants of The Church of Jesus Christ of Latter-day Saints*. Salt Lake City: The Church of Jesus Christ of Latter-Day Saints, 1949, 1952. ["Containing Revelations Given to Joseph, the Prophet, With Some Additions by His Successors in the Presidency of the Church."]

Smith, George Albert, *Pearl of Great Price*. Salt Lake City: The Church of Jesus Christ of Latter-Day Saints, 1949, 1952. ["A Selection from the Revelations, Translations, and Narrations of Joseph Smith, First Prophet, Seer and Revelator to the Church of Jesus Christ of Latter-Day Saints."]

Smith, Joseph. *Articles of Faith, Church of Jesus Christ of Latter-day Saints*. [See "The Fourteen Articles of Faith," on the 5th page following page 160 of "The Book of Commandments" in Wilford C. Wood, Joseph Smith Begins His Work, Vol. II]

Smith, Joseph Fielding, *Essentials in Church History*, 18th ed. Salt Lake City: Deseret Book Co., 1963. ["A History of the Church from the Birth of Joseph Smith to the Present Time with Introductory Chapters on the Antiquity of the Gospel and the 'Falling Away.' "]

Stenhouse, Mrs. T. B. H. *An Englishwoman in Utah: The Story of a Life's Experience in Mormonism*. "New and Cheaper Edition," London: Sampson Low, Marston, Searle & Rivington, 1882. [An autobiography by Mrs. T. B. H. (Fannie) Stenhouse of Salt Lake City, for more than twenty five years the wife of a Mormon missionary and elder, with introductory preface by Mrs. Harriet Beecher Stowe. Includes a full account of the Mountain Meadows Massacre, and of the life, confession, and execution of Bishop John D. Lee; fully illustrated.]

Stone, Irving. *Men to Match My Mountains*. New York: Doubleday, 1956. (Paperback edition, New York: Berkley Publishing Co, 1982.) [The story of the opening of the Far West and the men who braved a wilderness to bring a new nation to the shores of the Pacific, by an acclaimed author.]

Tanner, Jerald and Sandra Tanner. *The Changing World of Mormonism*. Chicago: Moody Press, 1980. ["A condensation and revision of *Mormonism: Shadow or Reality?*" Jerald Tanner is great-great-grandson of John Tanner, heavy financial contributor to Joseph Smith and LDS Church in 1835; Sandra is great-great-granddaughter of Brigham Young. These two have researched the origins of Mormonism since their teen years.]

Werner, M. R. *Brigham Young*. New York: Harcourt Brace & Co., First edition 1925. Printed by Quinn and Boden Co., Rahway, N.J. [The history of Mormonism, Joseph Smith, but especially Brigham Young. "Without Brigham Young, the Mormons would never have been important after the first few years of the institutional life, but without the Mormons Brigham Young might have been a great man. . . . it is due to his personality rather than to any other factor that Mormonism developed into a widespread creed and an extraordinary economic organization."]

Wood, Wilford C., comp. *Joseph Smith Begins His Work*, Volume I. Salt Lake City, Utah, 1958. [Volume I contains the *Book of Mormon*, reproduced by photo-offset from uncut original sheets of the 1830 first edition of the *Book of Mormon*.]

Wood, Wilford C., comp. *Joseph Smith Begins His Work*, Volume II. Salt Lake City, Utah, 1962. [Volume II contain copies of the *Book of Commandments* (1833); *Fourteen Articles of Faith*; and the *Doctrine and Covenants* (1835), composed of "The (7) Lectures on Faith," and "Covenants and Commandments."]

Young, Kimball. *Isn't One Wife Enough?* New York: Henry Holt, and Company, Inc, 1954. [The story of Mormon polygamy, by a grandson of Brigham Young.]

WHAT HAPPENS WHEN LONG-HELD *Secrets* COME TO LIGHT?

A Compelling Page-Turner from Beverly and David Lewis

She had hoped this day would never come.

Trembling, Melissa James returned the phone to its cradle and hurried to the stairs. She grasped the railing, nearly stumbling as she made her way to the second-story bedroom. Her heart caught in her throat as she considered the next move. Her only option.

You can do this, she told herself, stifling a sob. *You must….*

So begins *Sanctuary,* the first novel from the writing team of Beverly and David Lewis. A love story both poignant and harrowing, it captures the evil of revenge, the price of freedom, and the solace of friendship. Its characters, tender and wounded, are driven by a search for meaning that will bring them to a moment of shocking and profound truth.

Will the Light of Truth Direct Her Fight for Justice?

Historical Fiction by James Scott Bell and Tracie Peterson

Kit Shannon arrives in Los Angeles feeling a special calling to practice law despite the fact that her family doesn't understand her burning desire to seek justice for the poor and oppressed. Kit soon finds herself working with the city's most prominent criminal trial lawyer and drawn into a high-profile case. She longs to discover the truth but struggles with her personal doubts about the suspect she must defend.

◆ BETHANYHOUSE
www.bethanyhouse.com
1-800-328-6109